Praise for #1 *New York Times* bestselling author

NORA
ROBERTS

"America's favorite writer."

—The New Yorker

"Her stories have fueled the dreams of twenty-five million readers."

—Entertainment Weekly

"Nora Roberts is among the best."

—The Washington Post

"Roberts' bestselling novels are some of the best in the romance genre."

—USA TODAY

"Roberts' style has a fresh, contemporary snap."

—Kirkus Reviews

"You can't bottle wish fulfillment, but Nora Roberts certainly knows how to put it on the page."

—New York Times

NORA ROBERTS

O'HURLEY'S RETURN

Silhouette Books

Published by Silhouette Books

America's Publisher of Contemporary Romance

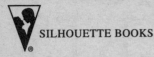 **SILHOUETTE BOOKS**

Recycling programs for this product may not exist in your area.

O'Hurley's Return

ISBN-13: 978-1-335-66644-4

Copyright © 2019 by Harlequin Books S.A.

The publisher acknowledges the copyright holder of the individual works as follows:

Skin Deep
Copyright © 1988 by Nora Roberts

Without a Trace
Copyright © 1990 by Nora Roberts

CONTENTS

SKIN DEEP

To my sisters,
Mary Anne, Carol, Bobbi, Carolyn, Maxine,
Reba, Barbara and Joyce, all of whom I've been
lucky enough to inherit through marriage.

Prologue

"I don't know what we're going to do with that girl."

"Now, Molly." With his eye on the mirror, Frank O'Hurley added a touch of pancake makeup to his chin to make certain his face didn't shine onstage. "You worry too much."

"Worry?" As she twisted to pull the zipper up the back of her dress, Molly remained at the dressing room door so that she could watch the corridor backstage. "Frank, we have four children and I love every one of them. But Chantel's middle name is trouble."

"You're too hard on the girl."

"Because you're not hard enough."

Frank chuckled, then turned around to scoop his wife into his arms. More than twenty years of marriage hadn't dulled his feelings for her a whit. She was still his Molly, pretty and bright, even though she was the mother of his twenty-year-old son and his three teenage daughters. "Molly, my love, Chantel's a beautiful young girl."

"And she knows it." Molly peeked over Frank's shoulder at the backstage door, willing it to open. Where was that girl? They had fifteen minutes before they were due onstage, and Chantel had yet to make an appearance.

When she had given birth to her three daughters, each within minutes of the next, she hadn't known that the first one would give her more to worry about than the other two combined.

"It's her looks that are going to get her in trouble," Molly muttered. "When a girl looks like Chantel, boys are bound to come sniffing around."

"She can handle the boys."

"Maybe that worries me, too. She handles them too well." How could she expect a man as simple and kind-hearted as her Frank to understand the complexities of women? Instead, she fell back on an old standard. "She's only sixteen, Frank."

"And how old were you when you and I—?"

"That was different," Molly said, but she was forced to laugh at the grin Frank sent her. "Well, it was." She straightened his tie, then brushed powder from his lapels as she spoke. "She might not have the good fortune to meet a man like you."

Cupping his hands under her elbows, he held her still. "What kind of man is that?"

With her hands on his shoulders, she looked at his face. It was thin, and already lined, but the eyes were the eyes of the smooth-talking boy she'd lost her head over. Though he'd never quite come up with that moon on a silver platter that he'd once promised her, they were partners in every sense of the word. For better or worse—through thick and thin. There had been a lot of thin. She'd spent more than half of her life with the man, Molly thought, and he could still charm her.

"A dear one," she told him, and brought her lips to his. At the sound of the back door closing, Molly pulled away.

"Now don't jump on her, Molly," Frank began as he caught his wife's arm. "You know it'll just put her back up, and she's here now."

Grumbling, Molly drew away as Chantel danced down the corridor. She was wearing a vivid red sweater and snug black slacks that showed off her blooming young shape. The brisk fall air had whipped color into her cheeks, highlighting already elegant bones. Her eyes were a deep, deep blue and held a breezy, self-satisfied expression.

"Chantel."

With her natural flair for drama and timing, Chantel paused outside the door of the dressing room she shared with her sisters. "Mom." Her lips turned up at the corners, and the smile spread farther when she saw her father wink at her over Molly's shoulder. She knew she could always count on Pop. "I know I'm a little late, but I'll be ready. I had the most wonderful time." Excitement added spark to beauty. "Michael let me drive his car."

"That fancy little red number—?" Frank began. Then he coughed into his hand as Molly leveled him with a look.

"Chantel, you've only had your license a few weeks." How she hated to lecture, Molly thought as she wound herself up for it. She knew what it was to be sixteen, and because of that she knew there was no way around what she had to do. "Your father and I don't think you're ready to drive unless one of us is with you. And in any case," she continued before Chantel could get out her first protest, "it isn't smart to get behind the wheel of someone else's car."

"We were on the back roads." Chantel came over and kissed her mother on both cheeks. "Don't worry so much. I have to have some fun or I'll just shrivel up."

Molly recognized the ploy too well, and she stood firm. "Chantel, you're too young to go off in some boy's car."

"Michael's not a boy. He's twenty-one."

"That only makes my point."

"He's a creep," Trace announced calmly as he came into the corridor. He only lifted a brow when Chantel turned on him, eyes flashing. "And if I find out he's touched you I'll rip his face off."

"It's none of your business," Chantel told him. It was one thing to be lectured by her mother, quite another to hear it from her brother. "I'm sixteen, not six, and I'm sick and tired of being hovered over."

"Too bad." He took her chin in his hand, holding it steady when she tried to jerk away. He had a rougher, masculine version of Chantel's beauty. Looking at them, Frank felt pride swell in him until he thought he was going to burst. They were the fire-eaters of the family, more like their mother than him. He loved them with all his heart.

"All right now, all right." Playing peacemaker, he stepped up. "We'll get into all this business later. Right now, Chantel has to change. Ten minutes, princess," he murmured. "Don't dawdle. Come on, Molly, let's go warm up the crowd."

Molly sent Chantel a quiet look that warned her the business wasn't over, then softened and touched her daughter's cheek. "We've a right to worry about you, you know."

"Maybe." Chantel's chin was still high. "But you don't need to. I can take care of myself."

"I'm afraid you can." With a little sigh, she walked with her husband down toward the small stage where they would earn their living for the rest of the week.

Far from mollified, Chantel put her hand on the knob of the door behind her before she faced her brother. "I decide who touches me, Trace. Remember that."

"Just make sure your friend with the fancy car behaves himself. Unless you'd like both his arms broken."

"Oh, go to hell."

"Probably will," he said easily. Then he tugged her hair. "I'll be clearing a path for you, little sister."

Because she wanted to laugh, Chantel yanked open the door, then shut it in his face.

Maddy glanced over as she buttoned the back of Abby's costume. "So, you decided to show up."

"Don't you start." Moving quickly, Chantel pulled a dress that matched her sisters' off an iron bar that spanned the width of the room.

"Wouldn't dream of it. Sounded interesting out in the hall, though."

"I wish they'd stop fussing over me." Chantel tossed the dress down, then peeled off her sweater. The skin below was pale and smooth, the curves already soft and feminine.

"Look at it this way," Maddy said as she finished Abby's buttons. "They're so busy fussing at you, they hardly ever pick on Abby and me."

"You owe me." Chantel slipped out of her slacks with brisk movements and stood in bra and panties.

"Mom really was worried," Abby interjected. Since her own makeup and hair were finished, she arranged the tubes and pots that would set Chantel's face for the stage.

Feeling a little pang of guilt, Chantel plopped down in front of the mirror the three of them shared. "She didn't have to be. I was fine. I had fun."

"Did he really let you drive his car?" Interested, Maddy picked up a brush to fix Chantel's hair.

"Yeah. It felt… I don't know, it felt important." She glanced around the cramped, windowless room with its concrete floor and dingy walls. "I'm not always going to be in a dump like this, you know."

"Now you sound like Pop." With a smile, Abby handed her a makeup sponge.

"Well, I'm not." With years of experience already behind her, Chantel added the color to her face in quick strokes. "One day I'm going to have a dressing room three times this big. All white, with carpet so thick you'll sink up to your ankles."

"I'd rather have color," Maddy said, dreaming herself for a moment. "Lots and lots of color."

"White," Chantel repeated firmly. Then she stood to put on her dress. "And it's going to have a star on the door. I'm going to ride in a limo and have a sports car that makes Michael's look like a toy." Her eyes darkened as she pulled on the dress, which had been mended too many times to count. "And a house with acres of garden and a big stone pool."

Because dreams were part of their heritage, Abby elaborated as she did up Chantel's buttons. "When you walk into a restaurant, the maître d' will recognize you and give you the best table and a bottle of champagne on the house."

"You'll be gracious to photographers," Maddy went on, handing Chantel her earrings. "And never refuse an autograph."

"Naturally." Enjoying herself, Chantel clipped the glass stones at her ears, thinking of diamonds. "There'll be two enormous suites in the house for each of my sisters. We'll sit up at night and eat caviar."

"Make it pizza," Maddy instructed, resting an elbow on her shoulder.

"Pizza *and* caviar," Abby put in, then stood on the other side.

With a laugh, Chantel slipped her arms around her sisters' waists. They were a unit now, just as they had been in the womb. "We're going to go places. We're going to be somebody."

"We already are." Abby tilted her head to look at Chantel. "The O'Hurley Triplets."

Chantel looked at the reflection the mirror tossed back. "And nobody's ever going to forget it."

Chapter 1

The house was big and cool and white. In the early-morning hours, a breeze came through the terrace doors Chantel had left unlatched, bringing in the scents of the garden. Across the lawn, hidden from the main house by trees, was a gazebo, painted white, with wisteria climbing up the trellises. Sometimes, when the wind was right, Chantel could catch the perfume from her bedroom window.

On the east side of the lawn was an elaborate marble fountain. It was quiet now. She rarely had it turned on when she was alone. Near it was the pool, an octagonal one affair skirted by a wide patio and flanked by another, smaller, white house. There was a tennis court beyond a grove of trees, but it had been weeks since she'd had the time or the inclination to pick up a racket.

Surrounding the estate was a stone fence, twice as tall as a man, that alternately gave her a sense of security or the feeling of being hemmed in. Still, inside the house, with its lofty ceilings and cool white walls, she often forgot about the fence and the security system and the electronic gate; it was the price she paid for the fame she had always wanted.

The servants' quarters were in the west wing, on the first floor. No one stirred there now. It was barely dawn, and she was alone. There were times Chantel preferred it that way.

As she bundled her hair under a hat, she didn't bother to check the results in the three-foot mirror in her dressing room. The long shirt and flat-heeled shoes she wore were chosen for comfort, not for elegance. The face that had broken men's hearts and stirred women's envy was left untouched by cosmetics. Chantel protected it by pulling down the brim of her hat and slipping on enormous sunglasses. As she picked up the bag that held everything she thought she would need for the day, the intercom beside the door buzzed.

She checked her watch. Five forty-five. Then she pushed the button. "Right on time."

"Good morning, Miss O'Hurley."

"Good morning, Robert. I'll be right down." After flipping the switch that released the front gate, Chantel started down the wide double staircase that led to the main floor. The mahogany rail felt like satin under her fingers as she trailed them down. Overhead, a chandelier hung, its prisms quiet in the dim light. The marble floor shone like glass. The house was a suitable showcase for the star she had worked to become. Chantel had yet to take any of it for granted. It was a dream that had rolled from, then into, other dreams, and it took time and effort and skill to maintain. But then she'd been working all her life and felt entitled to the benefits she had begun to reap.

As she walked to the front door, the phone began to ring.

Damn it, had they changed the call on her? Because she was up and the servants weren't, Chantel crossed the hall to the library and lifted the receiver. "Hello." Automatically she picked up a pen and prepared to make a note.

"I wish I could see you right now." The familiar whisper had her palms going damp, and the pen slipped out of her hand and fell soundlessly on the fresh blotter. "Why did you change your number? You're not afraid of me, are you? You mustn't be afraid of me, Chantel. I won't hurt you. I just want to touch you. Just touch you. Are you getting dressed? Are you—"

With a cry of despair, Chantel slammed down the receiver. The sound of her breathing in the big, empty house seemed to echo back to her. It was starting again.

Minutes later, her driver noticed only that she didn't give him the easy, flirtatious smile she usually greeted him with before she climbed into the back of the limo. Once inside, Chantel tipped her head back, closed her eyes and willed herself to calm. She had to face the camera in a few hours and give it her best. That was her job. That was her life. Nothing could be allowed to interfere with that, not even the fear of a whisper over the phone or an anonymous letter.

By the time the limo passed through the studio gates, Chantel had herself under control again. She should be safe here, shouldn't she? Here she could pour herself into the work that still fascinated her. Inside the dozens of big domed buildings, magic happened, and she was part of it. Even the ugliness was just pretend. Murder, mayhem and passion could all be simulated. Fantasyland, her sister Maddy called it, and that was true enough. But, Chantel thought with a smile, you had to work your tail off to make the fantasy real.

She was sitting in makeup at six-thirty and having her

hair fussed over and styled by seven. They were in the first week of shooting, and everything seemed fresh and new. Chantel read over her lines while the stylist arranged her hair into the flowing silver-blond mane her character would wear that day.

"Such incredible bulk," the stylist murmured as she aimed the hand-held dryer. "I know women who would sell their blue-chip stocks for hair as thick as this. And the color!" She bent down to eye level to look in the mirror at the results of her work. "Even I have a hard time believing it's natural."

"My grandmother on my father's side." Chantel turned her head a bit to check her left profile. "I'm supposed to be twenty in this scene, Margo. Am I going to pull it off?"

With a laugh, the stringy redhead stood back. "That's the least of your worries. It's a shame they're going to dump rain all over this." She gave Chantel's hair a final fluff.

"You're telling me." Chantel stood when the bib was removed. "Thanks, Margo." Before she'd taken two steps, her assistant was at her elbow. Chantel had hired him because he was young and eager and had no ambitions to be an actor. "Are you going to crack the whip, Larry?"

Larry Washington flushed and stuttered, as he always did during his first five minutes around Chantel. He was short and well built, fresh out of college, and had a mind that soaked up details. His biggest ambition at the moment was to own a Mercedes. "Oh, you know I'd never do that, Miss O'Hurley."

Chantel patted his shoulder, making his blood pressure soar. "Somebody has to. Larry, I'd appreciate it if you'd scout up the assistant director and tell him I'm in my trailer. I'm going to hide out there until they're ready to rehearse." Her co-star came into view carrying a cigarette and what Chantel accurately gauged to be a filthy hangover.

"Would you like me to bring you some coffee, Miss O'Hurley?" As he asked, Larry shifted to distance himself. Everyone with brains had quickly figured out that it was best to avoid Sean Carter when he was dealing with the morning after.

"Yes, thanks." Chantel nodded to a few members of the crew as they tightened up the works on the first set, a train station, complete with tracks, passenger cars and a depot. She'd say her desperate goodbyes to her lover there. She could only hope he'd gotten his headache under control by then.

Larry kept pace with her as she crossed the set, walking under lights and around cables. "I wanted to remind you about your interview this afternoon. The reporter from *Star Gaze* is due here at twelve-thirty. Dean from publicity said he'd sit in with you if you wanted."

"No, that's all right. I can handle a reporter. See if you can get some fresh fruit, sandwiches, coffee. No, make that iced tea. I'll do the interview in my dressing room."

"All right, Miss O'Hurley." Earnestly he began to note it down in his book. "Is there anything else?"

She paused at the door of her dressing room. "How long have you been working for me now, Larry?"

"Ah, just over three months, Miss O'Hurley."

"I think you could start to call me Chantel." She smiled, then closed the door on his astonished pleasure.

The trailer had been recently redecorated for her taste and comfort. With the script still in her hand, Chantel walked through the sitting room and into the small dressing area beyond. Knowing her time was limited, she didn't waste it. After stripping out of her own clothes, she changed into the jeans and sweater she would wear for the first scene.

She was to be twenty, a struggling art student on the down slide of her first affair. Chantel glanced at the script again. It was good, solid. The part she'd gotten would give her an opportunity to express a range of feeling that would stretch her creative talents. It was a challenge, and all she had to do was take advantage of it. And she would. Chantel promised herself she would.

When she had read *Strangers* she'd cast herself in the part of Hailey, the young artist betrayed by one man, haunted by another; a woman who ultimately finds success and loses love. Chantel understood Hailey. She understood betrayal. And, she thought as she glanced around the elegant little room again, she understood success and the price that had to be paid for it.

Though she knew her lines cold, she kept the script with her as she went back to the sitting room. With luck she would have time for one quick cup of coffee before they ran through the scene. When she was working on a film, Chantel found it easy to live off coffee, a quick, light lunch and more coffee. The part fed her. There was rarely time for shopping, a dip in the pool or a massage at the club until a film was wrapped. Those were rewards for a job well done.

She started to sit, but a vase of vivid red roses caught her eye. From one of the studio heads, she thought as she walked over to pick up the card. When she opened it, the script slid out of her hand and onto the floor. "I'm watching you always. Always."

At the knock on her door, she jerked back, stumbling against the counter. The scent of the roses at her back spread, heady and sweet. With a hand to her throat, she stared at the door with the first real fear she'd ever experienced.

"Miss O'Hurley... Chantel, it's Larry. I have your coffee."

With a breathless sob, she ran across the room and jerked open the door. "Larry—"

"It's black the way you—What's wrong?"

"I—I just—" She cut herself off. Control, she thought desperately. You lose everything if you lose control. "Larry, do you know anything about these flowers?" She gestured back, but couldn't look at them.

"The roses. Oh, one of the caterers found them while she was setting up breakfast. Since they had your name on them, I went ahead and put them in here. I know how much you like roses."

"Get rid of them."

"But—"

"Please." She stepped out of the dressing room. People. She wanted lots of people around her. "Just get rid of them, Larry."

"Sure." He stared at her back as she walked toward the set. "Right away."

Four aspirin and three cups of coffee had brought Sean Carter back to life. It was time to work, and nothing could be allowed to interfere with that—not a hangover, not a few frightening words printed on a card. Chantel had worked hard to project an image of glamour and style. She'd worked just as hard not to develop a reputation as a temperamental actress. She was ready when called and always knew her lines. If a scene took ten hours to shoot, then it took ten hours. She reminded herself of all of this as she approached Sean and their director.

"How come you always look as though you stepped out of the pages of a fashion magazine?" Sean grumbled, but

Chantel observed that makeup had dealt with the shadows under his eyes. His skin was tanned and shaved smooth. His thick, mahogany-colored hair was styled casually, falling across his brow. He looked young, healthy and handsome, the dream lover for an idealistic girl.

Chantel lifted a hand and let it rest on his cheek. "Because, darling, I did."

"What a woman." Because the aspirin had made him feel human again, Sean grabbed Chantel and leaned her back in a dramatic dip. "Let me ask you this, Rothschild," he said, calling to the director while his lips hovered inches from Chantel's. "How could a man in his right mind leave a woman like this?"

"It hasn't been established that you—or Brad," Mary Rothschild corrected, referring to the role, "is in his right mind."

"And you're such a cad," Chantel reminded Sean.

Pleased to remember it, Sean brought her up again. "I haven't played a real cad in about five years. I don't think I've properly thanked the writer yet."

"You can do it later today," Rothschild told him. "He's over there."

Chantel glanced over to the tall, rangy man who stood, chain-smoking nervously, on the edge of the set. She'd met him a handful of times in meetings and during preproduction. As she recalled, he had said little that hadn't dealt directly with his book or his characters. She sent him a vaguely friendly smile before turning back to the director.

As Rothschild outlined the scene, she pushed everything else out of her mind. All that would be left was the heartbreak and hope her character felt as her lover slipped away. Mechanically, their minds on angles and continuity, she and Sean went over their brief but poignant love scene.

"I think I should touch your face like this." Chantel

reached up to rest her palm on his cheek and looked plead-ingly into his eyes.

"Then I'll take your wrist." Sean wrapped his fingers around it, then turned her palm to his lips.

"I'll wait for you and so forth." Chantel skipped over the lines as one of the crew dropped a barn door into place with a clatter. She gave a small, broken sigh and pressed her cheek to his. "Then I'll start to bring my arms up."

"Let's try this." Sean took her shoulders, held her for a moment while they stared at each other, then placed two nibbling kisses on either side of her mouth.

"Oh, Brad, please don't go... Then I kiss you until your teeth rattle."

Sean grinned. "I'm looking forward to it."

"Let's run through it." Rothschild held up a hand. Women directors were still the exception to the rule. She couldn't afford to give herself, or anyone else, an inch. "I want a lot of steam when you get to the kiss," she told both of them. "Keep the tears coming, Chantel. Remem-ber, deep in your heart you know he's not coming back."

"I really am a cad," Sean said pleasantly.

"Places." Extras scrambled to their marks. A few mem-bers of the camera crew broke off making plans for a poker game. "Quiet on the set." Rothschild moved over, too, until she had the best angle for Chantel's entrance. "Action."

Chantel dashed out on the platform, looking around frantically while groups of people milled around her. It all showed on her face, the desperation, the last flames of hope, the dream that wasn't ready to die. There would be a thunderstorm brewing, thanks to special effects. Light-ning flashing, thunder rolling. Then she spotted Brad. She called out his name, pushing her way through the crowd until she was with him.

They rehearsed the scene three times before Rothschild

was satisfied enough to roll film. Chantel's make-up and hair were freshened. When the clapper came down, she was ready.

Throughout the morning they perfected the first part of the scene, her search, the impatience and rush of the crowd, her meeting with Brad. Take after take she repeated the same moves, the same words, at times with the camera no more than a foot away.

On the sixth take, Rothschild finally gave the signal for the rain. The sprinklers sent down a drizzle that misted over her as she stood facing Brad. Her eyes filled and her voice trembled as she begged him not to leave. Wet and cold, they continued to go over what would be five minutes on the screen until lunch break.

In her dressing room, Chantel stripped out of Hailey's clothes and handed them to the wardrobe mistress so that they could be dried. Her hair would be styled again, then soaked again, before she could call it a day.

The roses were gone, but she thought she could still smell them. When Larry came to the door to tell her that the reporter had arrived, she asked him to give her five minutes, then send him along.

She'd put it off too long, she told herself as she picked up the phone. It wasn't going to stop, and she'd reached the point where she could no longer ignore it.

"The Burns Agency."

"I need to speak to Matt."

"I'm sorry, Mr. Burns is in a meeting. May I—"

"This is Chantel O'Hurley. I have to speak to Matt now."

"Of course, Miss O'Hurley."

Chantel couldn't resist a slight smirk at how quickly the receptionist had changed her tune. Searching a drawer for the pack of cigarettes she kept for emergencies, she waited for Matt to come on the line.

"Chantel, what's up?"

"I need to see you. Tonight."

"Well, sweetheart, I'm kind of tied up. Why don't we make it tomorrow?"

"Tonight." Some of the panic fought its way through. Chantel lighted the cigarette and drew deeply. "It's important. I need help." She let the smoke out in a slow stream. "I really need your help, Matt."

Because he'd never heard fear in her voice before, he didn't question her. "I'll come by, what…eight?"

"Yes, yes, that's fine. I appreciate it."

"Can you tell me what it's about?"

"I can't. Not over the phone, not now." She was calming again, just knowing she was about to take a step seemed to help.

"Whatever you say. I'll be there tonight."

"Thanks." She hung up the phone just as the knock came at her door. Chantel carefully stubbed out her cigarette, tossed her still-damp hair back and ushered the reporter in with a gracious smile.

"Why in the hell didn't you tell me about this before?" Matt Burns paced around Chantel's spacious living room with an unfamiliar feeling of helplessness. In twelve years he'd scrambled his way up from mail clerk to assistant to top theatrical agent. He hadn't gotten there by not knowing what to do in any given situation. Now he had a hornet's nest on his hands, and he wasn't sure which way to toss it. "Damn it, Chantel, how long has this been going on?"

"The first phone call came about six weeks ago." Chantel sat on a low oyster-colored sofa and nursed a glass of mineral water. Like Matt, she didn't like the feeling of helplessness. She disliked having to ask someone else to do something about a problem of hers even more. "Look,

Matt, the first couple of calls, the first couple of letters, seemed harmless." Ice clinked in her glass as she set it down, then picked it up again. "With my face plastered all over magazines and all over the screen, obviously I'll attract attention. Not all of it's healthy. I figured if I ignored it it would stop."

"But it didn't."

"No." She looked down at her glass, remembering the words printed on the card. *I'm watching you always. Always.* "No, it got worse." She shrugged, trying to pretend to herself, and to him, that it wasn't as bad as it sounded. "I had my number changed, and for a while it worked."

"You should have told me."

"You're my agent, not my mother."

"I'm your friend," he reminded her.

"I know." She held out a hand. Real friendships were few and far between in the world she'd chosen. "That's why I called you before I went off the deep end. I'm not a hysterical woman."

He laughed, then released her hand to pour himself another drink. "Anything but."

"When those roses—Well, I knew I had to do something, but I didn't know what."

"The *what* is to call the police."

"Absolutely not." She lifted a finger when he started to object. "Matt, I imagine you can write the scenario as easily as I can. We call the police, then the press gets hold of it. Headline: Chantel O'Hurley Haunted by Twisted Admirer. Whispered Phone Calls. Desperate Love Letters." She pulled a hand through her hair. "We might be able to laugh that off, even use it to a point, but it wouldn't be long before a few more unbalanced personalities decided to write me some fan letters. Or camp out at the front gate. I don't think I can handle more than one at a time."

"What if he's violent?"

"Don't you think I've thought of that?" She plucked one of his French cigarettes from his pocket and waited for him to light it.

"You need protection."

"Maybe I do." She took a quick, hurried drag. "Maybe I'm just about ready to admit that, but I'm in the middle of a film. You bring cops on the set and people wouldn't stop talking."

"Since when has gossip worried you?"

"Never." She managed an easy smile. "Except when it's about something really personal. My, ah…extraordinary love affairs and hedonistic life-style are one thing. My life, as it really is, is quite another. No police, Matt, at least not yet. I need another alternative."

He took the cigarette from her and inhaled thoughtfully. Chantel's first job on the screen had been negotiated by him. He'd seen her through everything from shampoo commercials to feature films, and it was rare, very rare, for her to ask for help with something personal. In all the years he had known her, even Matt had seldom gotten beneath the image of the woman they had both manufactured.

"I think I have one. Trust me?"

"Haven't I always?"

"Sit tight. I'm going to make a call."

Chantel settled back and closed her eyes when Matt left the room. Maybe she was overreacting. Maybe she was being foolishly jumpy about a fan who'd taken admiration just a few steps too far.

I'm watching you…watching you…

No. Unable to sit, Chantel sprang up to pace around the room. She enjoyed being watched—on the screen. She could accept being photographed whenever she swept in or out of a club, whenever she attended a party or a premiere.

But this was…frightening, she admitted. As if someone were just outside the windows, looking in. The thought made her glance nervously over her shoulder. Of course there was no one there. She had the electronic gate, the walls, the security. But she couldn't stay locked in her house twenty-four hours a day.

She stopped by the antique mirror above the white marble fireplace. There was the face she was familiar with, the face critics had called devastating, incomparable, even heartlessly beautiful. A lucky accident, she sometimes thought, the combination of pearly skin, Nordic blue eyes and ice-sharp cheekbones. She'd done nothing to earn the face, the classic oval shape of it, the full, lush mouth or the thick mane of angel-blond hair. She'd been born with that, but she'd worked for the rest. And worked hard.

She'd been performing since she could walk, traveling endlessly around the country with her family in clubs and regional theater. She'd paid her dues long before she had come to Hollywood at nineteen, not starry-eyed but determined. In the years that had passed, she had won roles and lost them, had hawked shampoo and sold gallons of perfume in unapologetically sexy, often silly commercials. When her first break had come she'd been ready, more than ready, to play the soulless man-eater who stayed on screen less than twenty minutes. She'd stolen that movie from a pair of veterans and had gone on to star in one of her own. There'd been no looking back.

That first break had brought her the stardom she had always craved. And had, indirectly, nearly destroyed her life.

Yet, she'd survived, Chantel reminded herself as she faced her own reflection. She hadn't allowed what had happened all those years ago to ruin her. She refused to allow what was happening now to ruin her, either.

"He's coming right over."

She turned away from the mirror as Matt strode into the room again. "What?"

"I said he's coming right over. Let me fix you a real drink."

"No, I have to be on the set at six-thirty. Who's coming right over?"

"Quinn Doran. He might just be the answer, and since we go back a ways, I was able to...persuade him to think about it."

Chantel stuck her hands in the pockets of her white satin loungers. "Who is Quinn Doran?"

"He's sort of a private investigator."

"Sort of?"

"He runs a security business...corporate, small business, whatever. At one time he worked in some sort of covert operation. Might have been for our government, but I couldn't swear to it."

"Sounds fascinating, but I don't think I want a spy, Matt. A three-hundred-pound wrestler might be more appealing."

"And obvious," he reminded her. "You could hire yourself a couple of bruisers for bodyguards, sweetheart, but what you want here is brains—and discretion. That's Quinn." He finished off his drink and contemplated having another. "He doesn't do much of the legwork himself now. He has plenty of operatives or whatever they're called to handle that. Keeps himself available as a troubleshooter. But in this case I want you to have the best."

"And that's Quinn," Chantel mimicked, dropping onto the arm of the sofa. "What's he supposed to do?"

"I don't have any idea. That's why I called him. He's a moody bastard," he said reminiscently. "Not too, well... polished, but I'd trust him with my life."

"Or, in this case, mine."

Matt's expression changed immediately. "Chantel, if you're really that worried—"

"No, no." With a wave of her hand, she brushed off his concern. "I have the feeling that this Quinn Doran of yours is likely to listen to what I have to say, roll his eyes and give me a lecture on how to handle the obscene phone caller. I don't like him already."

"You're just nervous." Matt patted her knee as he crossed to the bar. "You're allowed to be nervous, Chantel."

"No, I'm not." She smiled, determined to lighten her own mood. "Nerves don't fit the image. It's an image you helped me mold."

"You didn't need any help with that." With a smile for her, he turned back and studied the flow of white satin that suited her so well. "You were born with the talent. I just helped you expand it."

She tilted her head and gave him a long, luxurious smile. "How'd we do?"

"I'll say this, no one looking at you today would think that you'd once mended your panty hose."

She laughed and slid down on the sofa. "You're so good for me, Matt."

"I've been telling you that for years. There's the bell. I'll get it."

Chantel picked up her warming mineral water and swirled it. If Matt thought Quinn Doran was an answer, she'd have to take his word for it. But it galled her, it galled her right down to the ground, to tell her personal problems to a stranger.

Then the stranger walked in.

If she had had to cast someone in the roll of a spy, a private investigator or an alley fighter, her choice would have been Quinn Doran. He filled the archway to her living room, inches taller than Matt, inches broader in the shoulders, yet with a wiry leanness that made her think he could move fast and move well. The quick flutter of feminine approval she accepted as natural even before she looked at his face. Then she thought it unnatural.

He wasn't leading-man handsome, but he had tough go-to-hell looks that would make any woman's pulse uneven. Dark, thick hair curled over his ears and trailed over the collar of a denim work shirt. His skin was tanned and taut over strong facial bones, and the pale shade of his eyes seemed almost startlingly cool. His lashes were too long, too thick for a man, but they were anything but feminine. There was nothing about him that wasn't totally masculine. When he walked, he walked with the soft, measured stride of a man who knew how to stalk. His mouth turned up slightly as he crossed to her, but Chantel didn't see humor or appreciation in his eyes. She saw, recognized and stiffened against derision.

"So this is the ice palace," he said in a surprisingly beautiful voice. "And the queen."

Chapter 2

He'd seen her before, of course. On the screen she looked larger than life, indomitable, untouchable. The face, almost mystically perfect, could rule a man's fantasies. A facade. Quinn understood facades, how they could be formed, altered or hacked away as circumstances demanded. He wondered, as with a casual glance he took in everything about her, how much substance there was beneath that silk-and-satin exterior.

Matt had known Quinn too long to be disturbed by his cavalier attitude. "Chantel, Quinn Doran."

Satin slid over satin as she crossed her legs. With a lazy kind of grace, she offered her hand. "Charming," she murmured, stiffening as his fingers curled firmly over hers. He didn't shake her hand, nor did he bring it to his lips in the casual-European gesture she suddenly felt he was capable of. He just held it while his pale green eyes held hers. Her skin was like the satin she wore, smooth, fragrant and coolly feminine. His was hard, unyielding and darkened by the sun. They froze for a moment, her on the sofa, him on his feet, with their hands still locked. Chantel had been in combat with men before, and only once had she lost. She understood that the glove had been tossed down, and she accepted the challenge.

"Is it still vodka rocks?" Matt asked Quinn as he turned to the bar.

"Yeah." With a slight inclination of his head, Quinn indicated that he knew the game was on. He relaxed his fingers slowly to let her hand slide from his. "Matt tells me you have a problem."

"Apparently I do." Chantel plucked a cigarette from a porcelain holder on the table, then lifted a brow. When Quinn drew a lighter out of his pocket and flicked it on, she smiled and leaned a bit closer. "I'm afraid I don't know if you're the man to deal with it—" her gaze lifted and held his before she leaned back again "—Mr. Doran."

"I'm inclined to agree with you… Miss O'Hurley." For the second time their gazes locked, and something not entirely pleasant hummed between them. "But since I'm here, why don't you tell me about it?" Quinn accepted the glass from Matt, then shot him a look before he could speak. "Why don't we let Miss O'Hurley fill me in, since it's her problem?"

As an agent, Matt knew when to negotiate and when to back off. "Fine, I'll just fill my mouth with a few of these canapés." He sat, leaving them to each other.

"I've been getting some annoying phone calls." She said it casually, but the tension showed briefly in the way her fingers curled and uncurled. Quinn was used to picking up on small details. At the moment he noticed that her hands were quite small and narrow, with long fingers, the rounded tips painted with clear lacquer. The fingers themselves were never quite still.

"Phone calls?"

"And letters." She moved her shoulders and the satin whispered quietly. "It started about six weeks ago."

"Obscene phone calls?"

Chantel lifted her chin, unable to resist the urge to look down her small, straight nose. "I suppose that would depend on your definition of obscene. Yours might be quite different than mine."

Humor touched his eyes and made them strangely appealing. She wondered fleetingly how many women had stepped into his lion's den and been devoured. "I'm sure it is. Go on."

"At first—at first you could say I was almost amused. It seemed harmless enough, though annoying. Then…" She moistened her lips and brought the cigarette to them. "Then he became a bit bolder, more explicit. It made me uneasy."

"You should change your number."

"I've done that. The phone calls stopped for about a week. They started again today."

As he leaned back, Quinn sampled the vodka. Like her, it was a quality brand. "You recognize the voice?"

"No, he whispers."

"You could change your number again." The ice clinked in his glass as he shrugged. "Or have the police put a tap on it."

"I'm tired of changing my number." With quick impatience, she stubbed out the cigarette. "And I don't want the police. I prefer to keep this discreet. Matt seems to think you're the answer to that."

Quinn drank again. The room was done in different shades of white, but it wasn't virginal. The very absence of color, with her at the center, was outrageously alluring. He was sure she knew it. In every one of her films she had acted the role of a woman who deliberately played on a man's needs, his weaknesses, his most private dreams. Quinn could drum up little sympathy for a woman who deliberately projected an image designed to arouse men, then complained about a few harmless phone calls.

"Miss O'Hurley, you're probably aware that men who make these kind of calls don't do anything but talk. I'd suggest you change your number again, then have one of your servants answer the phone for a while, until he gets tired of it."

"Quinn." Matt swirled his own drink. He had a habit of keeping in motion when under pressure, his hands, his feet. Now, he cleared his throat and tried to settle. "That's not much help."

"She can hire a bodyguard if it makes her feel better. Her security here could certainly be tightened."

"Maybe I need barbed wire, vicious guard dogs," Chantel interjected, and rose.

"That's the price you pay," Quinn told her coolly, "for being what you are."

"What I am?" Her eyes, already a vivid, searing blue, sharpened. "Oh, I see. I parade myself on the screen, I don't dress in burlap and wear a veil over my face, therefore I asked for what I got. And I deserve it."

Her cool beauty was compelling, but her passionate outburst was like seeing fire in ice. Quinn ignored the tightening in his gut and shrugged. "That's close enough."

"Thank you for your time," she said, and turned away. Before she could stop herself, she was whirling back. "Why don't you take a walk into the twentieth century? Just because a woman is attractive and doesn't disguise the fact doesn't mean she deserves to be abused—verbally, physically or emotionally."

"I don't believe I said an attractive woman, or any woman, deserves abuse," Quinn commented.

His careless tone only stoked the fires. "Just because I'm an actress and sexuality is part of my craft doesn't mean I'm fair game for any man who wants a piece of me. If I play the part of a murderer, it doesn't mean I should go on trial."

"You appeal to a man's most primitive fantasies, Miss O'Hurley, and you do it in Technicolor. There's bound to be a little backwash."

"So I should just take my medicine," she murmured. "You're an idiot. You're the kind of man who wears his brain below his belt. The kind who thinks if a woman agrees to have dinner with him she should pay for it with a romp between the sheets. Well, I can pay for my own dinner, Mr. Doran, and I can handle my own problems. I'm sure you can find the door."

"Chantel," Matt began, but she turned on him like a cat. "I'll just have a few more canapés," he muttered.

"Miss O'Hurley."

"What?" Chantel spun around to face her tall, aging majordomo, then drew in a long, cleansing breath. "Yes, Marsh, what is it?"

It was the tone that had Quinn narrowing his eyes. There was an underlying straightforward quality to it that ignored any domestic caste system and spoke human to human. Though nerves had her body strung tight, she smiled at the old man.

"These were just delivered for you."

"Thank you." Chantel crossed the room to him and took the vase of daylilies. "I won't need you any more to-night, Marsh."

"Very good, Miss."

Stepping behind Quinn, she went to a table by the windows. "Why don't you show your friend out, Matt? I don't think—"

She had the card in her hands and was staring at it. Her fingers trembled momentarily before she crushed the paper. Before she could drop it on the floor, Quinn had her wrist and was slowly drawing the mangled note from her. What he read made his stomach tighten, this time in disgust.

"No more than I deserve?" Chantel's voice was cold, almost detached, but her eyes, when Quinn looked into them, were terrified. He slipped the paper into his pocket as he took her arm.

"Why don't you sit down?"

"Was it another one?" Matt started toward them, but Quinn motioned to the bar.

"Get her a brandy."

"I don't want a drink. I don't want to sit down. I want you to go." When she started to pull her arm away, Quinn merely tightened his hold and led her to the sofa. "How often do you get one of these?"

"Nearly every day." She picked up a cigarette, then put it back.

"All of them as…direct?"

"No." She took the brandy and sipped at it, hating to admit she needed it. "That started a couple of weeks ago."

"What did you do with the notes?"

"I tossed out the first few. Then, when the tone started to change, I was going to burn them." The brandy warmed her but did nothing to settle her. "I kept them. I'm not sure why. I suppose I thought I should have them if things got out of hand."

"Call your servant back in. I want to ask him some questions. And go get the other letters."

His orders did what the brandy hadn't. Chantel felt her spine straighten. "It's none of your concern, Mr. Doran. We've already settled that."

"This just unsettled it." He drew the paper out of his pocket and watched her slight but definite recoil.

"I don't want your help."

"I didn't say I'd give it yet." He let that hang as they continued to stare at each other. "The letters? Unless you've got a better idea what to do about all this."

At that moment, at that one shimmering moment, she despised him. She could have hidden it. She was skilled enough. She didn't bother. Before she could speak, Matt laid a hand on her shoulder. His fingers moved as restlessly as hers.

"Please, Chantel. Think before you say anything."

She kept her eyes on Quinn's. "I wouldn't want to say what I'm thinking." When his lips curved again, she gritted her teeth. "Or perhaps I would."

"Chantel." Matt gave her shoulder a light squeeze. "I don't like ultimatums, but if we can't deal with Quinn, I'm going to call the police. No," he continued when her head shot back, "I mean it. You're a smart woman. Be practical."

She hated being backed into a corner. Quinn could see it. She was a woman who insisted on having the choice and the control in her own hands. It was something he could admire, even respect. Maybe, just maybe, there was more to Chantel O'Hurley than met the eye.

"All right, we'll do it your way. For now." She rose, at once regal and strong. "Don't badger Marsh." She met Quinn's eyes levelly. "He's old and getting frail. I don't want him upset."

"I haven't kicked a dog all day," Quinn told her.

"Only small children and kittens," she murmured, then swept from the room.

"Quite a woman, your client."

"She's all of that," Matt agreed. "And she's scared right down to her toes. She doesn't scare easily."

"I bet she doesn't." Quinn took out a cigarette and tapped it idly against the pack. He was forced to admit that he had thought she was simply dramatizing. The few sentences printed on the card had changed his mind. They were just short of vile. For Quinn, the line of demarcation between right and wrong was flexible, but the card fell well on the wrong side. Still, before he decided just how much he wanted to be involved, there were a few things he had to know.

He glanced back at Matt, watching him pace. "Just how close are the two of you?"

"We have a solid, mutually advantageous arrangement." Matt gave Quinn a sober smile. "And she doesn't sleep with me."

"You're slipping."

"She knows what she wants, and what she doesn't want. She wanted an agent. But I do care about her." He cast a worried look at the doorway. "She's already gone through enough."

"Enough of what?"

With a shake of his head, Matt sat again. "Another story, and nothing to do with this. Are you going to be able to help her?"

Quinn drew slowly on his cigarette. "I don't know."

"Excuse me." Marsh stood in the doorway, still dressed in his black suit and starched collar. "Miss O'Hurley said you wanted to speak with me."

"I wondered if you could tell me about the person who delivered the flowers." Quinn gestured toward them and watched the old man squint. Nearsighted, he thought.

"They were delivered by a young man, eighteen, perhaps twenty. He rang from the gate and explained that he had a delivery for Miss O'Hurley."

"Was he wearing a uniform?"

Marsh's brows knit as he concentrated. "I don't believe so. I can't say for certain."

"Did you happen to see his car?"

"No, sir. I took the flowers at the back door."

"Would you recognize him if you saw him again?"

"Perhaps. I think I might."

"Thank you, Marsh."

Marsh hesitated. Then, remembering his position, he bowed stiffly. "Very good, sir."

As he walked back into the hallway, Quinn heard Chantel stop him for a brief, murmured conversation. Her voice, he noticed, was soothing from a distance, quiet and easy. Up close, its smoky quality could twine around a man's nerve endings and make him want. She came back in, carrying a small pack of letters.

"I'm sure you'll find it fascinating reading," she said as she tossed them into Quinn's lap. "My guess is it's close to the technique you use to court women."

She'd regained her spirit, Quinn decided as he ignored her and opened the first envelope. The address on it, like the text inside, was printed in small block letters. The paper was dime-store quality. He could work for weeks and never trace it.

The first few notes he read were fawning in their admiration and subtly suggestive. And well written, Quinn added silently. The work of an educated person. As he went on, the prose and syntax remained good but the content deteriorated. Even a man who had seen and done what he had felt instant distaste. The writer went into graphic and pitiless detail, outlining his fantasies, his needs and his intentions. The last few letters added veiled hints that the writer was close by. Watching. Waiting.

When he'd finished, Quinn stacked the letters in a neat pile. "You sure you don't want the cops in on this?"

Chantel had seated herself across from him, and now she folded her hands in her lap. She didn't like him, she told herself. She didn't like the way he looked, the way he moved. She didn't like the fact that his voice was almost poetic, so very different from his lived-in face. So why, if all this was true, did she feel as though she wanted, even needed, his help? She kept her eyes on his. Sometimes you made bargains with the devil.

"No, I don't want the police. I don't want publicity on this. What I want is for this man to be found and stopped."

Quinn rose and poured himself another drink. Both the glasses and ice bucket were Rosenthal. He appreciated elegant things, just as he appreciated the cruder things in life. Beer from a bottle or wine from a crystal glass, it hardly mattered, as long as your thirst was quenched. He appreciated beauty, but he wasn't duped by it. An outer shell meant nothing. He'd shed plenty of his own when the occasion had called for it.

Chantel O'Hurley had beauty, had elegance. If he took the job, by the very nature of it he was bound to discover how much was shell, how much was substance. That was what had him hesitating. He understood just how dangerous knowledge of another person could be—to all involved.

He could control the attraction he felt for her looks, as long as he chose to. His mood on that could change from day to day. What he wouldn't control, had never been able to control, was his curiosity as to what lay beneath the skin.

Swallowing his vodka, he turned back around. She was sitting back in her chair, and one would have thought from looking at her that she was relaxed, even aloof. The fingers on her left hand moved, just a little, curling together, spreading apart, as if she had managed to center her nerves only there. He shrugged and matched his mood to hers.

"Five hundred a day, plus expenses."

She lifted a brow. It was the only movement she made. With it, she conveyed a range of feeling—amusement, consideration and dislike. What it didn't show was the surge of relief that passed through her.

"That's a princely sum, Mr. Doran."

"You'll get your money's worth."

"That's something I insist on." Leaning back, she steepled her fingers under her chin. Her wrists were slender, and her hands were as delicate as her face. A diamond flashed on her right hand, then became as white and cool as the rest of her. "Just what do I get for five hundred a day plus expenses?"

His lips curved just before he brought the glass to them. "You get me, Miss O'Hurley."

She smiled a little. Sparring helped. She was back in control again, and the fear was ebbing. "Interesting." The look she sent him was designed to pin a man to the wall and make him beg. Quinn felt the punch and acknowledged the power. "What do I do with you?"

"You've got it backward." He walked to her then, stopping by her chair to lean close. She caught a hint of scent, not cologne, not soap or powder, but raw and completely comfortable masculinity. Though she didn't retreat from it, she braced herself, recognizing her own attraction.

"Just what do I have backward, Mr. Doran?"

She looked like a painting, one he thought he'd seen in the Louvre a lifetime ago. "It's what I do with you. Five hundred a day, angel, and your trust. That's my price. You pay it and you get twenty-four-hour protection, starting with one of my men posted as a guard at that gate of yours."

"If I already have the gate, why do I need a guard?"

"Did it ever occur to you that a gate doesn't do a hell

of a lot of good if you're going to open it up to anyone who asks?"

"What didn't occur to me was that I'd have to lock myself in."

"Get used to it, because whoever's sending you flowers doesn't have a clean bill of health."

Panic came and went in her eyes. He gave her points for how quickly she mastered it. "I'm aware of that."

"I need your schedule. Starting tomorrow, one of my men goes with you every time you stick your pretty nose out the door."

"No." The O'Hurley stubbornness came through as she rose to face him. "For five hundred a day I want you, Doran. You're the one Matt trusts, and you're the one I'm paying for."

They stood close, very close. He could smell the scent that seemed to seep through her pores, neither quiet nor subtle. The perfection of her face could take a man's breath away. Her hair swept back from it in a glorious cascade, like an angel's. If a man touched it, would he find heaven or be cast from the clouds? When it came to that, Quinn wouldn't worry about the consequences.

"You might regret it," he murmured, then smiled slowly.

So she might. Chantel already knew that, but pride wouldn't let her back down. "I pay for you, Mr. Doran. That's the deal."

"You're the boss." He lifted his drink to her. "Two of my men will come by in the morning to wire the phone."

"I don't want—"

"I don't take the job if you tie my hands." His easy smile was gone as quickly as it had formed. "We tap the phone, maybe he says something to give himself away, maybe we get lucky and trace it. Just think of us as doctors." He smiled at her again, enjoying himself. "If you want to say something intimate to one of your…friends, don't worry. We've heard it all and more."

Temper had always been the most difficult of her emotions to master. It surged up and was fought back down before she spoke again. "I'm quite sure you have. What else?"

"I'll take the letters with me. It's doubtful we'll be able to trace the paper, but we'll give it a shot. Now, is there anyone you know who you think could be doing this?"

"No." The answer came immediately and with complete confidence. He decided to run a check on everyone close to her.

"Dump anyone in the last few months that may be carrying a torch for you?"

"Thousands."

"Cute." He drew a pad and the stub of a pencil out of his pocket. "I need the names of who you've slept with. We'll go back three months."

"Go to hell," she said sweetly, then started to sit. He caught her by the wrist.

"Look, I'm not going to play games with you. I'm not personally interested in how many men you've had in your bed. This is business."

"That's right." She tossed her head back. "My business."

Her skin was warmer than it looked. That was something he filed away to think about later. "One of them might just have gone off the deep end. Maybe you slept with him a couple times and it gave him delusions of grandeur. Think about it. This all started six weeks ago, so who were you with before that?"

"No one."

Annoyance covered his face as he tightened his hold. "Give me a break, angel. I haven't got all night."

"I said no one." She yanked her arm away. For a moment

she wished she could rattle off a dozen names, two dozen names, just to see him sweat. "Believe whatever you like."

"I tell you what I don't believe, and that's that you spend your evenings alone, darning socks."

"I don't jump into bed with every man who passes within five feet of me." In a calculated move, she dropped her gaze down as if measuring the distance between them.

"It looks like about ten inches to me," he murmured.

"Sorry to disappoint you, but I have to be interested first, and I haven't been. Besides, I've been working, and it tends to take up a great deal of my time." Unconsciously she rubbed at her wrist, where his fingers had pressed. "Satisfied?"

"Come on, Quinn, ease off." Feeling trapped in the middle, Matt moved over and put an arm around Chantel's shoulders. "She's had it rough enough."

"It's not my job to hold her hand." Quinn scooped up the letters, annoyed by the twinge of self-disgust he felt. "I'll be back tomorrow. What time do you get up?"

"Five-fifteen." She couldn't resist a smirk when he only stared at her. "I leave for the studio at five forty-five. That's a.m., Mr. Doran. Can you handle it?"

"You just write the check. Fifteen hundred in advance."

"You'll have it. Good night, Mr. Doran. It's been unusual."

"Do yourself a favor and don't answer your phone any more tonight." With that, he nodded to Matt and strode out. Chantel waited for the sound of the door closing behind him. She went to the coffee table and drew out another cigarette.

"Your friend's a bastard, Matt."

"Always has been," he agreed. "But he's the best."

Chapter 3

Chantel had thought she wouldn't sleep. The house had seemed so enormous around her, and so enormously quiet. But she had climbed into bed with a vision of Quinn Doran hovering in her mind. Just the thought of him made her furious, insulted her intelligence, nipped at her ego. And made her feel safe.

She slept only six hours, but she slept deeply.

Music woke her, pouring from the wall unit beside the bed. She rolled over, surrounded by pillows, covered with ivory linen sheets and nothing else.

The bed had been one of the first luxuries she had indulged herself with, almost before she could afford it. It was huge and old, with a carved cherrywood headboard that had made her think of princesses waking up from a hundred years of sleep. Growing up, she had invariably slept in hotel beds, and she'd decided that a sinfully beautiful bed was something she deserved to indulge herself in when she signed her first film contract. A small part in a full-length feature had been enough to pin her hopes on. Years later, when she awoke in the antique four-poster it still gave her the same satisfaction.

She thought back to the time when she had still lived in the small apartment in L.A. The bed had taken up the entire room, and she had had to crawl over it to reach the doorway. Her two sisters had visited once, and the three of them had stretched across it and talked and giggled for hours.

She wished they could be with her now. The feeling of safety would be more tangible.

She'd nearly told Maddy about the letters and calls when she'd gone to New York a few weeks before. Part of her had wanted to, needed to, but Maddy had been so preoccupied. She'd been entitled, Chantel reminded herself as she sat up and stretched. Her play had been nearly ready to open, and her heart had been wrapped up in the man who was backing it. All for a good cause, Chantel thought with a smile. The play was a smash, and Maddy was planning her wedding.

He'd better be good to her, Chantel thought as the old protective instinct rose up in her. She had had to watch one sister go through a miserable marriage. She couldn't bear it if Maddy was hurt, as well.

Maddy would be fine, she reassured herself. Just as Abby was fine. They had both found the right man at the right time. So she had one sister planning a wedding and the other preparing for the birth of her third child. She couldn't spoil all that by dumping her problems on them now. Besides, she was the eldest triplet, if only by a matter of minutes. To Chantel, that meant that she had the responsibility to be the strongest. They would be there for her, of course, just as she would be there for them. But she was the oldest.

They'd come so far. Chantel sat in the middle of the lush bed and looked around a room that was larger than the whole of her first apartment in California. Why was it she felt as though she still had so far to go?

Now wasn't the time for philosophizing. After turning up the volume on the radio, she climbed out of bed and prepared to face another day on the set.

Quinn wasn't accustomed to rising before dawn. It was much more his style to see the night through and find his bed at sunrise rather than climbing out of it at that hour. Not that he didn't appreciate an L.A. sunrise. It was simply more to his taste to watch the sky take on color after a night of celebration—in bed or out.

He drove across town under a pink and mauve sky, casting an occasional look of mild contempt at a jogger. Designer sweat suits weren't his style. If he wanted to tone up, he went to the gym. And not one of those pastel-walled spas where they piped in classical music, a real gym. You didn't see cute leotards there, and the sweat ran as free and healthy as the four-letter words. A man's world—and no one drank carrot juice frappé. A woman like Chantel O'Hurley wouldn't poke her million-dollar nose through the front door.

Quinn shifted in his seat and scowled at nothing in particular. He couldn't remember the last time a woman had made him uncomfortable. Chantel's looks were designed to make a man squirm—and ache. The hell of it was she knew it and, Quinn was certain, enjoyed it.

He couldn't let that be a problem. She was paying him to do a job. The only thing he could be concerned about from this point on was her security. The check she would give him entitled her to the best, and he *was* the best. Besides, he didn't care for the content of the letters she'd shown him.

Not that Quinn was a supporter of the women's movement. To his way of thinking, men and women were different. End of story. If a woman walking by a construction site was insulted because she got a few whistles or invitations, he figured she should walk someplace else. After all, that was just good clean fun. There'd been nothing clean, or fun, in the letters, though. And Chantel hadn't looked insulted, either. If he knew anything, Quinn knew what genuine fear looked like.

Sooner or later he would find out who had written them. That would take patience. In the meantime, he'd give Chantel the round-the-clock protection she was paying for. Remembering her face, Quinn acknowledged that that would take willpower. He had it, he thought with a shrug as he pulled up to the iron gates. Besides, chances were that she'd look like a hag at this hour of the morning.

He reached out the window and leaned on the buzzer.

"Yes?"

The frown moved into his eyes. Even in one word, Chantel's voice was easily recognizable. He hadn't expected her to answer the intercom herself. "Doran," he said curtly.

"You're prompt."

"You get what you pay for."

There was no answer, but the gates slowly swung open. Quinn cruised through them, then stopped to make certain they shut behind him.

In the daylight, he got a better look at the lay of the land. Anyone determined enough could find his way over the wall. He and a partner had once scaled a sheer cliff in Afghanistan with nothing more than rope and nerve.

The trees that flowered over the lawn sent up a sweet

scent. And would provide more-than-adequate cover for an intruder. He was going to have to get a good look at the alarm system in the house, though he knew anything that could be put in could be deactivated.

Quinn pulled up just beyond the steps, then got out to lean on the hood of his car. You couldn't hear any traffic from here. Just the sound of birds. He took out a cigarette. A glance around showed him a few floodlights, maybe a dozen ground lights, obviously placed more for aesthetic purposes than for added security. After a look at his watch, Quinn decided to walk around the house and check a few things out for himself.

Perhaps out of spite, Chantel decided to let Quinn cool his heels outside while she dallied in her dressing room. Under other circumstances she might have invited him in for a quick cup of coffee before the limo arrived. She wasn't feeling gracious. Instead, she took her time, bundling her hair back from her face, checking the contents of her bag, then writing a few instructions for her maid. When the buzzer from the gate rang again, she spoke to her driver, then gathered up her script. She turned toward the bedroom and walked into Quinn. He watched initial shock turn to anger.

"What the hell are you doing in here?"

"Just checked out your security system." He leaned against the doorway and noted, with a quick twinge, that regardless of the hour she looked fantastic. "It's pitiful. A Boy Scout with two merit badges could get past it."

Chantel settled the strap of her bag on her shoulder and promised herself she would pay Matt back if it was the last thing she ever did. "When it was installed I was assured it was the best on the market."

"Supermarket, maybe. I'll have my men beef it up."

She'd been born practical, and the years had done nothing to change that. "How much?"

"Don't know for sure until they're into it. Three to five, I'd say."

"Thousand?"

"Sure. Like I said, you—"

"Get what you pay for," she murmured, walking around him. "All right, Mr. Doran, you go right ahead." As she spoke, she moved to her nightstand. "But the next time you decide to check out the system, I wouldn't advise you sneaking into my bedroom." When she turned, she had a pearl-handled .22 in her hand. "I tend to be nervous."

Quinn regarded the gun with a raised brow. He'd been on the wrong end of one plenty of times before. "Know how to use one of those, angel?"

"You just pull this little trigger here." She smiled. "Of course, my aim's terrible. I'd point at your leg and end up shooting you right through the brain."

"There's only one rule about guns," he began, then scowled over her shoulder. When Chantel turned to look, he was on her. With a move too quick to judge, he had the gun in his hand and her beneath him on the bed. "The rule is, don't point one unless you intend to use it."

She didn't squirm beneath him, but lay still, letting the heat of fury and dislike pour out. With a casual gesture he flipped open the pistol's chamber.

"It's not loaded."

"Of course it's not. I wouldn't keep a loaded gun in the house."

"A gun's not a souvenir." He closed it again before he looked down at her. Her face was untouched by makeup, and it was as beautiful as it was furious. Despite himself, Quinn found the combination very much to his liking. Her body was small and strong beneath his, not as cushioned and feminine as he'd expected. But her scent was there, as it had been the night before, outrageously feminine.

"Nice bed," he murmured, unable to resist the urge to sweep his gaze down to her mouth. He thought, but couldn't be sure, that her heartbeat increased.

"Your approval means everything to me, Mr. Doran. Now, if you don't mind, I have to get to work."

How many other men had pinned her between their bodies and this wide, firm mattress? How many other men had felt this wild, edgy flare of desire? Both thoughts ran through his head before he could stop them. Because they did, he rolled aside and yanked her to her feet. But she was still close.

"Maybe we'll keep this business," he told her quietly. "And maybe we won't."

Though her pulse was racing, Chantel wasn't dishonest enough to blame it on temper. Desire was something she understood, even if she had rarely felt it for a man. It was also something that could be controlled. Instinct warned her that it was vital to do that now, and to continue to do so, when it applied to Quinn.

"You tempt me to put bullets in that gun, Mr. Doran."

"It wouldn't hurt." Quinn dropped it back in her bedside drawer. "And make it Quinn, angel. After all, we've been to bed together." Taking her arm, he escorted her downstairs and outside.

"Good morning, Robert." Chantel smiled at her driver as he opened the back door of the limo. "Mr. Doran will be accompanying me to the studio for a few days."

"Very good, Miss O'Hurley."

Quinn didn't miss the wistful look the driver sent him before they were closed in behind smoked glass. "How does it feel to infatuate the male of the species?"

Chantel settled back. "He's just a boy."

"Does that make a difference?"

Behind her dark glasses, Chantel shut her eyes. "Oh, I forgot. I'm one of those heartless women who tease and flaunt, then toss men aside after I've drained them, like empty pop bottles."

Amused, Quinn stretched out long legs. "That pretty much covers it."

"You have a remarkable disdain for women, Mr. Doran."

"No, you're wrong. Women happen to be one of my favorite pastimes."

"Past—" Chantel caught herself before she sputtered. She drew her glasses completely off, wishing she could see if he was baiting her or speaking the simple truth. Wanting to believe the worst of him, she went with the latter. "You're a classic chauvinist, Mr. Doran. I'd thought your species nearly extinct."

"We're a hardy breed, angel." He pushed a button and watched the compact bar rotate toward him. Quinn considered mixing a Bloody Mary but settled for straight orange juice.

Replacing her glasses, Chantel decided against beating her head against a brick wall. "I prefer not to introduce you as my bodyguard. I can do without that sort of speculation."

"Fine. How do you want to handle it?"

"They'll just assume you're my lover." Coolly she took the glass of juice from him and sipped. "I'm accustomed to that sort of speculation."

"I bet. It's your game. Play it any way you want."

She handed him back the glass. "I intend to. And what will you do?"

"My job." As they passed through the studio gates, he drained the glass. "You just smile pretty at the cameras, angel, and don't worry about it."

She found that her jaw was tensed so tightly it hurt. Acting on impulse, Chantel turned to him, and curled her fingers into his shirt. "Oh, Quinn, it's just that I'm so frightened. I'm so very frightened. Not knowing from one minute to the next if I'm safe." Her voice broke as she leaned closer. "I can't tell you what it means to me just to know you'll be there. Protecting me. I'm defenseless, vulnerable. And you're so...strong."

She was close, so close he could see her eyes flutter shut behind the tinted glasses. Her body trembled lightly as she leaned into him. Desire flared, along with a need to comfort and protect. She was soft, pliant and helpless. As he drew her nearer, her scent tangled around his senses until his head throbbed with it. "You don't have to worry," he murmured. "I'm going to take care of you."

"Quinn." Her head tilted up until her lips were only a whisper away from his. When she felt him tense, she jerked back and pressed something into his hand. "Your check," she said carelessly, then stepped out of the limo.

Quinn sat for a full ten seconds and wondered why he'd never entertained thoughts of strangling a woman before. When he stepped out beside her, he curled his fingers around her arm. "You're good. Very, very good."

"Yes, I am." She gave him a slow, easy smile. "And I get much better."

As Chantel went through her morning routine of makeup and hairstyling, Quinn simply observed. There were a dozen people Chantel came in contact with during the first hour alone. There were other actors, technicians and a parade of assistants. He'd want a list, and he was beginning to realize just how extensive it would be. Whoever was hounding her obviously knew her routine. That made the people she worked with his priority.

"Miss—ah, Chantel." Larry stopped by her side with a cup of fresh coffee.

"Oh, thanks. You read my mind."

He preened a bit, pleased. "I knew the hair was going to take longer this morning." He watched as the stylist patiently threaded pearls through the already complicated arrangement. "You're going to be just beautiful for the ballroom scene."

"A far cry from yesterday." She sipped the coffee. "If they'd watered me one more time, I'd have melted."

"Miss Rothschild said the dailies were great. I checked."

"Thanks." She caught sight of Quinn's reflection in the mirror and decided that moment was as good a time as any. "Larry, this is Quinn Doran, a friend of mine." Only years of training kept her from choking on the word as she held a hand over her shoulder for Quinn's. "Larry's my right hand. And often my left, as well. Quinn's going to watch the filming for a few days."

"Oh, well…" Larry cleared his throat. "That's nice."

Quinn saw that the young man thought it was anything but. Another conquest, he thought. But he couldn't afford to feel sympathy, only suspicion.

"I'll keep out of the way," Quinn promised, making the most of it by rubbing his thumb over Chantel's knuckles. "I just want to see Chantel at work."

"Isn't that sweet?" Chantel said with a brilliant smile. "Quinn's between jobs at the moment and has time on his hands. Now don't be sensitive, darling." She gave his hand a pat before drawing hers away. "We all understand how difficult the job market is, especially for botanists." Satisfied, Chantel rose. "I have to get into costume."

"They've scheduled publicity shots this morning," Larry told her after an uncertain glance at Quinn. "As soon as you're ready, you're supposed to go to the ballroom set."

"Fine."

"I'll go with you, darling." Quinn slipped an arm around her shoulders and squeezed, just a few degrees too hard. "You might need some help with buttons and snaps."

"Ease up, Doran," she muttered as they walked away. "I'm wearing a strapless dress for this scene, and I can't afford the bruises."

"You tempt me to put them where they won't show. A botanist?"

"I've always been attracted to the sensitive, introspective type."

"Like Larry?"

"He's my assistant. Leave him alone."

"Don't tell me how to do my job."

"He's a nice boy, he came with excellent references and—"

"How long ago?"

Annoyed, Chantel yanked open the door of her trailer. "About three months."

When the door shut at his back, Quinn drew out a notebook. "Let's have his full name."

"Larry Washington. But I don't see—"

"You don't have to. What about the makeup guy?"

"George? Don't be absurd, he's old enough to be my grandfather."

Quinn merely shifted his gaze until it met hers. "The name, angel. There's no age limit on a disturbed mind."

She muttered it, then swept back into the private dressing alcove. "I don't like the way you work, Doran."

"I'll notify the complaint department." Lowering to the arm of a chair, he took a quick, interested look around her dressing room. Like her home, it was meticulously decorated in white on white. "While we're at it, give me the names of the rest of the men you deal with on the set."

There was a brief, pregnant pause. "All of them?"

"That's right."

"That's impossible," she told him. "I couldn't possibly remember everyone. Oh, most by sight and by first name, but not everything about everyone."

"Then find out."

"I have a job to do. I can't—"

"So do I. Get me the names."

Chantel yanked up the zipper at her back and scowled at the wall that separated them. "I'll see if Larry can get me a list."

"No, you won't. I don't want to rouse anyone's suspicions."

"All right, all right." For a moment she was convinced the cure was more trouble than the problem. Then she remembered the contents of the last note. Like it or not, she needed Quinn. "The assistant director's name is Amos Leery. The cinematographer's Chuck Powers. And damn it, they didn't walk into town yesterday. They've been in the business for years. They have families."

"What difference does that make? An obsession's an obsession." When she walked back into the room, Quinn was still sitting, scribbling in his notebook.

"What about the director?"

"The director's a woman." Chantel slipped off her watch and laid it aside. "I think we can rule her out."

"What about the—" He made the mistake of looking up as he spoke. The words stopped because his thought processes simply disintegrated. She was wearing red, a hot, vibrant red that seemed to lick at her skin. The dress scooped low and snug at her breasts, then followed the lines of her body. The skirt hung straight, hitched up on one side nearly to the hip, where it was secured by a circlet of glittering stones. His mouth went suddenly and completely dry.

Chantel saw the look, recognized it. Normally it would have made her smile, either with pleasure or in automatic response. Now she found she couldn't, because her heart was thudding too hard. He rose slowly and she stepped back. It wouldn't occur to her until much later that it was the first time in her life she had retreated from a man.

"I'll have to give you the rest later," she said quickly. "They'll be waiting for me on set."

"What are you supposed to be in that?" He didn't take another step toward her. Self-preservation held him back.

Chantel moistened her lips. "A woman out for revenge."

He looked at her again, gradually, up, then down, then up again until their eyes met. "I'd say you get it."

Making a conscious effort, she drew in a breath, then let it out again. Play the role, she told herself. It was always possible to play the role. "Like it?" Deliberately she turned a slow circle, revealing the daring plunge at the back.

"It's a bit much for seven-thirty in the morning."

"Think so?" She smiled, more comfortable now. "Wait until you see the hardware that goes with it. Cartier's lending us a necklace and earrings. Two hundred and fifty thousand dollars worth of all that glitters. We'll have two armed guards and a very nervous jeweler here shortly."

"Why not use paste? It shines, too."

"Because the real thing makes for better publicity. Coming?"

He stopped her at the door with just a fingertip on her bare shoulder. Each of them felt the jolt. "One question. You wear anything under that?"

She managed another smile only because her hand was already on the knob. "This is Hollywood, Mr. Doran. We leave little details like that up to your imagination." She stepped out, hoping the constriction in her chest would ease before the first take.

* * *

By noon, Quinn had been forced to revise his opinion of Chantel at least in one area. She wasn't the pampered, temperamental prima donna he had expected. She worked like a horse—a thoroughbred, perhaps, but she went through her paces time and time again without complaint.

She'd been gracious to the photographers even when the session had run on for ninety minutes. She hadn't snapped at the makeup artist, as one of her co-stars had, when it had been time for yet another retouch. The temperature on the set was sizzling, thanks to the lights, but she didn't wilt. Between takes she sipped from an ever-present glass of mineral water, unable to sit, because wardrobe had fussed about creases in her costume.

Two armed guards kept their eyes trained on her, and on the quarter million in jewels she wore. They suited her, he was forced to admit—the thick gold band encrusted with diamonds and rubies that circled her neck, the symphony of diamonds and hot red stones that dripped from her ears. She wore them with the ease of a woman who knew she deserved them.

Quinn stayed well off the set and wondered how the actors could take the sheer monotony of repetition.

"Incredible, isn't it?"

Quinn turned his head and glanced at the tall, graying man beside him. "What's that?"

"How it takes them hours and hours to film a two-minute scene." He pulled out a thin black cigarette and lighted it from the butt of another. "I don't know why I come. It makes me nervous, but I can't stay away while they dissect my brainchild."

Quinn lifted a brow. "No, I suppose not."

He drew in smoke deeply before he smiled. "I'm not mad—or perhaps I am. I wrote the screenplay. Rather, I wrote what it appears this will loosely resemble." He offered a well-kept, rather thin hand. "James Brewster."

"Quinn Doran."

"Yes, I know. You're Miss O'Hurley's friend." He smiled again with a negligent shrug. "Word travels fast in small towns. She's quite brilliant, isn't she?"

"I don't know much about it."

"Oh, I assure you, she is. There was really no one else who could be Hailey. Cold, vindictive, clawing, and at the same time vulnerable and desperate for love. One of the few things I don't worry about as far as this little extravaganza goes is Chantel's interpretation of Hailey."

"She seems to know what she's doing."

"More, she feels what she's doing." Brewster took another quick puff as the crew set up for the next take. "It gives me enormous pleasure just to watch her."

Quinn slipped his hands into his pockets and mentally added Brewster to his growing list of men to check out. "She's an extraordinarily beautiful woman."

"That goes without saying. But then, to use a cliché, that's only skin deep. It's what's inside Chantel O'Hurley that fascinates."

Quinn's eyes narrowed fractionally. "And what's that?"

"I would say, Mr. Doran, that every man would have to discover that for himself."

The director called for quiet, and Brewster lapsed into a nervous silence. Quinn contemplated his own considerations.

She did seem to feel the part. The key scene called for her to confront her lover three years after he had left her, alone and abandoned. Even after a half a dozen takes, her eyes would frost over on cue, her voice would take on just the necessary hint of venom. On a dance floor crowded with people, she set out to seduce and humiliate. Chantel did both with such apparent ease that Quinn felt she must enjoy it.

Even to him, a man who'd learned how to look beyond illusions, it seemed that she was only aware of the man in whose arms she danced. There might not have been any cameras, any technicians, any dollies or lifts.

It went on for hours, but Quinn was patient. It interested him to see that whenever a break lasted longer than five minutes her assistant appeared at her elbow with a fresh glass of mineral water. More than once the assistant director came over to take her hand and murmur to her. The makeup artist retouched her face time and again, as though it were a rare canvas.

It was after seven before they wrapped. They had taken an hour for lunch, and apart from that, Quinn calculated, she had been on her feet for fourteen hours. All in all, he decided, he'd rather spend eight hours digging ditches.

"Ever think of another line of work?" Quinn asked her as they closed themselves in her trailer again.

"Oh, no." Chantel eased out of her shoes and felt her arches cramp instantly. "I love the glamour."

"Where was it?"

The smile came automatically. "You catch on fast. If she'd called for one more take, just one more, I was going to ask you to shoot her in the knee. Get the zipper for me, will you? My arms are like rubber."

"That's because you had them wrapped around Carter for most of the day."

"Just one of the perks of the job." She arched her back as Quinn brought the zipper down below her hips.

"He's okay, if you like the smooth poster-boy type."

She looked over her shoulder with a half smile. "I adore them."

"Ever think it might be Carter who's sending you flowers?"

She stiffened a bit, then walked into the dressing area. "He's too busy trying to untangle himself from his third wife. Besides, I've known him for years."

"People change, or do the unexpected. And you spend several hours a day in a clinch with him."

"That's work."

"Nice work if you can get it. In any case, you shouldn't trust anyone."

"Except you."

"That's right. Brewster seemed pretty taken with you, too."

"Brewster? The writer?" Really amused, Chantel walked back in, still buttoning her blouse. "James is much more interested in his characters than the people who play them. And he's been happily married for twenty-odd years. Don't you ever read the gossip-columns?"

"Never miss them." He stopped in the act of reaching for a cigarette when she sat abruptly and grabbed her foot. "Problem?"

"It's always after you take those damn things off that you're in agony." She winced, swore and kneaded. "I can tell you, it was a man who invented the high heel—the same one who invented the bra."

"It's you women who wear the things," he pointed out, but knelt down and took her foot in his hand. "Got you in the arch?"

"Yes, but—" Her protest died on her lips as he began to press. With a long, sincere sigh, she leaned back. "Yes, that's wonderful. You've missed your calling. You could make a fortune as a masseur."

"You should see what I could do for the rest of you."

She opened one eye. "We'll just stick with the feet, thanks. If I were a few inches taller, or Sean a few inches shorter, I could have gotten away with flats for most of the shots."

"I'll tell you this, his love scenes with you seemed pretty sincere."

"They're supposed to." Bone-tired, she opened both eyes. "Look, we're professionals. It looked that way because we played it that way, not because either one of us has any physical interest in the other."

"It looked like interest from my angle. Especially when he put his hand on your—"

"Try another tune, Doran."

"I think you're about to tell me how to do my job again."

"I'd like you to do your job," she shot back, "instead of harping on a man just because he's good at his work."

"Just checking him out, angel."

"I don't want my friends and associates spied on."

"If you want someone who's afraid to step on toes, you hired the wrong man."

"I've come to that conclusion several times myself." She couldn't have said why her temper was building so quickly, but his hands moving slowly up and down the arch of her foot were doing things they shouldn't to her system. She wanted him out and gone. "Why don't you take a walk, Doran?" She jerked her foot away. "You're just not my style." Rising, she stepped around him. "You can keep the change."

"Fine." He was as angry as she, and just as baffled as to the cause. He only knew that for one quick moment he'd felt something for her, something soft and easy. It was gone now, erased as if it had never been. In its place was the anger, and a need, just as strong, that demanded physical release. "I might as well take a bonus while I'm at it."

He grabbed her. She'd known he wouldn't be gentle. His hand tangled in her hair as his mouth came down on hers. She'd known he would show little finesse. What she hadn't known, or hadn't admitted, was that she could respond so completely.

No man held her when she didn't choose to be held. No man took from her what she didn't willingly offer. Yet he *was* holding her, and she found nothing within herself to make him stop. His face was rough against her, and his fingers dug into her skin as he held her close. Defending herself should have been simple, even automatic, yet she didn't struggle in his arms. Her knees trembled, but she didn't even feel it. Everything was bound up in the sensation of his mouth on hers and the explosion of the taste of him. Delectable. Her lips parted and invited him in.

He rarely worried about consequences, and even less frequently questioned his instincts. When he had felt the need to touch her, to take her this way, he had done so. He was already paying for it. She was more than he had imagined she could be. Softer, smoother, warmer. It wasn't an image he held in his arms but a passionate, hot-blooded woman. Even as he discovered and explored the flavor and texture of her lips, he understood that he needed more. That was the trap, and he'd fallen right into it.

He drew her away because he wanted to see her face after she had tasted him. Her eyes opened slowly, so dark, so very blue that for an instant he was more vulnerable to her than either of them could have guessed. He felt the need shift to an ache, and the ache to uncertainty, before he pulled himself back.

"It's been an interesting day, angel." And one he was afraid he wouldn't easily forget. "Why don't you tell Matt to find you somebody else?"

It had been a long time since she had felt rejection. It hurt more than she remembered. Training and pride had her straightening and kept her voice icy cool. "If you've finished your show of male dominance, you can go." The image was back, even before her pulse had started to level. "If I hear of someone who needs a bodyguard for their poodle, I'll give them your card."

Chantel turned away when the phone rang. She picked up the receiver, then looked over her shoulder until she saw Quinn open the door. With a toss of her head, she brought it back to her ear. "Yes, hello."

The voice was too familiar now, and a degree more frightening. "I've waited all day to talk to you. You're so beautiful, so exciting. All day I've been imagining how we would—"

"Why don't you stop?" Control snapped as she shouted into the phone. "Why don't you just leave me alone?" Before she could slam the receiver down, Quinn snatched it out of her hand.

"Don't be angry." The edgy desperation in the voice had him tensing. "I love you. I can make you happy, happier than you've ever been."

"Miss O'Hurley's happier without you," Quinn said calmly. "You really should stop bothering her."

There was a long silence, and Quinn heard the breathing on the other end of the phone grow heavier. "She doesn't need you. She needs me. She needs me," the voice repeated before the connection was broken. Quietly Quinn replaced the receiver. Chantel's back was to him, but after a moment she turned around.

He could see that she'd worked hard, even in those few moments, to regain her composure. But her skin was as white as the room around them. "I thought you'd gone."

"So did I." He made it a policy never to apologize for his actions. It was not that he didn't believe he could be wrong, just that apologies tended to weaken his position. In this case, he decided to come as close as possible without crossing the line. "Look, we don't have to like each other much to get this job done, and I don't like to leave things before they're finished. Why don't we just forget about what happened before."

She didn't care for compromises any more than Quinn did for apologies. But she cared less for the thought of going on alone. To satisfy both her needs and her pride, she gave him a bland smile. "Did something happen before?"

He acknowledged the gibe with a slight nod. "Not a thing. Let's get out of here."

Chapter 4

Chantel had long ago acknowledged that one couldn't have both privacy and fame. In order to achieve and maintain the second, the first almost invariably had to be sacrificed. If she went out for a quiet dinner with a friend, she would read about it the next day. If she danced with another celebrity, there would be pictures and speculation before the music stopped. According to the press, her life was full of men, full of wild, sizzling romance and blistering affairs. She accepted that. She was also shrewd enough to know that if she were rude or belligerent to the paparazzi both her reputation and her photographs would be unflattering. So she was willing, within reason, to court them and present a glamorous and unflappable image to the public.

But the tap on her phone and the guard at her gate were entirely different. They weren't part of the creamy silk-and-diamonds mystique she'd chosen to develop. If she had the choice... Every time that thought ran through her head, Chantel gritted her teeth and reminded herself that she didn't.

She should be grateful. It was difficult to acknowledge that fact, but she knew she should be. Since the phone call in her dressing room there had been nothing—no letters, no flowers, no whispering voice. She told herself she should be relieved. Instead, she felt as though she were waiting for the other shoe to drop.

During the week her work kept her too busy to think. She could, for a few hours a day, plunge herself into Hailey's character and her problems. As long as the film was rolling and the pressure was on, it was difficult to think of her own personal crises. Work had gotten her through other rough periods. She counted on its doing the same for her now.

But it was Saturday and the film was going smoothly, so she had no call. Normally she treasured mornings when she could lounge in bed for a few extra hours, indulging in the things that were reported to be part of her everyday life.

By seven she was awake. Disgusted, she ordered herself back to sleep. At seven-fifteen she was staring at the ceiling and thinking a great deal too much for her own peace of mind. Beautiful, glamorous women were supposed to sleep until noon, then pamper themselves with massages and facials. She'd have believed that herself if she hadn't been in the game so long.

Tossing the covers aside, she went into the office that adjoined her dressing room. Of all the rooms in her home, this one, and only this one, showed the other side of her. The furnishings, though sophisticated, were simple and functional; the material for the curtains might have been imported from Paris, but the space as a whole was imbued with a sense of organization and practicality. Her desk had been purchased for its usefulness as well as its appearance. And she did use it. She also used the computer that rested on it.

It was true that she had an agent and personal manager, a team of publicists and an assistant, but Chantel believed in keeping a handle on her own life, her own business. She knew what stocks she owned and the gross she received from the pictures she'd made. Copies of her contracts were meticulously filed. Chantel didn't simply sign them, she read them.

She went directly to her desk and, ignoring her thick appointment book and the pile of phone messages left by her maid, picked up a fat stack of papers. There were three scripts she hadn't so much as glanced at. The filming on *Strangers* wouldn't last forever. The sooner she started thinking about her next project, the less idle time she'd have.

Chantel got back into bed, propped the first script on her knees and told herself she would wait until eight o'clock for coffee. It only took half that time for her to discover that the first script was hopeless. The story itself had a few things going for it, but most of them were scenes with her naked, wrapped in one passionate embrace after another. She wasn't a prude, but neither was she willing to use her body as a selling point for a mediocre script. In any case, she was tired of playing the vamp or the victim. She tossed the script aside and picked up another. It caught her from the first page.

A comedy. At last someone had sent her an intelligent story that didn't rely exclusively on her sexuality to sell it. Not only was the dialogue sharp, the plot had twist after twist and made her chuckle out loud. The jokes were as much physical as verbal and would, she knew, exhaust her. Her character would make a fool of herself on-screen time after time. She'd end up with her face in the mud. And Chantel would love it.

Bless you, Matt. Halfway through the script, Chantel hugged it to her breast. He knew she wanted to do something at odds with the image they had both carefully created over the last six years. It would be a risk. Would people pay to see her face with mud on it? Chantel was willing to bet they would.

Happier than she'd been in weeks, Chantel pushed the intercom button and ordered breakfast brought up. She wasn't budging until she finished the last page. And when she did, she was going to call Matt. If she had to go to a casting call for this one, she would. If she had to read for the part, she'd read for it. She'd take a cut in salary if need be, but this was going to be hers.

Chantel snuggled back against the pillows, brought up her knees and turned the next page.

When the knock came at her door, she was totally absorbed. She answered absently, then began to chuckle as the character, *her* character, punched her way out of another crisis.

"Must be pretty funny stuff," Quinn commented.

Chantel's head whipped around. The amusement in her eyes turned instantly to annoyance. It was too bad, she thought, that he had to look so damn good. "A pity I didn't load that gun."

"You wouldn't shoot a man who's bringing you breakfast in bed." He moved across the room, set the tray on her lap, then made himself comfortable on the bed beside her. He wore a T-shirt and faded jeans and didn't seem to mind that his sneakers were on her handsewn spread. "What are you reading?" he asked, then stretched out his legs and crossed his arms behind his head.

"The stock market reports."

"Yeah, I always get a kick out of them, too." The pillows carried her scent, sexy, exotic and alluring. She was a bit rumpled from sleep, her hair tumbling around her shoulders and down her back. Even in the strong morning light he couldn't find a single flaw on her face. There were two skinny straps over her shoulders and a very little bit of lace low at her breasts. He remembered what he shouldn't have—what it felt like to hold her against him and kiss her until his mind went dim. He plucked a piece of toast off the tray and reached for the jelly.

"Help yourself," she muttered, fighting the urge to inch away.

"Thanks." He leaned over the tray as he spread on a healthy portion of jelly. When his breath whispered warm over her bare shoulder, she stiffened and reminded herself how much she disliked him. "Like I said before, this is a great bed."

"When I get the bill for laundering the spread, I'll deduct it from your fee." Determined not to show any reaction, Chantel reached for the pot of coffee and poured a cup. "What can I do for you, Doran?"

He nibbled on the toast and just looked at her. The smile bloomed slowly, very slowly.

"Don't embarrass yourself," she told him, and sipped the coffee while it was too hot. When it scalded her tongue, she decided she didn't simply dislike him. She detested him.

"Ask a silly question," he began, then proceeded to pour himself a cup of coffee.

"Look, I'm busy, so if—"

"Yeah, I can see that."

"I happen to be reading some scripts."

"Any good?"

Chantel drew a deep breath. Some men were more thickheaded than others, she reminded herself. Perhaps if she humored him a little... "As a matter of fact, yes. I want to finish this one this morning, so if we've business to discuss—"

"You going to chew up another man in this one?"

Patience, Chantel told herself. It was compassionate to show patience to an idiot. "No. As it happens, this is a comedy."

"A comedy?" He let out one quick laugh before he drank. "You?"

Her eyes narrowed. "Don't push your luck, Doran."

"Come on, angel. Yours isn't the kind of face that a man pushes a pie into."

"It's mud."

"What?"

"In this case, my face gets pushed in mud."

He chose a piece of melon from her bowl. "That I'd have to see."

"I'm counting on several million people having your attitude." With a natural flair, she whipped the napkin from its ring and passed it to him. "You are, after all, the common man, aren't you?"

"As common as they come," he said easily.

"Now, why don't you tell me why you're here this morning with your feet on my bed and your hands in my breakfast."

"Just part of the service. Great coffee."

"I'll give your compliments to the chef. Now, why don't you get to the point?"

"Aren't you going to eat?"

"Doran."

"Okay." He took a small folder out of the side basket of the tray and opened it. "I have a couple of preliminary reports. Thought you'd be interested."

"Reports on what?"

"Larry Washington, Amos Leery, James Brewster. Also have a bit on the makeup guy and your driver."

"My driver? You're investigating Robert?" Her appetite gone, Chantel pushed herself farther up in bed. Quinn saw dark rose silk beneath the lace and wondered how far down it went. "That's the most ridiculous thing I've ever heard."

"Angel, don't you ever read mysteries? The one you least suspect is always the one who done it."

"I'm not paying you to play Sam Spade, and I'm damned if I can see paying you to run investigations on people like Robert and George."

After brief consideration, Quinn decided on a strawberry. "Have you ever noticed how your Robert looks at you?"

The lace rose up, then settled again with her breathing. Deliberately Chantel tilted her head. "Darling, *all* men look at me like that."

He gave her a long stare before he sipped his coffee again. Even he had problems separating her act from reality. "Since I have to start somewhere, I'm starting with the men closest to you."

"The next thing you'll tell me is you're investigating Matt." When he said nothing, she looked at him again. "You must be joking. Matt's—"

"A man," Quinn finished for her. "You just said that was all it takes."

Furious, Chantel picked up the tray, then dumped it in his lap. Coffee sloshed over the rims of the cups. "Look, let's just stop this right now. I'm not going to have people I care about spied on and embarrassed. Matt's the closest friend I have, and I was under the impression he was your friend, too."

"This is business."

"Let's say our business is concluded. The calls have stopped, and so have the letters."

"For a whole forty-eight hours."

"That's enough for me. I'll pay your fee through today and we'll—" She broke off, the words sticking in her throat as the phone beside the bed began to ring. Without realizing it, Chantel found her hand in Quinn's, her fingers locked tight.

"They'll pick it up downstairs," he murmured. "Don't panic. If it's him, just keep calm. Try to get him to talk, to stay on the line as long as possible. We need time to run a trace." When the intercom buzzed, she jumped. "Pull yourself together, Chantel. You can handle it."

Working at keeping her breathing steady, Chantel spoke into the intercom. "Yes?"

"There's a man on the line, Miss O'Hurley. He won't give his name, but he says it's important. Shall I tell him you're unavailable?"

"Yes, I—" Quinn's hand curled around her wrist. "No, no, I'll take it. Thank you."

"Take it slow," Quinn told her. "Just let him talk."

Her fingers were stiff and cold as she picked up the receiver. "Hello." Quinn only had to look at her face to know she was hearing the familiar whisper.

"Don't lose it," he said quietly, keeping her free hand in his. "Just keep him on the line. Stay calm and answer him."

"Thank you," she managed, despite the block in her throat. "Yes, yes, I've gotten all your letters. No, I'm not angry." She closed her eyes and tried to pretend that the things he was saying didn't make her skin crawl. "I wish you'd tell me who you are. If you'd—" Caught between frustration and relief, she brought the receiver away from her ear. "He hung up."

"Damn." After setting the tray on the floor beside the

bed, Quinn leaned over her and punched a few buttons on the phone. "It's Quinn." He swore again. "Yeah, just keep on it. Right. Not enough time," he told Chantel as he hung up the phone again. "Did he say anything that rang a bell, anything that makes you think of someone you know?"

"No." She trembled once before she regained control. "No one I know has a mind like that."

"Drink some coffee." He poured more into her cup, then handed it to her. She drank to ease the tightness in her throat.

"Quinn." She had to swallow again. "He said—he said he had a surprise for me, a big surprise." When she turned her head to look at him, her eyes were huge and dark. "He said it wouldn't be much longer."

"Let me worry about him." He'd always had a soft spot for the defenseless. It had gotten him into trouble before— in South America, in Afghanistan, and in countless other places. Even though he knew it might be dangerous in a more personal way, he slipped an arm around her shoulders and brought her close. "That's what you're paying me for, angel."

"He's going to get to me." She said it with such flat finality that he tightened his hold. "I can feel it."

"He'll have a hard time doing that with me in the way. Listen, I've got two men patrolling the grounds, two others monitoring the phones."

"It doesn't seem to help." She closed her eyes and for a moment let herself lean on him. "Maybe it's because I can't see them."

"You can see me, can't you?"

"Yeah." And she could feel him, could feel the hard, working muscles of his arm and shoulder, the not-so-smooth skin of his face.

"Want to see more of me?"

Cautious, Chantel lifted her face to look into his. There was humor there, but—she was sure she was mistaken—it looked as though there were genuine concern, as well. "I beg your pardon?"

"I like the way you do that. Angel, you could cut a man off at the knees without lifting a finger."

"It's a talent of mine. Explain, Doran."

"Why don't I move in for a while? Now don't let your ego get the best of you," he warned as she started to stiffen. "You've got plenty of rooms in this place, and though I am developing a real fondness for your bed, I can make do with another. What do you say, angel? Want a housemate?"

She frowned at him, hating to admit how much safer she would feel with him around all the time. The house was certainly big enough to keep them out of each other's way, though privacy would go out of the window. The real problem would be remembering just how he'd made her feel during that one sizzling kiss. If he were around twenty-four hours a day, remembering might not be enough.

"Maybe I should buy that vicious dog," Chantel muttered.

"Your choice."

That was true. It was. And she knew exactly how to handle it—and him. "Go ahead and get your duffel bag, Doran. We'll find a corner for you to sleep in." Sitting up, she flipped through the script again. She felt better, she couldn't deny it. The icy fist in her stomach had loosened. "How much extra is this going to cost me?"

"Meals—and I want more than a bowl of fruit in the morning—use of the facilities and, since this is going to play hell with my social life, another two hundred a day."

"Two hundred?" Chantel gave a quick, unladylike snort. "I can't imagine your social life's worth more than fifty. Isn't that the going rate in the massage parlors?"

"What do you know about massage parlors?"

She slanted him a look. "Just what I see in the movies, darling."

"How about a hands-on demonstration?" He lifted a finger and slid a strap from her shoulder. Instead of replacing it, Chantel simply studied the script.

"No, thanks. I doubt if there's anything you could teach me."

"I was thinking more the other way around." When he nudged the other strap aside, Chantel lifted her gaze to his. He was baiting her, and she wasn't ready to nibble.

"Try me when I've got a few weeks to spare, Doran. With you, I'm afraid we'd have to start from scratch."

"I'm a fast learner." He slid his hand up her shoulder until his thumb brushed her jaw.

She grabbed his wrist before she could stop herself, but her voice remained steady. "Watch your step."

"If you watch your step, you miss too much."

He'd wanted to touch her again, to feel her skin smooth and warm under his hands. He'd wanted to see her eyes darken, partly from anger, partly from temptation, when he did. She looked ready to rake his face, but the bite of her nails wouldn't stop him from sampling the fire she held so well banked inside her. The fire she let flame so explosively on screen.

When her free hand came up, he grabbed it. She held one of his, he held one of hers. As far as Quinn was concerned, they were even. He thought it was pride that kept her from struggling, pride and the confidence that she could bring him to his knees whenever she chose. He wasn't as certain as he wanted to be that she couldn't.

He was just about to let her go when her chin lifted and her eyes dared him. He'd always been a sucker for a dare.

With his eyes open and on hers, he lowered his mouth.

But he didn't kiss her. Chantel felt the impact, both surprised and aroused, when he caught her bottom lip between his teeth. The chilly nonresponse she'd been determined to give him began to heat.

She could have stopped him. Her brother Trace had taught her and her sisters how to defend themselves from overamorous members of the male sex. Chantel was aware that she could take Quinn by surprise and have him bent over double and gasping for air with one quick jerk of her knee. She lay still, hypnotized by the green eyes that watched her.

She wasn't supposed to have these kind of feelings, this kind of hunger. She had blocked them out years before, when her emotions had made a fool of her. She wasn't supposed to have this slow, curling sensation in her stomach. Her bones weren't supposed to liquify at a touch. She'd done love scene after love scene—choreographed, blocked out, shot and reshot for the camera—and had felt nothing that hadn't been programmed into her character. She knew just how little the most passionate embrace could mean to the two people involved.

This light, nibbling sensation on her lip should have done nothing but annoy her. But she lay still, trapped by an urgent desire to absorb the rushing range of feeling it brought to her.

Impossible. It had to be impossible, but he felt innocence shimmering around her. If it was an act, she was more skilled than she had a right to be. If it wasn't—but he couldn't think. She did something to his mind that she shouldn't be permitted to do. She pushed her way into it and filled it until he was ready to forget everything but her.

Desire. Desire was something easily quenched and easily forgotten. It would pay to remember that. Any man was bound to want her. But he wasn't sure any man would be able to forget her. There was too much power in her, the power to make a man hunger, to make him ache, to make him weak. Quinn couldn't afford to lose his hold. With her lips warm and soft under his, he reminded himself that he had two priorities. One was to keep her safe. The other was to look out for himself.

When he felt himself sinking, he pulled back. The ground was too unsteady here. For once he would indeed watch his step. "You pack a punch, angel."

Steady, she told herself, struggling to find a foothold. It meant nothing to him, nothing more than the eternal war of wills men and women fought. He hadn't gone soft inside or felt the need to be loved, the need to believe that maybe, just maybe, this was right. She wouldn't give him the satisfaction of knowing she had.

"Next time it'll flatten you."

"You might be right," he muttered, and shifted away. "Your skin's a little pale." He skimmed his gaze over her bare shoulders and cursed himself for the twist of need he felt. "Get dressed and meet me out by the pool. I'll bring you up to date on what we have so far." He rolled from the bed and, taking the file with him, left her alone.

He needed some air, fast.

Quinn cut through the water of the pool like an eel, smooth, fast and quiet. When Chantel came onto the patio, she stood in the sunlight and watched him. She hadn't been wrong about the feel of his muscles. She could see them now, rippling with each stroke of his arm, bunching with each kick of his leg. He'd chosen brief black trunks from the stack she kept in the poolhouse for guests. They fit low and snug over his hips.

Still, she imagined he'd picked them for comfort rather than impact. As far as she could tell, Quinn Doran considered himself too irresistible to think about such things. She chose a chair by an umbrellaed table and waited for him to surface.

The physical exertion helped. Quinn realized he'd pushed himself closer to the limit with her than he'd intended. He still wasn't sure why he'd made a move toward her when he knew she was the kind of woman a smart man kept his distance from. He'd always been smart. That was the way you survived. But he'd also always had a habit of giving in to temptation. That was the way you lived. Though his life had never been dull, Chantel O'Hurley was his biggest temptation so far.

By the time he'd crossed the length of the pool and back thirty times, most of the tension had drained. Under other circumstances he would have used a punching bag to relieve it, but he was willing to make use of whatever was available.

Tossing wet hair from his face, he stood in the shallow end, water lapping at his thighs. And he saw her.

Tipped back in the chair, her face shaded by a big, white umbrella, she was the epitome of cool, gut-wrenching beauty. She'd pulled her hair up and back so that her face was unframed. It needed no framing. The sleek, severe style only accented that fact. The snug top she wore was cut deep at the shoulders and cinched into the waistband of cropped shorts that showed off long, long legs. His gaze lingered on those legs as he hauled himself out of the pool.

"You've got a hell of a foundation, angel."

"So I'm told." Reaching beside her, she picked up a towel. "I see you're finding your way around all right." She tossed the towel to him, but he did no more than sling it around his neck. The sunlight shimmered on the drops of water on his bronzed skin.

"Nice pool."

"I like it."

"Then you should use it more. Swimming's a great way to keep in shape."

"I'll worry about my shape, Doran." Temper was licking its way to the surface. Chantel coated it with sarcasm. "Is this going to take long? I want to get my nails done this afternoon."

"We'll fit it in."

"We?" She couldn't prevent a smile as he sat across from her. "Somehow I can't picture you in a chi-chi little place like Nail It Down."

"I've been in worse." He shifted the chair slightly, placing himself in full sunlight. "Anything else on your agenda today?"

"Oh, maybe a little window-shopping on Rodeo Drive," she said on the spur of the moment, just to make things tougher. "Lunch at Ma-Maison, I think, or perhaps the Bistro." She rested her chin on the back of her hand. "It's been *days* since I've seen anyone. You do have something appropriate to wear, don't you?"

"I'll get by. Then there's that charity dinner tonight."

Her smile faded. "How did you know about that?"

"It's my job to know." Though he didn't need them Quinn flipped through his notes. "My secretary contacted Sean Carter and explained you had another escort."

"Then she can contact him again. Sean and I arranged to go together to help promote the film."

"Are you willing to get into a dark limo with a man who might be—"

"It's not Sean." After cutting him off, Chantel reached for the pack of cigarettes Quinn had tossed on the table.

"We'll just play this my way." Quinn picked up his lighter and flicked it on. "I'll take you to your little party, and if you like you can cuddle with Sean for the cameras. What about tomorrow?"

Chantel gave him a poisonous look. "You tell me."

Quinn patiently flipped open his file. "You've got a reporter and photographer from *Life-styles* coming at one to do a story on you and the house. That's all I've got."

She dropped the cigarette in an ashtray and let it smolder. "Because that's all there is. I have some personal things to attend to here at home, then I go to bed early because Monday's a working day."

"Matt said you were practical." Quinn flipped the page over. "Larry Washington."

"Get on with it," she told him. "You won't be happy until you do."

"The kid looks clean enough on the surface. Graduated UCLA last year with a degree in business management. Seems he always had a thing for the theater, but preferred the setups and backstage stuff to the acting."

"Which is exactly why I hired him."

"Apparently he had a pretty heavy thing going with a co-ed until about six months ago. A very attractive blue-eyed blonde. She dumped him."

He didn't have to spell out the implications. "A lot of women have blue eyes, and a lot of college romances break up."

"Amos Leery," he continued, ignoring her. "Did you know his first wife divorced him because he couldn't keep his hands off other women?"

"Yes, I know. And it was fifteen years ago, so—"

"Old habits die hard. George McLintoch."

"That's pitiful, Doran. Even for you."

"He's been a makeup artist for thirty-three years. Has five grandchildren and another due in the fall. Since his wife died a couple of years ago, he's had a few problems with the bottle."

"That's enough." She rose and paced to the edge of the pool. The water was calm and crystal clear. So had her life been only a few weeks before. "That's really enough. I'm not going to sit here and listen to you dissect the personal problems of people I work with." She looked back over her shoulder. "You're in a filthy business."

"That's right." Not by a flicker did he reveal his feelings on the subject. "James Brewster. Seems like a pretty stable family life. Married twenty-one years, one son studying law in the east. Interesting that he's been in analysis for over ten years."

"Everyone in this town's in analysis."

"You're not."

"I will be if I keep you around."

He smiled briefly, then turned the page. "Your driver, Robert, is an interesting character. Young Robert DeFranco has himself a string of ladies."

"Just your kind of man."

"Can't help but admire his stamina. Matt Burns."

She turned all the way around then. This time he saw not anger but revulsion. It ripped at something inside him. "How could you?" She said it quietly and painfully. "He's your friend."

"This is my job."

"It's your job to spy into the personal lives of people you're supposed to care about?"

He kept his eyes on hers. "I can't afford to care about anyone but my clients when they're paying me. That's the service."

"Then keep this part of it to yourself. Whatever you dug up about Matt, I don't want to know."

He wouldn't allow her to make him regret what he'd

done. He'd done worse, much worse. He wondered how she'd look at him if she knew. "Chantel, you're going to have to consider all the possibilities."

"No, *you* are. And at this point you're getting seven hundred a day to do it. It's your job to find whoever's hounding me and to keep me safe while you're doing it."

"This is the way I do it."

"Fine. Since it is, all I want to see from you is the bill."

She started to storm back into the house, but he blocked her path. "Grow up." Taking her by the shoulders, he held her still. She was hurting, he realized, really hurting for the people she cared for. He had to convince her that she couldn't afford to. "Anyone at all could be making those calls. Maybe it's someone you've never even met, but my instincts tell me different. He knows you, lady." He gave her a quick shake to accentuate his point. "And he wants you real bad. Until we find him, you're going to do just like I say."

That morning's call was still too fresh in her mind. If a compromise had to be made, she'd make it. But she wouldn't like it. "I'll do what you say, Doran, to a point. I'll have my phone tapped, I'll have the damn guards at the gate and you in my house, but I won't listen to this garbage."

"In other words, you'll make a good showing, but you don't want the details."

"You got it."

He dropped his hands. "I thought you had more guts than that."

She opened her mouth to yell, then shut it again because he was right. She just didn't have the stomach for it. "Dry off, Doran."

She turned on her heel and walked away. As he stood watching her, Quinn decided his instincts were as reliable as ever. When push came to shove, she wouldn't crumble.

Chapter 5

When they got through the weekend without chewing any pieces off each other, Chantel decided they might make it. It hadn't pleased her to go to dinner with him and pretend, in front of three hundred other people, that she enjoyed being with him. Chantel had told herself to look at it as a job—a particularly difficult and unappealing job. Then Quinn had thrown her a curve. He'd been charming.

Surprisingly, black tie suited him. Though it didn't quite disguise his rough edges, it made them all the more appealing. He would never be suave or smooth or glossy. For some reason, Chantel found she was pleased to know that. He might wear a silk tie and the trappings of sophistication, but you knew—at least if you were a woman you knew—that a barbarian lay underneath.

Before the evening was over, he had drunk champagne with this year's top box-office draw and had danced with a three-time-Oscar-winning actress. The seventy-year-old veteran had patted Chantel on the knee and told her that

her taste in men was improving. Though that had been difficult to swallow, not once during the evening had Quinn
given Chantel the opportunity to smirk at him.

On Sunday he left her to herself. When the reporters
came and she gave them an interview and a tour of her
home, it was as if he weren't even there. She knew he was
around, somewhere, but he didn't infringe on her privacy.
She was free to get back to her reading, to indulge in a
long, soothing whirlpool bath and to catch up on corre-
spondence and a few niggling business matters. By the
time they left the house on Monday morning, Chantel was
almost ready to revise her opinion of him.

She felt rested and eager for work. The night before, she
had finished the script she'd begun on Saturday morning
and was more enthusiastic than ever. She'd woken Matt out
of a sound sleep to tell him to go after the part. It might
have been shy of 6:00 a.m., but Chantel felt wonderful.

She glanced over at Quinn beside her, legs stretched out,
eyes closed behind tinted glasses. From the look of him,
he hadn't shaved since Saturday. It seemed unfair that the
slightly dissipated aura suited him so.

"Rough night?"

He opened one eye. Then, finding it too much effort,
he closed it again. "Poker game."

"You played poker last night? I didn't know you'd gone
out."

"In the kitchen," he muttered, wondering how soon he
could get his hands on another cup of coffee.

"My kitchen?" Chantel frowned, a little annoyed that
she hadn't been asked to play. "With whom?"

"Gardener."

"Rafael? He hardly speaks English."

"Don't have to to know a full house beats a straight."

"I see." A smile tugged at her lips. "So you and Rafael played poker in the kitchen, got drunk and told lies."

"And Marsh."

"And Marsh what?" She stopped in the act of reaching for a glass. "Marsh played cards? *My* Marsh?"

"Tall guy, not much hair."

"Really, Quinn, he's nearly eighty and quite creaky. I'm surprised even you would take advantage of him."

"Took me for eighty-three dollars. Canny old son of a—"

"Serves you right," she said with satisfaction. "Sitting down in my kitchen, swilling beer and smoking cigars and bragging about women when I'm paying for your time."

"You were asleep."

"I hardly think that matters. You're being paid to watch out for me, not play five-card stud."

"Five-card draw, jacks or better. And I was watching out for you."

"Really?" She brought a glass of juice to her lips. "That's odd. I didn't see hide nor hair of you yesterday."

"I was around. You enjoy your whirlpool?"

"I beg your pardon?"

"You spent damn near an hour in that tub." He took the glass from her and drained it. Maybe it would wash the cotton out of his mouth. "Funny, I figured a woman like you would have two dozen bathing suits. Guess you couldn't find one."

"You were watching me."

He handed the glass back to her, then settled back again. "That's what you're paying me for."

Indignation rippled through her as she slammed the glass back in its holder. "I'm not paying you to be a Peeping Tom. Get your prurient kicks on your own time."

"My time is your time, angel. I saw nearly that much of

you when I plunked down ten bucks to see *Thin Ice*. Besides, if I'd been out for kicks, I'd have joined you."

"I'd have drowned you," she tossed back, but he only smiled and shut his eyes again.

His head was pounding like a jackhammer. He'd gotten less sleep before, but that had usually been of his own choosing. The poker game had been his way of distracting himself from the knowledge that she was sleeping upstairs, his way of trying to forget the way she'd looked stretched out in the foaming water of the spa that afternoon.

He hadn't, as he wanted her to believe, watched her. He'd seen her go into the poolhouse. Then, when she hadn't come out, he'd gone to check on her. She'd been lounging in the big tub, Rachmaninoff wafting from the overhead speakers. Her hair had been left down and floated in the frothing water. And her body...her body had been long and slender and pale. He could still feel the impact, like a sledgehammer straight to the solar plexus.

He hadn't stayed to tease and taunt, but had left as quietly as he'd come. There had been a fear, a definite fear that if she'd opened her eyes and looked at him he'd have crawled.

Thoughts of her haunted him day and night. He knew he should be able to prevent it. Nothing and no one was permitted to have power over him. But he was beginning to understand how a woman could become an obsession by simply existing. He was beginning to understand how a man could become overwhelmed by his own fantasies.

It made him worry about himself, but it made him worry more about her. If another man had become obsessed with her, and that other man had crossed certain lines, to what lengths might he go to have her? The letters and calls were gradually becoming more urgent. When would he stop them and try something more desperate?

As frightened as she was, Quinn didn't believe Chantel had any conception of just how far that kind of madness could push a man. The longer he was around her, the more he realized just how far that was.

They would shoot on the back lot that day. Another camera crew was already in New York filming exteriors. Chantel was looking forward to the time when she and other members of the crew would fly east for the handful of scenes to be shot on location. It would give her a chance to see her sister Maddy and, with any luck, catch her play on Broadway.

The thought of it brought back her earlier cheerful mood. It lasted even through an hour's delay while technicians worked out a few bugs.

"Looks like New England," Quinn commented as he glanced around the open-air set.

"Massachusetts, to be exact," Chantel told him, nibbling on a sticky bun. "Ever been there?"

"I was born in Vermont."

"I was born on a train." Chantel broke off another piece of her bun and laughed. "Well, nearly. My parents were on their way to a gig when my mother went into labor. They stopped off long enough to have my sisters and me."

"Your sisters *and* you?"

"That's right. I'm the oldest of triplets."

"There are three of you. Good God."

"There's only one of me, Doran." She popped a piece of the bun in his mouth, enjoying the fresh air and sunshine. "We're triplets, but each of us manages to be her own person. Abby's raising horses and kids in Virginia, and Maddy's currently wowing them on Broadway."

"You don't look like the family type."

"Really." She felt too good to be offended. "I also have

a brother. I can't tell you what he does, because no one's quite sure. I lean toward professional gigolo or international jewel thief. You'd get along beautifully with him." She watched one of the prop men pick up a boulder and move it a few feet. "Amazing, isn't it?"

Quinn studied the trees. They looked real, just like the ones back home, until you saw the wood base they sat on. "Anything real around here?"

"Not a great deal. Give them a few hours and they could make this a jungle in Kenya." Stretching her back, she toyed with the ice in her cup. She was used to waiting. "We were going to shoot this on location, but there were some problems."

"There's a lot of wait around in this business."

"It's not for the restless. I've gone back to my trailer and sat for hours to be called back for a five-minute scene. Other days you put in fourteen hours nonstop."

"Why?"

"Why what?"

"Why do you do it?"

"Because it's what I've always wanted to do." It was a stock answer. Why she felt obliged to elaborate on it, she didn't know. "When I was little and I sat in a theater and saw what could happen, I knew I had to be a part of it."

"So you always wanted to be an actress."

She tossed her hair back and smiled. "I've always been an actress. I wanted to be a star."

"Looks like you got what you wanted."

"Looks like," she murmured, shaking off a hint of depression. "What about you? Did you always want to be a—whatever it is you are?"

"I wanted to be a juvenile delinquent, and was doing a pretty good job of it."

"Sounds fascinating." She wanted to know more. To

be honest, she wanted to know everything about him, but she'd take care how she asked. "Why aren't you serving ten-to-twenty in San Quentin?"

"I got drafted." He grinned, but she sensed the joke was very much his own.

"The army builds men."

"Something like that. Anyway, I learned to do what I was good at, make a profit and stay out of jail."

"And what are you good at?" He turned his head, just enough that she could see the amusement and the challenge in his eyes. "Forget I asked. Let's try something else. How long were you in the army?"

"I didn't say I was in the army." He offered her a cigarette, then lighted it himself when she shook her head.

"You said you were drafted."

"I was. Drafted and government-trained. Want some more coffee?"

"No. How long were you in?"

"Too long."

"Is that where you learned not to give a direct answer?"

"Yeah." He smiled at her again. Then, before either of them realized his intention, he reached out to touch her hair. "You look like a kid."

Her heart shouldn't have been hammering, but it was. It was only a touch, after all, only a few words and a long look in a pretend world teeming with people. "That's the idea," she managed after a moment. "I'm twenty in this scene, innocent, eager, naive…and about to be deflowered."

"Here?"

"No, actually, just over there." She pointed to a small clearing in the forest the crew had created. "Brad the cad seduces me, promising me his everlasting devotion. He taps the passion that so far I've only given to my painting, then exploits it."

Quinn clucked his tongue. "With all these people watching."

"I love an audience."

"And you got mad because I watched you in the tub."

"You—"

"They're ready for you, Chantel."

After giving her assistant a nod, Chantel stood up, then carefully brushed off the seat of her pants. "Get yourself a good seat, Doran," she suggested. "You might learn something."

Taking her advice, Quinn watched her run through the scene several times on low power. From his angle, it seemed a lukewarm stock scene—a gullible woman, a clever man in a pretty springtime setting. Plastic, he thought, pure plastic, down to the leaves on the trees. Quinn kept his eyes on George as the makeup artist retouched Chantel's face to keep that dewy, never-been-touched look intact. One of the prop men handed her back her sketchpad and pencil.

"Places. Quiet on the set." The hubbub died away, to be replaced by silence. "Speed. Roll film." The clapper came down for take 1. "Action."

It began the same way, with Chantel sitting on a rock sketching. Sean made his entrance and stood watching her for a moment. When Chantel glanced up and saw him, Quinn felt his mouth go dry. Everything a man could want was in that look. Love, trust, desire. If a man had a woman look at him that way, he could win wars and scale mountains.

He'd never wanted to be loved. Love tied you down, made you responsible to someone other than yourself. It took as much as or more than it gave. That was what he'd thought, that was what he'd been certain of, until he'd seen the look come into Chantel's eyes.

A movie, he reminded himself when he realized he'd missed five minutes of shooting. They were already doing a second take. The look in her eyes was as much an illusion as the forest they were in. And it hadn't been aimed at him, in any case. It was a movie, she was an actress, and it was all part of the script.

The first time Sean Carter touched her, Quinn felt his jaw lock tight. Fortunately for him, the director cut the scene.

When they continued, Quinn told himself he was under control. He told himself that he was only there because he was paid to be. She meant nothing to him personally. She was a case. It didn't matter to him how many men she made love with, on or off camera.

Then he watched her touch her lips softly, hesitantly, to Sean's, and he thought of murder.

It was only a scene in a movie, with fake rocks, fake trees and fake emotions. But it seemed so real, so honest. There were dozens of people around him with machines to run the lights, the mikes. Even as Sean gathered Chantel closer, a camera edged in on them.

But she trembled. Damn it, he saw her quiver as Sean pulled the band from her hair and let it tumble free. Her voice shook when she told him she loved him, she wanted him, she wasn't afraid. Quinn found his hands were balled into fists in his pockets.

Her eyes shut as Sean rained kisses all over her face. She looked so young, so vulnerable, so ready to be loved. Quinn didn't notice the camera come in close. He only saw Sean unbuttoning her blouse, and her eyes, wide and blue, locked on her lover's. Hesitantly she unbuttoned his shirt. Color washed her cheeks as she drew the shirt aside and pressed her cheek to his chest. They lowered to the grass.

"Cut."

Quinn came back to reality with a thud. He watched Chantel sit up, then say something to Sean that made him laugh. She was wearing a brief strapless bra that would stay below camera range and a pair of baggy jeans. Larry draped her discarded blouse over her shoulder, and she gave him an absent smile.

"Let's take it again. Chantel, after you take off his shirt, I want you to lift your head." Mary Rothschild hunkered down as Chantel rebuttoned her blouse. "I want a kiss there, a good long one, before you two go down on the grass."

Sometime during the fifth take, Quinn found his objectivity. He searched the faces of those looking on. If there was an uncomfortable stirring in his stomach, he could ignore it now. His job was to find out who might be watching Chantel, not clinically, not approvingly as she completed the scene, but someone who might be eaten alive with jealousy. Or fantasizing. It wasn't going to do either one of them any good if it was him.

Quinn took out another cigarette and watched the faces around him. He had reports coming in on everyone from the cinematographer to the prop man. Gut instinct told him that whoever was sending her letters was someone she knew, someone she might speak to casually every day.

Quinn wanted to find him, and he wanted to find him quickly. Before he developed an obsession of his own.

The assistant director put his arm around Chantel's shoulders and, with his head bent close to her ear, led her off the set. Before they reached the trailer that was Chantel's dressing room, Quinn was in front of them.

"Going somewhere?"

Chantel shot him a narrow look but hung on to her temper. "As a matter of fact, I was going to get out of the sun for a while. Amos was giving me the rest of today's

schedule. You'll have to forgive Quinn, Amos. He's a bit…
possessive."

"Hard to blame him." Good-natured and a bit tubby
around the middle, Amos patted her shoulder. "You were
terrific, Chantel, just terrific. We'll call when we need
you for the close-ups and reaction shots. You should have
about a half hour."

"Thanks, Amos." She waited until he was out of earshot
before she turned on Quinn. "Don't do that."

"Do what?"

"All you needed was a knife between your teeth," she
muttered, jerking open the door of the trailer. "I told you
Amos was harmless. He—"

"Has a habit of touching women. One of those women
is my client."

Chantel chose a diet drink from the small refrigerator
and collapsed with it onto the sofa. "If I didn't want him
to touch me, I assure you, he wouldn't. This isn't the first
time I've worked with Amos, and unless you insist on acting like an idiot, it won't be the last."

Quinn opened the refrigerator and, to his satisfaction,
found a beer. "Look, angel, I can't narrow down the list of
suspects to suit your requirements. It's time you stopped
pretending that the person you're so afraid of isn't someone you know."

"I'm not pretending," she began.

"You are." He chugged back some of the beer before
he sat beside her. "And you're not pretending with half as
much style as you were out there rolling on the grass a
few minutes ago."

"That's work. This is my life."

"Exactly." He took her chin in a way that made her eyes
flash. "I'm supposed to take care of it. If it makes you feel
better, I've just about eliminated Carter."

"Sean?" She felt a quick surge of relief, then one of caution. "Why?"

"Simple enough reasoning." He took another sip of beer and kept her hanging. "Seems to me that if a man was obsessed with a woman—We'll agree that we're dealing with an obsession?"

"Yes, damn it." She snatched the bottle out of his hand. "What are you getting at?"

"Just that if I were going over the edge about a woman I wouldn't be able to stand up, dust myself off and turn aside after I'd spent a good part of the day tangled half-naked with her."

"Is that so?" Chantel handed him back his beer. "I'll be sure to keep that in mind." Relaxed again, Chantel leaned back against the pillows and stretched out her legs. "So, what did you think of the scene?"

"It ought to fog up a few bifocals."

"Oh, come on, Quinn." She held up her drink and watched moisture bead the sides of the bottle. "It wasn't just a matter of sex, you know. It was a betrayal of innocence and trust. What happened to Hailey in that New England wood will affect the rest of her life. A quick tumble on the pine cones doesn't do that."

"But a quick tumble on the pine cones sells tickets."

"This is television. We're after ratings. Damn it, Quinn, I put a lot into that scene. It's the turning point of Hailey's life. If it doesn't mean more than—"

"You were good," he cut in, and had her staring at him.

"Well." She set her drink down. "Mind repeating that?"

"I said you were good. I don't hand out the awards, angel."

She brought her knees up and dropped her chin onto them. With the thin slash of sunlight coming through the curtains, she still looked young and innocent. "How good?"

"How do you manage to feed that ego when you're alone?"

"I've never denied the size of my ego. How good?"

"Good enough to make me want to give Carter a black eye."

"Really?" Delighted, she caught her bottom lip between her teeth. She'd play it light. It wouldn't do to let him know just how much it meant to her to hear him praise her work. "Before or after the cameras were rolling?"

"Before, during and after." Unexpectedly he reached over and took the front of her shirt in his hand. "And don't push your luck, angel. I've got a habit of taking what looks good to me."

"You've such class, Doran." She uncurled his fingers from her blouse. "Such low class."

"Just keep that in mind. You know, angel, you gave me a twinge or two when I watched you and Carter paw each other."

"We weren't—"

"Give it any name you want. But good as you are, I didn't spend all my time watching you. I looked around and saw a few interesting things."

"Such as?"

"Brewster smoked a half a pack of cigarettes while you and Carter were…working."

"He's a nervous man. I've seen writers do worse when their script's being filmed."

"Leery practically fell in your lap trying to get a closer look."

"It's his job to look."

"And your assistant nearly swallowed his tongue when Carter took your shirt off."

"Just stop it." Springing up, she paced to one of the windows. They would call her soon. She wouldn't be any good if she let what Quinn was saying get her all churned up. "As far as I'm concerned, you're giving your own gutter-height views to everyone on set."

"That brings up another thought." He settled back and waited for her to look around at him. "Matt's yet to show up on the set. Strange. Aren't you his top client?"

She stared at him for a long moment. "You're determined to leave me without anyone, anyone at all."

"That's right." He ignored the quick, bitter taste in his throat. "For the moment, you trust me and only me."

"They'll be calling me soon. I'm going to go lie down." Without looking at him again, she walked to the back of the trailer and through a doorway.

Quinn had a sudden fierce urge to throw the bottle against the wall. Just to hear it shatter. She had no business making him feel guilty. He was looking out for her. That was what he was paid for. And it was easier all around if she was suspicious. If that meant she shed a few tears, it couldn't be helped. He wasn't worried about it. He didn't give a damn.

Swearing, he slammed the bottle down on the table beside him. Lecturing himself all the way, he strode through the trailer to the bedroom. "Look, Chantel—"

She was sitting at the foot of the bed, staring down at an envelope in her hands. He smelled the dark, sweet scent of wild roses before he saw them on the dresser.

"I can't open it," she murmured. When she looked up at him, something twisted in his stomach. It wasn't just her pallor. It wasn't just the fear he could see in the way her fingers shook. It was the complete and utter despair in her eyes. "I just can't take any more."

"You don't have to." With a compassion he thought had been erased in him years before, he sat beside her and gathered her close. "That's what I'm here for." He slipped the envelope out of her numb fingers. "I don't want you to open any more of the letters. If they come, you give them to me."

"I don't want to know what it says." She shut her eyes and hated herself for it. "Just rip it up."

"Don't worry about it." He stuffed the letter into his back pocket as he pressed a kiss to the top of her head. He had questions to ask, a lot of questions as to who might have gone into her dressing room that day. "Part of the deal is that you trust me. Just let me take care of things."

The head resting against his shoulder shook once in quick denial. "You can't take care of the way this makes me feel. I always wanted to be someone. I always wanted to feel important. Is that why this is happening?" With a dry sob, she pulled away from him. "Maybe you were right. Maybe I asked for this."

"Stop it." He took her hard by the shoulders and prayed she'd control the tears he could see were threatening. "I was out of line. You're beautiful, you're talented, and you've made use of it. That doesn't mean you're to blame for someone's sickness."

"But it's me that he wants," she said quietly. "And I'm afraid."

"I'm not going to let anything happen to you."

She let out a deep breath as her hand wrapped around his. "Sign that in blood?"

He smiled and ran a fingertip down her cheek. "Whose?"

Needing the contact, she rested her cheek against his for a moment. The gesture left him shaken. "Thanks."

"Sure."

"Look, I know I haven't been making this easy for you." She drew back again. As he'd hoped, the tears hadn't fallen. "I haven't wanted to."

"Trouble is my business. Besides, I like your style."

"While we're being nice to each other, I guess I'll say I like yours, too."

"A red-letter day," he murmured, and brought her hand to his lips.

It was a mistake. They both realized it the instant the contact was made. Over their joined fingers, their gazes met and held. She thought she could feel the tension jump from his palm to hers. This wasn't a matter of temptation, or of anger, or of passion flaring quickly, but of need. She needed to feel his arms around her again, holding her tight. She needed to feel his lips on hers, warm, hard, demanding. Everything else would fade, she knew, if only they came together now.

Their hands were still joined, but she didn't protest as his fingers tightened painfully on hers. What was he thinking? It suddenly seemed imperative that she understand, that she see, what he felt in his mind, in his heart. Did he want her, could he possibly want her as badly this moment as she wanted him…?

No other woman had ever made him ache like this. Not just from wanting. No other woman had ever made his blood swim. Not just from looking. He thought it would be possible to sit there through eternity and just look at that face. Was it only her beauty? Could it possibly be that he was twisted around inside because of a flawless facade?

Or was it something else, something that seemed to glow from within? There was something elusive, almost secretive, that showed in her eyes only if you looked quickly and carefully enough. He thought he saw it now. Then all he could think of was how much he wanted her.

With his free hand he reached up to trail his fingers through her hair. Spun gold, like an angel's. That's what it made him think of. But she was flesh and blood. Not a fantasy, a woman. He leaned closer, then watched her lashes flutter down.

The knock on the trailer door had her shooting up like an arrow out of a bow. She put both hands to her face but shook her head when Quinn reached for her.

"No, it's all right. That's just my call to go on the set."

"Sit down. I'll tell them you're not feeling well."

"No." She dropped her hands to her sides. "No, this isn't going to interfere with my work." The fingers of her left hand balled into a fist, but he could see she was working to regain control. "I can't let that happen." Turning her head, she stared at the roses on the table. "I won't let it."

He wanted to overrule her but knew this was the one thing he'd admired about her from the first. She was strong, strong enough to fight back. "Okay. You want a few more minutes?"

"Yeah, maybe." She walked to the window and drew the curtains aside to let in more sun. It was frightening, much too frightening to think about darkness. At night she was alone with her thoughts and her imagination. The sun was out, she reminded herself, sighing deeply. She had work to do.

"Would you mind letting them know I'll be out in a minute?"

"I'll take care of it." He hesitated, wanting to go to her, knowing it would be a mistake for both of them. "I'll be right outside, Chantel. Don't come out until you're ready."

"I'll be fine."

She waited until she heard him walk away before she dropped her forehead onto the glass. Weeping would be such a relief. Weeping, screaming, just letting go, would ease the hammerlock her nerves had on her system. But she couldn't let go, any more than she could allow herself to get churned up like this. There were hours more to put in that day. She needed her wits, and her stamina.

She'd make it, Chantel promised herself. Drawing a deep breath, she turned from the window. The flowers were gone. She stared at the table with a foolish sense of relief. He'd taken them away. She hadn't even had to ask.

What kind of a man was he? Rude and rough one moment, tender the next. Why couldn't he be easy to understand and easy to dismiss? With a shake of her head, she started down to the front of the trailer. He was impossible to understand. And he stirred things in her. He was anything but the kind of man a woman could be comfortable with. And she felt so safe knowing he was close by.

If she hadn't known herself so well, been so certain of her own control, she would almost have believed she was falling in love with him.

Chapter 6

It was anything but a quiet, restful week, though Chantel spent a good chunk of it in bed. The bed was big and plush and ornate—and it was on the set, on sound-stage D. The major scene to be shot was her wedding night—Hailey's wedding night—not to the man she loved but to the man she wanted to love.

The props included an ice bucket with champagne, a full-length sable draped over a chair and a table laden with roses that had to be spritzed constantly to keep them fresh under the lights. Don Sterling, a relative unknown, had been chosen to play the man she would marry. He'd been selected mainly because of looks and chemistry. Though his final reading with Chantel had been excellent, his nerves had him blowing the scene a half-dozen times during the morning.

Locked in his arms, Chantel felt him tighten up. Before he could do so himself, she flubbed the scene, hoping to take some of the pressure off him.

"Sorry." She gave a delicate shrug. "Can we take five, Mary? I'm getting stale."

"Make it ten," Rothschild ordered, then turned to consult with her assistant.

"How about a cup of coffee?" Chantel accepted the robe she was handed and slipped into it as she smiled at Don.

"Only if I can drown myself in it."

"Let's try drinking it first." She signaled to Larry, then found two seats in a relatively quiet corner. When she saw Quinn start to approach, she shook her head and leaned closer to Don. "It's a tough scene."

"It shouldn't be." He ran a hand through a mass of thick, dark hair.

"Look, the order they're shooting this miniseries in, we've only had a couple of scenes together so far. The first thing you know, we're married and on our honeymoon." She took the coffee from Larry. "I don't know about you, but I think it's easier to jump into bed with someone if you have more than a passing acquaintance."

He held the coffee in both hands and managed a chuckle. "I'm supposed to be an actor."

"Me, too."

"You could run through this scene with your eyes closed." He sipped the coffee, then, with a sound of disgust, set it aside. "I'll be honest. You intimidate the hell out of me." When she only lifted a brow, he let out a long breath and looked away. "When my agent called and told me I had this part and that I'd be playing opposite you, I almost went into a coma."

"That makes it tough to work up any passion." She put a hand on his. "Look, your reading with me was great. No one else even came close."

"The bit in Hailey's art studio." He picked up his coffee with a rueful look. "Not a bed in sight."

"The first love scene I ever played was opposite Scott Baron. Hollywood legend—the world's sexiest man. I had to kiss him, and my teeth were chattering, I was so scared. He took me aside, bought me a tuna-fish sandwich and told me stories, half of which were certainly lies. Then he told me something true. He said all actors are children and all children like to play games. If we didn't play the game well, we'd have to grow up and get real jobs."

The tension she'd spotted around his mouth had already relaxed. "Did it work?"

"It was either that or the tuna fish, but we went back on the set and played the game."

"You stole that movie from him."

She smiled. "I've heard it said." She continued to smile as she sipped coffee. "Don't think I'm going to let you steal this one from me."

"You blew that last line on purpose."

She could become a prima donna with little more than a tilt of her head. "I don't know what you're talking about."

"You have a reputation for being cold and driven," he mused. "I never expected you to be, well, nice."

"Don't let it get around." Rising, she offered him a hand. "Let's get this honeymoon off the ground."

The scene went like clockwork. Quinn didn't know what Chantel had said during her brief huddle with her co-star, but it had turned the trick. For himself, he was learning not to tense up when Chantel was in someone else's arms. It was difficult to work up any resentment when so much technology went into setting the scene. The lights had to be adjusted to simulate candlelight. Chantel and Don lay in the bed, he stripped to the waist, she in a thigh-length chemise. The camera was nearly on top of them. The director knelt on the bed and went over the moves. On cue, Chantel and Don turned to each other as if they were the only two people on earth.

It was so easy for her, Quinn reflected, to fabricate passion. When he watched her like this, he wondered if she had any real feelings at all. Her emotions were turned off and on as direction indicated. Like an exquisitely crafted puppet, he thought, beautifully formed on the outside, hollow within.

Yet he'd held her himself. He'd felt passion shimmer in her. The feelings, needs, uncertainties had been there for him to touch. Had that been just part of her act, as well? It shouldn't matter to him, he reminded himself as he lighted a cigarette. He couldn't let it matter. She was an assignment and nothing more. If she stirred feelings in him, as she did with uncanny regularity, he would just have to take a step back. Involvement with a woman like Chantel O'Hurley was suicide for a man who didn't have himself under complete control.

But when he looked at her, his mouth went dry.

Just desire, he told himself. Or, more accurately, lust. There was no denying that wanting her was as easy, as natural, as drawing breath. But it hadn't been desire or lust he had felt when he'd held her in his arms moments ago.

So he had some compassion left in him. Quinn found a chair, then discovered he was too wired to sit. He'd have been pretty low if he hadn't felt sympathy or been able to offer comfort to a frightened and vulnerable woman.

But it hadn't been sympathy, it had been rage. He recognized it even now, that hot, bubbling fury at the thought of his woman being threatened. His woman. That was the problem. The longer he was with her, the easier it became to think of her as his.

Take a step back from that, Doran, he ordered himself. And make it fast. If he didn't pull himself together soon, he was going to be in over his head. A man could only hold his breath for so long.

He crushed out his cigarette and wished the interminable day would end.

There had been two more letters that week, letters he hadn't shown her. The tone had shifted from pleading to near-whimpering. It worried Quinn more than the subtle menace the earlier letters had contained. The author was about to break. When he did, Quinn was certain it would be like a geyser, fast and violent. Because his own patience was thin, he hoped it would be soon. It would give him some outlet for the fury building inside him.

"That's a wrap, people. Don't have too much fun over the weekend. We want you alive and coherent on Monday."

Still in her chemise, Chantel sat on the edge of the bed and held an earnest conversation with Don. Jealousy. Where it had come from and why, Quinn couldn't begin to answer. Quinn had always been a live-and-let-live sort of person. If a woman, even a woman he was involved with, decided to look to another man, that was her prerogative. No strings, no pain, no complications. He'd managed very well that way for years. He'd never experienced this sharp twist in the gut over a woman before. He felt it now, and he didn't like it, or himself. Unable to stop himself, he walked over and drew Chantel to her feet.

"Playtime's over," he said, and pulled her with him.

"Let go of me," she told him under her breath as he walked toward her trailer. Larry started forward with her robe, saw the look on Quinn's face and backed away.

"Just shut up."

"Doran, this is my place of business, but if you keep it up I'm going to create the biggest, juiciest scene even your twisted brain can imagine. You'll read about it in the paper for weeks."

"Go ahead."

She set her teeth. "Just what is your problem?"

"You're my problem, lady. For a woman who should be watching her step, you were awfully chummy with that kid."

"Kid? Don? For God's sake, he's an associate, and he's not a kid. He's two years older than I am."

"You were steaming up his contact lenses."

"Don't you get tired of playing the same tune?" She jerked her arm free and pulled open her dressing room door herself. "If you've been doing your job, you already have a report on Don Sterling and you know he's practically engaged to a woman he's been involved with for two years."

"And the woman in question is three thousand miles away in New York."

"I know that." As she pushed her hair out of her face the chemise shifted, whispering silkily over her skin. "He was just telling me that he's going to catch the red-eye to the east coast so that he can spend the weekend with her. He's in love, Doran, though I realize you might not understand the term."

"A man could be in love with another woman and still want you."

She slammed the trailer door and leaned back against it. "What would you know about love? What would you know about any genuine emotion?"

"You want emotion?" He slapped his palms on the door at either side of her head. Though her eyes widened in shock, she stood firm. "You want a taste of the kind of emotion you push out of a man? The real thing, angel, not something out of the pages of a script. Think you can take it?"

Her heart was beating in her throat. It was crazy to actually *want* to be dragged against him, to be plundered, drained and weakened. She could see nothing but raw fury in his eyes, but somehow she relished it. If it was all he could feel for her, it was almost enough. She'd be willing to settle, and that scared the hell out of her.

"Just leave me alone," she whispered.

"You're smart to be scared of me."

"I'm not scared of you."

He leaned a little closer. "You're trembling."

"I'm furious." She pressed her damp palms against the door.

"Maybe you are. And maybe that's because you're not quite sure of what happens next. It's not written out for you, is it, Chantel? Not so easy to turn the switch off and on."

"Get out of my way."

"Not just yet. I want to know what you feel." His body pressed lightly against hers. "I want to know *if* you feel."

She was losing ground, and what she had left was shaky. If he touched her now, really touched her, she was afraid she would lose everything. How could she tell him what she felt, when what she felt was against all the rules? She wanted to be held, protected, cherished, loved. If she told him that, he'd only smile and take what he wanted. She'd been left empty before, and it would never, never happen to her again.

Chantel lifted her chin and waited until his lips hovered an inch from hers. "You're no better than the man I hired you to protect me from."

He stepped back as if she'd slapped him. The stunned look on his face made her want to reach out to him. Instead, she pressed back against the door and waited for his next move.

"Get some clothes on," he told her, and turned aside. As she walked away, he reached into the refrigerator for a beer. She was right. Quinn twisted off the top and took two long swallows. He'd wanted to frighten, to weaken, then take her there, on his terms. If he could have proven to himself that what happened between them was cold and calculated, he might have believed she meant nothing to him.

He'd wanted to hurt her. She was threatening his peace of mind, and he'd needed to strike back. He would have used sex to purge himself and to repay her for the restless nights. The wave of self-disgust was as unfamiliar and as unpalatable as the surge of jealousy he'd felt earlier.

He'd told himself to take a step back, yet he'd taken a leap forward and had landed in the mire. He'd done things and seen things in his life that would have left others pale and speechless. Yet, for the first time in his life, he felt truly soiled.

When he heard her coming back, he tossed the bottle into the trash. She wore rose-colored linen slacks and a jacket with a muted floral design. She looked cool, composed and nothing like the restless, questing character she'd played all day.

Without a word she walked by him and put her hand on the knob. Before she could open the door, Quinn placed his hand over hers. He cursed himself when she stiffened and sent him a cool, disinterested look.

"You're entitled to take a few shots," he said mildly. "I won't even duck."

For a moment she said nothing. Then, as the anger dissipated she sighed. She was tired, drained from the constant play and replay of emotion. "I'll take a rain check."

As she twisted the knob, he tightened his hand on hers. "Chantel…"

"What?"

He wanted to apologize. It wasn't his style, but he wanted badly to tell her he was sorry. The need was there, but the words wouldn't come. "Nothing. Let's go."

They rode home in silence while guilt ate at him. It

would fade, he assured himself. It was just one more of the odd emotions she drew out of him. She looked exhausted now, though he remembered she'd looked fine—in fact, she'd looked wonderful—before he'd…

Damn it, he couldn't waste his time worrying about things like that. He had a job to do, and if he'd stepped out of line, it wouldn't happen again. Case closed. He'd see her into the house, make certain the doors were locked and the alarm on. Then he'd relax. He needed to go over the report from his field man, though he was already aware they'd turned up nothing on the stationery. They needed a mistake. So far, no matter how mentally unstable Chantel's admirer was, he'd been smart.

Quinn sat back as the limo cruised through the gates, wishing he could say the same thing about himself.

He preferred to act on impulse. As he stepped out of the car, he didn't hesitate or think twice. Taking Chantel by the hand, he began to lead her around the side of the house.

"What are you doing?"

"It's Friday night and I'm sick of being cooped up in that house. We're going out to eat." He stopped by his car and nodded to one of the men who patrolled the grounds.

"Did it ever occur to you that I might not feel like going out?"

"Where I go, you go." He opened the door and started to nudge her inside.

"Doran, I've put in sixty hours this week and I'm tired. I don't want to go to a restaurant and be stared at."

"Who said anything about a restaurant? Just get in, angel. You don't want to embarrass yourself in front of my man over there."

"I'm not hungry."

"I am." He gave her a quick shove, then shut the door behind her.

"Has anyone ever mentioned that you're totally lacking in manners or any of the other social graces?"

"Constantly."

He gunned the motor and sent the car barreling down the drive. Chantel reached for her seat belt. "If you wreck this heap with me in it, the producers are going to have your head on a platter." For a moment she wondered if it wouldn't be worth it.

"Nervous?"

"You don't make me nervous, Doran, you simply annoy me."

"Everyone's got to be good at something." He turned the radio dial, and loud, throbbing rock poured out. Chantel closed her eyes and pretended to ignore him.

When the car came to a halt, she didn't move. Determined to show nothing but indifference, she sat still as the silence grew. Outside the car she heard the bump and grind of weekend traffic heating up. She had no idea where they were and told herself she didn't care. Quinn's door opened and closed, and she still didn't move. But she did open her eyes.

She saw him stride up to the little fast-food joint and fought back a chuckle. She would not be amused. At home she could have had a nice glass of wine and a crisp salad with her cook's special herb dressing. God knew what Quinn was carrying back to the car in the white bag. She simply wouldn't eat, she told herself. She'd let him get whatever he had in his system out, but she wouldn't eat.

Closing her eyes again, she tried not to react as aromas, really wonderful aromas, filled the car. He glanced over, smiled, then started the car again.

Again she didn't know where he was heading, but the road began to wind and the sounds of traffic faded. She very nearly dozed off as her system absorbed the quiet sunset drive. She hadn't realized how much she'd needed to get away, from work, from her house, maybe from herself. It was going to be hard not to be grateful to him. But Chantel told herself she would manage.

When the car stopped again, she refused to move. Curiosity gnawed at her, but she kept her eyes firmly shut. Saying nothing, Quinn reached for the bag, rattling it so that the scent seeped through the car. Then he stepped out and closed the door behind him.

Chantel's stomach contracted, reminding her that the plate of fruit and cheese she'd had for lunch wasn't enough. The least he could do was force her to eat something, the way he'd forced her to do other things she hadn't wanted to. But no, she thought as her temper began to rise, he would just go off and gobble up whatever was in that bag and let her starve.

Opening her eyes, Chantel pushed open her door. As she let it slam behind her, the noise seemed to echo forever. Astonished, she looked around her.

They were farther up in the hills than she had ever gone before. Below, miles below, L.A. stretched forever, glistening just a bit as lights winked on. She could see the separate levels of color in the sky as the sun went down. Deep blue led to paler blue, and paler blue to mauve and rose and pink, all glistening with gold. The first star blinked to life overhead and waited patiently for others to join it. The breeze whistled through the brush, but the city she knew so well seemed encased in glass, it was so quiet.

"Pretty impressive, isn't it?"

She turned and saw Quinn leaning against a giant H. The Hollywood sign, she realized, and nearly laughed. She'd seen it so often it no longer registered. From the hills it looked white, invulnerable and perhaps immortal. Up close, like the town it heralded, it was mostly illusion. It was big and bold, certainly, but a little grimy, a little shaky. Graffiti was etched in clumps near the base.

"It could use a fresh coat of paint," she murmured.

"No, it's more honest this way." He kicked aside a beer can. "Teenagers come up here to hang out—and make out."

She tilted her head. "And you?"

"Oh, I just like the view." He climbed over a few rocks effortlessly and planted himself on the base of an L. "And the quiet. If you're lucky, you can come up here and not hear a thing, except for a coyote now and again."

"Coyote?" She glanced over her shoulder.

"That's right." Not bothering to hide a grin, he dug in the bag. "Want a taco?"

"A taco? You dragged me all the way up here to eat tacos?"

"Got some beer."

"Lovely."

"It's getting warm. You'd better drink up."

"I don't want anything."

"Suit yourself." He unwrapped a taco and bit into it. "Got some fries, too," he said with a full mouth. "A little greasy, maybe, but they're not cold yet."

"I don't know how I can resist." She turned away from him to look down at the city again. As fate would have it, the breeze carried the spicy scents to her. Her mouth watered. Chantel scowled down at the lights and wished Quinn Doran to hell.

"I guess a woman like you turns her nose up if it isn't champagne and caviar."

Spinning around, Chantel stood with the city and the sunset at her back. Quinn felt his heart turn over in his chest. She'd never looked more beautiful. "You know nothing about me, nothing at all." Her voice had an edge to it now, a dull, gritty edge that had his eyes narrowing. "I spent nearly the first twenty years of my life shuffling from town to town, eating in greasy spoons or over a hot plate in a motel room. Sometimes, if we were lucky and the gig was good, we got to wolf down a meal in the hotel kitchen. If we weren't so lucky, there were always hard-boiled eggs and coffee. Don't you sit there in your smug little world and toss stones at me, Doran. You don't know what I am, or who I am. All you know is what I've made myself."

Slowly he set the beer on the rock behind him. "Well, well," he said quietly. "I wouldn't read any of that in your official bio, would I?"

She could only stare. What was it about him that made her lose control? Why had she been compelled to yank herself out and expose her roots to him?

"I want to go back."

"No, you don't." His voice wasn't curt now, but gentle. It was that gentleness that chipped away her defenses. "There's no one here but me, Chantel. Why don't we just sit up here and look down at the rest of the world for a while?"

Before she'd thought it through, she'd taken a step toward him. When he rose and held out a hand to help her up, she reached for it without hesitation. Hesitation came the moment his palm met hers. She remembered the feel of it, the strength of it, and her gaze lifted and locked with his. They stood there a moment with the sky darkening around them. Then he hauled her up.

"I'm sorry." The apology surprised him as much as it did her.

"For what?" She started to draw her hand from his, but he reached up to brush back her hair.

"For what happened before. I don't know why, but something about you makes me edgy."

She kept her eyes level with his. "Then we're even."

The wind tossed the hair back from his face. In every

situation, he knew, there came a time for honesty. Perhaps this was such a time. "Chantel, I want you. I'm having a hell of a time dealing with that."

Other men had wanted her, other men had told her so in more beautiful ways. But the words had never made it difficult for her to breathe. "I could fire you."

"It wouldn't matter."

"No, I don't suppose it would." She looked away, surprised at how strong a longing could be. "Quinn, I can't go to bed with you."

"I figured you'd feel that way."

"Quinn." She took his hand again as he started to step away. "I don't know what you think my reasons are, but I guarantee you, you're wrong."

"Not your style," he said, picking up his beer again. "Not your league."

Chantel snatched the bottle from him and heaved it. Spray spewed against the rocks before the glass shattered. "Don't tell me what I think. *Don't* tell me what I feel."

"Then you tell me." He grabbed her and pulled her against him.

"I don't have to tell you *anything*. I don't have to explain myself to you. Damn you, I just want some peace. I just want a few hours where the pressure's off. I don't know if I can take being squeezed at all sides for much longer."

"Okay, okay." His hold gentled immediately. As he murmured, his hand stroked up and down her back. "You're right. I didn't bring you up here to fight with you, but you make me edgy."

"Let's just go back."

"No, sit down. Please," he added, brushing his lips over her hair. "Let's see if we can stay here for an hour together and not pick on each other. Have a taco."

He smiled at her as he pulled her down to sit. Chantel took one look at the bag and gave up.

"I'm starving."

"Yeah, I figured as much." He handed her a wad of paper napkins. For the next few minutes they ate in companionable silence. "Was your childhood rough?"

Chantel stopped in the act of opening a little packet of salt for the fries. "Oh, no, I didn't mean that. It was just different. My parents are entertainers. They've been a song-and-dance team for over thirty years. The six of us trouped around the country, and some of the places we played were dives. But my family…" She smiled, absently accepting a beer. "They're wonderful. Trace did some routines, but he was best on the piano. It always used to frustrate me that no matter how hard I tried I couldn't play better than he did."

"Sibling rivalry."

"Sure. Life would be pretty dull without it. Trace and I were always so much alike that we couldn't stay off each other's backs for very long. There was never much of that between my sisters and me. We were just too much a part of each other." She sipped the beer straight from the bottle and looked down at the city below. "We still are. God, sometimes it's so hard to be away from them. When we were little we made all these plans for keeping the act together forever." She remembered them with a little pang of regret. "Then we grew up."

"What kind of an act?"

Laughing, she licked salt from her fingers. "You never heard of the O'Hurley Triplets?"

"Sorry."

"You'd probably be sorrier if you had heard of us. Three-part harmony, show tunes and popular music, a few old standards thrown in."

"You sing?"

"Doran, I don't just *sing*, I'm terrific."

"You never sing in your movies."

She shrugged a shoulder. "It hasn't come up. Matt keeps saying we should give the public a surprise one of these days and get a guest spot where I can do a few numbers, and dance, maybe too. Yes," she added when he slanted a look at her, "I can dance—my father would have died of shame otherwise."

"Why don't you do it?"

"The time just hasn't been right. Besides, I've been concentrating on what I'm best at."

He balled up the empty bag and set it beside his feet. "What's that?"

She gave him a quick, mocking look. "Playing roles."

Instead of smiling back, he tucked her hair behind her ear. "My guess is you're not playing one now."

She turned her head quickly and looked out. The sky was nearly dark, but there was only a smattering of stars. "You can't be sure. I'm not sure myself half the time."

"I think you're sure."

When she turned her head back, his mouth was close. Close and tempting. "Don't. I told you I can't—" But his lips brushed over hers, light as a whisper, and stopped her cold.

"Do you know how I felt when you were lying on that bed with Sterling today?"

"No. I don't want to know. I've told you, it's my job."

She was already half seduced; he could hear it in her voice. There was a thrill of anticipation along his skin as he thought of taking her beyond the next step. "I wasn't sure if I wanted to put my hands around his throat or yours, but I did know I wanted you to look at me the way you were looking at him."

"It's just a part. I'm supposed to—"

"There aren't any cameras here, Chantel. Just you and me. And that's what I think you're afraid of. No one's here to tell you what you're supposed to be feeling. No one's going to yell 'Cut' before things go just a little too far."

"I don't need anyone to tell me what to feel. I don't need anyone," she repeated, and tugged his mouth back to hers.

She wanted it. She wanted to experience the wild flood of sensation he could bring her. No one else. She could tell him there'd been no one else who had touched her just this way, but he'd never believe her. The image, her image, was all but carved in stone, and she'd polished it herself. What she was inside belonged to her. She was determined that no one would ever share that part of her again.

But she could have this, the heat, the need, the desperation. She could take this, and she could give it back to him as long as she promised herself she wouldn't give him too much. As long as she didn't give him everything.

The sky darkened above them, and the wind whistled through the brush.

She was pulling something from him, drawing something out of him. He couldn't seem to stop her. His hands weren't steady as they reached up to tangle in her hair. His mind was swimming in a mist of his needs, but the needs weren't as simple as he'd told himself they had to be. Desire could make you ache, but it shouldn't be allowed to slice you open.

He wanted to take her there, there in the rocks and dirt. He wanted to treat her like porcelain, delicately and with intense care.

His body was coiled tight, ready to explode. God, he had to touch her, even if it was only once. In one smooth stroke he brought his hand along her leg, over her hip, until he found and cupped her breast. She was small, incredibly fragile, and as soft as water. Compelled, he flicked open the two buttons on her jacket to feast on the warm flesh inside.

It had been so long, so long since she had allowed herself to be touched, since she'd felt the need for intimacy. She wanted his hands on her, his lips on her, his body hard and demanding against hers. The hell with where they were, who they were. The hell with the price she would surely pay for allowing herself to love him.

In an act of surrender that left him shaken, she brought her arms around him and buried her face against his throat.

"Chantel..." He started to tilt her face up, longing, for reasons he couldn't be sure of, to see what was in her eyes. Then he heard it, a rustling in the brush that came once, then twice, and had him tensing.

"What? What is it?" She had heard it, too, and she dug her fingers into his arm. "An animal?"

"Yeah, probably." But he didn't think so. His nerves were humming as he drew her aside.

"Where are you going?"

"To take a look. Just stay here."

"Quinn—" She was already standing.

"Just sit tight. It's probably just a rabbit."

It was no rabbit. She heard it in his voice. He wasn't nearly the actor she was. Fear made her want to cringe away. Pride had her matching him step for step. "I'm going with you."

"Chantel, sit down."

"No." She held his arm and scrambled over the rocks. Resigned, Quinn helped her regain her balance. "All right, then, be careful. You get any scratches on that skin and I'll get blamed for it."

"Damn right."

Because the light had faded, he went to his car and found a flashlight. "Why don't you just sit—"

"No."

Swearing under his breath, he took her by the arm again. He walked slowly toward the brush, casually angling his body to shield hers. "Lot of game up here," he began, but his muscles were coiled and ready. He moved softly, quietly pushing brush aside as Chantel hung on to his hand.

"I remember, coyote."

"Yeah." He crouched down when he spotted prints in the soft dirt. The beam of his light swept over them, then held.

Chantel pressed her lips together. "I guess coyote don't wear shoes."

"None that I've seen." He hated hearing that hint of fear in her voice. "Look, it was probably just a kid."

"No. You don't believe that and neither do I." She stared down at the scuffed prints. The brush where they were wasn't more than five yards from where they'd been sitting a moment before. "Someone was watching us, and I think we both know why. God." She pressed her fingers to her eyes. "He was here. He was right here, just watching. Why doesn't he stop? Why doesn't he—"

"Get a hold of yourself." Quinn took her by the shoulders and shook. She took a deep breath, then nearly screamed when the sound of an engine starting echoed back to them.

"He followed me." She stopped trembling. Her body felt too numb even for that. "How many other times has he been there, watching me?"

"I don't know." Frustrated, Quinn stared out at the darkening road. Even if he dared leave her there alone, he'd never catch up with the other car now. "Just remember, he's watching us now. I'm not going to let him get to you."

"For how long?" she said quietly, then turned away. "I want to go back."

Chapter 7

"It just doesn't seem like we're getting anywhere." Chantel poured herself a brandy, then freshened Matt's glass.

"I'm sorry, Chantel. I'd have sworn if anyone could dig up an answer it would be Quinn."

"I'm not blaming him." Cupping her brandy in both hands, she walked to the window. The sun was setting. It reminded her of another dusk. With the snifter at her lips, she watched night fall.

"You've changed your tune from the first time we talked about him."

More than you know, she thought, but shrugged her shoulders. "I can't claim he's not doing everything he can, that's all."

"Then maybe I have to," Matt returned, hating to hear the tired resignation in her voice. "He hasn't come up with anything solid. What about the letters?"

"The stationery the letters were written on could have

come from any of dozens of dollar or drugstores in the L.A. area. There's no way for him to trace it."

"But the flowers." Restless, Matt walked to the white baby grand, then back to the fireplace, his cigarette trailing expensive smoke behind him. "There has to be a way to trace where they were bought."

"Apparently not. Most of the time they just appear in my dressing room or somewhere on the set. So far no one's seen who delivers them."

"Florists keep records."

"If you pay cash and pick up the flowers yourself, there wouldn't be any reason to ask for ID." She pressed her fingers to the back of her neck, pressed and released, fruitlessly working at a knot of tension.

"Someone might remember who—"

"Quinn tells me his men have done a sweep of the florists in the area. There's nothing."

"The phone calls."

"They haven't been able to get a trace."

"Damn it." If something—or someone—existed, Matt felt there must be a way to find him. "Chantel, maybe you should reconsider the police."

She turned back. With him, she could allow the weariness to show. "Matt, do you really think they could do more than Quinn's done?"

"I don't know." The quiet desperation in her eyes was difficult to face. He scowled down at his brandy. "I just don't know." Setting down his drink, he crossed to her. "I was sure this thing would be tied up in a matter of days."

"It's not as simple as that. It seems he's clever, or cautious, at any rate."

"Are you sure you've told Quinn everything you know?"

"What I don't tell him, he finds out." Nerves had her swirling the brandy around and around in her glass but not drinking. "He's running investigations on everyone I know."

"Well, that—"

"Including you."

He stopped to stare at her. With a grimace, he stuck his hands in his pockets and nervously pulled out his lighter. "He's thorough, anyway."

"I don't like it, Matt." For the first time, real emotion came into her voice, into her eyes. "I feel... I don't know, sleazy when I think of him poking into the keyholes of people's lives, and on my account."

Not quite comfortable, Matt slipped an arm around her shoulder. "Look, baby, if rattling a few skeletons in my closet helps get to the bottom of this thing, then it's worth it." He was silent a moment, then cleared his throat. "So, what did he find out?"

"About you?"

"That's a good place to start."

"I don't know." Letting out a long breath, she leaned her head on his shoulder. The sun had disappeared completely, leaving only a hint of color streaking the clouds. "I told him I didn't want to know, Matt. He started to give me reports on people like Larry and James Brewster, and I hated it." She could still remember his cool disapproval of her cowardice. Chantel gritted her teeth against the memory. "We agreed that I'd take the precautions he'd outlined, and that he'd keep what information he had to himself."

With one hand he flicked on the silver monogrammed lighter he'd been toying with. "That's burying your head in the sand, Chantel."

"I don't care."

"Listen, there's no one, certainly no one who's made it past twenty, who hasn't done something they're ashamed of, something they'd prefer to keep covered." He shifted but made himself speak matter-of-factly. "Quinn's got a right to investigate, and because of who he is, nothing he finds out would go any farther."

"Thanks for the vote of confidence." Quinn paused in the doorway and studied them. Matt still had his arm around her. Chantel's head rested on his shoulder as the dim light through the window behind them settled over her hair. She looked comfortable with him, Quinn realized with a twinge of resentment. She looked as though she'd be content to snuggle up against him and sit for hours.

"I'm the one who recommended you," Matt said easily. "I'd hate to say I'd made a mistake."

"You didn't." Quinn crossed to the bar to pour himself a double shot of brandy. "How've you been, Matt? I thought we'd be seeing more of you."

"I've been tied up."

Sensing the restraint between them, Chantel took a step forward. "Just stop it," she told Quinn. "Don't start on him."

"You're telling me how to do my job again, angel."

"I'm not going to allow you to use your third degree on my friends."

Quinn tossed back his brandy. "Too bad I left my rubber hose upstairs."

"Why don't we sit down?" Matt put a hand on Chantel's shoulder. "I appreciate it, babe, but it isn't necessary." His gaze locked with Quinn's. "I guess when I told Chantel to hire you I should have figured you'd dig it up."

Quinn met the look, but there was nothing to show his feelings. "Yeah, you should have."

"Dig what up?" she demanded.

Quinn lifted his glass in a half salute. "Maybe you'd like to tell her yourself."

"Yes, I would. Sit down, Chantel." When she only

looked at him, Matt squeezed her shoulder. "Please, sit down."

She felt the now-familiar churning in her stomach as she chose a chair. "All right, I'm sitting."

"A few years back, almost ten now, I ran into some financial problems." He retrieved his brandy and took a deep swallow.

"Matt, you don't have to tell me about this."

"Yes, I do." He looked back at Quinn. "I want you to hear it from me." He held up a hand before she could protest again. "Just hear me out. When I'm finished maybe I won't feel as though the blade's about to fall on my neck."

"All right," she said evenly, but her left hand moved restlessly on the arm of her chair.

"Gambling," he said with a hint of fear in his voice.

"Matt, that's absurd." She nearly laughed. "You won't even play gin for matchsticks."

"That's now. This was then. I couldn't keep away from the horses." With a self-mocking smile, he looked back at her. "It's a fever, and mine ran pretty hot until I'd dropped more than I could afford. I was desperate. I'd borrowed money from a certain group of people—the kind who break small bones in your body if they don't get their weekly payment."

"Oh, Matt."

"I needed ten thousand I didn't have. I forged a check. A client's check." He closed his eyes before he took another swallow. Chantel sat in silence. "Of course, it didn't take long for it to come to light. My client didn't want the publicity, so he didn't press charges. I mortgaged my soul, then hocked the rest to pay him back. You could call it a turning point in my life." This time he laughed, but there was no humor in it. "My career was on the line, so I took a good hard look at myself. Because what I saw left me pretty shaken, I checked into an organization for obsessive gamblers. It's been nearly eight years since I've been to the track. Even though gambling nearly ruined my life, I have to fight the urge every day to place just one bet." He set down his glass and looked at her. "If you want another agent, I'll understand."

She rose slowly and walked to him. Without a word, she put her arms around him and gathered him close. Over his shoulder she sent Quinn a long, neutral look. "I don't want another agent. You know I insist on the best."

With a muffled laugh, he pressed a kiss to her brow. "You're a special lady."

"Someone's always telling me that."

He gripped her fingers hard, and she felt how damp his palms were. "I wouldn't let you down, Chantel."

"I know."

He kissed her again before he drew away. "I've got to get going. You'll call if there's anything I can do?"

"Of course."

He turned to Quinn. For a moment the men studied each other across the room. If there was regret on either side, they didn't show it. "Take care of her."

"I intend to."

With a brief nod, Matt let himself out.

Chantel turned on Quinn immediately. "How could you? How could you humiliate him that way?"

"It was necessary." But necessary or not, it left a foul taste in his mouth. Quinn poured another brandy, knowing that taste wouldn't be so easily washed away.

"Necessary? Why? What does a gambling debt nearly ten years ago have to do with what's happening to me now?"

"If a man can develop one obsession, he can develop another."

"That's ridiculous."

"No, that's a fact."

A quiver ran through her, not of fear but of anger. "Matt Burns has never attempted to be anything to me other than my agent and my friend. And he's had abundant opportunity."

"Would you have let him?"

Chantel took a cigarette, then flicked the table lighter three times before she managed to get it to flame. "What does that have to do with it?"

He came closer, curling his hand firmly around her arm. "Would you?"

"No." Tossing her head, she blew out smoke. "No."

"And he knows it." When she jerked her arm away, he watched her pace the room. "You're good with scenarios. Try this one. The man works with you for years, he watches you soar straight to the top. He's helped you, layer by layer, to build that illusion of cool, ice-hard sexuality. Maybe he wants what he helped to create."

A shiver ran down her spine, but her eyes were calm and level when she turned to him. "It doesn't play, Doran."

"It plays as well as anything else."

"No, it doesn't." The fear was back. She fought hard to keep it from showing. "Why wouldn't a man I know, a man I'm close to, just approach me openly?"

"Because he's a man you know, a man you're close to," Quinn countered. "He knows he doesn't have a chance with you on that level."

Impatient, she stubbed the cigarette out. "How would he know if he's never asked?"

Quinn put a hand to her cheek to stop her nervous pacing. "Don't you think a man knows when a woman's interested?" Running a thumb down her jaw, he brought her an inch closer. It was there, as it had been from the first, humming between them. She felt it, damn it, he knew she felt it, even though she refused to show that she did. "Don't you think he can look at a woman, see the way she looks at him, and know if they're going to be lovers?"

She put a hand to his wrist and carefully drew his away. Her skin felt as though it would stay warm for hours. "I'm tired," she told him. "I'm going to bed."

When he was alone, the brandy tempted him. Because it seemed too easy a way out, he turned his back on it. He went outside to walk the grounds.

Chantel was finding sleep harder and harder to come by. In the late hours she would toss and turn, then fall into a light doze, only to awake again, nervous and groggy, to toss and turn some more. Several times she had been tempted to give in and get a prescription for sleeping pills. Each time she remembered her promise never to tranquilize herself against pressure, personal or professional.

She thought of Matt, of the self-disgust and apology in his voice as he'd told her something she had no business knowing.

She thought of Quinn, firm and unyielding but offering Matt the chance to explain for himself.

Oddly enough, she thought of her brother and an argument they'd had when she'd been a teenager. Trace had threatened to knock some boy's block off if he got too familiar with her. Chantel remembered being furious at him for interfering, and telling everyone she could handle things.

Why wasn't she in control now?

She always had been. Even Trace had known then she hadn't needed him to stand up for her. Perhaps because she'd been one of three in the womb, she'd been born ready to handle her own problems. She'd faced tragedy, personal loss and disillusionment but had always managed to fight her way back. She wasn't fighting now, and she should be. It had never been necessary for her to look to a man for protection, and yet...

Then she thought of Quinn again and his promise to protect her. She wanted to believe him. When he was there, right beside her, she did.

But it was the middle of the night, and her brain was hazy. She only wanted to sleep. The sheets twisted around her as she turned again and finally drifted off.

When the phone rang, she groped for it. Half dreaming, she thought it was her mother calling to scold her for being late for rehearsal. "Yes," she mumbled into the receiver. "Yes, I'm coming."

"I can't sleep. I can't sleep for thinking of you."

The whisper had a low, desperate edge to it that shocked Chantel fully awake.

"You have to stop this."

"But I can't. I've tried, but I can't. Don't you know what you do to me? Every time I see you, every time I'm near you, I—"

"No!" she shouted into the phone. Then, to her disgust, she began to weep. "Please leave me alone. Please. I don't want to hear any more."

But she could hear him as she turned her face into the pillow. She could hear him still as she fumbled to hang up the phone. Even when she had the receiver cradled, she could hear his voice echoing in her head. Chantel curled into a ball and let the tears come.

Quinn was staring out his window when the phone rang. Cursing, he dashed across the room, hoping to get to it before it awakened Chantel. But the whispering had already started. For a moment he thought he recognized something—a speech pattern, accent, or turn of phrase.

He tried to focus on it, block out the words themselves and Chantel's terror. Then his mouth tightened to a grim line as he heard Chantel plead, then begin to cry. He heard her hang up, then heard a man sobbing before the connection was broken.

After slamming down the receiver, Quinn plunged his hands into his pockets, his fingers balling into fists. He'd lost something, maybe something vital because his concentration and his objectivity had been broken when she'd begun to cry.

The woman was making him soft. He couldn't allow it. Wouldn't allow it. He had to leave her alone. She'd *want* to be alone, he told himself. She wouldn't like to have him see her now that she'd lost control. A woman like Chantel would shed her tears in private. Even if she looked for consolation, the last person she'd want it from was him. Struggling against an overpowering sense of rage and helplessness, he stalked back to the window.

She'd sounded so frightened.

He couldn't leave her alone now. Not now, he thought as he pounded his clenched hand lightly against the windowsill. She might want to be alone, but she needed to be with him. He only hoped he could figure out what to do once he was with her.

There were a few slashes of moonlight coming through her windows. They turned everything to silver. He came in quietly, hoping she'd fallen asleep again and that he could just check on her, maybe sit with her awhile without her being aware of it. If she knew how badly he wanted to be with her, protect her—damn it, cherish her—wouldn't that give her all the more reason to push him aside?

He'd never had to use caution with a woman before. Because, he was forced to admit, no woman had really mattered until her. And she mattered too much.

She wasn't asleep. Quinn could hear her muffled weeping as he crossed to the bed. He stopped where he was, terrified by the small, helpless sound. He knew how a grenade sounded when it exploded in the dirt and sent shrapnel hurtling through the air. He'd heard the horrific noise of gunfire and the unspeakable sound of a bullet striking flesh. Those were things he'd faced with more confidence than he faced Chantel's quiet sobbing with now.

If she had been angry, he could have played on it. If she had merely been frightened, he could have insulted her out of it. But she was weeping.

Soundlessly he went to the side of the bed and crouched down. Wishing he knew the right words but knowing he didn't, he laid a hand on her hair. At his touch she sprang up, screaming.

"It's me. It's only me." He took both her hands and squeezed. "Relax. No one's going to hurt you."

"Quinn." Her hand went limp in his, then tensed again as she fought for control. "You startled me."

"Sorry." The moonlight was strong enough that he could see her face, and the tears damp on her cheeks. "You okay?"

"Yes." Her chest was hurtfully tight, her throat raw from unshed tears. "Yes, I'm fine. I guess you heard the phone."

"I heard it." He dropped her hands because he was afraid he'd break her fingers. "Why don't I get you something? Water." He stuck his hands in his pockets again. "Something."

"No. I don't need anything." She brought the heels of her hands over her face to dry her tears. "I couldn't keep him talking. I just couldn't do it."

"It's all right."

"No, it's not." Bringing her knees up, she dropped her head on them. "It's my problem, and as long as I keep running from it it's not going away. Everything you've said so far has been true, everything you've done has been right, and I haven't been holding up my end."

"Nobody's blaming you, Chantel." He started to reach out for her again, to touch her creamy shoulders, which were slumped in despair. Catching himself, Quinn clenched his hand. "You should try to get some sleep."

"Yeah."

He strained against his own helplessness. Where had he gotten the stupid idea that she needed him? He didn't know the way to comfort and soothe. He didn't have the pretty words that would relax her and help her sleep again. He had nothing but a rage boiling inside him and a fierce desire to keep her safe. Neither of those would help her now.

"Look, I can get you something. Go downstairs and make, I don't know, some tea."

With her face still pressed against her knees, she squeezed her eyes tight. "No, thanks. I'll be fine."

"Damn it, I want to do something." The explosion ripped out of him before he could stop it. "I can't stand seeing you like this. Let me get you some aspirin, or sit in the chair until you can get to sleep. Something. You can't ask me to just leave you alone."

"Hold me." The words came out in a sob as she lifted her head. "Could you just hold me a minute?"

He sat beside her and, gathering her close, pressed her head to his shoulder. "Sure. As long as you want. Go ahead and let go, angel."

She didn't have the strength to stop it, and she no longer wanted to. With his arms strong around her, she let the full force of the tears come. Quinn cradled her close and murmured things he hoped would help, things he wasn't even certain she heard. When she began to quiet, he stroked the hair back from her face and said nothing at all.

"Quinn?"

"Hmmm?"

"Thanks."

"Any time."

"I don't make a habit of it." She sniffled. "Got a handkerchief?"

"No."

Reluctant to shift away even slightly, she reached for a tissue on her bedside table. "I guess I figured a man like you would head for the hills when a woman started—" she sniffled again "—blubbering."

"This is different."

She tilted her head back. Her eyes were swollen, her cheeks tear-streaked. "Why?"

"It's just different." He brushed a tear from her lashes. Then, though he felt foolish, he let the moisture linger on his thumb. "Feel better?"

"Yes." She did, unaccountably, for she'd never believed tears solved anything. Now that they were shed she felt drained and embarrassed. "I'd, ah…appreciate it if we both forgot about this lapse in the morning."

"Never give yourself an inch, do you?"

"I hate to cry."

She said it with such bitter finality that he knew she'd shed hot tears over something before. Or someone. "Me, too."

That made her smile. "You're a nice guy when you put a little effort into it."

"I try not to let it happen often." He stroked her hair again before he shifted her closer. It hadn't been so hard to comfort, he discovered. It wasn't so hard to be needed. "Think you can sleep now?"

"I guess." She closed her eyes, discovering it felt enormously good to let her cheek rest against his.

He ran a comforting hand over her back, then tensed when he felt silk give way to flesh. "Tomorrow's Sunday. You can stay in bed all day."

"I have a photo session at one." With her eyes still closed, she explored the muscles of his shoulders with her fingertips.

"You can cancel it."

"I'll be okay. The photographer's accommodating me because of the shooting schedule."

"Then you'd better get some rest or you'll look like hell."

"Thanks a lot."

"You're welcome."

When he drew her back, she tilted her head up and smiled at him. His fingers tensed on her shoulders, and hers on his, and her smile faded. The need vibrated between them so urgently that it set the air humming.

"I'd better go."

"No." The decision had already been made, she knew, perhaps before they'd even met. Her heart had just accepted it. She loved. There was no changing it. Until now, until him, she hadn't known how much she needed to have the chance to love again. "I want you to stay." She slid her hands over his shoulders. "I want you to make love with me."

The ache that had begun to throb just from looking at her turned sharp and stabbing—a painfully sweet sensation. Her hands felt so cool on his skin. Her eyes looked so warm and dark. The moonlight dappled over her like a dream, but he couldn't afford to forget reality.

"Chantel, I want you so much right now I can hardly breathe. But…" He slid his hands up to her wrists. "I don't know if I could live with the fact that this happened between us because you were scared and shaky."

A smile curved her lips as she brought them closer to his. "Haven't you figured out yet that I know what I want?" She turned her head slightly so that her kiss brushed his chin. "Didn't you say that a man could tell just by the way a woman looked at him? Can't you see the way I'm looking at you?"

"Maybe I only see the way I want you to look." But his fingers had tangled in her hair.

"I want you to stay," she repeated, "not because I'm scared. I want you to stay because of the way you make me feel when you kiss me. When you hold me. When you touch me." She rubbed her cheek against his. "I want you to stay because you can make me forget there's anything outside of this room."

Something snapped inside him. Some would call it control. With an oath, he dragged his hands through her hair and plundered her mouth.

She was everything dark and desperate and desirable. She was pure aphrodisiac. As they knelt on the bed he let his dreams spring to life and rained kisses over her face, her hair, her throat. The scent that was so much a part of her misted through his brain like a fog. And she trembled. Not on cue but from pleasure, from the pleasure he gave her. Half-mad, he crushed his lips to hers again and tasted her passion.

Never before and, she was certain, never again, would a man bring her to life this way. Never before and never again would she want like this. Her body was like a furnace, pumping heat and energy while her mind was flooded with a brilliant kaleidoscope of sensation. No, never again would a man bring her this, because there was only one man. She'd known it, somehow, from the first.

Everything was so clear. She felt the scrape of his chin over her shoulder, felt the mattress sink under their combined weights as they knelt torso-to-torso. She could see the moonlight against his skin as she ran her hands over his shoulders and down. His muscles contracted at her touch, and she heard the soft hiss of his indrawn breath. Desperation flavored his kisses and fueled her own need. A kaleidoscope, a whirlwind, a race. The scents from her garden crept into the room. With a gurgle of delight, she lowered her lips to his shoulder and nipped.

A man could lose his mind and his soul to her. Quinn felt his chest constrict as he ran his hands freely over her. Pain and power…they were both twined together in his need for her. She made him hurt and made him soar just by being in his arms.

It wasn't just the perfection of form, of face, but the wild, wanton sexuality she had encased in glittering ice. Released, it was a Pandora's box of emotions, some dark, some dangerous, some desperately exciting.

He wouldn't resist her. He couldn't. He could feel her tremble, hear her moan as he touched and tasted and tempted. Her skin was hot, already damp. Her breath caught on his name. Tonight, even if it was just for tonight, he would make her as frenzied as he.

He gathered her hair in his hand, drawing her head back to expose the long white line of her throat. Her pulse beat frantically as he traced his tongue over it. Her hands moved over his chest, then lower, and his stomach muscles quivered at her touch. As she tugged at the snap on his jeans, he found her breast through the thin silk she wore. When he drew both silk and flesh into his mouth, she strained against him, shuddering. Her throat filled with indistinct murmurs of pleasure, she tugged the denim over his hips.

The feel of her hands on him drove every rational thought from his mind. In one crazed movement he ripped the silk from her, rending it down the middle. Her gasp was muffled against his mouth as he dragged her down beneath him.

He couldn't think. He could only feel. When he plunged into her she was so warm, so moist. He wondered if a man could die from being given his ultimate wish. Then she was wrapped around him, driving him even as he sought to drive her. He could see her, her hair spread out on tumbled white sheets, her eyes half closed, her lips slightly parted as the breath trembled out.

"Quinn." His name whispered from her as she was tossed by titanic waves of sensation. Heat, light, wind. Nothing had prepared her for this. She tried to tell him, but his lips were on hers again. She was a part of him. Release came in a torrent that left her too stunned for speech.

She didn't know what to say. Would he expect some clever phrase, some easy words? It wasn't possible to explain that she had given herself to only one other man and never, truly never, like this. If it hadn't mattered so much—if he hadn't mattered so much—she was sure she could have come up with something to break the long silence and the tension she felt building again.

He didn't know what to say. He'd taken her like a madman. She deserved better, more care, certainly more finesse. If only he hadn't lost control. But he had, Quinn reminded himself ruthlessly. He couldn't change that any more than he could change the fact that he'd damaged whatever might have been growing between them. He could only hope it wasn't too late to repair it.

Both of them tensed, then turned, then spoke each other's names at the same time. The awkwardness lasted only a moment before they grinned.

"I was thinking you were right," she began, "about me needing a script. I can't think of what I want to say."

"I've been having some trouble with that myself." He took her hand and brought it to his lips. "I guess I was a little rough."

"Were you?" Amused and relieved, Chantel groped for the remains of her silk teddy. Lifting a brow, she dropped it on his chest.

Quinn rubbed the material between his thumb and forefinger. "You could deduct it from my check."

"I intend to. Three hundred and fifty."

"Three hundred and fifty?" He rose on one elbow and examined the ripped silk more carefully. "You've got to be crazy to spend three-fifty on something you sleep in."

"I enjoy indulging myself." To prove her point, she leaned over and nibbled on his lips. "And under the circumstances, I think it only fair that I deduct half the price."

"Half?"

"It was a joint effort." She smiled and ran a fingertip over his chest. "Besides, it was worth it."

"Was it?" His hand came up her leg to rest on her hip. "You sure?"

"Well, I'm a cautious woman, and you know what they say in the business."

"No." Her hair teased his shoulders as she leaned over him. "What do they say in the business?"

"Take 2," Chantel sighed, lowering herself to him.

Chapter 8

"Quinn, I promise you, this is going to take a good three hours, maybe four." Chantel got out of the car, then leaned over to take her garment bag from the hook by the passenger door.

He noticed how nicely the slim skirt fit over her bottom. "I can be patient."

"A photo session is often very tedious for the people involved, much less for someone who just has to sit there."

"Let me worry about that," he advised, and took the bag from her.

"I have to worry about it. Knowing you're hanging around, grumbling under your breath, is going to make me tense." Chantel pressed a buzzer on the outside door, then tipped down her sunglasses to peer over them. "And tension will show in the pictures. This layout for *The Scene* is very important."

He pushed the glasses back up on her nose. "So are you."

It warmed her. She no longer knew how to pretend it

didn't. Chantel rose on her toes to brush a kiss over his lips. "I appreciate that. But I'll be perfectly safe. Margot will be there to do my hair, and the makeup artist is a freelancer I've worked with before. Mrs. Alice Cooke. They have to stay for the whole session. I'll be surrounded by well-meaning women."

"And the photographer," he reminded her. "I'm not letting you alone with this Bryan Mitchell or any other man."

Chantel started to correct him, then thought better of it. A woman was entitled to take every advantage offered. She ran a finger over the collar of his shirt. "Jealous?"

"Cautious."

"Bryan Mitchell." The voice coming through the intercom was low, smooth and feminine.

"It's Chantel O'Hurley for the one o'clock session."

"Right on time."

There was a mechanical buzz from inside the door, and then it unlatched.

"Bryan Mitchell is a tall, gorgeous blonde," Chantel began as they climbed the inside stairs. "We've been friends for years."

Quinn wrapped his fingers around hers. "All the more reason I'm not leaving you alone with him. Until this thing is settled, the only man you're having solitary dealings with is me."

"Well." Chantel paused at the studio door and wrapped her arms around him. "I like that," she murmured, and met his lips with hers.

"I bet you do." Bryan stood in the open doorway, grinning.

"Quinn Doran." Chantel laid a hand lightly on his arm. "Bryan Mitchell."

The photographer was indeed tall, blond and gorgeous. She was also a woman. Quinn shot Chantel a look as she smiled. "Nice meeting you."

Bryan offered him a hand, already wondering if she could convince him to sit for her. "Welcome to chaos," she told them as she gestured them inside. "I'm still setting up. Chantel, you know where the cold drinks are. Hairdressing and makeup are in the back room having an argument about fashion. Personally, I can't get emotionally involved over whether henna is back to stay." As she spoke, she walked over to a set of white umbrellas and adjusted them.

Chantel walked to a cramped little room off the side of the studio and poked in the refrigerator. "Quinn, it's going to be like this for hours. There must be something else you want to do."

He could hear the other two women chattering in the back room. Something about facial packs and eye tucks. "I can think of a couple dozen."

"Then go do them." Chantel set down the bottle of soda to take both of his hands. "Bryan had the security system installed a few months ago when there was a rash of robberies in the neighborhood. No one gets through the outside door unless she releases the lock. I'm surrounded by women who'll be fussing over me for hours, and you'll distract all of us. Go play some handball or something."

She was right. She'd be safe here, and he'd be in the way—as well as unmercifully bored. Then, too, it would help him to have a couple of hours away from her, a couple of hours of pure physical exertion. Would he work her out of his system?

"Gym's a couple of blocks down," he muttered.

"Jim who?"

"*The* gym," he corrected, putting his hands on her hips.

"You mean one of those places with weights and nasty machines that make you grunt and sweat?"

"More or less." Taking out his notebook, he wrote down

a name and number. "Call me when you're finished and I'll come back and pick you up."

"Rizzo's." She kept her face bland as she looked up at him. "Sounds serious."

"Just call." He leaned down to bite her lightly on the bottom lip. "Why don't you go make yourself beautiful?"

She kept her arms around him as she lifted a brow. "Aren't I already?"

He knew she hadn't so much as picked up a tube of mascara that morning. Her eyes were blue and brilliant, her skin luminous and pale. Fresh and dewy, as it was now, her beauty was heartbreaking. He lifted a hand to skim it over her cheek. "Such a hag."

Before she could retaliate he had her close, cutting off her breath in a kiss that seemed to last for hours. He needed to lift weights, Quinn thought. He had to sweat some of the need for her out of his system.

"Try to do something about that face, will you?"

"Take a walk, Doran."

He grinned at her, then slipped back into the studio. Chantel let out a shaky breath and leaned her palms against the cluttered counter beside the refrigerator. There was nothing she could do, and she was nearly ready to admit there was nothing she wanted to do, about the fact that she was in love with him. It was probably a mistake, a desperate one, but it had already been made.

Somehow, if she could somehow draw back a part of herself, she wouldn't be so devastated when he went his own way. And he would, wouldn't he? A man like Quinn lived alone, worked alone, walked alone. When his job was over he'd kiss her goodbye and go. She caught her bottom lip between her teeth and straightened. No, he wouldn't. Not if she had anything to do with it.

You're going to lose this match, Doran, she promised herself. No way was he going to walk away and leave her.

"Chantel, they're ready for you."

She was ready, too. Chantel left the drink on the counter. She was more than ready.

For two hours she worked nonstop. Her hair was frizzed, smoothed, sprayed and gelled. Her face was painted and powdered. Every time she changed her outfit her hair and face were subtly altered to enhance the look. Bryan worked with a slow, steady enthusiasm, as she always did.

"I haven't asked you how Shade is."

"Put your right hand on your left shoulder," Bryan instructed. "Spread your fingers. Good. Shade's terrific. He's home changing diapers." She caught Chantel's quick, mischievous grin on film.

"That I'd like to see."

"He's great at it. Organized, you know."

"Well, I can tell you, you don't look as though you had a baby two months ago."

"Who has time to eat? Tilt your chin up and try for aloof. That's it." She crouched, shifting angles. "Andrew Colby is a ten-pound slave driver."

"And you're crazy about him."

Bryan lowered her camera and beamed. "He's the most fantastic baby. Between Shade and me, we've taken at least five hundred rolls of film. Every day there's some little change." She tossed her long blond braid behind her back. "You can see how bright he is just by the way he looks at things. Just yesterday he—" She cut herself off with a laugh. "Stop me. It's an obsession."

"No." Chantel smiled, though the quick pang of envy she felt surprised her. "It's lovely."

"It is, you know. I never saw myself as a mother." She

lifted the camera back into place. "Now I can't imagine life without Andrew. Or Shade."

"The right man can change your outlook, I guess."

Bryan decided the wistful expression that flitted across Chantel's face would be the best shot yet. "You sure make my work easier."

Bringing herself back, Chantel looked at the camera. "How's that?"

"Turn to the side and look over your shoulder. A bit more. Smolder a little." She pressed the shutter four times in rapid succession. "A face like yours is always a pleasure to shoot, especially when you bring so much to it. But I didn't expect the bonus."

"What bonus?" Chantel asked as she shifted to look over her other shoulder.

"There's nothing more terrific than photographing a woman in love. Close your mouth," she ordered, then lowered her camera to stretch her shoulders.

Slowly Chantel turned to face Bryan again. "It's that obvious?"

"Don't you want it to be?"

"No…yes. I don't know." She pushed a hand through her carefully groomed hair. "I don't want to make a fool of myself."

"That kind of goes hand in hand with falling in love, but I think you'll survive it. He's got a great face. I don't suppose you could talk him into sitting for me."

"Maybe if you bound him hand and foot. Bryan, how did you handle Shade?"

Bryan took a chocolate bar out of her back pocket. "*You're* asking *me* for advice on men?"

Chantel accepted a sliver of the chocolate. "Don't let it get around."

"Have you felt like murdering him yet?"

"Several times."

"You're making progress. The best thing I can tell you is to let things happen. We're wrapped here." She bit into the candy. "If I were you, I wouldn't waste what's left of the weekend."

The gym smelt like men. Damp, athletic men. The air was filled with sweat and swearing. Most of the patrons had stripped down to shorts, and a few had added T-shirts. On a mat, a man with weights on his legs grunted his way through a series of sit-ups. On a bench press, another man swore repetitively every time he extended the bar over his head. The equipment was top-notch, but it had long since lost its shine.

Chantel strolled in and absorbed, both brows lifted. The first one who saw her was a young man pulling weights up the walls with two ropes. He was working steadily, the veins in his neck bulging out as he rotated his arms. His mouth dropped open and the ropes snapped back against the wall. Chantel smiled at him.

Careful to keep her skirts clear, she circled around the bench press. The man stopped swearing as his eyes bugged out. It took less than ten seconds for the noisy, steamy gym to drop into silence. Then she saw Quinn.

He hadn't noticed the sudden quiet. With his back to the room, he was systematically jabbing at a punching bag. Its buffeting noise was the only sound in the room. He looked magnificent, legs spread, eyes intense, his powerful back tensed as he concentrated on his timing. The small brown bag was a blur as his fists never let it rest. Chantel walked over to him, waited a moment, then ran a fingertip down his back.

"Hello, darling."

He swore and spun, his hand still fisted and lifted.

Chantel raised a brow, then her chin, as if inviting him to take his best shot.

"What the hell are you doing here?"

"Watching you." She took a finger and pushed at the bag. "Tell me, what's the purpose of beating at this little thing?"

"I told you to call me." He swiped sweat out of his eyes in order to glare at her better.

"I felt like a walk. Besides, I wanted to see where a man like you…played." Deliberately she looked over her shoulder and scanned the room. "Fascinating."

Every man in the room sucked in his stomach.

With an oath, Quinn took her by the arm. "You must be crazy. You don't belong in a place like this."

"Why ever not?" As they passed the man on the bench press, Chantel sent him a brilliant smile. The weights clattered against the safety bar.

"Cut that out," he muttered. "Rizzo, I'm using your office."

"Oh, where is he?" As he dragged her out, Chantel glanced back. "I'm dying to meet him."

"Shut up. Do you have to walk in here with legs like that?"

"They're all I have to walk on."

"Sit." He shoved her into a torn plastic chair. "What the hell am I supposed to do with you?"

"Would you like a multiple choice?"

"This isn't a joke, damn it." He pushed at the clutter on Rizzo's desk until he found a crumpled pack of Camels. "Look, Chantel, we made an arrangement. You were supposed to call. There are reasons." He shook out a cigarette and lit it.

"Quinn, it's a beautiful afternoon and it wasn't far. There isn't much opportunity to stroll in L.A., and I couldn't resist. If you're going to tell me I can't walk two blocks on a public street in broad daylight, I'll scream."

She glanced toward the door. "I can't imagine what your, ah, associates would make of that."

He exhaled a long stream of smoke, then crushed the cigarette into a mess of brown tobacco and white paper. "You go nowhere without me. You had instructions, Chantel, and I trusted you to follow them."

"Oh, lighten up." She rose and put her palms on his bare chest.

"I'm sweating like a pig," he muttered, taking her wrists.

"I noticed. I don't know what it is that attracts men to a place that smells like old athletic socks, but if this is how you keep in shape—" she glanced down approvingly "—I might just have to install a gym at home."

"Don't change the subject."

"What subject was that?"

"I don't want anything to happen to you."

She touched her tongue to her upper lip and edged closer. "Why? You've already been paid for this week."

"I don't care about the damn money," he said with violence.

"What do you care about, Quinn?"

"You." He said it between his teeth before he spun away. He'd thought he needed space, just some space and time to get his equilibrium back. There wasn't that much space in the whole world. "Don't pull anything like this again."

"All right. I'm sorry."

"I've got to shower. Stay in here."

When the door slammed at his back, Chantel sat again. He cared. She closed her eyes and hugged the knowledge to her. He cared about her. If she'd gotten him to say it, the next step was getting him to like it.

"How long are you going to be angry?"

They were driving home with the top down. Chantel had let the first fifteen minutes pass in silence.

"I'm not angry."

"You're clenching your teeth."

"Consider yourself lucky that's all I'm doing."

"Quinn, I've already said I was sorry. I'm not going to apologize again."

"No one's asking you to." He downshifted around a curve. "What I am asking is that you take the situation you're in seriously."

"You don't think I am?"

"Not after that little stunt of yours this afternoon."

She shifted in her seat. The wind picked up her hair and tossed it as her temper snapped. "Stop treating me like a child. I understand the situation I'm in perfectly. I live with it twenty-four hours a day, every day, every night. Every time the phone rings, every time I go through my mail. When I go to sleep at night, that's what I'm thinking of. When I wake up in the morning, that's what I'm thinking of. If I can't have an hour now and then when I can push it aside, I'll go crazy. I'm trying to survive, Doran. Don't talk to me as though I'm irresponsible."

She shifted away again, and again silence reigned. He was right, Quinn told himself as he slacked his speed. But so was she. There were times, because she put up such a good front, when he believed she'd forgotten she was in any danger. She never forgot, he realized. She just refused to buckle—except in her private moments. He didn't know how to tell her he loved her for that above everything else.

Loved her. That was a tough one to swallow, but then the truth often was. The more his feelings for her grew, the more he worried about her well-being. He knew she worked hard, and for long hours. With the kind of strain she was under, she could only keep up that pace for a limited time. Even a woman as strong-willed as Chantel would lose eventually.

Damn it, he wished he had something, anything, to go on. They were moving into their third week, and he was no closer to putting things right than he had been on the first day. He needed to see her safe, secure, content. Even though he was afraid that once she was she'd write him a check and kiss him off.

Quinn's hands tightened on the wheel, then gradually relaxed. She was going to have a fight on her hands when it came to that.

Relax, he told himself. She wasn't going to get away. Moving only his eyes, he took in the stiff, angry way she sat. Angel, he told her silently, I'm just the man to clip your wings.

Quinn tossed his arm casually over the back of the seat. "You're pouting."

"Go to hell."

"You're going to get lines all over your face if you keep that up. Then where will you be?"

"Kiss my—"

"Love to." He pulled over to the side of the road. She didn't even have the chance to snarl at him before he gathered her close. "Why don't I start with that homely face of yours and work my way down?"

"No."

"Okay, if you'd rather I take it from the bottom up."

When he started to shift her, she began to struggle in earnest. "Stop it. I don't want you to kiss me anywhere."

"Are you sure?" He brought her wrist to his lips and brushed them over the inside. "How about there?"

"No."

"Here, then." He pressed his mouth to the side of her throat. She stopped struggling.

"No."

"Well, other options are a little risky on the side of the road, but if you insist—"

"Stop." The laughter bubbled up as she shoved him away. Chantel leaned against the door and crossed her arms. "You creep."

"I love it when you insult me."

"Then you're going to love this," she began, but he was too quick. Whatever she'd had in mind was muffled against his mouth. Response came instantly, from the heart. Her arms went around him and her lips parted. For a moment there was nothing but the warm late-afternoon sun and sheer, unbridled pleasure.

Her eyes stayed closed, seconds after he'd drawn his lips from hers. When they opened, slowly, the irises were dark and clouded. "Are you trying to make up?" she murmured.

"For what?"

Her lips curved as she framed his face with her hands. "Never mind. Let's go home, Quinn."

He touched his lips to hers again, lingering, before he sat back and started the engine. "By the way, Rizzo wanted to know if he could have an autographed picture for his office."

Chantel laughed, then sat back to enjoy the rest of the drive. As they rode by the high wall surrounding her grounds, she began to toy with the idea of a long dip in the pool. Bryan was right. It would be a pity to waste what was left of the weekend. Even as she turned to ask Quinn to join her, he was bringing the car to a fast stop.

"Quinn, we really should wait until we're *inside*."

"There's a car in front of the gates." His tone had her tensing as she looked around. "A man's there, see? Looks like he's causing quite a bit of commotion."

"You don't think that—" She moistened her lips. "He wouldn't come right to the front gate."

"Why don't we find out?" He took the keys from the ignition and unlocked the glove compartment. Chantel watched as he drew out a revolver. It was nothing like her dainty little .22. And she was just as certain it wasn't unloaded.

"Quinn."

"Stay here."

"No, I—"

"Don't argue."

"But I don't want you to…" As the argument at the gate heated up, the voices drifted to her. Listening intently, Chantel tightened her grip on Quinn. "I don't believe it," she murmured. She squinted, trying to make out the figure in the distance. "I just don't believe it," she repeated, and sprang out of the car before Quinn could stop her.

"Chantel!"

"It's Pop." Laughing, she spun back to Quinn. "It's Pop. My father." Her long legs flashed as she sped up the rest of the road. "Pop!" Still laughing, she threw her arms wide.

Frank O'Hurley turned from his spirited argument with the guard. His thin face erupted into a grin. "There's my girl." Spry and wiry, he pumped down the remaining distance and caught Chantel close. With a whoop, he spun her in three dizzying circles. "How's my little princess?"

"Surprised." She kissed his baby-smooth face, then hugged him again. He smelled, as he always did, of powder and peppermint. "I didn't know you were coming."

"Don't need an invitation, do I?"

"Don't be silly."

"Well, tell that to the joker on the other side of the gate. The idiot wouldn't let me in even when I told him I was your own flesh and blood."

"I'm sorry, Miss O'Hurley." The stiff-faced man behind the gate speared Frank with a look. The crazy old man had threatened to pull out his tongue and wrap it around his neck. "There was no one here to verify."

"That's all right."

"All right?" Frank piped up. He was primed and ready for a donnybrook. "All right when your own father's treated like a trespasser?"

"Don't be cranky." Chantel brushed at his lapels. "I've added to the security, that's all."

"Why?" Immediately alert, he cupped Chantel's chin. "What's wrong?"

"It's nothing. We'll get into all that later. Now I'm just glad to see you." She glanced back at the dusty rental car. "Where's Mom?"

"Said she wasn't fit to see anyone until she'd been to the beauty parlor. I wasn't going to sit around cooling my heels while she's getting primped up. She'll be taking a cab out later."

"But tell me what you're doing here, how long you can stay. What—"

"God be praised, girl, can't it wait until a man's washed the dust out of his throat? Drove clear from Vegas today."

"Vegas? I didn't know you had a gig in Vegas."

"You don't know everything." He tweaked her nose, then looked over her shoulder as Quinn pulled up. "Now who might this be?"

"That's Quinn." She shot him a quick look. "Quinn Doran. You're right, Pop, we can talk better inside—especially after you've had a glass of the Irish."

"Now you're talking." Frank hopped back in his car, then sailed through the now-open gates. Chantel saw him look down his nose at the guard.

"Your father?" Quinn asked when she climbed back in the car.

"Yes, I wasn't expecting him, but that's nothing new." Her fingers twisted together. "You put the gun away?"

He lifted a hand to the guard as he drove through. "Don't worry."

"But I am. I didn't want to bring my family into all this." Chantel pressed the bridge of her nose between her thumb and forefinger. "I'm going to have to tell them something. He's seen the guard at the gates. He's bound to notice the men patrolling the grounds."

"Why don't you try the truth?"

"I don't want to worry my parents. Damn, I only get to see them three or four times a year, and now this." She looked at Quinn as he slowed at the end of the drive. "And I have to explain you."

"The truth," he repeated.

"All right. I can't think of anything else." She put a hand on his arm before he could climb out. "But I'll do it my way. I want to play it down as much as possible."

"Well now." Beaming and affable, Frank strolled over to the car. "Looks like you've got yourself a fine strong fellow here, Chantel."

"Quinn Doran, my father, Frank O'Hurley."

"Pleased to meet you." Frank offered a hand and pumped Quinn's exuberantly. "Wouldn't mind helping me in with the bags, would you, son?"

Chantel had to smile when Frank popped open his trunk and took out a small shoulder bag, leaving two large cases for Quinn. "You never change," she murmured hooking an arm through his to lead him into the house.

"Just leave them there," she told Quinn, gesturing to the base of the staircase. "You can take them up later."

"Thanks."

She met his sarcasm with an easy smile. "Why don't you two go into the living room and have a drink? I want to tell the cook there'll be two more for dinner." Leaving Quinn with a brief warning look, she started down the hall.

"Well, son, I don't know about you," Frank said, giving Quinn a solid slap on the back, "but I could use a drink." He trotted off into the living room and headed directly to the bar. "What's your pleasure?"

"Scotch."

Frank shrugged his narrow shoulders, then poured. "To each his own." Locating the bottle of whiskey, he gave a satisfied grunt and poured a generous three fingers. "Well, now… Quinn, is it? Why don't we drink to my girl?" He tapped his glass solidly against Quinn's without regard for the pricey Rosenthal crystal, then swallowed deeply. "Now that's a drink a man can wrap his heart around. Have a seat, son, have a seat." Still playing the congenial host, he gestured to a chair before finding one for himself. "Now…" He settled back and sighed. Then, abruptly, his eyes were shrewd and sharp. "Just what are you doing with my daughter?"

"Pop." Grateful for her timing, Chantel strolled into the room, then sat on the arm of her father's chair. "You'll have to excuse him, Quinn. He's never been subtle."

Quinn regarded his Scotch for a moment. "Seems like a reasonable question to me."

"There." Satisfied with what he saw, Frank nodded. "We're going to get along just fine."

"I wouldn't be surprised," she murmured ruffling her father's hair. "So tell me how it went in Vegas."

"Be glad to." He sipped his whiskey again, appreciating its smooth heat. "Just as soon as you explain why you have a trained gorilla at your front gate."

"I told you, I added some security." But when she started to rise, Frank put a firm hand on her knee.

"You wouldn't try to con an old hand like me, would you, princess?"

It would be useless, she admitted, and settled back.

"I've been getting some annoying phone calls, that's all. It seemed wise to take a few precautions."

"What kind of phone calls?"

"Just nuisance calls."

"Chantel." He knew his daughter too well. A few nuisance calls would have been brushed off, laughed off and forgotten. "Is someone threatening you?"

"No. No, it's nothing like that." Realizing she was being backed into a corner, she shot a pleading look at Quinn.

"I still opt for the truth," he said simply.

"Thanks for the help."

"Just be quiet," Frank told her, and there was such uncharacteristic authority in his tone that she closed her mouth instantly. "You tell me what's going on," he ordered Quinn. "And what you have to do with it."

"Quinn—"

"Chantel Margaret Louise O'Hurley, shut your mouth and keep it shut."

When she did, Quinn could only smile. "Nice trick," he said to Frank.

"I use it selectively to keep it fresh." Frank swallowed the rest of his whiskey. "Let's hear it."

Briefly, concisely, Quinn outlined what Chantel was dealing with. As he spoke, Frank's brows lowered, his thin face reddened and the hand still resting on Chantel's knee clenched.

"Slimy bastard." Frank rose out of the chair like a terrier ready to charge. "If you're a detective, Quinn Doran, why in hell haven't you found him?"

"Because he hasn't made a mistake." Quinn set down his glass and met Frank's outraged glare levelly. "But he will, and I'll find him."

"If he hurts my girl—"

"He's not going to get near her," Quinn interrupted flatly. "Because he has to go through me first."

Frank swallowed his fury—it was something he didn't often bother to do—and measured the man in front of him. He'd always prided himself on being a good judge of character. You needed to know whether to raise your fists or laugh and back off. The man in front of him was hard as a rock and mean as they came. If he had to trust his daughter to someone, this was the one.

"So. You're staying here, in the house, with Chantel."

"That's right. I'm going to take care of her, Mr. O'Hurley. You have my word on that."

Frank hesitated only a moment before his teeth showed in a smile. "If you don't, I'll skin you alive. And make it Frank."

Cool and regal, Chantel rose. "Perhaps I could say a word now."

"Don't put that face on with me, girl." Frank crossed to her, then gently framed her face in his hands. "You should have come to your family with this."

"There was no point in worrying you."

"Point?" Frank shook his head from side to side. "We're family. We're the O'Hurleys. We stick together."

"Pop, Maddy's getting married at the end of the week. Abby's pregnant. Trace is—"

"You'll kindly leave him out of it," Frank said stiffly. "Family business has nothing to do with your brother. That's his choice."

"Really, Pop, after all this time you should—"

"And don't change the subject. Your mother and me, and your sisters, are entitled to worry about you."

It wasn't the time to go to her brother's defense. And Chantel wasn't entirely sure he'd care one way or the other.

Now she wanted to smooth those lines of worry from her father's face.

"All right, then." She kissed him soundly. "Worry all you want, but everything that can be done is being done."

He kept his hand on her shoulder but turned to Quinn. "We're off to New York on Friday to see my daughter married off. You'll be going with us?"

"I didn't think it was necessary to drag Quinn to—"

"I'm going," he interrupted. His eyes met Chantel's in something like a challenge. "I've already made the arrangements."

"You never mentioned it to me."

"Why should I?" he countered for the simple pleasure of watching fury rise in her eyes.

"It hardly seems I'm necessary, does it?" Feeling squeezed from all sides, she bristled. "If you'll both excuse me, I'm going to go soak my head."

"Nasty little number, isn't she?" Frank asked with obvious pride as she stalked out.

"All that and more."

"It's the Irish, you know. We're either poets or fighters. O'Hurleys are a bit of both."

"I'm looking forward to meeting the rest of your family."

And they'll want to get a look at you, Frank said to himself. "Tell me, Quinn," he began in an amiable tone. "Do you intend to, ah, keep your eye on Chantel, so to speak, after this business is settled?"

Quinn studied the man across from him. It seemed it was still time for truths. "Yes. Whether she likes it or not."

Frank gave a quick laugh. "Let's have another drink."

Chapter 9

"Mom, there's no reason for you to do that."

Molly O'Hurley carefully folded a white silk jacket in tissue. "Why should you call a maid up here?" Years of experience had Molly packing Chantel's clothes with a minimum of fuss.

"It's her job."

Molly brushed her objections away with the back of her hand. "I never feel I can speak my mind in front of maids and butlers."

Chantel looked at the suitcase and at her stacks of clothes. She'd spent the first twenty years of her life packing and unpacking. As a matter of principle, she hadn't done so in years. But she'd never been able to win a fight with her mother. Resigned, Chantel began a careful selection of her toiletries.

"I'm sorry we haven't had much time together the past few days."

"Don't be silly." Brisk and practical, Molly rattled more tissue paper. "You're in the middle of that film. Your father and I didn't expect to be entertained."

"Pop seemed to be entertained the day you came to the set."

Chuckling, Molly glanced up. She was a pretty, trim woman who managed to look a decade younger than her years with a minimum of effort. Looking at her, Chantel acknowledged that the rush and craziness of her parents' life-style suited Molly just as much as it did Frank. "He did, didn't he? Still, I don't think he should have argued with the director about how to set the scene."

"Mary has a—a sense of humor."

"Good thing." For the next few moments, they packed in silence. "Chantel, we're worried about you."

"Mom, that's exactly what I don't want you to do."

"We love you. You can't expect us to love you and not be concerned."

"I know." She slipped a bottle of perfume into a padded travel box. "That's why I didn't want to tell you about what was going on. You had to worry enough about me when I was growing up."

"You don't expect a parent to turn off the juice just because a child's past the age of twenty-one?"

"No, I suppose not." She smiled and slipped her set of makeup brushes into their cases. "But it seems like you should have less to worry about after a certain age."

"I can only tell you that one day you'll find out differently yourself."

There was that pang again. Chantel's brows drew together as she tried to ignore it. "I don't know about that," she murmured. "I *do* know I don't want this business to affect the family."

"What affects one of us affects all of us. That's that."

Molly said it so matter-of-factly, Chantel was forced to smile.

"Your Irish is showing."

"And why shouldn't it?" Molly wanted to know. "Your father and I think we should come back with you after the wedding."

"Back here?" Chantel stopped to stare. "You can't. You have a gig in New Hampshire."

Molly folded a pair of linen slacks by the pleats and said with a little smile, "Chantel, your father and I have been performing for over thirty-five years. I don't think canceling one engagement is going to make much of a ripple."

"No." Chantel set down the bottles and pots in her hands to reach for her mother. "I can't tell you how much it means to me to know that you would. But what could you do?"

"We could be with you."

"You could hardly even do that. Mom, I'll be filming for weeks more. You've seen in the last few days how little I'm home. I'd be a wreck thinking about you sitting around here twiddling your thumbs when you'd want to be working."

"Sitting around here, as in lounging by the pool?"

Chantel's lips curved, but she shook her head. "If I could believe you'd be content for more than forty-eight hours, it would be different. Be logical, Mom. If you stayed I'd be worried because you were worried. Pop would drive the staff crazy, and I wouldn't even be around to enjoy it."

"I told Frank you'd feel this way." With a sigh, Molly touched Chantel's hair. "I always worried about you the most, you know."

"I guess I gave you the most cause."

"You did what you had to. And Trace also was going to go his own way, no matter what. Your father refused to see it, but it was there from the time he could walk. Somehow I always knew Abby and Maddy would be all right, even when Abby was going through the mess of her first marriage and Maddy was struggling to keep herself in dancing shoes. But you…" Molly caressed her daughter's cheek. "I was always afraid you'd miss what was beside you because you were always looking so far ahead. I want you to be happy, Chantel."

"I am. No, I am, really. These past few weeks, even with this other business hanging over my head, I've found something."

"Quinn."

Chantel made a restless movement before walking to the windows. "It's obvious to everyone but him the way I feel."

Molly had formed her own opinion of Quinn Doran. He wasn't an easy man, nor would he often be a gentle one, but her daughter didn't need an easy, gentle man. She needed one who'd give her a run for her money.

"Men are more thickheaded," Molly commented. She was a woman who knew well just how thickheaded men could be. "Why don't you tell him?"

"No." She turned back, then rested the heels of her hands on the windowsill. "At least not yet. This is going to sound foolish, but I want… I need him to respect me. Me," she repeated. "For what I am. I need to be certain he's not just passing the time."

"Chantel, you can't use Dustin Price as a yardstick."

"I'm not." Anger crept into her voice. She managed to control it only because her mother's eyes remained so steady. "No, I'm not. But it isn't something that's easy to forget."

"No, it's impossible. But you can't live your life with that as the foundation. Have you told Quinn about him?"

"No, I can't. Mom, there are so many complications now, why bring up another? It's been nearly seven years."

"Do you trust Quinn?"

"Yes."

"Don't you think he'd understand?"

She pressed her fingers to her eyes for a moment. "If I was sure he loved me, really sure that what's between us is real, I could tell him anything. Even that."

"I wish I could tell you there were guarantees, but I can't." Molly crossed to her and gathered Chantel close. "I can tell you that I wouldn't consider leaving you, not for a minute until everything was resolved, if I wasn't sure Quinn was going to protect you."

"He makes me feel safe. Until I met him, I didn't know anyone could." She squeezed her eyes shut. "I didn't know I needed anyone who could."

"We all need to feel safe, Chantel. And loved." Molly stroked her hair, the light silver-blond locks she'd brushed and braided so often in the past. "There's something I haven't told you. Something I should have told you a long time ago." She embraced Chantel. "I'm very proud of you."

"Oh, Mom." As the tears welled up, Molly shook her head.

"Now, none of that," she murmured. "If we go downstairs with puffy eyes, your father will be pinching at me to find out why we've been sitting up here crying." She kissed Chantel's cheek and held on for another moment. "Let's finish packing."

"Mom."

"Yes, dear."

"I've always been proud of you, too."

"Well." Molly cleared her throat, but her voice was still husky when she spoke. "That's quite a thing to hear from a grown daughter. You're going to be all right?"

"I'm going to be fine. I'm going to be terrific."

"That's my girl. Now let's be about our business." Turning away, Molly made herself busy. "Look at this." Clucking her tongue, she held up a brief nightgown fashioned of black silk and lace. "It looks like sin."

Chantel rubbed a knuckle under her eyes to dry them and giggled. "I can't give it an evaluation yet. I just bought it."

Molly held it up to the sunlight. "I think it speaks for itself."

"You like it." Pleased, Chantel came over, folded it carefully and handed it back to her mother. "A souvenir from Beverly Hills."

"Don't be silly." But Molly couldn't resist rubbing a thumb over the silk. "I couldn't wear a thing like this."

"Why not?"

"I'm the mother of four grown children."

"You didn't pick us from under cabbage leaves."

"Well, your father would…" She trailed off, speculating. Chantel watched a wicked gleam come into her eyes. "Thank you, dear." Molly set the nightgown apart from the rest of Chantel's lingerie. "And I'll thank you from your father in advance."

By the time they went downstairs again, Frank could be heard picking his banjo.

"He's practicing," Molly said, "so he can play at the reception. They'll have to knock him unconscious to keep him from performing."

"You know Maddy wouldn't have it any other way."

"It's about time, woman." Frank looked up as his family walked in, but his fingers never stilled. "A man needs some backup, you know. This one here——" he jerked his head toward Quinn "——won't sing a note."

"Just doing you a favor," Quinn said easily as he lounged back on the sofa.

"Never heard of a body that wouldn't sing," Frank commented. "Heard plenty that couldn't, but never one who wouldn't. Sit here, Molly, my love. Let's show the man what the O'Hurleys are made of."

Obligingly Molly sat beside him, picked up the count and launched into the song with a strong, practiced voice. Chantel sat on the arm of the sofa beside Quinn and listened to the familiar sound of her parents working together. It was good, it was solid. The tension of the past weeks drained away.

"Come on, princess, you remember the chorus."

Chantel joined in, the words and rhythm of the bright novelty number coming easily. She rarely sang on her own. To Chantel, singing was a family affair. Even now, as she added her voice to her parents', she thought of Trace and her sisters and the countless times they'd all sung that same old song.

She'd surprised him. Quinn sat back, enjoying himself, as Frank merged one tune into another. Chantel wasn't the cool movie star now, nor was she the restless, passionate woman he'd discovered beneath that facade. She was at home with the nonsense songs her father played. She was a daughter, a loving one. The innocence he'd once sensed in her was apparent as she laughed and accused her father of missing a note.

Her scent was there, dark and sultry, in contrast to her relaxed, playful behavior. He'd never seen her like this. Never known she could be like this. He wondered if she realized how much her family meant to her, if she knew how her Hollywood image faded when she was with them.

It had been a good week. Chantel didn't know of the letters that had come, because he'd intercepted them. Nor did she know that they had traced one of the calls to a phone booth downtown. Quinn saw no reason to tell her or to hit her with the fact that two of the letters had begged for a meeting in New York.

He knew her plans.

Quinn lifted a hand and ran it down her arm. Chantel's fingers linked naturally with his. There was no point in telling her. She wouldn't be alone in New York, not for a moment. He'd already arranged for three of his best men to fly to Manhattan. Every step Chantel took would be monitored.

Frank interrupted Quinn's train of thought as he shot a challenging look at his daughter. "Do you still play that thing? Or do you use it as a doorstop?"

Chantel glanced at the white baby grand, then examined her nails. "I manage to hit a few keys."

"With a big, beautiful instrument like that you should be able to do a lot more."

"I don't want to show you up, Pop."

"That'll be the day."

With a shrug, she stood and moved to the piano. Deliberately she fluttered her lashes, sat, then went into a long, complicated arpeggio.

"You've been practicing," Frank accused, then cackled with delight.

Chantel shot a look at Quinn. "I don't spend my evenings darning socks."

Quinn acknowledged the hit with a slight inclination of his head. "Your daughter's full of surprises, Frank."

"No need to tell me that. The stories I could tell you. Why, there was the time—"

"Requests?" Chantel interrupted sweetly. "Unless Pop wants me to tie his tongue in a nice, neat bow."

Always cautious, Frank cleared his throat. "Why don't you do that little number your mother wouldn't let you sing until you turned eighteen?"

"Abby always did that one best."

"True enough." Frank's grin was crooked and amiable. "But you weren't half-bad." Molly managed to hide a smile as Chantel's eyes narrowed.

"Half-bad?" She wrinkled her nose at him as she gave herself a flowing introduction.

The low, torchy ballad prickled along Quinn's skin. Her voice was as smooth as the Scotch in his hand, and just as potent. The words were plaintive, vulnerable, but with her voice they became seductive. She wore white as she sat behind the glossy white piano. But he no longer thought of angels. The room grew warmer just from the sound of her voice. It seemed to weigh on him, pressing down until he was no longer sure he was even breathing.

Then she brought her gaze up from the keys to meet his.

It wasn't a song of love, but of love lost. The thought came to him then that if he lost her there were no words written that could describe his desperation. She'd made him ache before. And she'd made him burn. Now, for the first time, she made him weak.

She played the last chords with her eyes still locked on his.

"Not half-bad," Frank repeated, pleased with her delivery. "Now if you'd—"

"It's late, Frank." Molly patted his hand, loving him for the knucklehead he was. "We should go up to bed. Tomorrow's going to be a long day."

"Late? Nonsense, it's barely—"

"Late," Molly repeated. "And getting later by the minute. I have a surprise for you upstairs."

"But I was just getting— A surprise?"

"That's right. Come along, Frank. Good night, Quinn."

"Molly." But he couldn't take his eyes off Chantel.

"All right, all right, I'm coming. Good night, you two.

Chantel, see if that cook of yours can make waffles in the morning, will you?"

"Night, Pop." She tilted her cheek for his kiss, but her eyes stayed locked on Quinn's.

As he climbed the stairs with his wife, Frank could be heard demanding what his surprise was.

"You were right," Quinn murmured when the room was silent again.

"About what?"

"You are terrific." He rose and came to her. Taking both her hands, he turned them palm up and pressed his lips to the center of each one. "The more I'm with you," he murmured, "the more I know you, the more I want."

With her hands still in his, she stood. Light glowed in her eyes. "I've never in my life felt about anyone the way I feel about you. I need you to believe that."

"And I need to believe it." They were close, very close, to taking that final step. Commitments, promises, dependence. He felt himself teeter on the edge, ready, but was afraid she would pull back and away if he pressed too soon. "Tell me what you want, Chantel."

"You." She could give that answer truthfully enough without demanding more than she thought he was ready to give. "I only want to be with you."

For how long? he wanted to ask, but fear stopped him. He would take today, tonight, and fight for tomorrow. "Come to bed."

Hands linked, hearts lost, they climbed the stairs.

They left a low light burning beside the bed. Odd, she thought, that her pulse should be hammering so hard, that her nerves should be fluttering so wildly when she already knew what they could bring to each other. Why should it feel so different this time? So special. So much, she realized dimly, like the first time. The only time.

She offered her mouth, anticipating the hard demand of his.

He was gentle. He was…tender. As he brushed his lips lightly over hers she felt her muscles go lax and her bones melt. He cupped her face with his hands so that his thumbs traced like whispers, like promises, over her throat. She sighed his name as she felt herself float.

What kind of passion was this that crept in so quietly? Desire was there, already thrumming, but with each caress he soothed it—and stoked it. His mouth was patient, gliding over her face as if he wanted to memorize the essence of her through touch and taste. He strung small, feathery kisses down her cheekbones, then sought her mouth. His tongue traced the outline, then lingered to stroke lazily over her bottom lip. The room began to whirl inside her head.

She was priceless. This time, he promised himself, he would show her. She had a beauty he knew now reached beneath the skin. He would cherish it. He combed his fingers through her hair, delighting in the silken feel of it. He murmured, and she sighed and pressed herself against him.

As his mouth continued to explore, he began to undo the row of buttons at her back. When the material parted, he ran his hands along her spine, gently, as a man touches fragile glass. As the silk slithered to the floor, she trembled. She was warm and naked beneath it. His heart hammered in his throat. It was as though she had waited all evening for this moment with him.

Quinn drew her away to look at her, all of her, in the lamplight. She was so small, so delicate, with skin like porcelain and a form that might have been carved from alabaster. Her hair tumbled over her shoulders, ending just before the curve of her breasts. Her rib cage was narrow. He ran his hands down it, amazed that the strength he knew she possessed came from such delicacy. Her waist tapered so that he could almost span it with his hands before flaring out gently to slender hips and long, slim thighs.

"You're so beautiful." His voice was strained as he brought his gaze back to hers. "You take my breath away."

She stepped forward into his arms.

The material of his shirt was rough against her bare skin. With her eyes half closed, Chantel moved against him, urging his mouth to take its fill. Her tongue found his and began a silent, exotic seduction. All the while, his fingertips played over her as exquisitely as hers had played over the piano keys.

Through the window the breeze stirred, threatening rain. Chantel inhaled the fragrances of the night as they tangled with the musky scent of passion. Slowly, and with as much care as he had shown her, she undressed Quinn.

She rubbed her palms over the hard, coiled muscles of his shoulders, delighting in the feel. Temptingly she pressed her lips to his chest. There was a power and discipline in his body that urged her to touch, to tease. The ridges of muscles in his torso fascinated her. With a murmur of approval, she bought her lips back to his.

They lowered themselves onto the bed.

No hurry. No rush. The moment was drawn out, dreamlike, as they pleasured each other. Chantel shifted to look down at him. How could she tell him what he'd come to mean to her? How could she explain how much she needed him to be with her—now, tomorrow, forever? Did a man like Quinn believe in forever? She shook her head quickly, thrusting the questions aside. She couldn't tell him, she couldn't ask him. But she could show him.

Softly Chantel brought her mouth to his, then ran her fingertip over it as if to test the warmth she'd elicited. Approving, she brought her lips to his again, to savor.

He hadn't known it could be like this. Even in the wildest rages of passion they'd incited in each other, he hadn't known there could be such wonder. He'd told himself before that she belonged to him, but now, with her pliant and soft in his arms, he could finally believe it. And what was more, he was hers. Completely, utterly. Love fueled by tenderness was more consuming than any madness.

He slipped into her easily, naturally. With a sigh, she accepted him. They rose together in a harmony of movement that was its own kind of beauty.

When there was nothing left to give, they gathered each other close and slept.

"Don't rush me, don't rush me." With a spring in his step, Frank waltzed in front of the skycap desk. "I'm going to make sure they don't send my banjo to Duluth."

"La Guardia." With a grin, the skycap showed Frank the stubs. "Don't worry about a thing."

"Easy for you to say. I've had that banjo longer than I've had my wife." Then, with a chuckle, he squeezed Molly's shoulder. "Not that you mean less to me, my love."

"But we run neck and neck. Did you take your Dramamine, Frank?"

"Yes, yes, don't fuss."

"Frank's a hideous air traveler," Molly put in as she pocketed the tickets and boarding passes. "That's where Chantel got it from."

Surprised, Quinn stopped in the act of hefting his small carry-on bag. "You don't like to fly?"

"I'm fine." She'd already downed half a roll of antacids and two air-sickness pills.

Molly glanced at the watch on her wrist. "We'd better get moving."

"Women. Always rushing." Frank gave Quinn a slap on the back. "Why do we put up with it, boy?"

"Only game in town."

"Right you are." Delighted with the world in general, Frank cackled as he strolled through the automatic doors.

"You're feeling chipper this morning," Chantel commented dryly, refusing to acknowledge the leaden feeling in her own stomach.

"And why not?" Frank beamed as they rode up the escalator toward their gate. "A good night's sleep's just the ticket." He quirked his brow at Molly and wondered if she'd wear that little black number again anytime soon.

As they passed through gate security, Chantel began the slow and even breathing technique that helped her get on board.

"Angel." Quinn drew her off to the side. "Don't you have a tranquilizer or something?"

"I don't take them." She twisted the strap of her bag in her fingers. "Besides, I'm fine."

He unclenched her fingers and soothed them with his. "Your hands are like ice."

"It's chilly in here."

Quinn noted a man mopping his brow as the room filled with body heat. "I didn't realize you were nervous about flying."

"Don't be silly, I fly all the time."

"I know. It must be rough."

Disgusted with herself, she stared over his shoulder. "Everyone's entitled to a phobia."

"That's right." He brought her hand to his lips. "Let me help."

She started to draw her hand away but found it held firmly. "Quinn, I feel like an idiot. I'd rather you just let it go."

"Fine. But you wouldn't mind holding my hand during the flight, would you?"

"It's six hours," she muttered. "Six incredibly long hours."

He tilted her face to his. "We ought to be able to think of something to pass the time." As he lowered his mouth to hers, neither of them noticed a man wearing dark glasses slip into a seat in the corner of the departure lounge. Neither of them noticed the way his hands clenched into fists as he watched them.

"If we do what you're thinking of, we'll be arrested," Chantel murmured, but the tension in her shoulders eased.

Quinn nipped at her lip. "I'm surprised at you. I was thinking of gin rummy."

"Like hell." When their flight was called, she drew a deep breath and kept her hand in his. "A dollar a point?"

"You're on."

Laughing, she walked with Quinn and her parents through the gate.

The man in dark glasses rose and pulled a low-brimmed hat over his head, then took out his boarding pass. He merged with the crowd that surged onto the plane.

Chapter 10

"Are you sure you don't mind being drafted into the family?" Chantel carefully zipped a dress into her garment bag. She'd hired one of Hollywood's leading designers to create it, but it wasn't for the stage or the screen. It wasn't every day she was maid of honor at her sister's wedding.

"Is that what you call it?" Amused, Quinn sat on the unmade bed, dressed only in a towel. There was a freshly pressed suit in the closet that he didn't even want to think about.

"I don't know what else." Preoccupied, Chantel checked her makeup bag. If she'd forgotten anything, Maddy was sure to have it—probably still in the box. "Pop said you had to be at Reed's suite an hour before the ceremony." She paused and glanced back at him. "Just what is it men do before a wedding?"

"State secret, and no, I don't mind."

She stopped again, tapping a brush against her palm. "What did you think of Reed, Quinn? I know we only had a few hours together last night, but you must have formed an impression."

"Worried about your sister?"

"It goes with the territory."

He settled back against the pillows and looked at her. Trim slacks, a silk blouse, silver-blond hair pulled back from an extraordinary face with hammered-gold combs. Chantel O'Hurley didn't look anything like a mother hen, but he'd learned to see farther than skin deep. When it came to her family, she was a marshmallow.

"Dependable, certainly successful. Meticulous, I'd guess. Conservative."

"And Maddy?"

"Scattered, theatrical and a shade wide-eyed."

"That's Maddy," Chantel murmured. "It doesn't seem as though they'd have enough in common for more than a ten-minute conversation. But—"

"But?"

"It feels right." With a sigh, she dropped the brush into her bag. "It just feels right."

"Then what are you worried about?"

"She's my baby sister."

"By how many minutes?" he asked dryly.

"Time has nothing to do with it." She said it with such offhand certainty that he was sure the question had been put to her before. "She *is* my baby sister, and she's always been the most trusting one, the most loving one. Abby's so…solid," she said. "And I've got enough meanness in me to keep my head above water. But Maddy… Maddy's the kind of woman who believes the check *is* in the mail, the alarm didn't go off or the gas gauge was broken."

"I think your sister knows exactly what she wants and how to make it work."

"So do I, really. I guess I'm just being sentimental."

Quinn arched a brow. "Why don't you come over here and be sentimental?"

She sent him a slow smile. "I thought you were waiting for room service."

"Hate to wait alone."

"Quinn, if I get back in that bed..."

"Yeah?"

"I'm going to make incredible love to you."

"Threats, huh?" He lay back and crossed his arms behind his head. "Why don't you come over here and say that?"

She tossed her cosmetic bag aside and walked to him. "You haven't got a chance."

"Big talk."

"I can do more than talk," she murmured, and ran her fingertips up his leg to where the towel skimmed the top of his thigh. "Much more."

Before she could prove it, Quinn grabbed her wrist and yanked so that she tumbled across his chest. Her laughter came first, then was muffled to a sigh against his lips.

It didn't seem possible that she could want him as much as she had the night before, when they'd first slipped between the linen hotel sheets, but the excitement was just as new now, just as vital.

The scent of his shower was on him, fresh and tangy. His hair was slightly damp as it brushed across her face. His body was there for her, strong, virile, unclothed. With another laugh, she pressed her lips to his throat.

"Something funny?"

"I feel safe." She tossed back her head to smile at him. "So wonderfully safe."

He brushed the hair away from her face, holding it a moment, then letting it stream through his hands. How had she come to mean so much to him in so short a time?

"Safe's not the only thing I want you to feel."

"No?" She lowered her lips to his shoulder and let her tongue glide across his skin. "What else?"

Love, loyalty, devotion. It was frightening that those were his first thoughts. To protect himself, and maybe to protect her, he didn't tell her that. The physical loving wouldn't hurt either of them—not the way emotions could.

"Why don't I show you?" In one quick move he had Chantel on her back beneath him. The towel around his waist was held in place only by the press of their bodies. When his lips found hers, she began to tug the towel aside. Aroused, he laughed and made quick work of the buttons on her blouse. A knock on the door of the adjoining parlor had them both groaning. Chantel rose on her elbow and tossed her mussed hair back.

"You had to have breakfast, didn't you?"

"Let him bring it back later." Quinn slipped a hand under her skirt to explore her thigh. The knock came again, more insistently this time.

"I'll get it." Shifting away from Quinn, she adjusted her blouse. Then, with a grin, she picked up the towel and tossed it across the room. "You stay here." She kissed him again, quickly. "Right here."

"You're the boss."

"Keep that in mind." Chantel was smiling as she hurried into the parlor. Quinn would have his breakfast, but he was going to eat it cold.

In bed, Quinn reached over and idly turned on the radio. A little music, he thought. With the drapes still drawn, the room was dim. They might be anywhere. For a moment he let himself imagine they were in their bedroom—not in her house, not in his, not in some plush hotel, but in a home they'd made between them. When you loved, he realized, you didn't just think of now, but of always.

Maybe it was time to tell her, time to admit to her, not

just to himself, that he loved her and wanted to share his life with her. His life—that meant past, present, future, not just the fleeting urge to satisfy passion, to quench desire. There was passion, but it would never be satisfied. Desire would never be quenched. And more, much more, there was emotion that swelled and expanded every moment he was with her.

He wanted her for his wife. That should have terrified him, but it almost amused him. He wanted her in all the traditional ways, the ways he'd always shrugged aside as restrictive and unimportant. A home, a family, his ring on her finger and hers on his. Quinn Doran, family man. It suddenly seemed to fit.

She might balk. She probably would. He'd just have to apply the right kind of pressure. Thinking of it made him smile a little. Persuading Chantel O'Hurley to marry him might just be the toughest nut he'd ever cracked.

"Quinn."

"Yeah?"

"Would you come out here a minute?"

He heard it in her voice, just a hint of tension. Quinn pushed aside his fantasies and reached for his robe. He saw the flowers as soon as he stepped into the parlor. A dozen blood-red roses with their petals just opened sat on the table by the door. Chantel stood beside them, her face as white as the card she held in her hand.

"He knows I'm here." She managed to keep her voice even, almost calm. "He says he'd follow me anywhere." Her fingers were steady as she handed the card to Quinn, but when his brushed over them, he found them cold. "He says he's waiting for the perfect time."

Quinn took the note and glanced briefly at the message. In the corner of the envelope was the printed name of the florist's shop. "He's made his first mistake," he murmured. "Who brought these up?"

"A bellboy." She stared at the far wall, at a Monet print, and wondered why she felt nothing, nothing at all. "I didn't even tip him."

"Stop it."

His voice snapped her back. After one long shudder, Chantel looked at him. She wouldn't get sympathy from Quinn, or soothing words or empty promises. She didn't want them. She wanted the truth. "He's here, isn't he? He might even be in this hotel."

"Sit down." He started to take her arm, but she backed away.

"I don't need to sit down. I need some answers."

"Chantel—"

At the next knock, she pressed a hand to her mouth to muffle a scream. Swearing, Quinn pushed her into a chair, then went to the door. Through the peephole he saw a room-service waiter with a breakfast tray. "It's all right," he tossed over his shoulder. "Just room service."

Quinn opened the door to let the waiter roll the cart to the table by the window. After scrawling his name on the tab, he followed the waiter to the door to take a quick scan of the hall.

"You could use some coffee," Quinn said, moving past Chantel to the breakfast tray.

"No, answers." Though her knees were wobbly, she rose. "I'm not sure why, but I think you have them. You knew he'd be here."

Despite her refusal, Quinn poured two cups. "Yeah."

"Yeah." A dry laugh came from nowhere as she pressed her fingers to her temple. "You're not a man to elaborate, are you, Quinn? How did you know he'd be here? Sixth sense, gut hunch, instinct?"

"Any of those would do." He felt a sick curling in his stomach as he turned to face her again. "I expect him to go where you go, but in addition to that he said he'd be here in the last few notes he sent."

She crossed her arms over her chest. The chill had sprung to her skin quickly. She was beginning to feel now, and feel sharply. "You didn't think I should know?"

"If I'd thought you should know I'd have told you. Why don't you eat something?"

Yes, there were feelings now. They were boiling inside her, threatening to bubble out with the first word she spoke. Chantel walked to the table and, keeping her eyes on Quinn's, picked up a plate and very deliberately dropped it on the floor.

"Just who the hell do you think you are?" Her voice carried more venom when it was low and steady. "How dare you treat me as though I'm some brainless, gutless female who needs to be led around by the nose? I had a right to know he intended to follow me, that things would be the same here as they were on the Coast."

He could let his temper go or he could control it. Quinn sat down and picked up his coffee. Anger had taken the dazed look out of her eyes. He'd let her take it as far as she could. "I handled it my way. You pay me to handle things my way."

Caught off guard, she stepped back. She paid him. How could she have forgotten he was only doing a job? An arrow of pain passed through her. Even that, somehow, was better than the numbness. "I expect to be kept informed of your progress, Doran."

"Fine." He picked up a piece of toast and began to heap on jelly.

"I'll just leave you to enjoy your breakfast."

"Chantel." His voice was soft, but it had enough punch

to stop her before she crossed the room. "You might as well sit down. You're not going anywhere by yourself."

"I'm going down to Maddy's room."

"You can try to leave." He set his knife very deliberately on the side of his plate. "You won't make it. I'll take you down myself as soon as I'm dressed." He sent her a cool, challenging look. "And you'll stay there, inside the room, until I come back for you."

"I don't—"

"I've got a man stationed in the room across the hall, and another in the room across from your sister's. You're perfectly safe inside, but I want to take you down myself."

She was almost angry enough to take her chances. Chantel measured the distance to the door, and the look in Quinn's eyes. Without a word, she dropped down onto a chair and ignored him while he finished his breakfast.

Quinn found the cramped little flower shop in the West Sixties. In spite of the air-conditioning, the air was sultry inside and heavy with a barrage of floral scents. Three customers were crowded in, two of them in front of a long, chipped counter covered with scraps of papers and a shrilling phone the harried little man behind the counter ignored. Another customer stood in front of a display window and studied arrangements.

"Can't have them there before four. Can't." The owner scrawled on a form and kept shaking his head. He took a credit card and ran it through a machine for authorization. "Yes, it'll be pretty," he answered to the customer's murmured question. "Big pink carnations, some sprays of baby's breath. Tasteful, very tasteful. Sign here."

Quinn wandered to a grouping of lilies while the man dealt with the other customers.

"Okay, okay, you want to buy flowers or just look at them?"

Quinn glanced over to see the man piling the papers on the counter. "Pretty busy today."

"You're telling me nothing." The little man pulled out a handkerchief to wipe the back of his neck. "Got problems with the air conditioner, my clerk gets appendicitis, and too many people are dying." When Quinn lifted a brow, the man settled down a bit. "Funerals. Got a run on gladiolas this week."

"Tough." Quinn skirted a spray of daisies in a watering can. "This one of yours?"

He glanced at the card in Quinn's hand. "Says so right there." The man's squat finger punched at the name. "Flowers by Bernstein. I'm Bernstein. You have a problem with a delivery?"

"A question. Red roses, a dozen, delivered to the Plaza this morning. Who bought them?"

"You ask me who bought them?" Bernstein gave a long, nasal laugh. "Young man, I sell twenty dozen roses this week if I sell one. How am I supposed to know who buys?"

"You keep records?" Quinn gestured toward the register. "Receipts. You should have a receipt for a dozen red roses delivered to the Plaza at, let's say, ten-thirty, eleven this morning."

"You want me to go through my receipts?"

Quinn reached in his pocket and drew out a twenty. "That's right."

The little man stood straight. His drooping jowls quivered with indignation. "I don't take bribes. You got twenty dollars, you buy twenty dollars' worth of flowers."

"Fine. How about the receipts?"

"You a cop?"

"Private."

Bernstein hesitated. Then, grumbling, he went into the drawer that held the day's receipts. He mumbled to himself as he flipped through them. "Nobody bought red roses today."

"Yesterday."

That earned Quinn a disgusted look, but Bernstein went into another drawer. "Red roses to Maine, two dozen to Pennsylvania, a dozen to Twenty-seventh Street…" He mumbled out a few more addresses. "A dozen to the Plaza Hotel, suite 1203, for delivery this morning."

"Can I take a look at that?" Without waiting for an answer, Quinn plucked it out of his hand. "Paid cash."

"I got no problem taking cash."

But cash meant no signature. Quinn passed the receipt back. "What did he look like?"

"What did he look like?" The man let out another snort of laughter. "How am I going to remember what you look like tomorrow? People come in here and buy their flowers. I don't care if they got an eye in the middle of their forehead so long as their credit's good or their cash is green."

"Just think about it a minute." Quinn pulled out another twenty. "You got some great flowers here."

The florist gave him a shrewd look. "The carnations on display here are getting wilted."

"I happen to be very fond of carnations."

With a nod, the man pocketed the two twenties, then took the slightly drooping carnations from behind the glass. "I remember he said to send the roses to Chantel O'Hurley. Things were pretty busy here yesterday. They hauled my clerk out in an ambulance. My other clerk's on vacation, and we've got two weddings." Because the florist had a genuine love for flowers, he took out a plastic bottle and spritzed the carnations. "Anyhow, he says to send them to her, so I say, hey, is that the actress? You know, the wife and I go to the movies a lot. Oh, yeah, I ask him if he's from California. He was wearing a hat, one of those panama types, and dark glasses."

"What did he say?"

"I don't think he did. And don't ask me what he looked like again, 'cause I don't know. I had Mrs. Donahue in here fussing about her daughter's wedding. Rose petals—bags of 'em. Pink." He shook his head. "He was a guy, and I never saw much of his face."

"How old?"

"Could've been younger than you, could've been older. But he wasn't built so big. Nervous hands," he remembered suddenly, and in a moment of conscience added some fresh greenery to the carnations.

"Why do you say that?"

"Came in here smoking some foreign cigarette. I don't allow smoking, no matter how classy the tobacco. Not good for the flowers."

"How do you know it was foreign?"

"How do I know? How do I know? I know an American cigarette when I see one," the florist said testily. "And this wasn't one of them. Made him put it out too. Don't care how much money you spend in here, you ain't gonna pollute my flowers."

"Okay, so he had nervous hands."

"Couldn't keep them still once he put the thing out. Look, I had enough trouble in here yesterday without this character. Mrs. Donahue was driving me to grief and my clerk was getting her appendix out. Next thing you know, she'll want to claim it on workman's compensation."

"Anything else?" Quinn steered him patiently away from his clerk's appendectomy. "Anything he did or said that sticks in your mind?"

"Money clip," he said abruptly. "Yeah, he took the cash

out of a clip instead of a wallet. A nice one, nothing you'd pick up on the street. Silver. Monogrammed."

"What initials?"

"Initials?" The florist began to file away his stack of receipts. "What do I know from initials? It had squiggly lines on it."

"Any rings? A watch?"

"I don't know. I notice the clip because the guy's got a nice fat wad tucked into it. Maybe he's got jewelry, maybe he doesn't. I'm taking his cash, not giving him an appraisal."

"Thanks." Quinn took out a card and wrote his number at the hotel on the back. "I'd appreciate it if you'd call if you remember anything else. Or if he comes back."

"He in trouble?"

"Let's just say I'd like the chance to talk to him."

"Don't forget your carnations."

Quinn tucked the arrangement under his arm and headed for the door.

"Guess you get some weirdos out in California," Bernstein commented.

"Our share."

"Movie stars." He gave another quick snort. "Guy said he worked close with Miss O'Hurley. Real close."

Quinn's fingers tightened around the knob. "Thanks." As he stepped onto the sidewalk, he thrust the flowers into the arms of a woman dragging a shopping cart. He didn't look back to see her staring at him. There was a sick feeling starting in his stomach. He knew someone who occasionally carried a silver money clip. A clip that had been a present from Chantel. Matt Burns.

He didn't want to believe it. Matt was a friend, and no one knew better than Quinn how hard it was to make and keep friends in his business. Yet how well did he really know Matt Burns?

He hadn't known about the gambling until he'd dug it up. Matt had betrayed a client then because of a weakness. Didn't that make him first in line to betray Chantel because of another kind of weakness?

A lot of men carried money clips, Quinn reminded himself as he headed away from the hotel rather than toward it. He needed to think things through before going back to Chantel. A lot of men carried silver money clips, Quinn continued, just the way a lot of men smoked foreign cigarettes. But he wondered how many men who knew Chantel, who worked closely with Chantel, did both.

He was being stupid, Quinn decided as he stopped at a phone booth. The word was soft, he corrected. That's what the woman had done to him. It wasn't his job to find reasons why it couldn't be Matt, but find reasons why it could.

Flipping open his notepad, he scanned for Matt's number and dialed.

"Answering for Matt Burns."

"I need to speak with him."

"I'm sorry, Mr. Burns is unavailable until Monday."

"Make him available, sweetheart. It's important."

The voice became very prim. "I'm sorry, Mr. Burns is out of town."

Nerves skimmed down Quinn's spine. "Where?"

"I'm not permitted to give out that information."

"This is Quinn Doran. I'm calling for Chantel O'Hurley."

"Oh, I'm sorry, Mr. Doran. You should have told me who you were. Mr. Burns is out of town, I'm afraid. Should I have him get in touch with you if he checks in?"

"I'll get in touch with him on Monday. Where is he?"

"He flew to New York, Mr. Doran. On some personal business."

"Yeah." He bit off an oath as he hung up the phone. It was very personal. This was going to hurt her, Quinn thought. And it was going to hurt deep.

"Three more hours." Maddy O'Hurley jumped up from her chair, paced across the room and plopped onto the sofa. "We should have gotten married in the morning."

"It'll be afternoon soon enough." Chantel sipped at her third cup of coffee and wondered when she would hear from Quinn again. "Shouldn't you be enjoying your last hours as a single woman?"

"I'm too wired to enjoy anything." Maddy was up again, her mop of red hair bouncing with the movement. "I'm so glad you're here." She stopped long enough to give Chantel a quick squeeze. "I'd be going crazy now if you weren't. I wish Abby would come down."

"She will, as soon as she dumps Dylan and the boys on Pop. Think about something else."

"Something else." Maddy's slim dancer's body spun in a circle. "How can I think of something else? Walking down that aisle is the biggest entrance I'll ever make."

"Speaking of entrances, tell me about the play."

"It's terrific." Her amber eyes lighted with love of the theater. "Maybe I'm prejudiced because it was the play that brought Reed and me together, but it's the best thing I've done. I was hoping you'd be able to see it."

"I'll be back in New York shooting on location soon. You'll be back from your honeymoon and onstage." Chantel reached restlessly for a cigarette. "And if the reviews are any indication, the thing's going to be running for years."

Maddy watched her sister toy with, then light, the cigarette. It was something she did rarely, and only when she was tense. "How's the filming going?"

"No complaints."

"And this Quinn? Is it serious?"

Chantel moved her shoulders. "He's just a man."

"Come on, Chantel, this is Maddy. I've seen you with just a man before. Did you have an argument?" She managed to keep herself still long enough to sit on the arm of Chantel's chair. "Last night you seemed so happy. You practically glowed every time you looked at him."

"Of course I'm happy." She gave Maddy's arm a quick pat. "My baby sister's getting married to a man I've decided is nearly worthy of her."

"Don't hedge, Chantel." Abruptly serious, Maddy took Chantel's restless hands in hers. Nerves seemed to leap from one sister to the other. "Hey, something's really wrong, isn't it?"

"Don't be silly, I—" She broke off at the knock on the door. Maddy felt her sister's fingers tense.

"Chantel, what is it?"

"Nothing." Disgusted with herself, Chantel made her muscles relax. "Just make sure who it is, darling. We don't want an overexuberant bridegroom walking in."

Far from satisfied, Maddy rose and walked to the door. "It's Abby," she said as she looked through the peephole. And with Abby's help, she thought, she'd get to the bottom of what was worrying their sister. "How come you're not fat yet?" she accused as she opened the door.

With a laugh, Abby put one hand on her stomach and the other on Maddy's cheek. "Because I have over five months to go. How come you're not getting ready yet?"

"Because the wedding's not for three hours."

"Just enough time." Abby draped a garment bag over the back of a chair and went to Chantel. "Think we can whip her into shape?"

"Maybe. At least if we start on her she can't pace around

the suite. Thank God Reed talked you into giving up that apartment. We'd have been sitting on top of each other."

"I still miss it." With a grin, Maddy moved over to wrap an arm around each of her sisters. "I have such a hard time picturing me in a penthouse uptown. Are Dylan and the boys with Pop?"

"I left them at his door. Mom's getting her hair done, and Pop was about to talk Dylan into a prewedding toast. I can't wait to see Ben in his tux again. He looks like such a little man. And Chris is annoyed that we're renting them instead of buying them. He thinks it's just the thing to show off to his friends at home. And by the way—" she gave Chantel a squeeze before she released her "—I liked your Quinn."

"The possessive pronoun's a bit premature," Chantel managed a smile. Then, on impulse, she went to the phone. "I know what's missing here," she told them, punching up room service. "I'd like a bottle of champagne, three glasses. Dom Pérignon '71. Yes, Madeline O'Hurley's suite. Thank you."

Abby arched a brow and leaned her arm on Maddy's shoulder. "It's barely eleven."

"Who's counting?" Chantel wanted to know. "The O'Hurley Triplets are going to celebrate." Without warning, her eyes filled. "Oh, God, sometimes I miss the two of you so much I can hardly stand it."

In an instant they were together, holding close in the bond that had cemented them even before birth. Maddy sniffled, Abby soothed, and then, to her sisters' amazement, Chantel broke down completely.

"Oh, baby." Abby lowered her to the sofa, casting a quick, concerned look at Maddy. "What's wrong, Chantel?"

"It's nothing, nothing." She brushed her tears aside. "Just being sentimental. I guess I'm a little edgy, working too hard. Just seeing the two of you, you with your beautiful family, Abby, and Maddy about to start one of her own. I wonder if things had been different..." She let her words trail off with a shake of her head. "No, I made my choices, now I have to deal with them."

Abby brushed the hair from Chantel's face. Her voice was always calm, her hands always gentle. "Chantel, is this about Quinn?"

"Yes—No." She lifted both hands, then dropped them. "I don't know. I'm having a little trouble with an overenthusiastic fan," she said, downplaying her problem. "I hired Quinn to more or less keep him at a distance, and then I fell in love with him and..." She trailed off again, letting out a deep breath. "I just said it out loud."

Maddy bent down to kiss the top of her head. "Did it help?"

Some of the tension uncurled. "Maybe. I'm being an idiot." She fumbled for a tissue. "And I'll be damned if I'm going to walk down the aisle as maid of honor with puffy eyes."

"That sounds more like Chantel," Maddy murmured. "And besides, if you're in love with Quinn, everything's going to work out."

"Always the optimist."

"Absolutely. Abby found Dylan, I found Reed, so it's your turn. Now if we could just pin down Trace..."

"You're really reaching," Chantel said with a laugh. "If there's a woman out there who can put a hobble on big brother, I'd love to meet her." She started at the knock on the door, but brought herself back quickly. "Must be the champagne." Stuffing the tissue in her pocket, Chantel went to the door but checked the peephole first. "Uh-oh." A smile hovered on her lips as she glanced over her shoulder. "We've got the champagne, all right, but there's more.

Abby, drag Maddy into the bedroom. There's a lovesick maniac at the door."

"Reed? Is it Reed?" Maddy was halfway to the door before her sisters headed her off.

"No way." She might be nearly four months pregnant, but Abby was still agile. She had an arm hooked around Maddy's waist. "Bad luck, honey. You get into the bedroom. Chantel and I can transmit any messages."

"This is silly."

"I'm not opening the door until you're out of the room," Chantel said simply, and leaned back on it. "All the way out."

After wrinkling her nose, Maddy slammed the door behind her. As a precaution, Abby posted herself in front of it. With a nod of satisfaction, Chantel pulled open the door to the hall. "Just over there," she told the waiter. "And you—" she put a slender, manicured finger to Reed's chest "—not a step farther."

"I just want to see her for a minute."

Chantel managed to force back a smile and shook her head. She could almost feel the love coming from him, the nerves, the longing. He hadn't changed into his tux yet, and he was wearing a pair of casual slacks and a shirt that reflected his conservative style. He looked like an executive. He *was* an executive, she thought with another shake of her head. And the farthest thing from the type one would have imagined with her free-spirited, bohemian sister. Yet they fit. Chantel imagined Maddy had fallen for those calm gray eyes first. The rest would have been a smooth drop.

"Look, I have something for her." Used to getting his own way, Reed took a step forward, only to be blocked easily by Chantel. "I'll be in and out before you know it."

"You won't be in at all," Chantel corrected. "We're Irish,

Reed, and we're theater people. You're not going to find a group more superstitious. You'll see Maddy at the church."

"That's right." Hearing a stirring behind her, Abby hooked her hand firmly around the knob of the bedroom door. "I'm sure you're too much of a gentleman to try to get through both of us." Using the ultimate weapon, she smiled and put a hand to her stomach. "Or should I say all three of us?"

Reed wasn't so sure. He wanted to see Maddy, touch her, if only for a minute, to assure himself it was all real. Abby smiled at him with warm, sympathetic eyes, but she didn't budge. Chantel signed the receipt for the wine without moving from the doorway.

"Go down to the eighth floor and have a drink with Pop," she advised.

"I just want to—"

"Forget it." Then she softened and kissed his cheek. "Just a couple of hours, Reed. Believe me, it'll be worth the wait."

Only minutes before, Reed had managed to talk his way around Dylan and override Frank's objections. But he knew when he was out of his depth. "Would you give her this?" He took a small box from his pocket. "It was my grandmother's. I was going to give it to her later, but, well, I'd like her to wear it today."

"She'll wear it." She started to hustle him out again, then stopped. "Reed."

"Yeah?"

"Welcome to the family." Then she shut the door in his face. "Lord, another minute of that and I'd have been in tears again. Let her out."

"What did he give you?" Maddy was already nudging past her sister. She took the box from Chantel and opened it. Inside was a tiny heart of diamonds on a thin silver chain. "Oh, isn't it lovely?"

"It's going to look even lovelier against your dress." Abby ran a fingertip over the stones. "Here, I'll clasp it for you."

"Now *I'm* going to cry." Maddy closed her hand over the heart. He was going to be hers, truly hers, in a matter of hours. And her new life would begin.

"No more tears." Chantel released the cork from the wine with a swoosh. It landed on the carpet, to be ignored as she poured wine to overflowing into three glasses. "We're going to get just a little drunk— Well, two of us are going to get a little drunk, and Abby's going to have half a glass. Then, between the three of us, we're going to create the most beautiful bride to ever walk down the aisle at St. Pat's. Here's to you, little sister."

"No." Maddy touched her glass to Chantel's, then to Abby's. "Here's to us. As long as we have each other, we're never alone."

Chapter 11

At Chantel's insistence, she and Quinn caught the red-eye to L.A. Saturday night. New York hadn't been the haven she'd hoped for. With the wedding over and her sister off on a Caribbean honeymoon, Chantel could only think of getting home.

The reception had been a strain. She'd caught herself watching strangers, studying familiar faces and wondering. Even when she willed herself to sleep on the plane, she promised herself that the next time she came back to New York, it would be without fear.

And what could she say to Quinn? She felt betrayed by his silence, yet had she, by the extent of her dependence on him, asked for it? Was she so weak, so cowardly, that he felt it necessary to shield her from everything? She wanted his protection, but she also wanted his respect. Had she forfeited that by refusing to listen to his reports, by allowing him to intercept the notes and keep the contents from her? It was time that stopped. All her life, except for one brief period, she had had her hand on the controls. Now, through fear, she'd relinquished them. Starting now, she was taking back the helm.

Quinn wondered how long it would take her to unfreeze. She'd certainly been cool enough throughout the afternoon and evening. Cool, aloof, distant. It was something he had no choice but to accept. Yet when he'd seen her walking down the aisle in front of her sister, wearing that pale blue dress, all filmy and romantic, he'd wanted to step out of his seat, scoop her up and carry her off. Somewhere. Anywhere.

He wondered what it would feel like to stand where Reed Valentine had stood, to watch Chantel, as Reed had watched Maddy, walk toward him wearing white lace. What would it be like to hear her make the promises her sister had made? He shook himself out of the mood.

They were almost ready to land, and Chantel was dozing restlessly beside him. Couldn't she understand that he'd done what he'd done for her sake, because he'd needed so badly to see her relax, even if only for a couple of days? She didn't understand, or wouldn't, and he hadn't tried to explain. He didn't know how.

He didn't have the flair of one of her leading men. He didn't have the words all neatly typed in a script he could memorize. He had only what was inside him, and there didn't seem to be a way to explain that. Words weren't feelings. Phrases weren't emotions. And emotions were all he had.

When they landed, Chantel looked fresh and rested, as though she'd spent eight hours sleeping on a soft bed rather than snatching naps on a plane. They got their luggage without incident and within twenty minutes were riding in the back of a limo toward Beverly Hills.

Chantel lighted a cigarette, then glanced casually at her

watch. Right now she felt wired, restless. Jet lag would hit tomorrow, but she would function.

"I'd like to see your reports, all of your reports, by noon tomorrow."

Streetlights flashed intermittently against the windows. His face was in shadow, but Chantel doubted she would have been able to read his expression in any case. "Fine. I have the file at your place."

"I'd also like an update on anything you came up with in New York."

"You're the boss."

"I'm glad you remember that."

He could have strangled her. He thought about ways that were quick and quiet, but instead he simply sat back and bided his time. He stepped out of the limo at the gate. Though Chantel had been gone, he'd thought it best to leave the twenty-four-hour guard in place. A few brief words and he was back in the limo, gliding through the open gates.

At the entrance, Chantel sailed past him. She had reached the head of the main staircase before he caught her.

"Something eating you, angel?"

"I don't know what you're talking about. You will excuse me now, Quinn?" Delicately she peeled his fingers from her arm. "I want to take a long, hot bath."

No one did it better. He had to give her that as he watched her walk down the hall to her room. She could, with a look, with an inflection, slice a man in half without leaving a drop of blood.

He thought he was calm. He thought he was controlled—until the moment he heard the lock click on her door. Then the rage he'd held in throughout the day clawed free. He didn't hesitate. Maybe he wasn't even thinking. Quinn walked to her bedroom door and kicked it in.

She wasn't often speechless. Chantel just stood there. The jacket of her suit had already been discarded, leaving her in a pale pink teddy and a rose-colored skirt. One hand remained frozen on top of her head where she had begun to pin up her hair.

She'd seen fury before, real and simulated, but she'd never seen anything like what was boiling in Quinn's eyes.

"Don't you ever lock a door on me." His voice was so quiet after the crash of splintering wood that she shivered. "Don't you ever walk away from me."

Slowly she lowered her hand so that her hair tumbled to her shoulders. "I want you to leave."

"Maybe it's time you learned even you can't have everything you want. I'm here to stay. You're going to have to do a hell of a lot more than turn a key to keep me out."

When he came toward her, she stiffened but refused to retreat. She was through backing away from anything, even him. He took her hair and wrapped it around his hand.

"You wanted to slap me down, and that's fine. But I'll be damned if I'll take it from you for doing my job."

"I won't be treated like a fool, or a weakling." The lace of the teddy trembled over her breasts as she took an unsteady breath. "You knew he was going to follow me to New York. You knew I'd be no safer there than I was here."

"That's right. I knew, you didn't. And you had one night when you didn't toss in your sleep."

"You had no right—"

"I had every right." The hand in her hair tightened. She wanted to wince, but she didn't seem to be able to move at all. "I have the right to do anything, everything, to keep you safe, to give you some peace of mind. And I'm going to keep on doing it, because there's nothing that matters to me more than you."

Chantel let out a breath she hadn't been aware of holding. She'd seen it in his eyes, beneath the anger, beneath the frustration, but she hadn't been certain she could believe it. "Is that your—" She stopped, pressing her lips together. It wouldn't do for her voice to tremble now. She wanted to be strong, for him, as well as herself. "Is that your way of telling me you love me?"

He stared down at her, a good deal more stunned by his announcement than she. He hadn't meant to throw it at her like a threat. He'd wanted to give them both time, to give them both room, so that he could coax her along until she realized she needed him. But he'd never been good at coaxing.

"Take it or leave it."

"Take it or leave it," she repeated in a murmur. How like him. "Would you mind letting go of my hair? I need it for a couple of scenes on Monday. Besides, that way you'd have both arms to put around me."

Before he could, she was pressed against him, holding tight and hard and praying it wasn't a dream.

"I guess this means you're taking it." He buried his face in her hair and wondered how he'd ever survived without her scent, without her touch.

"Yeah. I've been trying to figure out a way to make you fall in love with me so you wouldn't be able to walk away." She tossed her head back to look at him. "Tell me you're not going to walk away."

"I'm not going anywhere." Then he found her mouth and made it a promise. "Let me hear you say it." He took her hair again but drew it back gently until their eyes met. "Look at me and say it. No lights, no camera, no script."

"I love you, Quinn, more than I thought it was possible to love. It scares the hell out of me."

"Good." He kissed her again, harder. "It scares the hell out of me, too."

"We've got so many things to talk about."

"Later." He was already drawing down the zipper of her skirt.

"Later," she agreed, tugging his shirt out of the waistband of his slacks. "Want to take a bath?" As she asked, she yanked his shirt over his shoulders.

"Yeah."

"Before?" With a laugh, she nipped at his chin. "Or after?"

"After." And he pulled her with him onto the bed.

It had been wild before, fierce, violent, passionate, and it had also shimmered with gentleness. But now there was love, felt, spoken, answered. She'd stopped believing that her life would lead her to this—love, acceptance, understanding. In the end she'd only had to open her hand and take it. In a burst of emotion they were caught close, mouths open and hungry, bodies heated and aware. She heard his long indrawn breath as he buried his face in her hair, as if he, too, had just realized what a gift they'd been given.

She thought he trembled. Her hands, pressed against his back, felt the quick tensing of muscle. She didn't want to soothe it. She wanted him to be as she was: stunned, a little afraid, and deliriously happy. When she pressed her lips to his throat she felt the throb of excitement, tasted the heat. In one long, possessive stroke she ran her hands down his back, then up again. He was hers. From this moment, he was hers.

She was there for him, soft, yielding, yet strong enough to hold him. He'd never looked for her. Quinn understood himself well enough to know he'd never looked for anyone to share his life. Still, he'd found her, and in her he'd found everything. A mate. There was something primitive yet soothing in the word. It meant someone to tumble between the sheets with on hot, sultry nights. It meant someone to wake with in the cool, lazy mornings. It was someone to confide in, someone to protect, someone to reach out to.

Just the thought of it made him close his eyes, as if to keep the fantasy trapped forever. With his fingertips he traced her face so that her image hovered there, in his mind.

"So beautiful," he murmured. "Here…" His finger lingered on her cheek. "And here." Slowly he slid his hand down her body. Then he opened his eyes to look into hers. "And inside."

"No, I—"

"Don't contradict the man who loves you." He brought her palm to his lips, watching her. He turned her hand over, kissing each finger. The diamond glittered on one, a symbol of what she was to the world. Cool sex, glamour with a hard polish. Her hand trembled like a young girl's.

He brushed kisses along her jawline, and her breath came in slow, quiet gasps. She could almost hear her skin hum as his fingers whispered over it. With each touch she drifted deeper into a dark, liquid world where sensations were her only guide.

Only he could make her forget the boundaries she'd once set for herself. Only he could make her forget that when you loved, you risked. With him she could give without fear, without reservations or restrictions. There would be a tomorrow with Quinn. There would be a lifetime of tomorrows.

He wasn't sure he knew how to show her how he felt. He wasn't used to pampering. Romance was for books, for movies, for the young and foolish. Yet he had a need, a growing one, to show her that his feelings went so far beyond desire that he couldn't measure them.

Rising to his elbow, he brushed the hair carefully away from her face, combing his fingers through it as it fell, silvery-blond, over the spread. Gently, as though she might crumble at the slightest touch, he cupped her face in his hand. Could she be more beautiful now? Somehow it seemed so to him as he watched the first beams of daylight steal through the windows and over her skin.

He ran his thumb over her lips, fascinated by the shape, by the softness, by the flavor he imagined would linger on his own flesh. As if it were the first time—and perhaps it was—he touched his lips to hers.

Her body went weak. As his lips lingered, the hand she had pressed to his back slipped down, limp. She'd thought she understood possession, but she'd been wrong. She'd thought she could imagine what it was like to be loved, loved fully. But she'd had no idea. Something fluttered through her, so softly that it might have been a dream. But it expanded within her, and a promise was made.

The heat centered, focused and grew. Strength flooded back into her, and with it a passion so rich that she moaned from the pleasure. Together they rolled until she lay over him. Together they let themselves go.

His hands were quick, but no more urgent than hers. His lips were hungry, but his desperation had met its match. Sanity was discarded as easily as silk and lace. They came together like thunder, in a storm that lingered into the morning. As dawn rose, they took each other into the dark.

"I'm so glad it's Sunday." Chantel eased her shoulders down into the hot, frothy water. She picked up a wineglass from the side of the tub and laughed at Quinn over the rim. "You're not supposed to scowl at the bubbles. You're supposed to enjoy them."

Quinn shifted to reach for his own glass. Chantel's tub was easily big enough for two, and the skylight overhead showed a perfect blue sky. The water that lapped nearly to the edge was layered with white, fragrant bubbles.

"I'm going to smell like a woman."

"Darling." She touched her tongue to the rim of her glass. "No one's going to smell you but me."

"With all the stuff you dumped in here, I'll be lucky if it wears off in a week." He shifted again, and his leg slid over hers. "But it has its compensations."

"Mmmm." With her eyes half closed, she leaned back. "For both of us. I need this. The shooting schedule next week is murder. There are three scenes in particular that I know will leave me limp. The one where Brad and Hailey nearly die in the fire is the worst."

"What fire?"

"Read the script," she said lazily, smiling when he tossed bubbles at her. "I trust Special Effects, but it doesn't make it any easier to crawl around in a shack on the back lot or on the set on the soundstage while they're shooting flames and pumping smoke in. That's why it's especially nice that it's Sunday and I can lie in the tub and think about making love with you." She looked at him through eyes that were hardly more than slits. "Again."

"You can lie in the tub *and* make love with me." He twisted his body, bringing it forward until his face was close to hers. "At the same time."

Chantel laughed and linked her hands behind his head as water lapped over the tub and onto the floor. "Too much water."

"You filled it up."

"My mistake. I usually bathe alone."

"Not anymore." Bubbles burst between them as he kissed her. "Why don't you pull the plug?"

"Can't get to it." She tilted her head to change the angle

of the next kiss. "It's, ah, behind me. Now I bet a big strong man like you could manage it all by himself."

"Back here?" His hand trailed over her breast, then slipped to her rib cage.

"Close. Very close." She felt his fingers slide over her hip. "Getting closer. Why don't we—" The words were cut off as she found herself submerged, his mouth hard on hers. Up again, she drew in air, swiped at her face and squinted at him. "Quinn!"

"Slipped." He found the lever easily and flipped it down.

"I bet. Now I've got soap in my eyes." He started to grin, but his mouth went dry when she rose up, magnificent, and let water drain from her skin as she reached for a towel. "Remind me to bring a snorkel next time we take a bath."

"Chantel."

She was holding the towel to her face, but she lowered it with a half smile that faded when he stood beside her. Without a word, he gathered her to him. They stood where they were while the bubbles drained beneath them and dried on their skin.

"I never knew it could be like this," she murmured. "Not like this."

"That makes two of us." He'd found her. It seemed so incredible that he'd found her, found everything, without looking. "You're getting cold." Feeling the chill on her skin, he took a towel and wrapped it around her. "I guess I'd have a lot to answer to if you went to work tomorrow with a red nose."

"I never get a red nose." She took a towel in turn and wrapped it around him. "It's in my contract."

"Think you could take a break when you finish filming?"

"That depends." She smiled again. "On where and with whom."

"With me. We can talk about the where."

"I should be wrapped in three weeks. You pick the where." She started to step from the tub, then braced herself against the wall. "Careful. We've flooded the place."

"Just toss down a couple towels." Quinn plucked another from the shelf and let it fall to the floor to soak up the water.

"My housekeeper's going to love you." Out of habit, Chantel picked up a jar of moisturizer and began to rub a light cover over her skin.

"After we're married, there's going to have to be a change in the rules of the tub." He was hooking the towel at his waist and didn't notice the way her fingers froze in place on her cheek. "Bubbles are okay, but they've got to be unscented. It's one thing for the staff to sniff, but we can't have the kids wondering if their father wears perfume."

Somehow she managed to get the lid back on the jar and set it down without dropping it. "We're getting married?"

He didn't have to look at her to know she'd taken three paces back. He heard it in her voice. "Absolutely."

Her heart was hammering in her throat, but she'd trained herself to speak clearly over nerves. "You want children?"

"Yeah." One by one, the muscles of his stomach knotted. "Is that a problem?"

"I... Things are moving pretty fast," she managed.

"We're not teenagers, Chantel. I think we both know what we want."

"I have to sit down." She didn't trust her legs, so she moved quickly back to the bedroom and took a chair. She held the towel together in front of her with hands that had gone white at the knuckles.

Quinn waited a moment. The steam had fogged the wall-length mirror opposite the tub, but he could imagine her sitting there, her beauty reflected, slim, young, perfect. She was a dream and, more, she was a star, someone who lighted up the screen and created fantasies. His jaw was tight when he walked into the bedroom.

"Looks like I pushed the wrong buttons." Digging up his shirt, he found his cigarettes. "I thought that's what you wanted, too." Lighting one, he drew smoke in deeply. "I guess a husband and kids don't go with the image."

She looked up slowly. Her eyes were dry, but he recognized pain, something deep and dull and lasting.

"Chantel—"

"No." She stopped him with a gesture of her hand. "Maybe I deserved that." Rising, she went to the closet and chose a robe. With deliberate motions she dropped the towel, then slipped the robe on and belted it. She linked her fingers a moment, then let them fall to her sides. "My career is important to me, but I've never let it interfere with my personal life—or vice versa. My work is demanding. You've seen for yourself that the hours can be brutal."

"So there's no room for me and a family?"

Something came into her face again. Pain again, but with a touch of anger this time. "My parents raised four children on the road. There was always room, always time for family."

"Then what is it?"

She dipped her hands into her pockets, then took them out again, unable to keep them still. "First, I want to tell you that there's nothing I want more than to marry you and start a family. Please, don't," she said quickly when he started to come to her. "Sit down, Quinn. It would be easier for me if you would sit."

"All right."

When he had, she drew a deep breath. "There are things you have to know before we go any farther. It's difficult, at least for me, to admit past mistakes, but you have a right to know. If I'd listened to my mother, I would have told you before. It might have been easier then."

"Look, if you want to tell me you've been with other men—"

Her low laugh cut him off. It was strained. "Not exactly. This doesn't fit the image, either, but I only slept with one other man before you. Surprise," she said quietly when he simply stared. She went to stand at the window. "I was barely twenty when I met him. I was doing commercials, going to acting classes. I even had a part-time job selling magazines on the phone. I kept telling myself it was just a matter of time, and I believed it, but it was tough. Oh, God, it was so tough to be alone. Then Matt called and said he'd gotten me a test for a small part on a feature. *Lawless*, my first real break. The producer was—"

"Dustin Price."

Chantel turned back from the window. Her hand was curled in a fist. "Yes. How do you know that?"

"A lot of movie buffs might, but the fact is, I already know about Price. He turned up when I did a background check on you."

"You did a check on me?" She found herself braced against the windowsill. "On me?"

"It's standard, Chantel. I do a run on you, maybe somebody turns up you've forgotten, or forgotten to mention. Like Dustin Price. He's clean, by the way. Been in England eighteen months."

"Standard," she repeated, letting the rest sift away like sand. "I guess I should have expected it."

"What difference does it make now? So you slept with him. You needed a break, he could give you a break. It was years ago, and I don't give a damn."

Every muscle in her body went rigid. "Is that what you think? You think I slept with him to get a part?"

"I'm telling you I don't care."

"Don't touch me." She whipped away from him as he reached for her. "I don't have to sleep with anyone to get a part, and I never have. I may have made compromises, I may have given up more than I should, but I never prostituted myself."

"I'm sorry." This time he took her arms, ignoring her resistance. "I'm trying to tell you that whatever happened between you and Price doesn't matter."

"Oh, it matters." She pulled away and poured wine into a fresh glass. "It matters. When Matt called me to tell me I had the part, I was so happy. I knew it was the beginning. I was going places, I was going to be somebody." She pressed her fingers to her lips until she was sure she could speak calmly. "Dustin sent me a dozen roses, a bottle of champagne and a lovely letter of congratulations. He said he knew I was going to be a star and suggested we have dinner to discuss the film and my career."

She drank because her throat was dry, then set down the glass, refusing to rely on wine to get her through the story. "Of course, I agreed. He was one of the top producers, riding on a wave of three box-office smashes. Of course, he was married, but I didn't think of that." The derision was in her voice again, self-derision, self-disgust.

"Chantel. It was years ago."

"There are some things you never stop paying for. I was going to be sophisticated. We were just having dinner, colleagues. God, he was charming." The memory still hurt, but the pain was dull now, covered with scar tissue. "The flowers kept coming, the dinners. He knew so much about the business, the people. Who to talk to, who to be seen with. All of that was so important to me then. I thought I could handle it. The truth was I was just a naive young girl on her own for the first time.

"I fell in love with him. I believed everything he said about him and his wife living together for appearances only, about the quiet divorce that was already in the works. About the two of us making the best and brightest team Hollywood had seen since the golden age. The whole thing might have run its natural course as I got a little smarter, and he a bit bored, but before all that happened, I made a mistake." She ran her damp palms down her robe, then linked them. "I got pregnant." She managed to swallow. "You didn't find that in your background check, did you?"

Rage hit, and he smothered it. "No."

"He had enough money, enough influence, to keep it quiet. And it wasn't an issue for very long."

He was struggling, fighting desperately to understand. "You had an abortion?"

"That's what he wanted. He was furious. I suppose a lot of men would be when their mistress—and that's what I was, really—turns up pregnant and threatens his very comfortable marriage. Of course, he'd never planned on getting a divorce or marrying me. All of that came out when I told him I was going to have his baby."

"He used you," Quinn spit out. "You were twenty years old and he used you."

"No." Strange that she could say it so calmly now. "I was twenty years old and I pretended I knew all the rules. I pretended very well. I made one mistake, then I made another mistake. I told him he could go to hell, but I was keeping the baby. Things got ugly then. He threatened to destroy my career if I didn't play his way. Well, there's no use going into what was said, except that the affair was over and my eyes were wide open."

"You're still hurting," Quinn said quietly.

"Yes, but not for the reasons you might think. I thought I loved him, but as soon as the glitter washed off I knew I never had. I called my parents. I was ready to run home and leave everything behind. I bought plane tickets. Quinn, I don't know what I would have ultimately done once I was thinking clearly. That's the worst of it, not knowing. There was an accident on the way to the airport." She took a deep breath, struggling to finish. "Nothing major, the taxi driver had a couple of broken bones, and I—I lost the baby."

With a broken sob, she pressed her fingers to her eyes. "I lost the baby, and I tried to tell myself it was for the best. But all I ever could think was that it had never had a chance. I was only six weeks pregnant. Six weeks. Here, then gone. Matt pulled me out of it, got me back to work almost as soon as I was out of the hospital. Everything clicked for me then, the parts, the people, the fame I'd always wanted. All I had to do was lose a baby."

"Chantel." He came to her, running his hands over her face, her hair, her shoulders. "There's nothing I can say. Nothing I know how to do."

"There's more."

"No more." He started to gather her close, but she backed away.

"When I lost the baby, there were complications. The doctors told me, well, they said it was possible I could have other children, but it wasn't something they could guarantee. Possible, just possible, not even probable. There might never be another baby, another chance. Do you understand?"

He took her hands. "Are you going to marry me?"

"Quinn, aren't you listening? I just told you—"

"I heard you." His fingers linked with hers and held firm. "You might not be able to have children. I want them, Chantel—yours, mine. If we can have them, that's great. But first, always…" He bent to touch his lips to hers. "I want you. I need you, angel. The rest is up to chance."

"Quinn, I love you."

"Then let's get married tomorrow."

"No." She put her hands to his chest to hold him off. "I want you to think about this, really think about it. You need some time."

"I need you," he corrected. "I don't need time."

"I feel I owe it to you. Let's leave things as they are. A few days."

He could have pushed. He could have won. But the hurt seemed too close to the surface just then. "A very few days. Come here." This time she went willingly into his arms. "I'm not going to let anyone hurt you again," he murmured.

She closed her eyes, hoping she could promise him the same thing, even if she were speaking of herself.

Chapter 12

The day started at six and never let up. Filming began at a shack on the back lot. The interior was no more than that, a small frame building that had been used in a handful of films. For *Strangers* it had been given a face-lift, a false front that had turned it into a rustic cabin in the woods of New England. In a climactic scene, Special Effects would burn it down, the fire starting under mysterious circumstances with Hailey and Brad inside.

The interior scenes would be shot later, on a two-story set on the soundstage, but the morning was spent on exteriors. Chantel drove Hailey's Ferrari to the deserted cabin. She was older now, but still caught between the man she had married and the man who had betrayed her. The scene called for her, on the verge of a breakdown, to seek solace in the remote cabin, searching for the roots of her art, which she'd lost in the tangle of success.

All the scenes were shot out of sequence and then would

be edited together. For several hours of this shoot there was no dialogue. She was filmed unloading her art equipment, setting an easel on the narrow porch, walking through the door and out again with costume changes. There was a long, lingering close-up of her leaning on the porch rail with a cup of coffee in her hand. Without words, Chantel could use only her face to show the turmoil her character was feeling.

She painted on the porch, sketched on the porch steps, planted flowers. Through posture and gestures and by relaxing the set of her face, Chantel showed her character's gradual healing.

From the sidelines, Quinn watched her and felt his pride in her grow. He didn't know the story, but he understood the woman she became for the cameras. And he began to root for Hailey.

There was a poignant scene in which Hailey sat on the porch and poured out her heart to a stray dog. It was the examination of a life, with all its flaws, its wrong turns, its regrets. Even when it was reshot to change the angle, the emotion generated remained intense. Quinn saw more than one member of the crew wipe their eyes.

Before lunch they had wrapped a number of scenes, including a short, vicious argument between Hailey and Brad on the porch. During an hour's break Chantel took a quick, necessary nap, then shored up her energy with fruit, cheese and a protein drink before going to the soundstage for the interiors.

The set was as rustic as the outside of the cabin had promised, but there were a few of Hailey's paintings on the wall. The props included a large carved music box that had been a wedding present from her husband. The earlier tension was back in her character as Chantel opened the box and let the strains of the *Moonlight Sonata* out.

Dissatisfied with the way the scene was going, Chantel and the director went into a discussion on mood and motion.

"What do you think of our little story?"

James Brewster appeared beside Quinn. The two of them watched Larry Washington bring Chantel a glass of juice.

"Hard to say when you see it chopped up this way." Quinn kept his eye on Larry as the young man hovered around Chantel, ready to jump at the tiniest gesture. "But I expect it'll sell. It has it all—sex, violence, melodrama."

"You don't write a best-seller by leaving them out," Brewster said easily. "Of course, Hailey is the key, the hinge. What she does, what she feels, affects every character. When I started the book, I thought I was telling a tale of betrayal and birth. But it became a story of how one woman—and what happens to her—determines the destiny of everyone she touches." He broke off with a laugh. "It sounds pretentious, and perhaps it would be without Chantel. She is Hailey."

"She does make you believe," Quinn murmured.

"Exactly." Pleased, Brewster gave a quick nod. "As a writer, there's no greater reward than watching one of your characters come to life, particularly one you feel strongly about. I nearly killed her in the fire, you know."

Quinn stiffened. "What do you mean?"

Brewster laughed again and drew out a cigarette. "You're a very literal man, Mr. Doran. I meant I nearly ended the book here, in this cabin, with Hailey losing everything, including her life, in a fire set by the only man who really loved her. I found it impossible. She had to go on, you see, and survive."

They both watched as the stage was set for the next take.

"An extraordinary woman," Brewster murmured. "Every man here is just a little bit in love with her."

"And you?"

A wry smile in his eyes, Brewster turned. "I'm a writer, Mr. Doran. I deal in fantasies. Chantel is very much flesh and blood."

At the assistant director's signal, the set fell silent and filming began again.

Quinn watched Brewster carefully. The writer seemed less nervous than he had in the early days of shooting. Perhaps he was pleased with the progress. It was Larry Washington who seemed on edge now. Chantel's assistant was never still for long, was always moving from one spot to the next. Did the tension Quinn felt on the set come from him? It was there. Quinn sensed it sparking the air, something nervy and desperate. Yet, everywhere he looked, people were going about their jobs with the drum-tight efficiency the director insisted on.

Perhaps the tension was just within himself. There was plenty of cause. Chantel was still just out of reach, not yet ready, or not yet able, to commit herself. When a man who had lived his life avoiding commitments finally found one he wanted, he was bound to be impatient. So Quinn told himself as he watched Chantel listen to the music box with pain and indecision in her eyes.

Were her thoughts on him, he wondered, or was she in character? Her talent made it nearly impossible to separate the actress from the role.

Every eye was on her, but she was alone, in a cabin in the woods, at a turning point in her life.

"Cut. Print. Wonderful." Mary Rothschild straightened from her position behind the camera operator. "Really wonderful, Chantel."

"Thanks." She drew a deep breath and tried to shake off

the emotion that had carried her through the scene. "I'm glad I don't have to do that again."

"We're going to go to the confrontation with Brad." As she spoke, Mary began to knead Chantel's shoulders. "You know what you're feeling. You still want him. After everything he's done, everything you know, you can't quite remove yourself from the young woman who fell in love with him. You want to love your husband, you've tried, but the only thing you've managed to do is hurt him. You're on the edge of your life here. You know if you go with Brad you'll never survive. Yet you're drawn."

"I'm fighting myself more than him."

"Exactly. Let's run through it."

They worked until six. Before it was over, Special Effects had pumped smoke onto the set. Hailey, dazed by the smoke, terrified of the fire that had begun to roar through the cabin, crawled along the wooden floor in a desperate search for the door. All she carried was the music box.

"Hell of a day," Quinn commented later when they were in Chantel's trailer.

"Tell me about it." Weary, she creamed off the streaks of soot Makeup had smeared her face with. "I don't even want to eat, just sleep."

"I'll tuck you in."

She smiled and, after drying her face, swung her bag over her shoulder. "Tuck me in? I prefer having someone to snuggle against."

"You'll have that, too, in a few hours." They walked out of the trailer, past the soundstage, where the director and cinematographer were having an impromptu meeting.

"Going somewhere?"

"I've got some business." He thought of Matt, his friend,

and of Chantel, the woman he loved. "I'll tell you about it when I get back."

"I'd rather you told me now." When they were outside, Chantel headed straight for the waiting limo. "Quinn, I don't want to be protected this way. Not anymore."

She was right, and he'd known that sooner or later he'd have to tell her. When she settled into the limo, he slid his arm behind, ready to comfort her.

"I didn't want to get into it in New York. You had your sister's wedding, and we had our own problems to deal with. Yesterday…" He hesitated, still not sure how to describe what that one twenty-four-hour-period had meant to him. "I wanted yesterday for both of us."

"I understand." She lifted a hand to his. "So, what is it, Quinn?"

"I got a lead on the man who ordered the flowers." He felt her tense, but didn't try to soothe her. She wouldn't want soothing now. "He paid cash, so there's no record. The florist couldn't give me much of a description. The guy wore dark glasses and a hat. There were a couple things the florist noticed, though." He hesitated, hating to be the one to destroy a trust and a friendship. She was more important than both. Than anything. "He smoked a foreign brand of cigarette and carried a monogrammed silver money clip."

For a moment her mind was blank. Slowly, the meaning came through. Rather than disillusionment, he saw a quick flash of determination. "A lot of men prefer foreign tobacco and clips."

"A lot of men don't work closely with you. This one said he did."

"He could have been lying."

"Could have been. We both know he wasn't. All along the one thing we could bank on was that this man knows you, and you know him. Chantel, you gave a silver money clip to someone who works with you."

"It's not Matt."

"Angel, it's time to separate what you want from what is, or at least what might be."

"It doesn't matter what you say, I won't believe it."

"I called Matt while we were in New York." He lifted a hand to cup her face. His grip was firm. "He was out of town, Chantel."

"So he was out of town." There was a quick flutter just beneath her heart, but she ignored it. "A lot of people go out of town on weekends."

"He was in New York on personal business."

She paled, but just as quickly shook her head.

"Quinn—"

"I have to go talk to him."

"I don't want you to accuse—" A look from him cut her off. "All right," she murmured, turning her head to stare out the window. "I'm not supposed to tell you how to do your job."

"That's right, angel. Look." He took her shoulder and turned her toward him. "Look at me." When she did, he swore under his breath and brushed the hair back from her face. "I don't want this to hurt you."

"You're telling me that my closest friend is your top suspect. I can't help but be hurt."

"Go home." He leaned closer and touched his lips to hers. "Go to bed. Stop thinking about it tonight. For me," he said before she could speak. "I love you, Chantel."

"Stay home and show me."

"No." He caught her face in his hands. "I won't be long. And this is going to be over. I promise you that."

They went through the gate and up the long, quiet drive.

"I trust you," she told him, and forced herself to relax. "I'm going to wait for you."

"Wait for me in bed," he murmured, hoping for her sake that she'd fall asleep quickly.

They stepped out of the limo. "You'll be careful?"

"I'm always careful."

She started up the steps, then stopped and turned back. "I hate this, but I can't regret it anymore, because it brought you. Come back soon." She walked into the house without looking back.

She wouldn't think. The day's work had drained her body, and she would concentrate on that. She'd have a late supper brought upstairs when Quinn came back. For now, she would wind down with a swim and a whirlpool.

If it was Matt, it could all be over tonight. Over. For a moment, her hope centered there. Abruptly she felt the sickness hit the pit of her stomach. No, she wouldn't wish for that. Running away from her own thoughts, she hurried upstairs to change.

"I'm glad I caught you in."

"Even superagents don't party every night." Matt was dressed in a casual sweater and slacks and comfortable boat shoes and was wound tight as a spring. "Actually, I'm having a quiet dinner at home tonight. I didn't expect to see you. Want a drink?"

"No. Thanks."

Matt set the decanter down. "How's Chantel?"

"She's fine." Rather, he was going to see that she was fine, no matter what he had to do. "Funny, I thought you'd be checking a bit more closely on that yourself."

"I figured she'd be in good hands with you." Matt rocked back and forth on his heels, not sitting, not offering Quinn a chair. "And I've been a little tied up on some personal business."

"The business take you into New York over the weekend?"

"New York?" Matt's brows drew together. "What makes you think that?"

"The florist got a pretty good look." Quinn drew out a cigarette, watching Matt as he lighted it.

"Yeah?" With a half laugh, Matt finally sat. "What the hell are you talking about, Quinn?"

"The roses you sent to Chantel. You made a mistake this time. The envelope for the card had the florist's name on it."

"Roses I sent?" Matt dragged a hand through his hair as he shook his head. "I don't know what you're getting at. I—" He stopped then, as understanding came into his eyes. "Good God, you think I've been doing this to her? You think it's me? Damn it, Quinn." He sprang out of the chair. "I thought we knew each other."

"So did I. Where'd you spend the weekend, Matt?"

"None of your damn business."

Blowing out smoke, Quinn remained in his chair. "You can tell me, or I can find out. Either way, I'm going to see to it that you're out of her life."

Fury showed in clenched fists. Quinn glanced at them, almost hoping Matt would put them to use. A physical outlet would be more to his taste than this psychological sparring, hoping to wear down his opponent's resistance. "I'm her agent, I'm her friend. When she hit rock bottom, I was there for her. If I'd had those kind of feelings, I could have acted on them then."

"Where were you over the weekend?" Quinn demanded, determined to play this through to the bitter end.

"I was out of town," Matt snapped. "Personal business."

"You've had a lot of personal business going lately. You haven't shown up at all during the filming. You're such a good friend of Chantel's, but you've only seen her twice since you found out what was going on."

Guilt flashed briefly in his eyes, but then temper obscured it. "If Chantel had wanted me, she would have called me."

"I wonder if it's you who's been calling her."

"You're crazy." But Matt's hands shook a bit as he went to pour a drink.

"You use a money clip, Matt. A silver one," Quinn continued. "One Chantel gave you. The florist picked up on a couple little details like that."

"You want to see my money clip?" Furious, Matt reached into his pocket and yanked out a wad of bills held together by a small metal clip. It hit the table with a quiet thud.

Frowning, Quinn picked it up. It was gold, not silver, with Matt's initials engraved on it.

"I've been using that for two months, since you're so interested. Ever since Marion gave it to me." He picked up his drink and tossed it back. "If it wasn't for Chantel, I'd take a shot at tossing you out."

"You're entitled to try." Quinn dropped the clip again. "Maybe you'd be smarter to level with me. Where were you over the weekend, Matt?"

"New York." Swearing, he walked to the window and back. "Brooklyn. From Friday night until Sunday afternoon—I was meeting Marion's parents. Marion Lawrence, a twenty-four-year-old schoolteacher. Twenty-four," he repeated under his breath, rubbing a hand over his face. "I met her about three months ago. She's twelve years younger than me, bright, innocent, trusting. I should have walked away. Instead, I fell in love with her." After sending Quinn a furious look, he fumbled for a cigarette of his own.

"I've spent the last three months thinking about how I relate to houses with picket fences. This young, beautiful woman is going to marry me, and I spent the weekend trying to convince her conservative and very concerned parents that I wasn't some Hollywood playboy out to take their daughter for a ride. I'd rather have faced a firing squad." He puffed on his cigarette without inhaling.

"Listen, Quinn, if I haven't been around as much as Chantel needed, it was because I've lost my head over an elementary-school teacher. Look at her." Matt flipped a photograph out of his billfold. "She looks like she could still *be* in school. I've been living on nerves for weeks."

Quinn believed him. With a mixture of relief and frustration, Quinn shut the billfold. It could have been a lie, but one man in love easily recognizes another. "What the hell does she see in you?"

Matt gave a shaky laugh. "She thinks I'm terrific. She knows about the gambling, about everything, and she thinks I'm terrific. I want to marry her before she finds out any different."

"Good luck."

"Yeah." Matt put the billfold away. His temper was gone, as were his embarrassment and his nerves. But guilt remained. "If we've got that straightened out, I'd like you to fill me in about Chantel. This character sent her flowers in New York?"

"That's right."

"He looked like me?"

"I don't know what he looked like."

"But you said—"

"I lied."

"You always were a bastard," Matt said without heat. "How's she holding up?"

"She's struggling. She's going to be better knowing you're clear."

"Let me ride out with you." He rubbed the back of his neck. "I would've told her about Marion before, but I felt—I guess I felt like an idiot. Here lies Matt Burns, agent of the stars, knocked unconscious by a woman who helps kids tie their shoelaces all day."

With her hair wet and loose, Chantel came into the poolhouse after a quick swim. The water and exercise had helped clear her head. Now all she wanted was to soothe her body. Hitting the switch for the whirlpool, she sent the bubbles gushing. A sigh of gratitude purred out as she lowered her body into the hot, churning water.

Quinn would be back soon, and one way or the other they would work things out. She had to concentrate on that, and not on the circumstances that had brought them together. Not on the circumstances that had taken him away tonight.

Beams from the setting sun came through the ribbon of high windows. The skylights above were deep blue with early evening. Chantel let the jets of water beat the fatigue out of her muscles and soothe the lingering tension from her limbs.

She was on the verge of having everything she wanted. She had only to say yes to Quinn. He loved her. Chantel closed her eyes on that thought. He loved her for what she was, not what she appeared to be on the surface. No one but her family had ever accepted her totally, with her flaws, her insecurities, her mistakes. Quinn did. A woman could live a lifetime and not find a man who loved what she was on the inside.

What held her back from taking what she needed was the fear that she might not be able to give him everything—not a family of his own.

She wanted children. His children. What if she ultimately disappointed him that way? What if he, too, had to pay for her past mistakes? If she didn't love him so much, it would be so easy to say yes.

She wanted him to come back, to be with her now. If he could just hold her now, she'd know, somehow, the right answer to give him. Chantel closed her eyes and let herself sink a little deeper. When he came back to her she would know, and whatever she did would be right for both of them.

She heard a sound, a soft one, at the back of the poolhouse. Straightening, Chantel pushed the wet hair away from her face. "Quinn? Don't say anything now." She closed her eyes again. "Just come here."

Then she heard the music, and her heart shot to her throat.

It was quiet, lovely, with the bell-like quality only the best music boxes achieve. The sky was nearly dark as the strains of the *Moonlight Sonata* flowed over the sound of churning water.

"Quinn." But she said his name knowing he wasn't there. Her hand shook as she reached over and turned off the jets. In the silence, the music box continued to play. Putting the heels of her hands behind her, Chantel pushed herself out of the tub.

"I've waited so long for this."

At the whisper, the air clogged in her throat. She had to breathe, she told herself. If she was to get to the door she had to breathe, and the door was so far away. The lights dimmed, and the fear raced along her skin.

"You're so beautiful. So incredibly beautiful. Nothing I

could imagine or create could be as perfect. Tonight, we'll finally be together."

He was in the shadows near the rear door. Chantel forced herself to look, but even then she couldn't see who it was. "There are guards outside." She balled her hand into a fist, refusing to allow her voice to quiver. "I could scream."

"There's only the guard at the gate, and he's too far away. I had to hurt the others. Sometimes you have to hurt when you love."

She gauged the distance to the front door. "How did you get in?"

"Over the wall by the tennis courts. You haven't been using the tennis courts. I've been watching for you."

"The alarm—"

"I took care of the alarm. I have some knowledge. My reputation for careful research is well deserved." Brewster stepped out of the shadows with the music box in his hands.

"James." The air in the poolhouse was sultry, but Chantel began to shiver. "Why are you doing this?"

"I love you." His eyes were glazed, and she could see no emotion in them as he walked closer. "When you first formed in my mind, I knew I had to have you. Then you were there, flesh, blood. Real. I had this made for you."

He held out the music box, and Chantel stepped back.

"Don't be afraid of me, Hailey."

"James, I'm Chantel. Chantel."

"Yes, yes, of course." He smiled at her, then set the box down on a little table beside the tub. It continued to play, romantic and sweet. "Chantel O'Hurley, with the perfect face. I've dreamed of you for months. I can't write. My wife thinks I'm agonizing over my new book. But there is no book. There'll never be another book. Chantel, you wouldn't keep my flowers."

"I'm sorry." Quinn would be back, she told herself. The

nightmare would be over. She felt exposed in her brief suit, so she reached for her wrap. Training kept her gestures casual, even as her heart roared in her head. "It was the way you sent them, James. You frightened me."

"I never meant to. Hailey—"

"Chantel," she corrected, a flutter of panic in her voice. "I'm Chantel. James, I think we should go into the house and talk about this."

"Chantel?" He looked momentarily puzzled. "No, no, I want to be alone with you. I've waited too long for tonight. The perfect night, when the moon is full. The song." He looked at the music box. "It was meant for you."

"Why didn't you just talk to me?"

"You would have rejected me. Rejected me," he repeated in a rising voice. "Do you think I'm a fool? I've seen you with those young men, all muscles and smooth faces. But none of them love you like I do. You've driven me mad with waiting. You were obsessed with Brad. It was always Brad."

"There is no Brad!" she shouted. "He's a character. There is no Hailey. You made them up. They're not real."

"You're real. I've seen you with him. I've watched the way you look at him, let him touch you, when it should be me. But I've been patient. Tonight." He started toward her. "I've waited for tonight."

Chantel raced for the front door, knowing that if she could beat him she'd have a chance. Grabbing the knob, she pulled, but it held firm.

"I locked it from the outside," Brewster told her quietly. "I knew you'd try to run away. I knew you'd throw my love back in my face."

Chantel spun around, pressing her back to the door. "You don't love me. You're confused. I'm an actress, I'm not your Hailey."

He winced as if in pain and pressed his fingers to his eyes. "Such headaches," he murmured. "No, don't," he warned when she edged toward the back door. He blocked her way, then stepped back into the shadows to pick something up. "I know what I have to do, and there's no running for either of us now, Hailey."

"I'm not—"

"It's too late," he said viciously. "Too late. I guess I've always known. I hate what you've done to me." He pressed his fingers to his temple as tears welled up in his eyes. "But as God is my witness, I can't let another man have you. You're mine. From the first moment, you were mine. If you could only understand that."

"James." She was afraid to touch him, but she took a small step closer. "Please, come into the house with me. I'm—I'm cold," she said quickly. "I'm wet, I need to change. Then we can sit down and talk."

He looked at her, but saw only what he wanted to see. "You can't lie to me. I created you. You're going to try to leave. You want to see them put me away. My doctor wants to put me away, but I know what I have to do. For both of us. It ends here, Hailey."

He held up the can, and she smelled the gasoline. "Oh, God, no."

"You were meant to die in the fire before, but I couldn't do it then. Now I have to."

He turned the can over as she lunged at him. It hit the floor with a clatter, then skidded, gas soaking into the wood. She fought to get past him. Chantel heard him sob as he shoved her down and her head hit the table. Suddenly there were shooting stars in front of her eyes.

"Chantel's going to want to open a bottle of champagne."

"I think we could all use it," Matt commented as they

walked into the house. "Quinn, I'd appreciate it if you'd let me tell her."

"You're entitled." He looked around the cool, quiet hall. "You were entitled to take a swing at me back there."

"You're bigger than I am," Matt said easily.

"I overreacted, Matt. I'm not used to that." He thought about Chantel waiting for him upstairs, and what he would have done, would continue to do to keep her safe. "The thing is I jumped on you with both feet because it was the first solid lead I've had in this whole mess."

"From what you told me, it looks like everything the florist told you fit me."

"What fits you fits someone else. I'm missing it," Quinn murmured. "I'm missing it because I'm too close. You know what the first rule of law enforcement, private or public service, is? Don't get involved."

"A little late for that I take it."

"Way too late. She believed in you," he added. "I think you should know that. Even after I spelled it all out for her she stood behind you."

Touched, Matt fiddled with the lapel of his jacket. "She's a very special woman."

"She's the most beautiful woman I've ever met, inside and out. Integrity. You don't see the integrity when you look at her, or the guts, or the loyalty. It's taken me a while to get under the surface and see all there is to her." He moved his shoulders, restless, dissatisfied. "Maybe if I'd had a little more of her faith in the people she cares for, I wouldn't have chased down a blind alley."

Matt followed Quinn's gaze up the stairs. If Quinn had overreacted, he thought, then he himself had underreacted. The past few weeks he'd been too involved with his own world to give one of his closest friends the kind of time and attention she needed. He turned the bottle in his hand. He was going to start making up for it now.

"Look, I was pretty steamed before, but I think you're as crazy about Chantel as I am about Marion. I probably would have done the same thing myself."

"Maybe." Quinn glanced at the stairs again. He didn't want champagne. He only wanted to be alone with Chantel, but she needed to see Matt, needed to talk to him. She'd be relieved, and yet he wondered if she would feel the same frustration he was experiencing. They'd come so far, yet they'd gone nowhere. "I hate what she's going through."

"So do I." Matt laid a hand on his shoulder. "The past couple months have taught me that love can drive anybody crazy. I guess it's like Brewster said in that interview."

"What interview?"

"It was in the paper tonight. They did an article on *Strangers*, focusing on Hailey. The way he described her, hell, you'd have thought she was real. But he said something that rang true—about how when a man really loves a woman, he sees her as no one else does, that no matter what he accomplishes, what he fails at, she stays at the center of his life, rules it just by being. I guess I was feeling sentimental when I read it," Matt said with a trace of embarrassment. "But I thought I knew what he meant. He even got Chantel and Hailey's names mixed up once."

"What?"

"You could tell the reporter got a charge out of that. He played up how Chantel must be turning in an Emmy-winning performance to have the writer confuse the actress with the character."

"Damn." Quinn slammed his fist against the newel post and started up the stairs. "He practically confessed this afternoon. He all but spit it in my lap."

"What are you—" But Quinn was gone. Matt just shrugged and wondered if he had time to telephone Marion.

"Call the fire department," Quinn shouted, taking the steps three at a time. "The poolhouse is going up."

"It's on fire?"

"She's in there." Quinn was at the door before Matt picked up the phone. "He's got her in there."

Chantel shook her head to try to clear it. The room swam, and she struggled to her hands and knees. She smelled the smoke first, thick and pungent, as it had been that afternoon during the filming. But this wasn't special effects, she remembered. She heard the crackle of flames and looked over to see the floor turn to fire.

He was still blocking the back door, standing there as if hypnotized by the fire, which was spreading fast. He wasn't trying to leave. He would die here, he wanted to die here. And he would take her with him.

Chantel stood, choking on smoke as she looked around frantically. Her head throbbed and spun, but she couldn't allow herself the luxury of passing out. The windows were too high. She'd never get out that way. The front door was barred. There was only one exit. She had to get past him before the fire closed it off.

Her breath came in a fit of coughing, but he didn't hear. The flames held his attention as they ate greedily at the far wall. The heat was growing, visible in waves that shimmered between her and the door. Moving fast, Chantel grabbed a towel and dumped it in the tub. Then, draping it over her face, she looked for a weapon.

The music box sat on the table, playing though the tune was muffled by the sound of flames. She took it and, on legs that threatened to buckle, walked behind Brewster.

He was crying. She heard it now as she raised the heavy

wooden box over her head. Tears were streaking her own face, blurring her vision. It was so much like the scene she had studied, rehearsed, tried to understand.

Hailey, she thought as smoke clouded her brain. It was the cabin, her New England retreat. She was Hailey and she'd brought tragedy on herself, on those who had loved her. Past mistakes, past loves, past lives. If only she hadn't given her love and her innocence to Brad.... To Dustin?

Her vision went gray, and she fought to clear it. There was no Brad. Only Quinn. Quinn was real and she was Chantel. An O'Hurley. O'Hurleys were survivors.

Weeping, she smashed the box down on Brewster's head.

When he crumpled at her feet, she could only crouch, panting, struggling to find air in a room consumed by smoke and flame.

Had she killed him? She looked at the doorway, framed now by flames. Her only way out. Survival. She took a step forward, stopped, then bent over Brewster.

He'd loved her. Mad or sane, whatever he'd done had been tied to her. Somehow, later, she would sort it out, but she couldn't save herself without trying to save him.

She snatched off the towel and covered his face with it. The ceiling gave an ominous crack, but she didn't dare look. She didn't think. Everything was centered on living. Hooking her hands under his armpits, Chantel began to drag him toward the door and closer to the flames.

She was losing. There was no air to fill her lungs as she dragged the deadweight of Brewster's unconscious body. The fire was winning, edging closer. She felt the furnace blast of heat on her skin and wished desperately that she'd taken the time to wet some towels.

Inches from the door, she stumbled and fell, light-headed from lack of oxygen. A little farther, she demanded, dragging herself and Brewster across the floor. Oh, God, just a little farther.

She watched, too dazed to be frightened, as a beam fell, flaming, into the hot tub.

"Chantel!"

She heard the shout dimly as her consciousness started to waver. Somehow she managed to gain another two inches.

Quinn kicked in the front door and saw nothing but a wall of flame. He screamed for her again and heard nothing but fire. The roof was going. He ran for the doorway, but the heat drove him back. It was then he saw her, or thought he did, slumped by the far wall, with the flames separating them.

Coughing on the smoke he'd swallowed, he raced around the building, praying for the first time in his adult life.

She'd almost made it. That was his first thought as he saw her, collapsed against Brewster near the door. Burning wood showered from the ceiling as he hurled his body over hers. He felt it hit and sear his hand before he dragged her out onto the grass.

"In the name of God—" Matt began as he raced to them.

"Brewster's in there," Quinn managed. "Take care of her."

Quinn fought the heat again, nearly giving way at what had been the back doorway. Crawling on his belly, he inched closer, until he managed to grip Brewster's wrist. If there was a pulse, he couldn't feel it, but he dragged him back. As the roof collapsed inward, he left Brewster lying on the grass and rolled onto his back to draw in air.

"Chantel." Still coughing, he crawled to her. Her face was smeared with soot. He heard the sirens as she opened her eyes to look at him.

"Quinn. He—"

"I got him out. Don't try to talk now." She began to

shiver, though the heat was still intense. Quinn stripped off his shirt and covered her. "She's in shock," he said tersely. "Smoke inhalation. She needs the hospital."

"I told them to send an ambulance." Matt peeled off his sweater and added it to Quinn's shirt. "She's going to be all right. She's tough."

"Yeah." Quinn cradled her head in his lap. "Yeah."

"He thought I was Hailey." She groped for his hand as she wavered in and out of consciousness.

"I know. Shhh." He took her hand and squeezed. The pain from his burns was real. She was real. And they were alive.

"I...for a little while in there, so did I. Quinn, tell me who I am."

"Chantel O'Hurley. The only woman I've ever loved."

"Thanks," she whispered, and drifted off.

By the time he was allowed to see her, Quinn had gone twenty-four hours without sleep. He'd refused to leave the hospital to change, and his clothes were streaked and reeking of smoke. Throughout the night he'd paced the halls and driven the nurses crazy.

She'd been treated for shock and smoke inhalation. The doctors had assured him that all she needed was rest. He intended to see and speak to her himself before he went anywhere. And when he went, she was going with him.

At dawn the day after the fire, Chantel awoke from a drugged sleep. When the doctor came out of her room, he was shaking his head. He looked at Quinn, noting his bandaged hand and singed clothing. "You can see her now. I'm going to process her discharge papers, though if you have any influence you should talk her into staying one more day for observation."

"I can take care of her at home."

The doctor sent a dubious look in the direction of the door. "Maybe you can. Mr. Doran?"

Quinn stopped with his hand on the knob. "Yes?"

"She's a very strong-willed woman."

"I know." For the first time in hours, Quinn smiled. He opened the door to see Chantel sitting up in bed, frowning into a mirror.

"I look horrible."

"Beauty's only skin deep," he said as she lowered the mirror to look at him.

"It's a good thing, because you look worse than I do. Oh, Quinn…" She spread her arms wide. "You're really here," she whispered as she used all her strength to squeeze. "It's all right now, isn't it? Everything's going to be all right."

"It's over. I should have taken better care of you."

"I'll dock your pay."

"Damn it, Chantel, it's not a joke."

"You saved my life," she told him as she drew away.

"When I think of what might have happened—"

"No." She put her fingertips to his mouth. "I don't want to think of 'what ifs' anymore, Quinn. I'm safe and so are you. That's all that matters now. And…and James…"

"He'll live," Quinn said, answering her unspoken question. He stood and began to prowl the room. "He's going to be put away, Chantel. I'm going to help see to that."

"Quinn, he was so pathetic, so confused. He created something that overwhelmed him."

"He would have killed you."

"He would have killed Hailey," she corrected. "I can only pity him."

"Forget him," Quinn told her, knowing he would have to if he didn't want to be eaten alive by bitterness. "Your family's coming."

"Here? All of them?"

"Your sisters, your parents. Nobody knows how to reach Trace."

"Quinn, I don't want to disrupt Maddy's honeymoon. And everyone else—"

"Wants to make sure you're all right. That's what families are for, right?"

"Yes." She folded her hands. "It is. Quinn, you deserve a family, your own family."

He turned to her, ready to fight for what he needed. "I know what I want, Chantel."

"Yes, I think you do." She'd made her decision when she'd opened her eyes on the grass and seen his face. "Quinn, before all of this happened last night, I was waiting for you. I knew when you came back and held me I'd make the right choice, for both of us." She glanced around the room, then into the mirror. With a grimace she set it facedown on the table beside her. "This isn't exactly how I expected things to be, but it would help a lot if you'd come here and put your arms around me."

He sat on the bed beside her and gathered her close. "Listen, I have to tell you this. When I got there last night and the poolhouse was burning, I knew you were inside because my heart had stopped. If I had lost you, it would never have started again."

"Quinn." She lifted her head, searching for his lips. Finding them, she found all the answers she needed. "I'd like a short engagement," she said, smiling. "Very, very short."

* * * * *

WITHOUT A TRACE

To black sheep

Prologue

"**P**ick up the beat on the intro, Tracey boy, you're dragging it."

Frank O'Hurley stood on his mark, stage right, and prepared to go through his opening routine again. The three-night run in Terre Haute might not be the highlight of his career, and it certainly wasn't the apex of his dreams, but he was going to give the audience their money's worth. Every two-bit gig was a dress rehearsal for the big break.

He counted off the beat, then swung into the routine with the enthusiasm of a man half his age. The calendar might put Frank's age at forty, but his feet would always be sixteen.

He'd written the little novelty number himself, with the wide-eyed hope that it would become the O'Hurley trademark. At the piano, his oldest child and only son tried to put some life into a melody he'd played too many times to count—and dreamed of other things and other places.

On cue, his mother spun onstage with his father. Even

after endless routines, endless theaters, Trace still felt a
tug of affection for them. Just as, after endless routines,
endless theaters, he felt what had become a familiar tug
of frustration.

Would he always be here, beating out a second-rate
tune on a second-rate piano, trying to fill his father's big
dreams that hadn't a hope in hell of coming true?

As she'd been doing most of her life, Molly matched her
steps to Frank's. She could have done the number blind-
fold. As it was, while she dipped, spun and double-stepped,
her mind was more on her son than her timing.

The boy wasn't happy, she thought. And he wasn't a
child any longer. He was on the brink of manhood and
straining to go his own way. It was that single fact, she
knew, that terrified Frank to the point that he refused to
acknowledge it.

The arguments had become more frequent, more heated.
Soon, she thought, all too soon, something was going to
explode, and she might not be able to pick up all the pieces.

Kick, ball change, dip, and her three daughters tapped
onto the stage. With her heart close to Frank's, Molly could
feel him swell with pride. She would hate for him to lose
that pride or the hope that kept him the youthful dreamer
she'd fallen in love with.

As Molly and Frank moved offstage, the routine eased
smoothly into the opening song. The O'Hurley Triplets—
Chantel, Abby and Maddy—launched into three-part harmony as if they'd been born singing.

They practically had, Molly thought. But, like Trace,
they weren't children any longer. Chantel was already
using her wit and her wiles to fascinate the men in the audience. Abby, steady and quiet, was just marking time. And
it wouldn't be long before they lost Maddy. As a mother,
Molly felt both pride and regret at the thought that her

youngest had too much talent to remain part of a roving troupe for long.

Yet it was Trace who concerned her now. He sat at the scarred piano in the dingy little club, his mind a thousand miles away. She'd seen the brochures he collected. Pictures and stories on places like Zanzibar, New Guinea, Mazatlán. Sometimes, on the long train or bus rides from city to city, Trace would talk of the mosques and caverns and mountains he wanted to see.

And Frank would brush those dreams off like dust, desperately clinging to his own—and to his son.

"Not bad, darlings." Frank bounced back to center stage to give each of his daughters a hug. "Trace, your mind's not on the music. You need to pump some life into it."

"There hasn't been any life in that number since Des Moines."

A few months before, Frank would have chuckled and rubbed a hand over his son's hair. But now he felt the sting of criticism, man to man. His chin came up to a stubborn point. "Nothing wrong with the song and never has been. It's your playing that's lacking. You lost tempo twice. I'm tired of you sulking over the keys."

Playing peacemaker, Abby stepped between her father and brother. The growing tension had been keeping the family on edge for weeks. "We're all a little tired, I think."

"I can speak for myself, Abby." Trace pushed away from the piano. "No one's sulking at the keys."

"Hah!" Frank brushed Molly's restraining hand away. Lord, the boy was tall, Frank thought. Tall and straight and almost a stranger. But Frank O'Hurley was still in charge, and it was time his son remembered it. "You've been in a black mood since I told you I wouldn't have a son of mine harking off to Hong Kong or God knows where like some

Gypsy. Your place is here, with your family. Your responsibility is to the troupe."

"It's not my damn responsibility."

Frank's eyes narrowed. "Watch your tone, boy-o, you're not so big I can't take you down."

"It's time somebody took that tone with you," Trace went on, spewing out everything he'd held back for too long. "Year after year we play second-rate songs in second-rate clubs."

"Trace." Maddy said it quietly, adding a pleading look. "Don't."

"Don't what?" he demanded. "Don't tell him the truth? God knows he won't hear it anyway, but I'll have my say. The three of you and Ma have protected him from it long enough."

"Temper tantrums are so boring," Chantel said lazily, though her nerves were strung tight. "Why don't we all break to neutral corners?"

"No." Quivering with indignation, Frank stepped away from his daughters. "Go on, then, have your say."

"I'm tired of riding a bus to nowhere, of pretending the next stop's the brass ring. You drag us from town to town, year after year."

"Drag you?" Frank's face flushed with fury. "Is that what I'm doing?"

"No." Molly stepped forward, her eyes on her son. "No, it's not. We've all of us gone willingly, because it was what we wanted. If one of us doesn't want it, he has a right to say so, but not to be cruel."

"He doesn't listen!" Trace shouted. "He doesn't care what I want or don't want. I've told you. I've told you," he rounded on his father. "Every time I try to talk to you, all I get is how we have to keep the family together, how the big break is right around the corner, when there's nothing around the corner but another lousy one-night stand in another two-bit club."

It was too close to the truth, too close to what would make him feel like a failure when all he'd wanted was to give his family the best and the brightest. Temper was the only weapon Frank had, and he used it.

"You're ungrateful and selfish and stupid. All my life I've worked to pave the way for you. To open doors so you could step through. Now it's not good enough."

Trace felt tears of frustration burn his eyes, but didn't back down. "No, it's not good enough, because I don't want to walk through your doors. I want something else, I want something more, but you're so wrapped up in your own hopeless dream you can't see that I hate it. And that the more you push me to follow your dream instead of my own, the closer I come to hating you."

Trace hadn't meant to say that, and shocked himself speechless with his own bitter words. Before his stunned eyes, his father paled, aged and seemed to shrivel. If he could have taken the words back, he might have tried. But it was too late.

"Take your dream, then," Frank said in a voice rough with emotion. "Go where it takes you. But don't come back, Trace O'Hurley. Don't come back to me when it leaves you cold. There'll be no killing of the fatted calf for you."

He strode off, stage left.

"He didn't mean it," Abby said quickly, taking Trace's arm. "You know he didn't."

"Neither of them did." Her own eyes welling, Maddy looked helplessly at her mother.

"Everyone just needs to cool off." Even with her flair for the dramatic, Chantel was shaken. "Come on, Trace, we'll go for a walk."

"No." With a little sigh, Molly shook her head. "You girls go on now, let me talk to Trace." She waited until they were alone, then, feeling old and tired, sat on the piano bench. "I know you've been unhappy," she said quietly. "And that you've bottled things up. I should have done something about it."

"None of it's your fault."

"Mine as much as his, Trace. The things you said cut deep in him, and that won't heal for a while. I know some were said in temper, but others were true." She looked up, studying the face of her firstborn and only son. "I think it was true what you said about coming to hate him if he didn't let you go."

"Ma—"

"No. It was a hard thing to say, but harder if it came true. You want to go."

He opened his mouth, on the edge of caving in yet again. But the rage he had felt for his father was still too close, and it frightened him. "I have to go."

"Then do it." She stood again to put her hands on his shoulders. "And do it quick and clean, else he'll charm or shame you into staying and you'll never forgive him. Take your own road. We'll be here when you come back."

"I love you."

"I know. I want to keep it that way." She kissed him, then hurried away, knowing she had to hold off her own tears until she had comforted her husband.

That night, Trace packed his belongings—clothes, a harmonica, and dozens of brochures. He left a note that said simply, "I'll write." He had $327.00 in his pocket when he walked out of the motel and stuck out his thumb.

Chapter 1

The whiskey was cheap and had the bite of an angry woman. Trace sucked air through his teeth and waited to die. When he didn't, he poured a second shot from the bottle, tipped back in his chair and watched the open expanse of the Gulf of Mexico. Behind him, the little cantina was gearing up for the evening's business. Frijoles and enchiladas were frying in the kitchen. The smell of onions was coming on strong, competing with the odors of liquor and stale tobacco. The conversations were in rapid-fire Spanish that Trace understood and ignored.

He didn't want company. He wanted the whiskey and the water.

The sun was a red ball over the Gulf. There were low-lying clouds shimmering with pinks and golds. The fire of the whiskey was settling into a nice, comfortable heat in the pit of his stomach. Trace O'Hurley was on vacation, and by God he was going to enjoy it.

The States was only a short plane ride away. He'd

stopped thinking of them as home years before—or at least he'd convinced himself he had. It had been twelve years since he'd sailed out of San Francisco, a young, idealistic man riddled with guilt, driven by dreams. He'd seen Hong Kong, and Singapore. For a year he'd traveled the Orient, living by his wits and the talent he'd inherited from his parents. He'd played in hotel lounges and strip joints at night and soaked up the foreign sights and smells by day.

Then there had been Tokyo. He'd played American music in a seedy little club with the idea of making his way across Asia.

It had simply been a matter of being in the right place at the right time. Or, as Trace thought when he was feeling churlish, the wrong place at the wrong time. A barroom brawl was a common enough occurrence. Frank O'Hurley had taught his son more than how to keep the beat. Trace knew when to swing and when to retreat.

He hadn't started out with the intention of saving Charlie Forrester's life. And he certainly hadn't known that Forrester was an American agent.

Fate, Trace thought now as he watched the red sun sinking closer to the horizon. It was fate that had caused him to deflect the knife meant for Charlie's heart. And it was fate and its wily ways that had embroiled him in the grim game of espionage. Trace had indeed made his way across Asia, and beyond. But he'd been bankrolled by the International Security System.

Now Charlie was dead. Trace poured himself another shot and drank a toast to his friend and mentor. It wasn't an assassin's bullet or a knife in a dark alley that had gotten him, but a stroke. Charlie's body had simply decided his time was up.

So Trace O'Hurley sat in a little dive on the Mexican coast and held his own wake.

The funeral was in fourteen hours in Chicago. Because he wasn't ready to cross the Rio Grande, Trace would stay in Mexico, drink to his old friend and contemplate life. Charlie would understand, Trace decided as he stretched out long legs clad in dingy khaki. Charlie had never been one for ceremony. Just do the job, have a drink and get on with the next one.

Trace pulled out a crushed pack of cigarettes and searched in the pocket of his dirt-streaked shirt for a match. His hands were long and wide palmed. At ten he'd dreamed of becoming a concert pianist. But he'd dreamed of becoming many things. A battered bush hat shadowed his face as he struck the match and touched it to the end of the cigarette.

He was very tanned, because his last job had kept him outdoors. His hair was thick and, because he hadn't bothered to have it trimmed, long enough to curl beyond the hat in dark blond disarray. His face was damp from the heat, and lean. There was a scar, small and white, along the left side of his jaw—an encounter with a broken bottle. His nose had been slightly out of alignment ever since he'd been sixteen. A fight over a girl's honor—or lack thereof.

His body was on the lanky side at the moment, due to a prolonged hospital stay. The last bullet he'd taken had nearly killed him. Even without the whiskey and the grief, he had a dangerous look. The bones were prominent, the eyes intense. Even now, when he was on his own time, they made occasional sweeps of the room.

He hadn't shaved in three days, and his beard was rough enough to give his mouth a surly look. The waiter was happy to leave him with his bottle and his solitude.

As dusk fell, the sky became quieter, and the cantina noisier. A radio played Mexican music interrupted by occasional bursts of static. Someone broke a glass. Two men started to argue about fishing, politics and women. Trace poured another shot.

He saw her the minute she walked in. Old habits had his eye on the door. Training had him taking in the details without seeming to look at all. A tourist who'd made a wrong turn, he thought as he took in the ivory skin dashed with freckles that went with her red hair. She'd burn to a crisp after an hour under the Yucatán sun. A pity, he thought mildly, and went back to his drink.

He'd expected her to back out the moment she realized the type of place she'd wandered into. Instead, she went up to the bar. Trace crossed his ankles and whiled away the time by studying her.

Her white slacks were spotless despite the dusty heat of the day. She wore them with a purple shirt that was loose enough to be cool. Even so, he noted that she was slender, with enough curve to give the baggy slacks some style. Her hair, almost the color of the setting sun, was caught back in a braid, but her face was turned away, so he could see only her profile. Classic, he decided without much interest. Cameo style. The champagne-and-caviar type.

He tossed back the rest of the drink and decided to get very drunk—for Charlie's sake.

He'd just lifted the bottle when the woman turned and looked directly at him. From the shadow of his hat, Trace met the look. Tensed, he continued to pour as she crossed the room toward him.

"Mr. O'Hurley?"

His brow lifted only slightly at the accent. It had a trace of Ireland, the same trace his father's had taken on in anger or in joy. He sipped his whiskey and said nothing.

"You are Trace O'Hurley?"

There was a hint of nerves in the voice, as well, he noted. And, close up, he could see smudges of shadows under what were extraordinary green eyes. Her lips pressed together. Her fingers twisted on the handle of the canvas bag slung over her shoulder. Trace set the whiskey down and realized he was just a bit too drunk to be annoyed.

"Might be. Why?"

"I was told you'd be in Mérida. I've been looking for you for two days." And he was anything but what she'd expected. If she wasn't so desperate, she'd already have fled. His clothes were dirty, he smelled of whiskey, and he looked like a man who could peel the skin off you without drawing blood. She pulled in a deep breath and decided to take her chances. "May I sit down?"

With a shrug, Trace kicked a chair back from the table. An agent—from either side—would have approached him differently. "Suit yourself."

She wrapped her fingers around the back of the chair and wondered why her father believed this crude drunkard was the answer. But her legs weren't as steady as they might be, so she sat down. "It's very important that I speak with you. Privately."

Trace looked beyond her to the cantina. It was crowded now, and getting noisier by the minute. "This'll do. Now why don't you tell me who you are, how you knew I'd be in Mérida, and what the hell you want?"

She linked her fingers together because they were trembling. "I'm Dr. Fitzpatrick. Dr. Gillian Fitzpatrick. Charles Forrester told me where you were, and I want you to save my brother's life."

Trace kept his eyes on her as he lifted the bottle. His voice was quiet and flat. "Charlie's dead."

"I know." She thought she'd glimpsed something, some flash of humanity, in his eyes. It was gone now, but Gillian still responded to it. "I'm sorry. I understand you were close."

"I'd like to know how you understand anything or why you expect me to believe Charlie would have told you where to find me."

Gillian wiped a damp palm over the thigh of her slacks before reaching into her bag. In silence, she handed a sealed envelope to him.

Something told Trace he'd be better off not taking it. He should get up, walk out and lose himself in the warm Mexican night. It was only because she'd mentioned Charlie that he broke the seal and read the note inside.

Charlie had used the code they'd communicated with during their last assignment. As always, he'd kept the message brief: "Listen to the lady. No involvement with the organization at this time. Contact me."

Of course, there was no way to contact Charlie now, Trace thought as he folded the letter again. With the feeling that, even dead, Charlie was still guiding his moves, he looked at the woman again. "Explain."

"Mr. Forrester was a friend of my father's. I didn't know him well myself. I was away a lot. About fifteen years ago they worked together on a project known as Horizon."

Trace pushed the bottle aside. Vacation or not, he couldn't afford to dull his senses any further. "What's your father's name?"

"Sean. Dr. Sean Brady Fitzpatrick."

He knew the name. He knew the project. Fifteen years before, some of the top researchers and scientists in the world had been employed to develop a serum that would immunize man against the effects of ionizing radiation-injury—one of the nastier side effects of nuclear war. The ISS had been in charge of security and had monitored and maintained the project. It had cost hundreds of millions, and it had been a whopping failure.

"You'd have been a kid."

"I was twelve." She jolted and turned around nervously when something crashed in the kitchen. "Of course, I didn't know about the project then, but later..." The smell of onions and liquor was overpowering. She wanted to get up, wanted to walk along the beach, where the air would be warm and clear, but she forced herself to continue. "The project was dropped, but my father continued to work on it. He had other obligations, but whenever possible he resumed experimenting."

"Why? He wouldn't have been funded for it."

"My father believed in Horizon. The concept fascinated him, not as a defense, but as an answer to the insanity we're all aware exists. As to the money—well, my father has reached a point where he can afford to indulge his beliefs."

Not only a scientist, but a rich scientist, Trace thought as he watched her from under the brim of his hat. And this one looked as if she'd gone to a tidy convent school in Switzerland. It was the posture that usually gave it away. No one taught proper posture like a nun.

"Go on."

"In any case, my father turned all his notes and findings over to my brother five years ago, after he suffered his first heart attack. For the past few years, my father has been too ill to continue intense laboratory work. And now..."

For a moment, Gillian closed her eyes. The terror and the traveling were taking their toll. As a scientist, she knew she needed food and rest. As a daughter, a sister, she had to finish. "Mr. O'Hurley, might I have a drink?"

Trace shoved both bottle and glass across the table. He was nibbling, but he wasn't ready to bite yet. She interested him, certainly, but he'd learned long ago that you could be interested and uninvolved.

She'd have preferred coffee or at the most, a snifter of warm brandy. She started to refuse the whiskey, but then caught the look in Trace's eye. So he was testing her. She was used to being tested. Her chin came up automatically. Her shoulders straightened. Steady, she poured a double shot and downed it in one swallow.

She drew in breath through a throat that felt as if it had been blowtorched. Blinking the moisture from her eyes, she let it out again. "Thank you."

The light of humor flashed in his eyes for the first time. "Don't mention it."

Hot and bitter though it was, the whiskey helped. "My father is very ill, Mr. O'Hurley. Too ill to travel. He contacted Mr. Forrester but was unable to fly to Chicago himself. I went to Mr. Forrester in his place, and Mr. Forrester sent me to you. I was told that you're the best man for the job."

Trace lit another cigarette. He figured he hadn't been the best man for anything since he'd lain bleeding in the dirt, a bullet two inches from his heart. "Which is?"

"About a week ago, my brother was taken, kidnapped by an organization known as Hammer. You've heard of them?"

It was training that kept his face blank over a mix of fear and rage. His association with that particular organization had nearly killed him.

"I've heard of them."

"All we know is that they took my brother from his home in Ireland, where he had continued, and nearly completed, his work on the Horizon project. They intend to hold him until he has perfected the serum. You understand what the repercussions could be if a group like that possessed the formula?"

Trace tapped the ash of his cigarette onto the wooden floor. "I've been told I have a reasonably developed intelligence."

Driven, she grabbed his wrist. Because she was a

woman in a man's field, physical contact was usually reserved for family and loved ones. Now she held on to Trace, and the only hope she had. "Mr. O'Hurley, we can't afford to joke about this."

"Careful how you use *we*." Trace waited until her fingers uncurled. "Let me ask you, Dr. Fitzpatrick, is your brother a smart man?"

"He's a genius."

"No, no, I mean does he have two grains of common sense to rub together?"

Her shoulders straightened again because she was all too ready to lay her head on the table and weep. "Flynn is a brilliant scientist, and a man who under normal circumstances can take care of himself quite nicely."

"Fine, because only a fool would believe that if he came up with the formula for Hammer, he'd stay alive. They like to call themselves terrorists, liberators, rebels. What they are is a bunch of disorganized fanatics, headed by a rich madman. They kill more people by mistake than they do on purpose." Frowning, he rubbed a hand over his chest. "They've got enough savvy to keep them going, and pots of money, but basically, they're idiots. And there's nothing more dangerous than a bunch of dedicated idiots. My advice to your brother would be to spit in their eye."

Her already pale skin was ghost white. "They have his child." Gillian placed a hand on the table for support as she rose. "They took his six-year-old daughter." With that, she fled the cantina.

Trace sat where he was. Not his business, he reminded himself as he reached for the bottle again. He was on vacation. He'd come back from the dead and intended to enjoy his life. Alone.

Swearing, he slammed the bottle down and went after her. Her anger had her covering ground quickly. She heard him call her name but didn't stop. She'd been an idiot to believe that a man like him could help. She'd be better off attempting to negotiate with the terrorists. At least with them she wouldn't go in expecting any compassion.

When he grabbed her arm, she swung around. Temper gave her the energy that lack of sleep and food had depleted.

"I told you to wait a damn minute."

"You've already given me your considered opinion, Mr. O'Hurley. There doesn't seem to be any need for further discussion. I don't know what Mr. Forrester saw in you. I don't know why he sent me to look for a man who would rather sit in a seedy little dive swilling whiskey than help save lives. I came looking for a man of courage and compassion and found a tired, dirty drunk who cares about no one and nothing."

It stung, more than he'd expected. His fingers stayed firm on her arm as he waved away a small boy with a cardboard box filled with Chiclets. "Have you finished? You're making a scene."

"My brother and niece are being held by a group of terrorists. Do you think I care whether I embarrass you or not?"

"It takes more than an Irish redhead on a roll to embarrass me," he said easily. "But I have a policy against drawing attention to myself. Old habit. Let's take a walk."

She very nearly yanked her arm away. The part of her that was pride burned to do it. The part that was love triumphed, and she subsided. In silence she walked beside him, down the narrow planks that led to the water.

The sand was white here against a dark sea and a darker sky. A few boats were docked, waiting for tomorrow's fishing or tomorrow's tourists. The night was quiet enough that the music from the cantina carried to them. Trace noted that somebody was singing about love and a woman's infidelity. Somebody always was.

"Look, Dr. Fitzpatrick, you caught me at a bad time. I don't know why Charlie sent you to me."

"Neither do I."

He stopped long enough to cup his hands around a match and a cigarette. "What I mean is, this situation should be handled by the ISS."

She was calm again. Gillian didn't mind losing her temper. It felt good. But she also knew that more was accomplished with control. "The ISS wants the formula as badly as Hammer. Why should I trust my brother's and my niece's lives to them?"

"Because they're the good guys."

Gillian turned toward the sea, and the wind hit her dead on. Though it helped clear her head, she didn't notice the first stars blinking to life. "They are an organization run by many men—some good, some bad, all ambitious, all with their own concept of what is necessary for peace and order. At the moment, my only concern is my family. Do you have family, Mr. O'Hurley?"

He drew hard on the cigarette. "Yeah." Over the border, he thought. He hadn't seen them in seven years, or was it eight? He'd lost track. But he knew Chantel was in L.A. filming a movie, Maddy was in New York starring in a new play. Abby was raising horses and kids in Virginia. His parents were finishing up a week's gig in Buffalo.

He might have lost track of the time, but not of his family.

"Would you trust the lives of any of the members of your family to an organization? One that, if they considered it necessary for the common good, might sacrifice them?" She closed her eyes. The wind felt like heaven, warm, salty and strong. "Mr. Forrester understood and agreed that what was needed to save my brother and his child was a man who would care more about them than the formula. He thought you were that man."

"He was off base." Trace pitched his cigarette into the surf. "Charlie knew I was considering retiring. This was just his way of keeping me in the game."

"Are you as good as he told me?"

With a laugh. Trace rubbed a hand over his chin. "Probably better. Charlie was never much for back patting."

Gillian turned again, this time to face him. He didn't look like a hero to her, with the rough beard and the grimy clothes. But there had been strength in his hand when he'd taken her arm, and she'd sensed an undercurrent of violence. He'd be passionate when it was something he wanted, she thought, whether it was a goal, a dream or a woman. Under usual circumstances, she preferred men with cool, analytical minds, who attacked a problem with logic and patience. But it wasn't a scientist she needed now.

Trace dipped his hands into his pocket and fought the urge to squirm. She was looking at him as though he were a laboratory rat, and he didn't like it. Maybe it was the hint of Ireland in her voice or the shadows under her eyes, but he couldn't bring himself to walk away.

"Look, I'll contact the ISS. The closest field office is in San Diego. You can feed them whatever information you have. Inside of twenty-four hours, some of the best agents in the world will be looking for your brother."

"I can give you a hundred thousand dollars." Her mind was made up. She had discarded logic for instinct. Forrester had said this man could do it. Her father had agreed. Gillian was throwing her vote with theirs. "The price isn't negotiable, because it's all I have. Find my brother and my niece, and with a hundred thousand dollars you can retire in style."

He stared at her for a moment, and then, biting off an oath, he walked toward the sea. The woman was crazy. He was offering her the skill of the best intelligence organization in the world, and she was tossing money in his face. A tidy sum.

Trace watched the sea roll up and recede. He'd never been able to hang on to more than a few thousand at a time. It just wasn't his nature. But a hundred thousand could mean the difference between retiring or just talking about retiring.

The spray flew over his face as he shook his head. He didn't want to get involved, not with her, not with her family, and not with some nebulous formula that might or might not save the world from the big blast.

What he wanted was to go back to his hotel, order up a five-star meal and go to bed on a full stomach. God, he wanted some peace. Time to figure out what to do with his life.

"If you're determined to have a freelancer, I can give you a couple of names."

"I don't want a couple of names. I want you."

Something about the way she said it made his stomach knot. The reaction made him all the more determined to get rid of her. "I just came off nine months of deep cover. I'm burned out, Doc. You need someone young, gung ho and greedy." For the second time he ran his hands over his face. "I'm tired."

"That's a cop-out," she said, and the sudden strength in her voice surprised him enough to have him turning around. She stood straight, loose tendrils of hair flying around her face, pale as marble in the light of the rising moon. It suddenly struck him that in fury and despair she was the most stunning woman he'd ever seen. Then he lost that thought as she advanced on him, her Irish leading the way.

"You don't want to get involved. You don't want to be responsible for the lives of an innocent man and a young child. You don't want to be touched by that. Mr. Forrester saw you as some kind of a knight, a man of principle and compassion, but he was wrong. You're a selfish shell of a man who couldn't have deserved a friend like him. He was a man who cared, who tried to help for nothing more than the asking, and who died because of his own standards."

Trace's head snapped up. "What the hell are you talking about?" His eyes caught the light and glittered dangerously. In one swift, silent move he had Gillian by both arms. "What the hell do you mean? Charlie had a stroke."

Her heart was beating hard in her throat. She'd never seen anyone look more capable of murder than Trace did at that moment. "He was trying to help. They'd followed me. Three men."

"What three men?"

"I don't know. Terrorists, agents, whatever you chose to call them. They broke into the house when I was with him." She tried to even her breathing by concentrating on the pain his fingers were inflicting on her arms. "Mr. Forrester pushed me through some kind of hidden panel in his library. I heard them on the other side. They were looking for me." She could remember even now how hot and airless it had been behind the panel. How dark. "He was putting them off, telling them I'd left. They threatened him, but he stuck by the story. It seemed that they believed him."

Her voice was shaking. Trace watched her dig her teeth into her lower lip to steady herself. "It got very quiet. I was more frightened by the quiet and tried to get out to help him. I couldn't find the mechanism."

"Two inches down from the ceiling."

"Yes. It took me almost an hour before I found it." She didn't add that she'd fought hysteria the entire time, or that at one point she'd beaten against the panel and shouted, prepared to give herself up rather than stay in the suffocating dark. "When I got out, he was dead. If I'd been quicker, I might have been able to help him… I'll never be sure."

"The ISS said stroke."

"It was diagnosed as one. Such things can be brought on by a simple injection. In any case, they caused the stroke, and they caused it while looking for me. I have to live with that." Trace had dropped his grip, and she'd grabbed his shirtfront without realizing it, her fingers curled tight. "And so do you. If you won't help me for compassion or for money, maybe you'll do it for revenge."

He turned away from her again. He'd accepted Charlie's death once. A stroke, a little time bomb in the brain set to go off at a certain time. Fate had said: Charlie, you've got sixty-three years, five months, on earth. Make the best of it. That he'd accepted.

Now he was being told it wasn't fate, it was three men. Fate was something he was Irish enough to live with. But it was possible to hate men, to pay men back. It was something to think about. Trace decided to get a pot of black coffee and do just that.

"I'll take you back to your hotel."

"But—"

"We'll get some coffee and you can tell me everything Charlie said, everything you know. Then I'll tell you if I'll help you."

If it was all he'd give, she'd take it. "I checked into the same hotel as you. It seemed practical."

"Fine." Trace took her arm and began to walk with her. She wasn't steady, he noted. Whatever fire had pushed her this far was fading fast. She swayed once, and he tightened his grip. "When's the last time you ate?"

"Yesterday."

He gave a snort that might have been a laugh. "What kind of a doctor are you?"

"Physicist."

"Even a physicist should know something about nutrition. It goes like this. You eat, you stay alive. You don't eat, you fall down." He released her arm and slipped his around her waist. She would have protested if she'd had the energy.

"You smell like a horse."

"Thanks. I spent most of the day bumping around the jungle. Great entertainment. What part of Ireland?"

Fatigue was spreading from her legs to her brain. His arm felt so strong, so comforting. Without realizing it, she leaned against him. "What?"

"What part of Ireland are you from?"

"Cork."

"Small world." He steered her into the lobby. "So's my father. What room?"

"Two-twenty-one."

"Right next door to mine."

"I gave the desk clerk a thousand pesos."

Because the elevators were small and heated like ovens, he took the stairs. "You're an enterprising woman, Dr. Fitzpatrick."

"Most women are. It's still a man's world."

He had his doubts about that, but he didn't argue the point. "Key?"

She dug into her pocket, fighting off the weakness. She wouldn't faint. That she promised herself. Trace took the key from her palm and stuck it in the lock. When he opened the door, he shoved her against the wall in the hallway.

"What's wrong with you?" she asked. She swallowed

the rest when she saw him draw a hunting knife out of his pocket.

It was all he had. He hadn't considered it necessary to strap on a gun while on vacation. His eyes were narrow as he stepped into the room and kicked aside some of the debris.

"Oh, God." Gillian braced herself in the doorway and looked. They'd done a thorough job. Even someone inexperienced in such matters could see that nothing had been overlooked.

Her suitcase had been cut apart, and the clothes she hadn't unpacked were strewn everywhere. The mattress and the cushions from the single chair had been slit, and hunks of white stuffing littered the floor. The drawers of the bureau had been pulled out and overturned.

Trace checked the bath and the access through the windows. They'd come in the front, he concluded, and a search of a room this size wouldn't have taken more than twenty minutes.

"You've still got your tail, Doc." He turned but didn't sheath the knife. "Pick up what you need. We'll talk next door."

She didn't want to touch the clothes, but she forced herself to be practical. She needed them, and it didn't matter that other hands had touched them. Moving quickly, she gathered up slacks and skirts and blouses. "I have cosmetics and toiletries in the bath."

"Not anymore you don't. They dumped the lot." Trace took her arm again. This time he checked the hall and moved quietly to the room next door. Again he braced Gillian against the wall and opened the door. His fingers relaxed on the handle of the knife, though only slightly. So they hadn't made him. That was good. He signaled to her to come in behind him, double-locked the door, then began a careful search.

It was an old habit to leave a few telltales, one he followed even off duty. The book on his nightstand was still a quarter inch over the edge. The single strand of hair he'd left on the bedspread hadn't been disturbed. He pulled the drapes, then sat on the bed and picked up the phone.

In perfect Spanish that had Gillian's brow lifting, he ordered dinner and two pots of coffee. "I got you a steak," he said when he hung up the phone. "But this is Mexico, so I wouldn't expect it for about an hour. Sit down."

With her clothes still rolled in her arms, she obeyed. Trace pushed himself back on the bed and crossed his legs.

"What are they after?"

"I beg your pardon?"

"They've got your brother. Why do they want you?"

"I occasionally work with Flynn. About six months ago I spent some time with him in Ireland on Horizon. We had a breakthrough." She let her head tilt back against the cushion. "We believed we'd found a way to immunize the individual cell. You see, in ionizing radiation injury the main structure affected is the single cell. Energy rays enter the tissue like bullets and cause localized injury in the cells. We were working on a formula that prevented molecular changes within the affected cells. In that way we could—"

"That's just fascinating, Doc. But what I want to know is why they're after you."

She realized she'd nearly been reciting the information in her sleep and tried to straighten in the chair. "I took the notes on this part of the project with me, back to the institute, to work on them more intensely. Without them it could take Flynn another year, maybe more, to reconstruct the experiment."

"So you're the missing piece of the puzzle, so to speak?"

"I have the information." The words began to slur as her eyes closed.

"You're telling me you carry that stuff with you?" God save him from amateurs. "Did they get it?"

"No, they didn't get it, and yes, I have it with me. Excuse me," she murmured, and went to sleep.

Trace sat where he was for a moment and studied her. Under other circumstances he would have been amused to have a woman he'd known for only a few hours fall asleep in the chair of his hotel room in the middle of a conversation. At the moment, his sense of humor wasn't what it might have been.

She was deathly pale from exhaustion. Her hair was a fiery halo that spoke of strength and passion. Clothes lay balled in her lap. Her bag was crushed between her hip and the side of the chair. Without hesitation, Trace got up and eased it out. Gillian didn't move a muscle as he dumped the contents on the bed.

He pushed aside a hairbrush and an antique hammered-silver compact. There was a small paperback phrase book—which told him she didn't speak the language—and the stub of a ticket for a flight from O'Hare. Her checkbook had been neatly balanced in a precise hand. Six hundred and twenty-eight dollars and eighty-three cents. Her passport picture was better than most, but it didn't capture the stubbornness he'd already been witness to. She'd worn her hair loose for it, he noted, frowning a bit at the thick riot of curls that fell beyond her shoulders.

He'd always had a weakness for long, luxuriant, feminine hair.

She'd been born in Cork twenty-seven years before, in May, and had kept her Irish citizenship, though her address was listed as New York.

Trace pushed the passport aside and reached for her wallet. She could use a new one, he decided as he opened it. The leather had been worn smooth at the creases. Her driver's license was nearly up for renewal, and the picture on it carried the same serious expression as the passport. She had three hundred and change in cash, and another two thousand in traveler's checks. He found a shopping list folded into the corner of the billfold along with a parking ticket. A long-overdue parking ticket.

A flip through the pictures she carried showed him a black-and-white snapshot of a man and a woman. From the clothes he judged that it had been taken in the late fifties. The woman's hair was as neat as the collar and cuffs on the blouse she wore, but she was smiling as though she meant it. The man, husky and full-faced, had his arm around the woman, but he looked a bit uncomfortable.

Trace flipped to the next and found a picture of Gillian in overalls and a T-shirt, her head thrown back, laughing, her arms around the same man. He was older by perhaps twenty years. She looked happy, delighted with herself, and nothing like a physicist. Trace flipped quickly to the next snapshot.

This was the brother. The resemblance to Gillian was stronger than with the people Trace assumed were her parents. His hair was a tamer red, almost a mahogany, but he had the same wide-set green eyes and full mouth. In his arms he held a pixie of a girl. She would have been around three, he concluded, with that telltale mane of wildly curling red hair. Her face was round and pleased, showing a dimple near the corner of her mouth.

Before he realized it, Trace was grinning and holding the photo closer to the light. If a picture told a story, he'd bet his last nickel the kid was a handful. He had a weakness for cute kids who had the devil's gleam in their eyes. Swearing under his breath, he closed the billfold.

The contents of her bag might have told him a few things about her, but there hadn't been any notes. A few phone calls would fill in the blanks as far as Dr. Gillian Fitzpatrick was concerned. He glanced at her again as she sat sleeping, then, sighing, dumped everything back in her purse. He might have to wait until morning to get anything else out of her.

When the knock came at the door, she didn't budge. Trace let the room-service waiter set up the table. After giving Gillian three hefty shakes and getting no more than a murmur in response, he gave up. Muttering to himself, he slipped off her sandals, then gathered her up in his arms. She sighed, cuddled and caused him an uncomfortable pressure just under the ribs. She smelled like a meadow with the wildflowers just opening. By the time he'd gotten her into bed, he'd given up on the idea of sleeping himself.

Trace poured his first cup of coffee and settled down to eat his dinner—and hers.

Chapter 2

Gillian woke after a solid twelve hours of sleep. The room was dim, and she lay still, waiting for her mind to clear. Quickly, and in order, the events of the previous day came back to her. The bumpy, nerve-racking flight from Mexico City to Mérida. The fear and fatigue. The frustrating search from hotel to hotel. The dingy little cantina where she'd found the man she had to believe would save her brother and her young niece.

This was his room. This was his bed. Cautiously she turned her head—and let out a small groan. He was sleeping beside her, and in all probability he was as naked as the day he was born. The sheet slanted across his bare back, from below the shoulder blade to the waist. His face, a little less harsh, a little less forbidding, in sleep, was inches from hers. She felt then, as she had felt when she'd first seen him the evening before, that it was the face of a man a woman would never be safe with.

Yet she'd spent the night with him and had been safe—safe from him and from whatever forces were after her. More significantly, the moment she had stepped into the room and had finished unburdening herself, she had felt a wave of relief and confidence. He would help, reluctantly, resentfully, but he would help.

Sighing, she shifted in bed, preparing to get up. His hand shot out. His eyes opened. Gillian froze. Perhaps she wasn't as safe as she'd thought.

His eyes were clear and alert. His grip was firm, and just shy of being painful. Under his fingers, he felt her pulse speed up. Her hair was barely mussed, which told him that exhaustion had held her still through the night. The hours of sleep had faded the shadows under her eyes, eyes that watched him warily.

"You sleep like a rock," he said mildly, then released her and rolled over.

"The traveling caught up with me." Her heart was bumping as though she'd run up three flights of stairs. He was dangerous to look at, and too close. Perhaps it was the morning disorientation that caused her to feel that dull sexual pull.

Before she managed to resist it, her gaze had flicked down—the strong column of neck, the broad chest—and froze. A long red scar marred the tanned skin just right of his heart. It looked as though he'd been ripped open, then put back together. And recently.

"That looks…serious."

"It looks like a scar." His voice held no inflection at all as she continued to stare at the wound with horrified eyes. "You got a problem with scars, Doc?"

"No." She made herself look away, back at his face. It was as hard and blank as his voice. Not my business, she reminded herself. He was a violent man who lived by violent means. And that was exactly what she needed. She got out of bed to stand awkwardly, smoothing her clothes. "I appreciate you letting me sleep here. I'm sure we could have arranged for a cot."

"I've never had a problem sharing a bed." She was still pale. It gave her a delicate bone-china look that made him edgy. "Feel better?"

"Yes, I—" She reached a hand to her hair as she felt the first wave of embarrassment. "Thank you."

"Good, because we've got a lot of ground to cover today." He tossed the sheet aside and noted her instinctive flinch. His own discomfort turned to amusement. He wore flesh-colored briefs that left little room for modesty or imagination. Rising without any sign of self-consciousness, he gave her a slow, cocky grin. He liked the fact that she didn't avert her eyes. Whatever her thoughts, she stood where she was and watched him coolly.

Her throat had gone dry as dust, but she made a passable stab at casualness. "You could use a shower."

"Why don't you order up some breakfast while I do?" He turned toward the bath.

"Mr. O'Hurley…"

"Why don't you make it Trace, sweetheart?" He looked over his shoulder and grinned again. "After all, we just slept together."

The water was running in the shower before she managed to free the breath that was trapped in her lungs.

He'd done it on purpose, of course, she told herself as she sat on the edge of the bed. It was typical of the male of the species to flaunt himself. The peacock had his plumage, the lion his mane. Males were always strutting and preening so that the female would be impressed. But who would have guessed the man would be built like that?

With a shake of her head, Gillian lifted the phone. She didn't care how he was built as long as he helped her.

He'd have preferred it if she hadn't looked so frail and vulnerable. Trace kept the water cold to make up for three hours' sleep. His problem. Lathering his face, he began to shave in the shower by feel. He'd never been able to resist the damsel-in-distress routine. It had nearly gotten him killed in Santo Domingo. And nearly gotten him married in Stockholm. He wasn't sure which would have been worse.

It didn't help a hell of a lot that this one was beautiful. Beautiful women had an edge, no matter what modern-day philosophy said about intellect. He could admire a mind, but—call him weak—he preferred it packaged well.

By God, she was some package, and she'd dumped him into an international mess when all he wanted to do was wander around some ruins and go snorkeling.

Hammer. Why in the hell did it have to be Hammer? He'd thought he was done with the half-baked, destructive group of renegades. It had taken him more than six months to infiltrate the organization at one of the base levels. He'd been working his way up, nicely, keeping a low profile with a Slavic accent, his hair dyed black and a lot of facial hair to complete the disguise.

Ten miles out of Cairo, he'd made the mistake of discovering that the man he'd been working with on a small-arms deal had been making a few deals of his own on the side. Nothing to him, Trace thought now, bitterly. God knew he'd tried to tell the man he didn't give a damn about his private ventures. But in a panic, the terrified entrepreneur had blown a hole in Trace's chest and left him for dead rather than risk being reported.

It was well-known that the man who wielded the power and money at Hammer had little patience with private enterprise.

For nothing, Trace thought in disgust. The months of work, the careful planning, all for nothing because one half-crazed Egyptian had had a sweaty trigger finger.

As a result, he'd brushed close enough to death to want to spend some time appreciating life. Get drunk, hold a willing woman, lie on white sand and look at blue skies. He'd even started thinking about seeing his family.

Then she'd come along.

Scientists. He rubbed a hand over his chin and, finding it smooth enough, let the water beat over his head. Scientists had been screwing up the order of things since Dr. Frankenstein's day. Why couldn't they just work on a cure for the common cold and leave the destruction of the world to the military?

He turned off the taps, then reached for two undersized towels. Two phone calls the night before had given him enough information on Gillian Fitzpatrick to satisfy him. She was the genuine article, though he'd been wrong about the Swiss school. It was Irish nuns who'd taught her posture. She'd completed her education in Dublin, then gone on to work for her father until she'd accepted a position with the highly respected Random-Frye Institute in New York.

She was single, though there was a link between her and a Dr. Arthur Steward, head of research and development at Random-Frye. Three months ago she'd spent six weeks in Ireland, on her brother's farm.

A busman's holiday, Trace decided, if she had indeed worked on Horizon while she'd been there.

There was no reason to disbelieve her, no reason to refuse to do as she asked. He'd find Flynn Fitzpatrick and the angel-faced little girl. And while he was at it he'd find the men who'd killed Charlie. He'd get a hundred thousand for the first and a great deal of satisfaction for the second.

The towel covered him with the same nonchalance as

the briefs. He walked back into the bedroom to find Gillian shaking out what was left of her clothes.

"Shower's yours, Jill."

"Gillian," she told him. Fifteen minutes alone had done a great deal to help her regain her composure. Since she was going to have to deal with Trace O'Hurley for some time, she'd decided to think of him as a tool rather than as a man.

"Suit yourself."

"I usually do. I don't have a toothbrush."

"Use mine." He pulled open a drawer of the bureau. He caught her look in the mirror and grinned. "Sorry, Doc. I don't have a spare. Take it or leave it."

"It's unhygienic."

"Yeah, but then, so's kissing if you do it right."

Gillian took her clothes and retreated to the bath without commenting.

She felt almost human when she came out again. Her hair was damp, her clothes were wrinkled, but the scent of food and coffee brought a very healthy pang to her stomach. He was already eating, poring over the newspaper as he did. When she moved to join him, he didn't bother to look up.

"I wasn't sure what you liked."

"This is fine," he told her over a mouthful of eggs.

"I'm so glad," she murmured, but the sarcasm bounced off him without making a dent. Because her hunger was urgent, she applied herself to her own plate and returned the compliment by ignoring him.

"They make it sound like it's only going to take a couple of nice chats to ratify the new SALT Treaty."

"Diplomacy is essential in any negotiation."

"Yeah, and—" He looked up. He knew exactly what it felt like to take a hard fist in the solar plexus. He knew how the body contracted, how the air vanished and the head spun. Until now he hadn't known he could experience the same sensation by looking at a woman.

Her hair curled damply past her shoulders, the color of a flame. Her skin was ivory, touched with a rose brought back by rest and food. Over the rim of her cup her eyes, as deep and rich a green as the hills of Ireland, looked into his questioningly.

He thought of mermaids. Of sirens. Of temptation.

"Is something wrong?" She was nearly tempted to reach out and take his pulse. The man looked as though he'd been struck on the back of the neck. "Trace, are you all right?"

"What?"

"Are you ill?" Now she did reach out, but he jerked back as if she'd stung him.

"No, I'm fine." No, he was an idiot, he told himself as he lifted his own coffee. She wasn't a woman, he reminded himself, she was his ticket to an early retirement and sweet revenge. "We need to clear up a few points. When did they snatch your brother?"

Relief came in a tidal wave. "You're going to help me."

He smeared more butter on a piece of toast. "You said a hundred thousand."

The gratitude in her eyes dulled. The warmth in her voice cooled. He preferred it that way. "That's right. The money is in a trust fund that came to me when I turned twenty-five. I haven't needed it. I can contact my lawyer and have it transferred to you."

"Fine. Now when did they take your brother?"

"Six days ago."

"How do you know who took him and why?"

It didn't matter that he was a mercenary, she told herself, only that he would save her family. "Flynn left a tape. He'd been recording some notes when they came for him.

He left the tape on, and I suppose no one noticed during the struggle." She pressed a hand to her mouth for a moment. The sounds of the fight had come clearly over the tape, the crashing, the screams of her niece. "He didn't go easily. Then one of the men held a knife to Caitlin's throat. His daughter. I think it was a knife because Flynn said not to cut her. He said he'd go quietly if they didn't cut her."

She had to swallow again. The breakfast she'd eaten with such pleasure rolled toward her throat. "The man said he'd kill her unless Flynn cooperated. When Flynn asked what they wanted, he was told he was working for Hammer now. They instructed him to bring all his notes on the Horizon Project. Flynn said…he told them he'd go with them, he'd do whatever they wanted, but to let the child go. One of the men said they weren't inhuman, it would be too cruel to separate a child from her father. And he laughed."

Trace could see what this was doing to her. For both their sakes, he offered her no comfort. "Where's the tape?"

"Flynn's housekeeper had been at the market. She found the mess in the laboratory when she got back, and she phoned the police. They contacted me. Flynn's recorder had an automatic shutoff when he reached the end of the tape. The police hadn't bothered with it. I did." She linked her hands together as Trace lit a cigarette. "Ultimately I took the tape to Mr. Forrester. It was gone when I found him dead."

"How do you figure they know about you?"

"They would only have to have read Flynn's notes. It would have been recorded that I worked with him and took part of the project back with me."

"The men on the tape, they spoke English?"

"Yes, accented… Mediterranean, I think, except for the one who laughed. He sounded Slavic."

"Anyone use a name?"

"No." On a deep breath, she ran both hands through

her hair. "I listened to the tape dozens of times, hoping I might catch something. They said nothing about where they were taking him, only why."

"Okay." Trace tipped back in his chair and blew smoke toward the ceiling. "I think we can get them out in the open."

"How?"

"They want you, don't they? Or the notes." He was silent for a moment as he watched that sink in. "You said you had them with you. I didn't find them in your bag."

The consideration in her eyes turned to indignation. "You looked through my belongings?"

"Just part of the service. Where are they?"

Gillian pushed away from the table to pace to the window. It seemed nothing was hers alone any longer. No part of her life could be private. "Mr. Forrester destroyed them."

"You told me you had them with you."

"I do." She turned back and placed a fingertip to her temple. "Right here. With a true photographic memory, one sees words. If and when it becomes necessary, I can duplicate the notes."

"Then that's what you're going to do, Doc, with a few alterations." He narrowed his eyes as he thought the plan through. It could work, but it all hinged on Gillian. "How are you fixed for guts?"

She moistened her lips. "It's not something I've had to test to any extent. But if you mean to use me as bait to find out where Flynn and Caitlin are being held, I'm willing."

"I don't want any grand sacrifices." He crushed out his cigarette before he rose and walked to her. "Do you trust me?"

She studied him in the hard, brilliant light of the Mexican sun. He was scrubbed and shaven and, she realized, no less dangerous than the man she'd met in the cantina. "I don't know."

"Then you'd better think it through, real careful." He cupped a hand under her chin. "Because if you want to stay alive, you're going to have to."

It was a long, mostly silent drive to Uxmal. Trace had made certain everyone in the hotel knew they were going. He'd asked for brochures, gotten directions in both English and Spanish, then gone to the gift shop to buy another guidebook and some film. He'd asked the clerk about mileage, restaurants along the way, and insect repellent. In general, he'd played the enthusiastic tourist and made a spectacle of himself.

Anyone looking for Gillian would know she could be found at the ruins of Uxmal.

The vegetation on either side of the road was thick and monotonous. The Jeep was canopied, but it didn't have air-conditioning. Gillian drank bottled lemonade and wondered if she'd be alive for the drive back.

"I don't suppose we could have found someplace closer."

"Uxmal's a natural tourist spot." The road was straight and narrow. Trace kept an eye on the rearview mirror. "We'll have some company, but not enough, I think, to put our friends off. Besides, one of the reasons I'm here is to check out the ruins." If they were being followed, the tail was first-class. Trace shifted in his seat and adjusted his dark glasses. "It's not as big or as popular as Chichén Itzá, but it's the most impressive site on the Puuc Route."

"I didn't think a man like you would be interested in ancient civilizations and pyramids."

"I have my moments." In truth, he'd always been fascinated by such things. He'd spent two months in Egypt and Israel using a cover as an anthropology major early in his career. It had given him a taste for both history and danger. "We should be able to pull this off, and soak up the atmosphere, as long as you follow orders."

"I agreed, didn't I?" Even with the thin buff-colored blouse and slacks she wore, the heat was irksome. Gillian concentrated on it rather than the anxiety that was gnawing at her gut. "What if they're armed?"

Trace took his eyes off the road long enough to shoot her a grimly amused look. "Let me worry about that. You're paying me to handle the details."

Gillian lapsed into silence again. She must be mad, she thought, trusting her life and the lives of her family to a man who was more interested in money than humanity. Taking another swig of warming lemonade, she tried to comfort herself by remembering what Charles Forrester had said of him.

"A bit of a renegade, and certainly not a man who would be considered a good team player. If he was, he'd be running the ISS by now. That's how good he is. If you want a man who can find a needle in a haystack—and you don't care if the hay gets a bit mangled in the process—he's the one."

"This is my brother's life, Mr. Forrester. And the life of a little girl, not to mention the possibility of nuclear repercussions."

"If, out of all the agents I've worked with, I had to pick one to trust my life to, it would be Trace O'Hurley."

Now she was trusting her life to him, a man she'd known less than twenty-four hours. He was crude, and more than a little rough around the edges. Since she'd met him he hadn't offered one word of sympathy about her family, and he hadn't expressed more than a passing interest in a formula that could change forever the balance of power in the world.

And yet…there was the quietly supportive way he'd

slipped an arm around her waist when she'd been staggering with fatigue.

Who was he? A quick bubble of panic started in her throat as the question finally broke through. Who was this man she was trusting everything to?

"How long have you been a spy?"

He looked at her again, then back at the road, before he burst out laughing. It was the first time she'd heard the sound from him. It was strong, careless, and more appealing than she'd counted on. "Honey, this ain't James Bond. I work in espionage—or, if you like a cleaner term, intelligence."

Unless she was mistaken, there was a trace of bitterness there. "You didn't answer my question."

"Ten years, more or less."

"Why?"

"Why what?"

"Why are you in this kind of work?"

Trace punched in the cigarette lighter and ignored the little voice in his head that reminded him he'd been smoking too much. "That's a question I've been asking myself lately. Why physics?"

She wasn't foolish enough to think he cared. It was simply a way to switch the conversation away from himself. "Family tradition, and I had a knack for it. I was all but born in a laboratory."

"You're not living in Ireland."

"No, I was offered a position at Random-Frye. It was an excellent opportunity." To finally slip out from under her father's shadow.

"Like the States?"

"Yes, very much. At first it seemed everything moved faster than it should, but you find yourself catching up. Where are you from?"

He pitched the cigarette out into the road. "Nowhere."

"Everyone's from somewhere."

His lips curved at some private joke. "No, they're not. We're nearly there. Want to go over anything?"

Gillian drew a long, steadying breath. The time for small talk was over. "No."

The parking lot was half full. When the winter season got under way, the ruins, less than a two-hour drive from Cancun, would do a brisk business. With his camera slung over his shoulder, Trace took Gillian's hand. Her initial resistance only caused him to tighten his grip.

"Try to look a little romantic. We're on a date."

"You'll understand if I find it a bit difficult to look starry-eyed."

"Shoot for interested." He pulled the guidebook out of his back pocket. "The place dates back to the sixth and seventh centuries. That's comforting."

"Comforting?"

"Over a thousand years and we haven't managed to destroy it. Up for a climb?"

She looked at him but couldn't see his eyes behind the dark lenses. "I suppose."

Hands linked, they started up the rough steps of the Pyramid of the Magician. She wasn't immune to the atmosphere. Even with sweat trickling down her back and her heart thudding with dull fear, she was moved by it. Ancient stones lifted by ancient hands to honor ancient gods. From the top she could look out over what had once been a community filled with people.

For a moment she indulged herself and held herself very still. The scientist in her would have cocked a brow, but her ancestors had believed in leprechauns. Life had been in this place. Spirits still were. With her eyes closed, Gillian felt the power of the atmosphere.

"Can you feel it?" she murmured.

It was captured memories, lingering passions, that drew him to places. The realist in him had never completely over-shadowed the dreamer. "Feel what?" he asked, though he knew.

"The age, the old, old souls. Life and death. Blood and tears."

"You surprise me."

She opened her eyes, greener now with the emotion that was in her. "Don't spoil it. Places like this never lose their power. You could raze the stone, put a high-rise on this spot, and it would still be holy."

"Is that your scientific opinion, Doctor?"

"You *are* going to spoil it."

He relented, though instinct told him they would both be better off it he kept the distance. "Have you ever been to Stonehenge?"

"Yes." She smiled, and her hand relaxed in his.

"If you close your eyes and stand in the shadow of a stone, you can hear the chanting." His fingers had linked with hers, intimately, though neither of them were aware of it. "In Egypt you can run your hand along the stone of a pyramid and all but smell the blood of slaves and the incense of kings. Off the coast of the Isle of Man there are mermaids with hair like yours."

He had a fistful of it, soft, silky. He imagined it heating his skin with the kind of fire magicians conjure without kindling or matches.

She could do nothing but stare at him. Though his eyes were still hidden, his voice had become soft and hypnotic. The hand on her hair seemed to touch every part of her, slowly, temptingly. The little twist of need she had felt that morning became an ache, that ache, a longing.

She leaned toward him. Their bodies brushed.

"The view better be worth it, Harry. I'm sweating like a pig."

Gillian jerked back as if she'd been caught with her hand in the till as a middle-aged couple dragged themselves up the last of the stairs.

"A pile of rocks," the woman said when she took off her straw hat to fan her flushed face. "God knows why we had to come all the way to Mexico to climb a pile of old rocks."

The magic of the place seemed to retreat. Gillian turned to look out over the ruins.

"Young man, would you mind taking a picture of my wife and me?"

Trace took the disc camera from the slightly overweight man, who had an Oklahoman accent. It was the least he could do after they'd prevented him from making a mistake. Letting his mind wander off the task at hand and into more personal matters wouldn't get him his revenge, and it wouldn't get Gillian her family.

"Little closer together," he instructed, then snapped the picture when the couple gave two wide, frozen grins.

"Kind of you." The man from Oklahoma took back his camera. "Want me to take one of you and the lady?"

"Why not?" It was a typical tourist device. After handing over his camera, he circled Gillian's waist. She went stiff as a board. "Smile, honey."

He wasn't sure, but he thought he heard her call him an unflattering name under her breath.

As they started back down, Trace maneuvered so that Gillian's bag was between them. Looking down from the pyramid, he'd seen three men come onto the site together, then separate.

"Stay close."

Gillian set her teeth and obeyed, though at the moment she would have liked nothing better than to put as much distance as possible between them. It must have been too much sun, she decided, that had made her go so soft and light-headed. It certainly hadn't had anything to do with genuine emotion. Sunstroke, she told herself. Add that to the fact that she had always been highly sensitive to atmosphere, and it made a plausible answer to why she had nearly kissed him, and wanted to kiss him, had felt as if she were meant to kiss him.

"This isn't the best time to be daydreaming." Swinging an arm around her shoulders, Trace drew her tight against his body and steered her under an arch into the Nun's Quadrangle.

The position pleased him. The grand plaza was flanked on all four sides by structures that were really a series of interior rooms and doors. It left them enough in the open, while providing cover if cover proved necessary. If he had a choice, he wanted to deal with their friends one at a time.

"You're supposed to be appreciating the detail work on the stones."

Gillian swallowed a little ball of fear. "The carved arches and facades are classic Mayan architecture. The Puuc construction is recognizable in the finely cut stone."

"Very good," Trace murmured. He saw one of the men slip into the quadrangle. Just one, he thought. So they had, as he'd hoped, spread out to find her. Turning, he pressed her against a column and ran his hands down her body.

"What are you—?"

"I'm making a lewd suggestion," he said softly as he leaned close to her ear. "Understand?"

"Yes." It was the signal for her to act, but she found herself frozen. His body was hard and hot and, for reasons she didn't want to dissect, made her feel safe.

"A very lewd suggestion, Gillian," Trace repeated. "It

has something to do with you and me naked in a twenty-five-gallon tub of whipped cream."

"That's not lewd, that's pathetic." But she sucked in a deep breath. "You filthy-minded swine." Putting her heart into it, Gillian swung back and brought her palm hard—a bit harder than necessary—across his face. She shoved him away and made a production of smoothing her hair. "Just because I agreed to an afternoon's drive doesn't mean I intend to spend the night playing your revolting games."

Eyes narrowed, Trace ran a hand over his cheek. She packed a punch, but they'd discuss that later. "That's fine, sweetheart. Now why don't you find your own way back to Mérida? I've got better things to do than to waste my time on some skinny broad with no imagination." Swinging around, he left her alone. He passed the man who stood three yards away, ostensibly studying an arch.

Gillian had to bite her tongue to keep herself from calling Trace back. He'd asked her if she had guts, and now she was forced to admit she didn't have as many as she'd hoped. Her hands trembled as she cupped her elbows. It didn't take long.

"Are you all right, miss?"

This was it. She had no trouble recognizing the voice from her brother's tape. Gillian turned around, hoping her overbright eyes and unsteady voice would be taken as indignation. "Yes, thank you."

He was dark, and not much taller than herself, with olive skin and a surprisingly kind face. She forced herself to smile. "I'm afraid my companion wasn't as interested in Mayan architecture as he pretended."

"Perhaps I could offer you a ride back."

"No, that's kind of you, but—" She broke off when she felt the prick of a knife at her side, just above her waist.

"I believe it would be for the best, Dr. Fitzpatrick."

She didn't have to feign terror, but even as her mind threatened to freeze with it, Gillian remembered her instructions. Stall. Stall as long as possible so that Trace could even the odds.

"I don't understand."

"It will all be explained. Your brother sends his best."

"Flynn." Regardless of the knife, Gillian reached out and grabbed the man's shirt. "You have Flynn and Caitlin. Tell me if they're all right. Please."

"Your brother and niece are in good health and will remain so as long as we have cooperation." He put his left arm around her shoulders and began to walk.

"I'll give you whatever you want if you promise not to hurt them. I have some money. How much—?"

"We're not interested in money." The knife urged her forward. However kind his face had been, the hand on the knife was merciless. "There is a matter of the missing experiments and the notes."

"I'll give them to you. I have them right here." She gripped the strap of her bag. "Please don't hurt me, or my family."

"It's to your advantage that you are more easily persuaded than your brother."

"Where is Flynn? Please, tell me where you're holding him."

"You'll be with him soon enough."

Trace found the second man behind the Governor's Palace. He strolled by, clicking his camera, then pressed the man's face into one of the twenty thousand intricately carved stones.

"Fascinating stuff, isn't it?" He had his hand around the man's neck in what would look like a brotherly embrace. They both knew it would take only a jerk to break bone. "If you want to keep the use of your right arm, don't look around. Let's make this quick while we've got some privacy. Where are you holding Flynn Fitzpatrick?"

"I don't know a Flynn Fitzpatrick."

Trace hitched the man's arm up another quarter inch. He could hear bone grinding against bone. "You're wasting my time." After a quick look around, Trace pulled out his hunting knife and placed the blade where ear met skull. "Ever heard of van Gogh? It only takes a few seconds to remove an ear. It won't kill you—unless you bleed to death. Now, once more—Flynn Fitzpatrick."

"We weren't told where he was taken." The blade nipped into flesh. "I swear it! Our instructions were to take him and the girl to the airport and turn them over. We were sent back for the woman, his sister."

"And your instructions for her?"

"A private plane at the airport in Cancun. We were not told of the final destination."

"Who killed Forrester?"

"Abdul."

Because time was pressing, Trace had to forgo the pleasure of making the man suffer. "Go to sleep," he said simply, and rammed his head into the stone.

Where was Trace? Gillian thought as she approached a small white compact. If he didn't come soon, she and the altered notes would be on their way to... She didn't even know where.

"Please, tell me where you're taking me." She stumbled, and the knife slashed through the cotton of her blouse to flesh. "I feel faint. I need a moment." When she leaned heavily against the hood of the car, the man relaxed enough to draw the knife away from her side.

"You can rest in the car."

"I'm going to be sick."

He made a sound of disgust and pulled her upright by

the hair. Trace's fist sent him reeling back three feet. "She may be a bit of a bitch," he said mildly, "but I can't stand to see a woman manhandled. Look, honey, I just wanted to get you naked. No rough stuff."

Gillian let the bag slip out of her hands and fled.

"That's a woman for you. No appreciation." Trace shot the man, whose mouth was spurting blood, a grin. "Better luck next time."

The man swore. Trace knew enough Arabic to catch the drift. When a knife was drawn, he was ready. He wanted badly to pull out his own, to go head-to-head with this man he knew had killed his closest friend. But it wasn't the time, and it wasn't the place. He wanted not only the instrument, but also the man who'd given the order. Keeping his gaze locked on the blade, Trace lifted both hands and backed off.

"Listen, you want her that bad, she's all yours. One woman's the same as another as far as I'm concerned." When the man spit at his feet, Trace bent down as if to wipe off his shoe. He came up with a nickel-plated .45 automatic. "Abdul, isn't it?" The half-amused light in his eyes had become deadly. "I've already taken care of your two friends. The only reason I'm not going to put a hole in your head is that I want you to take a message to your boss. Tell him Il Gatto's going to pay him a visit." Trace saw the quick widening of the dark eyes and grinned. "You recognize the name. That's good. Because I want you to know who kills you. Deliver the message, Abdul, and put your affairs in order. You don't have very long."

Abdul still had the knife in his hand, but he was aware that a bullet was faster than a blade. He was also aware that Il Gatto was quicker than most. "Il Gatto's luck will run out, the same as his master's."

Trace leveled the gun to a point just under Abdul's chin.

"Yeah, but yours is ticking away right this minute. My finger's starting to sweat, Abdul. You'd better move."

He waited until the man had gotten behind the wheel and driven off before he lowered the gun. It had been close, Trace realized as he slipped the gun back into the holster strapped to his calf. He'd nearly taken his revenge there and then. Trace straightened again. When his blood was cool and his mind clear, revenge would be that much sweeter.

He spun quickly when he heard footsteps behind.

Gillian had seen that look before—when she'd told him that Forrester had been murdered. She thought she'd seen it again when her head had been jerked up by the hair. But even now, though she was seeing it for the third time, her skin prickled cold.

"I thought I told you to stay with a crowd."

"I saw," she began, then walked over to pick up her bag. It would sound foolish to say she'd stayed close in case he'd needed her help. "I didn't know you had a gun."

"You figure I was going to get your brother out with fast talk and a charming smile?"

"No." She couldn't meet his eyes now. She'd disliked but at least understood the world-weary, slightly grungy man she'd first met. She'd nearly liked and again had understood the cocky, smart-mouthed man she'd breakfasted with. But this one, this hard-eyed stranger who carried death within easy reach, she didn't understand at all. "Did you...the other two men, did you..."

"Kill them?" He said the word simply as he took her arm and led her back to the Jeep. He'd seen both fear and revulsion in her eyes. "No, sometimes it's better to leave people alive, especially when you know what's left of that life is going to be hell. I didn't get a lot out of either of them. They dropped your brother and the kid at the airport and were sent out for you. They didn't know where he was being held."

"How do you know they were telling you the truth?"

"Because these guys are the bottom of the food chain. They haven't got the brains to lie, especially when they know you'll slice off little pieces of their bodies."

The adrenaline washed out of her. "God, then how are we going to find him?"

"I've got some leads. And the word is *I*, not *we*. As soon as I find a safe house for you, you're going under."

"You're mistaken." She stopped in front of the Jeep. Her face was beaded with sweat but no longer pale.

"Sure, we'll discuss it later. Right now, I want a drink."

"And as long as you're working for me you'll drink in moderation."

He swore, but more good-naturedly than she'd expected. "Name ten Irishmen you know who drink in moderation."

"You, for one." She turned to walk around to her side of the Jeep when he swore again and grabbed her. She was about to snap at him when he pulled her shirt loose from the waistband of her slacks. "What the hell do you think you're doing?"

"You're bleeding." Before she could protest, he'd yanked her slacks down enough to expose her hipbone. The cut wasn't very deep, but it was rather long. Blood had seeped through to stain her shirt. For an instant—and an instant was often too long—the dull red haze of fury clouded his vision. "Why didn't you tell me he'd hurt you?"

"I didn't realize." She bent to examine the wound clinically. "I was trying to slow him down and stumbled. He gave me a jab, I guess for incentive. It isn't serious. Nearly stopped bleeding."

"Shut up." It didn't seem to matter at the moment that the cut was shallow. It was her skin, her blood. Trace half

lifted her into the Jeep, then popped open the glove compartment. "Just be still," he ordered as he broke open a
first-aid kit. "I told you not to take any chances, damn it."

"I only— For heaven's sake, that hurts worse than the
cut. Will you stop fussing?"

"I'm cleaning it, damn it, and you're going to shut up."
He worked quickly, and none too gently, until she was
cleaned and bandaged.

"Congratulations, Doctor," she said dryly, and only
smiled when he lifted angry eyes. "I never expected a man
like you to get so flustered at the sight of a little blood. As
a matter of fact, I would have taken bets that—"

She was cut off quickly and completely when his mouth
covered hers. Stunned, she didn't move a muscle as his
hands came to her throat and passed up into her hair. This
was the promise, or the threat, she had glimpsed from the
top of the pyramid.

His mouth, hard and hungry, didn't gently persuade, but
firmly, unarguably possessed. The independence that was
an innate part of her might have protested, but the need,
the desire, the delight, overlapped and won.

He didn't know why in hell he'd started this. It seemed
his mouth had been on hers before he'd even thought of it.
It had just been. He'd been frightened when he'd seen her
blood. And he wasn't used to being frightened—not for
someone else. He'd wanted to stroke and soothe, and he'd
fought that foolishness back with rough hands and orders.

But, damn it, why was he kissing her? Then her lips
parted beneath his and he didn't ask any longer.

She tasted as she smelled, of meadows and wildflowers and early sunlight on cool morning dew. There was
nothing exotic here, everything was soft and real. Home...
Why was it she tasted of home and made him long for it
as much as he did for her?

What he'd felt at the top of the pyramid came back a hundredfold. Fascination, sweetness, bewilderment. He coated them all with a hard-edged passion he understood.

She didn't cringe from it. She lifted a hand to his face. The echo of her heartbeat was so loud in her head that she could hear nothing else. His kiss was so demanding, she could feel nothing else. When he drew away as abruptly as he had come to her, she blinked until her blurred vision cleared.

He was going to have to get rid of her, and fast, Trace thought as he stuck unsteady hands in his pockets. "I told you to shut up," he said briefly, and strode around the Jeep.

Gillian opened her mouth, then shut it again. Perhaps, until she could think clearly, she'd take his advice.

Chapter 3

Trace nursed a beer. He figured that if Abdul was smart the message would be delivered to the right people before nightfall. He intended to be out of Mexico in an hour. He gave a brief thought to warm Caribbean waters and lazy snorkeling, then picked up the phone.

"Make yourself useful and pack, will you, sweetheart?"

She turned from the window. "The name is Gillian."

"Yeah, well, toss the stuff in the suitcase. We're going to check out as soon as—Rory? Well, so how the devil are you? It's Colin."

Gillian's brows went up. In mid-sentence his voice had changed from a lazy American drawl to a musical Irish brogue. Colin, was it? she thought, folding her arms.

"Aye. No, I'm fit. Right as rain. How's Bridget? Not again. My God, Rory, do the two of you plan to populate Ireland by yourselves?" As he listened, Trace glanced up long enough to give her a mild look and gestured toward the bureau. With more noise than grace, Gillian began yanking out his clothes.

"I'm glad to hear it. No, I don't know when I might be back. No, no trouble, nothing to speak of, in any case, but I wondered if you'd do me a favor." He watched Gillian heap his clothes into the suitcase and took a pull on the beer. "I'm grateful. There was a plane, probably private, that left the airport in Cork ten days ago. I don't want you to ask who was on board or why. Understand? That's a lad. Just nose around and see if you can find out the destination. Lacking that, find out how many miles she was fueled for and where she might have put down to be refueled. I'll take it from there… Important enough," he went on after a pause, "but nothing you should take risks for… No." And this time he laughed. "Nothing to do with the IRA. It's more of a personal matter. No, I'm traveling. I'll get back to you. Kiss Bridget for me, but try to keep it at that. I don't want to be responsible for another baby."

He hung up and looked at the twisted, mangled clothes in his suitcase. "Nice job."

"And what was that all about… Colin?"

"That was about finding out where your brother is. You'd better toss whatever you want to keep in there, too. We'll deal with getting you another suitcase later." He was up and stuffing his snorkeling gear into a tote.

"Why the accent and the false name? It sounded to me as though that man was your friend."

"He is." Trace went to gather up the things in the bath.

"If he's your friend," Gillian insisted as she tailed behind him, "why doesn't he know who you are?"

Trace glanced up and caught his own reflection in the mirror. His own face, his own eyes. Why was it that too often he didn't recognise himself? He dumped toothpaste and a bottle of aspirin into a travel kit. "I don't use my name when I'm working."

"You checked in as Trace O'Hurley."

"I'm on vacation."

"If he's your friend, why do you lie to him?"

He picked up his razor and examined the blade very carefully before he dropped it in the case. "He was a kid mixed up in a bad situation a few years ago. Gunrunning."

"That's what you meant by the IRA?"

"You know, Doc, you ask too many questions."

"I'm trusting the most precious things in my life to you. I'll ask questions."

He zipped the travel kit in one impatient movement. "I was on assignment when I ran into him, and I was using the name Colin Sweeney."

"He must be a very good friend to agree to do you this kind of a favor without any questions."

Trace had saved his life, but he didn't want to think about that. He'd saved lives, and he'd taken them. He didn't want to think about either at the moment. "That's right. Now can we finish packing and get out of here before someone pays us a visit?"

"I have another question."

He let out a little laugh. "Am I surprised?"

"What was the name you gave that man this afternoon?"

"Just a nickname I picked up a few years back in Italy." He stepped forward, but she didn't move away from the door.

"Why did you give it to him?"

"Because I wanted whoever gives the orders to know who was coming for him." Brushing past her, he dumped the rest of his things into the suitcase and snapped it shut. "Let's go."

"What does it mean?"

He walked to the door and opened it before turning back to her. There was a look in his eyes that both frightened and fascinated. "Cat. Just cat."

He'd known some day he would go back to the States. There had been times in a jungle, or a desert or a grimy hotel room in a town even God had forgotten when he'd imagined it: the prodigal son returns, brass band included. But that was the theatrical blood in him.

Other times he'd imagined slipping quietly into the country, the way he'd slipped out a million years before.

There were his sisters. At the oddest times he would think of them, want to be with them so badly he'd book a flight. Then he'd cancel it at the last minute. They were grown women now, with lives of their own, and yet he remembered them as they'd been the first time he'd seen them. Three scrawny infants, born in one surprising rush, nestled in incubators behind a glass nursery wall.

There had been a bond between them, as he supposed was natural between triplets, and yet he'd never felt excluded. They'd traveled together from the time they'd been born until he'd stuck out his thumb on a highway outside Terre Haute.

He'd seen them only once since then, but he'd kept track. Just as he'd kept track of his parents.

The O'Hurleys had never been the huge commercial success his father had dreamed of, but they'd gotten by. They were booked an average of thirty weeks of the year. Financially they were solvent. That was his mother's doing. She'd always had a knack for making five dollars stretch into ten.

It was Molly, he was certain, who had tucked a hundred dollars in fives and tens into the pocket of his suitcase a dozen years before. She'd known he was going. She hadn't wept or lectured or pleaded, but she had done what she could to make it easier for him. That was her way.

But Pop… Trace closed his eyes as the plane shuddered a bit with turbulence. Pop had never, would never, forgive him—not for leaving without a word, but for leaving.

He'd never understood Trace's need to find something of his own, to look for something other than the next audience, the next arrangement. Perhaps in truth he'd never been able to understand his son at all, or in understanding, hadn't been able to accept.

The only time Trace had gone back, hoping perhaps to mend a small portion of his fences, Frank had greeted him with tight-lipped disapproval.

"So you've come back." Frank had stood icily rigid in the tiny dressing room he'd shared with Molly. Trace hadn't known that his presence had made Frank see it for what it was. A dim little room in a second-rate club. "Three years since you walked out, and only a letter now and again. I told you when you left, there'd be no fatted calf for you."

"I didn't expect one." But he'd hoped for some understanding. Trace had worn a beard then, part of an affectation he'd grown for an assignment. The assignment had taken him to Paris, where he'd successfully broken up an international art fraud. "Since it was Mom's birthday, I thought… I wanted to see her." And you—but he couldn't say it.

"Then run off again so she can shed more tears?"

"She understood why I left," Trace had said carefully.

"You broke her heart." And mine. "You're not going to hurt her again. You're either a son to her, or you're not."

"Either the son you want me to be, or nothing," Trace had corrected, pacing the cramped little room. "It still doesn't matter to you what I need or feel, or what I am."

"You don't know what matters to me. I think you never

did." Frank had to swallow the obstruction in his throat that was part bitterness and part shame. "The last time I saw you, you told me what I'd done for you hadn't been good enough. That what I could give you never would be. A man doesn't forget hearing that from his son."

He was twenty-three. He'd slept with a whore in Bangkok and gotten roaring drunk on ouzo in Athens, and he had eight stitches in his right shoulder from a knife wielded by a man he'd killed while serving his country. Yet at that moment he felt like a child being scolded without justice or cause.

"I guess that's the only thing I ever said to you that you really heard. Nothing's changed here. It never will."

"You've chosen your way, Trace." His son had no way of knowing that Frank wanted nothing more than to open his arms and take back what he'd thought he'd lost forever. And was afraid Trace would only turn away. "Now you'll have to make the best of it. At least have the decency to say goodbye to your mother and sisters this time."

It had been Frank, his eyes blurred with tears, who had turned away. Trace had walked out of the dressing room and had never gone back.

He opened his eyes now to find Gillian watching him steadily. She looked different with the short, dark wig he'd made her wear. But she'd stopped complaining about it— and the horn-rimmed glasses and drab, dun-colored dress. It was padded to make her look frumpy, but he couldn't quite get his mind off what was hidden underneath. In any case, she'd blend into the scenery, which was just what he wanted.

No one would mistake the woman sitting beside him for the spectacular-looking Doctor Gillian Fitzpatrick.

He'd switched planes and airlines in San Diego, charging the tickets to a credit card under one of his cover names.

After rerouting in Dallas, he'd picked up the fielder's cap and sideline jacket he was wearing. Now, as they headed into Chicago, they looked like a couple of dazed, weary tourists who wouldn't rate a second glance.

Except he could see her eyes, those deep, dark, intense green eyes through the clear lenses.

"Problem?" he asked.

"I was going to ask you the same thing. You know, you've been brooding ever since we boarded."

He pulled out a cigarette and played with it. "I don't know what you're talking about."

"I'm talking about the fact that you're ready to bite my head off if I so much as say pass the salt. I'm wearing this hideous wig, aren't I? And this very fashionable dress."

"Looks great."

"Then if you're not upset about my disguise, what is it?"

"Nothing's wrong with me," he said between his teeth. "Now back off."

Holding on to her temper, Gillian sipped the white wine she'd been served—with a pitying look from the flight attendant, she thought with some disgust. "There certainly is something wrong with you. I'm the one who should be having an anxiety attack, but I'm not, because we're actually doing something. But if there's a problem... I should be concerned about, I'd appreciate you telling me."

His finger tapped on the armrest between them. "Do you always nag?"

"When it's important. Lives are at stake, lives that mean the world to me. If you're worried about something, then I need to know."

"It's personal." Hoping to dismiss it, he pushed back his seat and closed his eyes.

"Nothing's personal now. How you feel will affect your performance."

He opened one eye. "You'd be the first woman to complain, sister."

She flushed, but didn't let up. "I consider myself your employer, and as such, I refuse to have you keep secrets from me."

He swore at her, quietly but with considerable imagination. "I haven't been back in a while. Even I have memories, and they're my business."

"I'm sorry." She took a deep breath. "I haven't been able to think about anything but Flynn and Caitlin. It never occurred to me that this might be difficult for you." He didn't seem like a man of deep feelings or genuine emotions. But she remembered the pain in his eyes when she'd spoken of Forrester. "Chicago…is it a special place for you?"

"Played Chicago when I was twelve, and again when I was sixteen."

"Played?"

"Nothing." He shook his head and tried to relax. "I spent a few days there with Charlie a few years back. Last thing I saw of the States was O'Hare Airport."

"Now it'll be the first thing you see again." She had a magazine in her lap, but instead of opening it she just ran a thumb along its edge. "I've never seen much of America except New York. I've always meant to. Flynn brought Caitlin to visit a couple of years ago, just after her mother died." She let out a long breath. "They were both like lost souls. We went up the Empire State Building and to Rockefeller Center and had tea at the Plaza. Flynn bought her a little windup dog from a street merchant. She slept with it every night." The emotion came so quickly, she could do nothing to block it. "Oh, God." She pressed both hands to her face. "Oh, God, she's only six."

There hadn't been a woman in his life to comfort in too many years to count, but he hadn't forgotten how. "Take it easy." His voice was soft as he put an arm around her. "They're not going to hurt her. They need your brother's cooperation too much to risk it."

"But what are they doing to her inside? She must be so frightened. The dark— She still can't sleep in the dark. Would they give her a light? Do you think they'd give her a light?"

"Sure they would." His hand stroked her hair just as his voice stroked her fears. "She's going to be fine, Gillian."

Tears ran down her cheeks even as she struggled to calm herself. "I'm sorry. The last thing I want to do is make a fool of myself."

"Go ahead." His hand ran rhythmically over her shoulder. "I don't mind."

With a watery laugh, she fumbled for a tissue. "I try not to think of her too much. I try to concentrate on Flynn. He's very strong and capable."

"And he's with her. He's taking care of her."

"Aye, they're taking care of each other." God, she needed to believe that. She needed to believe that before long she'd see them, whole and healthy and safe. "We're going to get them out, aren't we?"

There were no promises in this kind of game. He knew that better than most. But she was looking at him now with brimming eyes and such desperate trust that he had no choice. "Sure we are. Didn't Charlie tell you I was the best?"

"He did." She let out a little breath. Control was back, but she didn't have as tight a grip on it as she would have liked. If she didn't think about something else, every minute that passed seemed like an hour. "Tell me about your family. Do you have brothers?"

"No." He drew his arm away, because it would have been entirely too easy to leave it around her. "Sisters."

"How many?"

"Three."

"That must have made life interesting."

"They were okay." His lips curved as he lit a cigarette. "Chantel was the brat."

"Every family has one," she began. Then it hit her, and she sat up straight. "Chantel O'Hurley? Chantel O'Hurley's your sister? I've seen her movies. She's wonderful."

The pride came, more intense than he'd expected. "She's okay. Always leaned toward the dramatic."

"She's the most beautiful woman I've ever seen."

"And knows it."

"Then Maddy O'Hurley's your sister, too." More than a little stunned, Gillian shook her head. "I saw her on Broadway a few months ago. She's very talented. The stage just lights up when she's on it."

It always did, Trace thought. "She's nominated for a Tony."

"She deserves it. Why, the audience nearly brought down the roof when she went into the number at the end of the first act. You should have seen…" Her words trailed off when she realized that he should indeed have seen, but, for reasons yet unknown to her, hadn't. "Your third sister?" she asked, wanting to give him both time and room.

"Abby raises horses in Virginia." He crushed out his cigarette and wondered how he'd ever gotten started on his family.

"Yes, I think I read something about her. She married Dylan Crosby, the writer, recently. There was a write-up in the *Times*. Oh, of course, triplets. Your sisters are triplets."

"I thought scientists would be too busy causing and solving the ills of the world to read gossip columns."

She lifted a brow and decided against taking offense. At least until she'd learned everything she wanted to know.

"I don't keep my head buried in a test tube. The article mentioned that they grew up in show business, traveling around the country. Your parents still do. I don't remember reading anything about you."

"I've been gone a long time, remember?"

"But didn't you travel with them?" Intrigued by the idea, she smiled and shifted in her chair. "Did you sing and dance and live out of a trunk?"

"You know, for a doctor, you tend to glamorize the mundane." He felt the slight dip that meant they were starting their descent. "It's like going to the circus and seeing only the spangles and the red lights. Backstage there are elephant paddies up to your ankles."

"So you did travel with them." Gillian continued to smile. "Did you have a speciality?"

"God save me from plane rides with nosy women. I've been out of it for twelve years." He jerked his seat belt on. "I prefer thinking about today."

Gillian clicked her own belt into place. "I wanted to be a singer when I was a little girl. I always pictured myself in the spotlight." With a little sigh, she slipped the magazine back into the pocket of the seat. "Before I knew it, I was my father's lab assistant. Strange, isn't it, how our parents seem to map out our routes even before we're born?"

Charlie's house was behind a five-foot stone wall and was equipped with an elaborate security system. He left behind, as far as Trace knew, only an older sister who lived in Palm Beach and a nephew who ran a brokerage firm somewhere in the Midwest.

Gillian sat in the rented car while Trace pressed a series of buttons on the panel outside the gates. They opened soundlessly. He hadn't spoken since the airport, not once during all the cruising and backtracking, looking for signs of surveillance or a tail. She was holding back her questions now. It was grief that silenced him here, and she knew he'd have to deal with it in his own way.

The trees were fading as winter closed in, but they still held a stubborn touch of color. Wind tore at the leaves and moaned through the branches. The elms would shade the drive in the summer, she thought, giving the old brick house a stately, sturdy feel. It was something she'd barely noticed on her first trip here, and it was something that she tried to concentrate on now.

The house didn't look deserted, but as if it were simply waiting to be occupied again. She thought of the man who had listened to her, who had given her brandy and a sliver of hope.

"He was crazy about this place," Trace murmured. He shut off the engine but sat looking at the two stories of worn brick and white trim. "Whenever he was away, he'd always talk about coming back. I guess he'd have wanted to die here." He sat a moment longer, then pushed open his door. "Let's go."

He had keys. Charlie had given them to him once.

"Use them sometime," he'd said. "Everybody has to have a home."

But he hadn't used them, not until now. The key slipped into the lock and turned with a quiet click.

The hallway was dim, but he didn't switch on the lights. He remembered the way well enough, and in truth he didn't yet have the heart to look at anything of Charlie's too closely.

He took her into a library that smelled of lemon and leather. The heat had been turned down because there was no one left to need the warmth. "You can wait here."

"Where are you going?"

"I told you I was coming here to find out where they

took your brother. I'm going to find out, and you're going to wait here."

"And I told you that I'm involved with anything that has to do with Flynn. Besides, I might be able to help."

"If I need a physicist, I'll let you know. Read a book."

"I'm not staying here."

She was two steps behind him when he reached the doorway. "Look, Doc, there's such a thing as national security. I'm already bending the rules because Charlie seemed to think it was worth it."

"Then bend them a little more." She took his arm. "I'm not interested in state secrets and international affairs. All I want is to know where my brother is. I've worked on sensitive projects, Trace. I have clearance."

"You keep interfering with me, it's going to take a lot longer."

"I don't think so."

"Have it your way. But keep your mouth shut for once." He went up the stairs, trying to convince himself he wasn't making a mistake.

The carpet was new since Trace had been there, but the wallpaper was the same. So was the room three doors from the top of the stairs that Charlie had used for an office. Without hesitating, Trace went to the desk and pushed a button under the second drawer. A four-foot span of paneling swung out.

"Another tunnel?" Gillian asked. Her courage was fading fast.

"Workroom," Trace said as he stepped through. He threw a switch and discovered that Charlie had updated his equipment.

Along the top of the far wall were clocks, still running, that gave the time in every zone around the globe. The computer system spread beneath them, then continued in an L along the next wall. With the radio equipment opposite it, he could have contacted anyone from the local deejay to the Kremlin. "Pull up a stool, Doc. This could take a while."

Gillian jolted only a bit when the panel slid shut behind them. "What are you trying to do?"

"You want to bypass some paperwork, so I'm going to patch into the ISS computer."

"Do you think they know where Flynn was taken?"

"Maybe, maybe not." He switched on the terminal and sat. "But they should have a pretty good idea where Hammer's new headquarters are. Charlie had to go and get state-of-the-art on me." He punched a series of buttons. When the machine requested his code, he gave Charlie's. "Okay, that's a start. Let's see what this baby can do."

He worked in silence, but for the tapping of his fingers and the beeping of the machine, as Gillian looked on. He inched past one security block to ram into the next.

Patience, Gillian noted, more than a little surprised to find he had the quality, as he broke one code and slowly drew out more data. She began to find a rhythm to the numbers and symbols that appeared on the screen, then blinked out again, at Trace's command. As he worked, she began arranging and rearranging the system in her head.

"So damn close," Trace muttered as he tried another series. "The problem is there are enough variables to keep me at it for a week."

"Maybe if you—"

"I work alone."

"I was only going to say that—"

"Why don't you go down to the kitchen and dig up some coffee, sweetheart?"

Her eyes narrowed at the tone, and temper trembled on

the tip of her tongue. "Fine." She whirled and faced the closed panel. "I don't know how to open the door."

"Button's on the left. Just put your finger on it and push."

Her mouth opened again, but, all too aware of what might come flying out, she pushed the button.

Typical hardheaded, egocentric male, Gillian decided as she marched down the stairs. Hadn't she lived with one, tried to please one, nearly all of her life? Why had fate decreed that in this, the most important thing she'd ever had to do, she'd be chained to another man who had no use for her opinion.

Make coffee, she thought as she found the kitchen. And if he called her sweetheart one more time, she'd give him what men like him deserved. The back of a woman's hand.

She started the coffee, too incensed to feel uncomfortable with rooting through a dead man's cupboards.

He'd had no business dismissing her. Just as he'd had no business kissing her the way he had. It had felt as if she were being devoured. And yet when it had finished she'd been whole. It had felt as if she'd been drugged. And yet her mind had been clear, her senses sharp.

However she'd felt, however it had finished, she would never be quite the same. She could admit that here, alone, to herself. She was too practical a woman for self-deception. Her feelings were perhaps more easily touched, perhaps more readily given, than she would have preferred, but they were her feelings, and she would never have denied them. She'd enjoyed the feel and taste of Trace's lips on hers. She would remember it for a long time. But she was also an expert on self-discipline. Enjoyable or not, she wouldn't allow it to happen again.

Trace was still working when she came back into the room. Without ceremony, she slammed the coffee cup down next to him. He acknowledged her with a grunt. Gillian took a turn around the room, told herself to keep her mouth shut, then jammed her hands into her pockets.

"Access, number 38537/BAKER. Tabulate access code five. Series ARSS28." Gillian blurted the series out almost like an obscenity. "And if you're not too pigheaded to try it, it may work. If not, switch the first number sequence with the second."

Trace lifted his coffee, pleased she'd left it black, surprised she'd made it well. "And what makes you think you can figure out the access code to one of the most sophisticated computer systems in the free world?"

"Because I've been watching you for the past hour and I do a little hacking as a hobby."

"A little hacking." He drank again. "Broken into any good Swiss bank accounts?"

She crossed the room slowly, almost, Trace thought not without admiration, the way a gunslinger might approach a showdown. "We're talking about my family, remember? Add to that the fact that I'm paying you, and the least you could do is try my suggestion."

"Fine." Willing to humor her to a point, Trace tapped out the sequence she'd recited.

ACCESS DENIED

With only a slight smirk, he gestured toward the screen.

"All right, then, transpose the numbers." Impatient, she reached around him and began hitting the keys herself. The only thing Trace noticed for a moment was that his shampoo smelled entirely different on her.

REQUEST FILE

"There we are." Pleased with herself, Gillian leaned closer. "It's rather like working out a system for blackjack. A professor and I played around with that last semester."

"Remind me to take you with me the next time I go to Monte Carlo."

They were closer. One step closer. Smiling, she turned her face to his. "What now?"

There wasn't a hint of amber or gray in her eyes. They were pure green and brilliant now. Even as he watched them, they changed, filling with speculation, awareness, memory. "You talking about the computer?"

She needed to swallow badly. "Of course."

"Just checking." Trace turned away again. They both let out a quiet breath. He began typing, and within seconds data came up on the screen.

He moved from screen to screen. After all, he knew quite a bit about Hammer already. He'd been briefed intensely before he'd gone undercover, and had learned more during his stint as a low-level delivery boy. During his assignment, he'd managed to pass along names, places and dates to the ISS, and he'd been on the verge of being transferred to the newly implemented main base before he'd been shot.

Frowning at the screen, he rubbed a thumb over the scar.

But he'd been sedated for days, hanging between life and death. His recovery had taken two months of hospital care. He'd been debriefed, the assignment had been blown and he'd taken off for a long—supposedly peaceful—vacation.

Quite a bit could change in two or three months. Charlie, being Charlie, would have keyed into it.

He breezed by the basic data. Hammer had been founded in the Middle East in the early seventies. With a combination of luck and money, and a complete disregard for life, they had pulled off a number of bombings, taken hostages. The last hijacking the organization had attempted had ended with someone's itchy finger pushing a detonator and blowing eighty-five innocent people and six terrorists to oblivion.

That was their style, he thought. Win some, lose some.

"Husad," Gillian said, honing in on one name as Trace flipped screens. "Isn't he the leader?"

"He's the one with the bucks. Jamar Husad, political outcast, self-proclaimed general and complete lunatic. Come on, Charlie," he muttered at the machine. "Give me something."

"You're hardly looking," she began.

"I already know all this."

"How?"

"I worked for them for six months," he said half to himself.

"You *what*?" She took a step back.

Annoyance flickered in his eyes as he glanced up. "Relax, sweetheart, all for the good of the cause. I infiltrated."

"But if you were inside, then you should know where they would have taken Flynn and Caitlin. Why are we fooling with this computer when—"

"Because they moved. They were just getting set up in the new location when I got taken out."

"Taken out?" Puzzlement veered into horror. "You were shot?"

"Part of the job description."

"You were nearly killed—a scar like that…" She trailed off and laid a hand on his shoulder. "You were nearly killed by those people, but you're doing this."

He shook her hand away. He couldn't afford to let her feelings soften toward him. Then it would be too easy to let his soften toward her. "I got a personal investment here. There's a matter of a hundred thousand—my ticket to paradise."

She curled her fingers into her palm. "Do you expect me to believe you're only doing this for the money?"

"Believe what you like, but keep it to yourself. I've never known anybody who asks so many questions. I'm trying to concentrate. Yeah, yeah," he muttered. "I know they were in Cairo, that's old—

"All *right*. I knew I could count on Charlie." Trace leaned back. "New base of operations: Morocco."

"Morocco? Could they have taken Flynn and Caitlin all that way?"

"They'd want the best security for them. In Morocco, Hammer would have allies close." He continued to flip from screen to screen until he came to the end of the file. "Nothing on your brother here yet." He instructed the computer to print out the pages that interested him, then turned to Gillian. "It would only take a phone call to bring the ISS in on this. I want you to think about it."

She had thought about it, worried about it. "Why didn't Mr. Forrester do that?"

"I've got some ideas."

"But you're not going to tell me what they are."

"Not yet. Like you said, it's your family, you make the choice."

She moved away from him. It was more logical to call the ISS. They were an organization with sophisticated equipment, with manpower, with political clout. And yet... Every instinct told her to go with this one man, the man Charles Forrester had called a renegade. With her hands linked, Gillian turned to him. He still didn't look like a hero. And she was still going with her instincts.

"One hundred thousand, Mr. O'Hurley, and I go with you every step of the way."

"I told you I work alone."

"Perhaps you haven't seen me at my best, but I'm a very strong and capable woman. If I have to, I'll go to Morocco alone."

"You wouldn't last a day."

"Maybe not. Hammer's agents are looking for me. If they find me, they'll take me to my brother. At least that way I'd know he and my niece were all right. I'd rather do it another way."

He stood up to do some pacing himself. She'd slow him down, but not by much. And if she stayed with him, he'd be able to keep an eye on her. He couldn't deny she'd held up in Mexico. If he had to play that kind of game again, he could use her.

"We go together, it doesn't mean we're partners, it means you take orders."

Gillian inclined her head but didn't say anything.

"When the time comes for me to move, you stay out of the way. I won't be able to worry about you then."

"You won't have to worry about me." She took a deep breath. "What do we do now?"

"First I check with Rory." He moved to the phone. "But I have a feeling we're catching a plane."

Chapter 4

Casablanca. Bogart and Bergman. Pirates and intrigue. Foggy airports and sun-washed beaches. The name conjured up images of danger and romance. Gillian was determined to accept the first and avoid the second.

Trace had booked adjoining rooms in one of the more exclusive hotels near United Nations Square. Gillian remained silent while he spoke to the desk clerk in fluent French and was addressed as Monsieur Cabot.

André Cabot was the name on the passport he was using now. He wore a conservative three-piece suit and shoes that had a mirror gleam. His brown-rinsed hair was a bit mussed from the drive, but he'd shaved. He stood differently, too, she noted. Ramrod-straight, as though he'd come through some military academy. Even his personality had changed, she thought as she stood to the side and let him deal with the details of checking in. He'd slipped so effortlessly into the role of the brusque, slightly impatient

French businessman, she could almost believe she'd lost Trace O'Hurley along the way and picked up someone else.

For the second time she felt as if she were putting her life into the hands of a stranger.

But the eyes were the same. A little shock passed through her when he turned and looked at her with the dark intensity she recognized but had yet to become accustomed to.

She remained silent as Trace took her arm and led her to a bank of elevators. Gillian still wore the wig, but the glasses were gone and the drab dress was replaced by an elegant silk outfit more suited to the image of Cabot's current mistress. Twenty stories later they were entering their suite and he hadn't said a word. Trace passed bills to the bell man in a slow, methodical fashion that indicated that he was a man who counted his francs.

She expected Cabot to disappear the moment the door was closed, but instead he spoke to her in lightly accented English. "For rooms of this price, the sheets should be threaded with gold."

"What—"

"See if the bar is stocked, *chérie*." He was moving around the room, checking lamps, lifting pictures from the wall. He turned to her only briefly, with a warning glance. "I would prefer a small glass of vermouth before I have the pleasure of undressing your lovely body." He picked up the phone, unscrewed the mouthpiece, and then, after a quick search, fastened it again.

"Would you?" She understood he was staying in character until he was certain there was no surveillance equipment in the rooms. Though it was unnerving, she accepted it. It was only the fact that he'd portrayed his character and hers as lovers that grated. Deciding two could play, she moved to a small wet bar and opened a cabinet door.

"I'm more than happy to fix you a drink, sweetheart." She saw his brow lift as he checked the headboard, then the mattress. "But, as to the rest, I'm a bit tired after the flight."

"Then we'll have to see what can be done to bring your energy back." Satisfied the first room was clean, Trace walked to her. There was a long moment of silence before he accepted the glass she'd poured. "Let's move into the next room," he murmured, then turned and left her to follow. "Perhaps you're not as tired as you think."

As he began the same procedure on the second room, Gillian sat on the bed. "It was a long flight."

"Then you should rest. Let me help you." He lifted a print of the Cathedral of the Sacré Coeur. His hands, long-fingered and sure, ran over the frame and the back. "You'll rest better unconfined."

Gillian slipped out of her shoes to massage her arches. "You seem to have only one thing on your mind."

"A man would be foolish to have more than one thing on his mind once alone with you."

Gillian considered a moment. Perhaps she could grow to like this André Cabot. "Really?" She lifted the glass he'd discarded and sipped from it. "Why?"

He'd come closer to check the headboard. Pausing a moment, he looked at her. There was a grin on her face that said, "I dare you." She should have known better. "Because you have skin like a white rose that grows only warmer and softer when I touch you." His hand brushed her thigh, making her jolt. Trace continued to check the mattress, but his eyes stayed on hers. "Because your hair is fire and silk, and when I kiss you... When I kiss you, *ma belle,* your lips are the same."

Her breath caught as he circled his hand around her neck. He leaned closer so that when it was released again it mingled with his. "Because when I touch you like this I can feel how much you want me. Because when I look at you I can see you're afraid."

She couldn't look away. She couldn't move away. "I'm not afraid of you." But she was fascinated. Whoever he was, he fascinated.

"No? You should be."

She didn't notice that his voice had changed, had become his own again, just before his mouth closed over hers. It was the same heat, the same strength, as before. Had it only been once before? she thought as her body went fluid, sliding beneath his onto the bed. Without a thought to reason, without a thought to consequences, she wrapped her arms around him.

Why did it seem so easy? His mouth was hard and hot, his hands were anything but gentle. And yet it seemed so easy to be with him now, so natural. So familiar. Surely his taste was a taste she'd woken to before. If she ran her hands over his back, she knew what muscles she would find. If she drew in a breath so that the scent of him filled her, it would be no surprise.

Perhaps she had known his face for only a matter of days. But there was something here that she had known all her life.

He must be going mad. It was as though she'd always been there for him. Would always be there. The feel of her body beneath his wasn't like that of any other woman. It was like that of the only woman. He knew, somehow, how her sigh would sound before he heard it, how her fingers would feel on his face before she lifted them to touch him.

He knew, he expected, yet it still stunned.

He could feel his pulse speed up until it beat in hundreds of points throughout his body. He could hear his own crazed murmuring of her name as he tore his mouth from hers to let it roam desperately over her face and throat. Then there was the need, growing to a rage inside him that was nothing like the desire he'd felt for other women.

He wanted all of her, mind, body, soul. He wanted her now. He wanted her for a lifetime.

It was that shocking thought that stopped him. There were no guaranteed lifetimes, especially not in the game he'd chosen to play. He'd learned to live for the moment. Tomorrow was up for grabs.

Whatever she was doing to him had to stop—if he wanted to live to collect his hundred thousand.

He ached. He could have hated her for that, but he rolled off her with a carelessness that left her still and speechless. "The room's clean." He picked up the glass to drain the last of the vermouth. And wished it was whiskey.

Her breathing was uneven, and her limbs were unsteady. There was nothing she could do about that, or about the unsated need crawling inside her. But she could hate him. With her whole heart and soul she could hate him.

"You bastard."

"You asked for it, sweetheart." He pulled out a cigarette and focused his mind on what lay ahead, instead of what had lain beneath him only moments before. "I've got some things to do. Why don't you take a nap?"

She came off the bed slowly, with the look in her eye that he'd noted before. It occurred to him that it was fortunate for both of them that his weapons were out of sight and reach.

She'd been humiliated before. She'd been rejected before. But she didn't intend to be either at his hands ever again. "Don't you ever touch me. I'll put up with your crude manners because I have no choice, but don't you ever put your hands on me again."

He wasn't sure why he did it. Anger had a way of urging

a man to make a wrong and reckless move. He yanked her against him, even enjoying her fast and furious struggles as he clamped his mouth down on hers again. She was wild-fire now, hot, volatile and dangerous. He had an image, steamy and strong, of pulling her to the bed and letting violence feed violence. Before he could top one mistake with another, he let her go.

"I don't take orders, Gillian. Remember that."

Her hands curled into fists. Only the knowledge that she'd lose kept her from landing a blow. "There'll come a time you'll pay for that."

"Probably. Right now, I'm going out. Stay inside."

When the door closed behind him, she had the small satisfaction of cursing him.

He was gone only an hour. Most of Casablanca was as he remembered it. The little shops along the Boulevard Hansali still catered to the tourist trade. The port was still busy with European ships. He had walked through the original Arab town, still surrounded by old rampart walls. But he hadn't gone sightseeing. His contact in the bidon-ville, the shantytown near the shopping district, had been pleased to see him again, and agreeable enough after an exchange of a few dirham to give birth to a certain rumor about a hijacked shipment of American arms.

Trace arrived back at the hotel, satisfied that the first step had been taken and ready to start the next. The rooms were empty. He didn't panic, not at first. His training was a natural extension of his mind, just as his arm was a nat-ural extension of his body.

After unstrapping his revolver from his calf, he began to search both rooms and baths. The balcony doors were still locked from the inside, though the curtains had been drawn. She'd taken her things out of his suitcase. Trace found them neatly put away in closets and drawers. The cosmetics she'd bought to replace those she'd lost stood on the counter in the bath. There were bath salts the color of sea foam, and a short cotton robe shades darker hanging on the back of the door.

Her purse was gone, and so were the notes inside it. The drumming at the back of his neck, slow and steady, was growing louder.

There was no sign of a struggle. It was hard for him to believe that a woman like Gillian would have submitted to anyone without a fight. It was just as difficult for him to believe that anyone could have traced them so quickly.

So where the hell was she? Trace thought as he felt the first twinges of panic. He ran a hand through his hair and tried to think calmly. If they had her… If they had her, then he would…

He couldn't think calmly when he kept seeing how Abdul had dragged her up by the hair. He couldn't think calmly when he remembered how her blood had felt on his hands.

When he heard the key in the lock, he whirled. It took only an instant to pull back control. Before the knob turned, he was behind the door, gun pointed up, body tensed. As the door opened, he grabbed a wrist. And yanked Gillian inside. Both of them received a shock when he dragged her into his arms.

"Damn it, where were you? Are you all right?"

She'd drawn in her breath to scream. The collision with Trace had knocked the air out of her again. She managed to nod, and then, feeling the tension in his body, she soothed him automatically.

"I'm fine." She ran a hand over his back. "Did something happen? I was only gone a few minutes."

And in a few minutes his imagination had worked at

top speed. Trace cursed himself, then her. "I told you to stay inside. What the hell's wrong with you?" Furious with himself, he shoved her away. "I don't have time to babysit, damn it. When I give an order, you're to follow it."

To think she'd felt a flow of concern, Gillian thought, berating herself. She'd even felt a warmth at what she'd thought was his concern for her. Both those emotions froze quickly enough. "I hired you to find my brother, not to spend every spare moment shouting at me."

"If you'd show some sense, I wouldn't have to shout at you. You've been cut once, sweetheart." He could only hope the memory of that would shake her as much as it did him. "Keep this up and I might not be around next time to make sure it's not any worse than that."

"You're not my bodyguard. In any case, you're the one who went off without telling me where you were going or how long you'd be."

He didn't care to be reminded why he'd left so abruptly. "Listen, sister, the only reason you're here with me is because I might be able to use you to get your brother out. You won't be of much use if they've already got you."

"No one has me," she tossed back as she hurled her purse on the bed. "I'm here, aren't I?"

He hated to argue with logic. "I told you to stay inside. If you can't do what you're told, you're going to find yourself on the first plane back to New York."

"I go where I want, when I want." She planted her feet and almost hoped he'd try to put his hands on her again. "But, for your information, I did stay inside."

"That's strange. I could have sworn I pulled you into the room a few minutes ago."

"That you did, and nearly dislocated my shoulder in the process." She yanked a small bottle out of the bag she carried. "Aspirin, O'Hurley. There's a gift shop off the lobby downstairs, and I had a headache. Now, if you'll excuse me, I think I'm about ready to take the whole bottle." She stormed across the room. The bathroom door shut with a resounding slam.

Women, Trace thought as he strode into the adjoining room. He rarely thought they were more trouble than they were worth, but he was making an exception in Gillian's case.

After nearly a dozen years of fieldwork, he was still alive. And that was why he was considering retiring more and more seriously. The law of averages was against him. He was a man who believed in fate and believed in luck just as passionately. Sooner or later luck ran out. As it had for Charlie.

Lighting a cigarette, he stood at the window and looked out at Casablanca. The last time he'd been here it had had to do with smuggling. He'd nearly gotten his throat cut, but luck had still been with him. He'd been Cabot then, as well, the French businessman who didn't mind a shady—if profitable—deal.

His cover would hold. The ISS had invented it with the meticulousness they were best at. His nerve would hold, as long as he remembered that the woman in the next room was a means to an end and nothing more.

He heard the water running in Gillian's bath and checked his watch. He'd give her an hour to stew. Then they had business to attend to.

Gillian's temper wasn't the kind that flashed quickly and vanished. She knew how to hold it off, and how to nurse it along when it suited her. At the moment, she was reaping enormous satisfaction from keeping herself on the edge of fury. It gave her energy and blocked her fear.

She told herself she wasn't the least bit concerned about

what was going on in the room next door as she changed into a simple blouse and skirt.

He probably intended to make her stay locked up in her room, eating a solitary dinner from room service. She attached a wide leather belt almost as if it were a holster. She'd be damned if she'd hole up here like a mouse. She might not be sure what she could do to help with Flynn's and Caitlin's release, but there had to be something. Trace O'Hurley was going to have to accept the fact that she was part of this thing. Starting now.

She moved to the door that joined the rooms and nearly ran into him.

"I was just coming in to see if you'd stopped sulking."

Her chin angled. "I never sulk."

"Sure you do, but since you've apparently finished we can go."

She opened her mouth, then shut it again. He'd said *we*. "Where?"

"To see a friend of mine." Eyes narrowed, he backed up to look at her. "Is that what you're wearing?"

Her automatic response was to look down at the wide circle skirt and blouse. "What's wrong with it?"

"Nothing, if you're going to tea at the rectory." While she sputtered and slapped at his hand, Trace unfastened two more buttons. He stood back, frowned, then nodded. "Helps a little."

"I've no desire to display myself for your benefit."

"Personally, I don't give a damn if you wear a cardboard box, but you've got a role to play. Don't you have any gaudy earrings?"

"No."

"Then we'll get some. And darker lipstick," he muttered before he stepped back. "Can you do anything with your eyes?"

"My eyes? What's wrong with my eyes?" Natural feminine vanity began to war with bafflement as Trace strode into her bath.

"Cabot's woman hasn't come straight out of a convent, know what I mean?" As he began to root through her cosmetics, she shoved him aside.

"No. Just what do you mean?"

"I mean you need a little more paint, a little more cleavage and a little less breeding." He picked up a smoky green eye shadow, examined it, then held it out. "Here, try for tart, will you?"

"Tart?" The word came out of her mouth with beautiful Irish indignation. "Tart, is it? Do you really believe I'd paint myself up so you can display me like a...like a..."

"Bimbo is what I had in mind. A nice-looking, empty-headed bimbo." He picked up her scent and gave the atomizer a squeeze. It smelled warmer on her skin, he thought, and he quickly pulled himself back. "This is drawing room stuff. Is this the only perfume you have?"

She unclenched her teeth only because it hurt to keep them clamped together. "It is."

"It'll have to do, then," he decided and sprayed it at her. "The hair, Doc."

She touched a hand to her wig almost protectively. "What's wrong with it?"

"Mess it up. The guy I'm going to see would expect me to travel with a pretty, empty-headed and very sexy woman. That's Cabot's style."

This time her eyes narrowed. "Oh, it is, is it?"

"Right. And you have to look the part. Don't you have anything slinky?"

"No, I don't have anything slinky." Her lower lip moved into a pout as she turned to look at herself in the mirror. "I wasn't coming on this trip to socialize."

"I've never known a woman not to have something slinky."

If looks really could have killed, he would have dropped like a stone. "You've never known this one."

Taking it in stride, Trace reached for her blouse again. "Well, maybe one more button."

"No." She pulled her blouse together. "I'm not parading around half dressed so you can keep up your image." Teeth gritted, she snatched the eye shadow from him. "Go away. I don't want you hovering over me."

"Five minutes," he told her, and with his hands in his pockets he strolled out of the bath.

She took ten, but he decided not to quibble. Anger had brought on a flush that she'd added to with blusher. She'd used shadow and liner liberally so that her eyes were big as saucers and had that heavy bedroom look.

He'd wanted flamboyant, and she'd delivered. For the life of him, he couldn't figure out why it made him angry.

"Cheap enough for you, Monsieur Cabot?"

"It'll do," he said, already at the door. "Let's go."

She felt like a fool, and as far as she was concerned she looked the part. Still, she had to remind herself she wasn't being left behind to worry and fret while Trace went about the business of finding Flynn. Drawing a breath, Gillian told herself that if she was playing a part she should play it well.

As they stepped out of the hotel, Gillian tucked her arm through his and leaned against him. He gave her a quick, wary look that had her smiling. "Am I supposed to be crazy about you?"

"About my money, anyway."

"Oh, are you rich?"

"Loaded."

She looked over her shoulder as she stepped into a cab. "Then why don't I have any jewelry?"

A smart aleck, he thought, and wished he didn't like her better for it. He put his hand firmly on her bottom. "You haven't earned it yet, sweetheart."

The makeup couldn't disguise the fire and challenge that leaped into her eyes. Because he'd gotten the last word, he felt a great deal better as he settled into the cab beside her. He gave the driver an address, then turned to her. "Speak any French?"

"Only enough to know whether I'm ordering calf's brains or chicken in a restaurant."

"Just as well. Keep your mouth shut and let me do the talking. You're not supposed to be too bright, in any case."

He was telling her to keep her mouth shut too often for her taste. "I've already deduced that your taste in women runs to the type in men's magazines. Glossy and two-dimensional."

"As long as they don't talk back. If you have to say anything, ditch the Irish. You've lived in New York long enough to have picked up the tone."

They were driving out of the section of the city marked by hotels and large, modern shops. Inland from the port and harbor was the old medina, the original Arab town, enclosed by walls and mazed with narrow streets. At any other time, it would have fascinated her. She would have wanted to get out and look, smell, touch. Now it was only a place where a clue might be found.

Trace—or Cabot, as Gillian was training herself to think of him—paid off the cab. She stepped out to look at the hodgepodge of little shops and the mix of tourists they catered to.

The charm was there, the age, the Arab flavor. Exotic colors, open bazaars, men in robes. The avenue was shaded, the shop windows were crammed with souvenirs and silks and local crafts. The women she saw were for the most part European, unveiled and trousered. The wind was mild and carried the scents of the water, of spice, and of garbage left too long.

"It's so different." With her arm tucked through Trace's again, she began to walk. "You read about such places, but it's nothing like seeing them. It's so…exotic."

He thought of the bidonville he'd visited that afternoon, the squatters' shacks, the squalor hardly a stone's throw away from charming streets and neat shops. A slum was a slum, whatever the language or culture.

"We're going in here." Trace stopped in front of a jeweler's with gold and silver and brightly polished gems in the window. "Smile and look stupid."

Gillian lifted a brow. "I'm not sure I'm that talented, but I'll do my best."

The bells on the door of the shop jingled when it opened. Behind the counter was a man with a face like a burnt almond and hair growing white in patches. He glanced up, and recognition came quickly into his eyes before he went back to the customers bargaining over a bracelet. Trace simply linked his hands behind his back and studied the wares in a display case.

The shop was hardly more than ten feet by twelve, with a backroom closed off by a beaded curtain. There was music playing, something with pipes and flutes that made Gillian think of a tune shepherds might play to their flocks. The scent in here was all spice—cloves and ginger—and a paddle fan lazily twirled the air around and around.

The floor was wooden and scarred. Though the jewelry gleamed, most of the glass was dull and finger-marked. Remembering her role, Gillian toyed with necklaces of blue and red beads. She sighed, thinking how delighted little Caitlin would be with a few strands.

"Bon soir." His transaction completed, the shopkeeper cupped one hand in the other. "It's been a long time, old friend," he continued in French. "I did not expect to see you in my shop again."

"I could hardly come back to Casablanca without dropping in on an old and valued friend, al-Aziz."

The shopkeeper inclined his head, already wondering if a profit could be made. "You have come on business?"

"A little business…" Then he indicated Gillian by turning his palm upward. "A little pleasure."

"Your taste is excellent, as always."

"She's pretty," Trace said carelessly. "And not smart enough to ask too many questions."

"You would purchase her a bauble?"

"Perhaps. I also have a commodity to sell."

Annoyed with being shut out of the conversation, Gillian moved to Trace. She twined an arm around his neck, hoping the pose was sexy enough. She tried for the clipped New York accent of her assistant at the institute. "I might as well have stayed back at the hotel if you're going to speak in French all night."

"A thousand pardons, *mademoiselle*," al-Aziz said in precise English.

"No need to apologize," Trace told him after giving Gillian's cheek a light, intimate pat. The trace of Ireland was still there, but he doubted anyone who wasn't listening for it would have noticed. "There now, *chérie*, pick yourself out something pretty."

She wanted, quite badly, to spit in his eye, but she fluttered hers instead. "Oh, André, anything?"

"But of course, whatever you like."

She'd make it good, Gillian decided as she bent over the

display counter like a child in an ice cream parlor. Good and expensive.

"We can speak freely, *mon ami*," Trace went on. He too rested against the counter, but he moved his hands quickly, competently, then folded them together on the glass top. "My companion understands no French. I assume you're still…well connected."

"I am a fortunate man."

"You'll remember a few years ago we made a deal that was mutually profitable. I'm here to propose another."

"I am always happy to discuss business."

"I have a similar shipment. Something that was liberated from our capitalist friends. I find the shipment, shall we say, too volatile to store for any length of time. My sources indicate that a certain organization has relocated in Morocco. This organization might be interested in the supplies I can offer—at the going market rate, of course."

"Of course. You are aware that the organization you speak of is as volatile as the supplies you wish to sell?"

"It matters little to me, if the profit margin is agreeable. Are you interested in setting up the negotiations?"

"For the standard ten-percent commission?"

"Naturally."

"It's possible I can help you. Two days. Where can I reach you?"

"I'll reach you, al-Aziz." He smiled and ran a fingertip along the side of his jaw. It was a trait peculiar to Cabot. "There is a rumor I find interesting. A certain scientist is, let us say, employed, by this organization. If I had more information about him, the profit could very well increase, by perhaps twenty percent."

Al-Aziz's face was as bland as his voice. "Rumors are unreliable."

"But simple enough to substantiate." Trace drew out a

money clip and extracted some bills. They disappeared like magic into the folds of al-Aziz's cloak.

"Such things are rarely impossible."

"Oh, darling, can I have these?" Gillian grabbed Trace's arm and drew him over to a pair of long gold earrings crusted with red stones. "Rubies," she said with a long, liquid sigh, knowing perfectly well they were colored glass. "Everyone at home will simply die of envy. Please, darling, can I have them?"

"Eighteen hundred dirham," the shopkeeper said with a complacent smile. "For you and the lady, sixteen hundred."

"Please, sweetheart. I just adore them."

Trapped in his own game, Trace nodded to al-Aziz. But he also managed to pinch Gillian hard as the shopkeeper drew the earrings out of their case.

"Oh, I'll wear them now." Gillian began to fasten them on as Trace took more bills from his clip.

"Two days," Trace added in French. "I'll be back."

"Bring your lady." The shopkeeper's face creased with a smile. "I can use the business."

Trace steered her out to the street. "You could have picked out some glass beads."

Gillian touched a fingertip to one earring and sent it spinning. "A woman like me would never be satisfied with glass beads, but would probably be foolish enough to believe paste was rubies. I wanted to do a good job."

"Yeah." The earrings glittered with a lot more style on her than they had in the case. "You did okay."

With a hand on his arm, Gillian pulled up short. "Wait a minute. I'm nearly breathless after that compliment."

"Keep it up."

"There, that's better. Now are you going to tell me what that was all about?"

"Let's take a walk."

Chapter 5

At least she wasn't cooped up in a hotel room. Gillian tried to comfort herself with that as she sat in a noisy club that was fogged with smoke and vibrating with recorded music. Nursing a glass of wine, she sat observing the life around her. The clientele was young, and again mostly European. Though her traveling had been limited by her work, Gillian thought you could have found an almost identical place in London or Paris.

It occurred to her that she'd seen more of the world in the past two weeks than she had in all her life. Under other circumstances she might have enjoyed the noise and confusion, the edgy party atmosphere. Instead, she leaned closer to Trace.

"You have to tell me what was said, what's being done."

He'd chosen the club because it was loud and the clientele were self-absorbed. Whatever they said wouldn't carry beyond the table at which they sat. He'd chosen it for those reasons, and because he was postponing going back to the hotel, where he would be alone with her.

"Al-Aziz is a businessman. So is Cabot." Trace nibbled on a stale bread stick. "I made him a business proposition."

"What does that have to do with Flynn?"

"I get al-Aziz interested. With any luck he gets Hammer interested. We set up a meeting and I find out a hell of a lot more than we know now."

"You're going to meet with those people?" For some reason, her blood froze at the thought. For him, she realized. She was afraid for him. "But they know who you are."

Trace took a sip of his whiskey and wondered how long it would be before he was back in a country that served a proper drink. "Abdul knows who I am. Goons like him aren't generally in on arms transactions."

"Yes, but— Arms?" Her voice dropped to a passionate whisper. "You're going to sell them guns?"

"They damn well better think so."

"That's crazy. Setting up business transactions, pretending you'll be selling arms to terrorists. Certainly there has to be a better way."

"Sure. I could have walked into al-Aziz's and told him you were Dr. Gillian Fitzpatrick, whose brother had been kidnapped by Hammer. I could have appealed to his humanitarian instincts. Before the sun came up in the morning you'd be in the same position your brother's in now. And I'd be dead."

Gillian frowned into her wine. "It certainly seems a roundabout way of accomplishing something."

"You stick to your equations, Doc, I'll stick to mine. In a few days I should be talking with the general himself. I have a feeling that wherever he is, your brother's close by."

"You really think Flynn's near here?" As she leaned

closer, her fingers gripped his. "I wish I could be sure. I wish I could feel something."

"The computer said Morocco. Rory confirmed that the plane was logged for Casablanca. Wherever he is now, he was here. So we start here."

He seemed so confident, so sure of the plan of attack. There was nothing she wanted, needed, more than to believe in him. "You'd met al-Aziz before, hadn't you? He seemed to know you."

Trace felt an itch between his shoulder blades. He'd have preferred sitting with his back to the wall. "We've dealt before."

"You've used him to sell guns before."

"The ISS used him," Trace said. He broke another bread stick in half. "A few years back there were plans for a coup the ISS wanted to endorse. Anonymously. Cabot made a nice profit, al-Aziz made his commission, and democracy took a giant step forward."

She knew such things happened. She'd grown up in a country divided by war. She lived in a country whose faith had been strained by secret deals and political machinations. But that didn't make it right.

"It's wrong."

"This is the real world," he countered. "And most of it's wrong."

"Is that why you do it?" She'd drawn away from him, but she couldn't ignore the impulse to move closer. "To make things right?"

There'd been a time—it seemed a lifetime ago—when he had been idealistic enough to believe that things could be made right. When he'd lost that, where he'd lost that, he couldn't have said. And he'd stopped looking.

"I just do my job, Gillian. Don't try to make a hero out of me."

"It didn't occur to me." She said it dryly enough to make his lips curve. "I just think it would make it easier if I understood you."

"Just understand that I'm going to get your brother and his kid out."

"And then?" She made a conscious effort to relax. There was nothing she could do now but wait. Wait, and try to probe beneath the surface of the man who held her life in his hands. "Will you retire?"

"That's the idea, sweetheart." The smoke around him was expensive—French, Turkish. The music was loud, the liquor just tolerable. He wondered when it had hit him that he'd spent too much time in places like this. He nearly laughed out loud. For all intents and purposes, he'd been born in a place like this. Sometime over the past year he'd realized he wanted out as badly as he'd wanted out a dozen years before. Only he was long past the point where he could just stick out his thumb.

"Trace?"

"What?"

She wasn't sure where he'd gone, but she knew it wasn't the time to ask. "What will you do...when you retire?"

"There's a place in the Canary Islands where a man can pick fruit right off the tree and sleep in a hammock with a warm woman. The water's clear as glass, and the fish jump right in your lap." He took another long sip. "A hundred thousand dollars in a place like that, I could be king."

"If you didn't die of boredom first."

"I've had enough excitement to last me the next thirty or forty years. Honey-skinned women and a salt-free diet." He clicked his glass against hers. "I'm going to enjoy myself."

"André!"

Trace twisted in his chair and found his mouth captured in a long, steamy kiss. About halfway through, recognition dawned. He could remember only one woman who smelled like a hothouse flower and kissed like a vampire.

"Désirée." Trace ran a hand down her bare arm as she snuggled into his lap. "Still in Casablanca."

"Of course." She gave a throaty laugh and tossed back a mane of spiky midnight hair. "I'm partners now in the club."

"Come up in the world."

"But yes." She had skin like a magnolia and a heart that pumped happily with poison. Despite it, Trace had maintained a distant affection for her. "I married Amir. He's in the back, or he'd slit your throat for putting your hands on me."

"Nothing's changed, I see."

"You haven't." Blithely ignoring Gillian, Désirée ran her fingertips over Trace's face. "Oh, André, I waited weeks for you to come back."

"Hours, anyway."

"Are you staying long?"

"Few days. I'm showing my friend the charms of North Africa."

Désirée glanced around, took a sweeping up-and-down look, then cast Gillian into oblivion. "There was a time when my charms were enough for you."

"Your charms were enough for any army." Trace lifted his drink and kept his eye on the door of the back room. He knew Désirée wasn't exaggerating about Amir. "I've got a little business, *ma belle*. Do you still listen well at keyholes?"

"For you—and a price."

"Flynn Fitzpatrick. Scientist. Irish, with a small daughter. How much will it cost me to find out if they're in Casablanca?"

"For such an old, dear friend…five thousand francs."

Trace shifted her off his lap before taking out his money clip. "Here's half now. As an incentive."

She bent down and slipped the money into her shoe. "It's always a pleasure to see you, André."

"And you, *chérie*." He rose and brushed his lips over her knuckles. "Don't give Amir my best."

With another laugh, Désirée weaved her way through the crowd.

"You have fascinating friends," Gillian commented.

"Yeah. I'm thinking of having a reunion. Let's go."

Gillian made her way out of the smoke and into the clear night. "What were you saying?"

"Just reminiscing about old times."

She lifted a brow. "I'm sure they were fascinating."

Despite himself, he had to smile. Désirée had a heart of coal, but what an imagination! "They had their moments."

She fell silent for a moment, struggling. At last she gave up. "That woman was your type? Slinky?"

Trace knew enough about women to know when laughter was dangerous. He coughed instead. "Let's just say she's *a* type."

"I'm aware of that, and I doubt she's terribly attractive once you've scraped off the three layers of makeup."

"No need to be jealous, sweetheart. We're old news."

"Jealous?" She made the word sound like a joke and despised herself because it wasn't. "I would hardly be jealous of any woman you'd…you'd…"

"Come on, you can spit it out."

She shrugged off the arm he'd draped companionably around her shoulders. "Never mind. What did you pay her for?"

"To dig up some information."

"How would a woman like that be able to get any information?"

Trace looked down at her, saw that she was serious, and could only shake his head. "Diplomacy," he said.

She couldn't sleep. The energy that had been so sorely depleted only days before was back in full force. She was in Africa, a continent she had only read about in books. The Sahara was to the south. She was only steps away from the Atlantic, but from this side of the world it seemed a different ocean. Even the stars seemed different.

She didn't mind the strangeness. During her childhood she'd often dreamed of going to faraway places, but she'd contented herself with books. Her decision to emigrate to America had been the result of a craving to see something new, to be her own woman in a way she could never have been if she'd remained in Ireland with her father. So she'd gone to America to pursue her own goals, to live her own life. Now her father was ill and her brother was missing.

Gillian pulled on her robe, then threw open the terrace doors. How many times had she asked herself if things would somehow have been different if she'd stayed. It seemed foolish, even egotistical, to believe it. And yet the nagging doubt remained.

Now she was in Africa with a man who changed his identity in the blink of an eye. It would be through him and her own determination that things were put right again.

Put right. With a sigh, Gillian leaned on the railing and looked out at the lights and shadows of Casablanca. He said he didn't believe in putting things right, only in doing his job. Why didn't she believe that? It seemed to fit the style of the man. What it didn't fit were her feelings about him.

Almost from the first moment, she'd felt both drawn and repelled. There was something in his eyes, though only rarely, that told her he could be both kind and compassionate. There was the way he'd looked at her, looked to her, at the top of the Pyramid of the Magician. Part of him was a dreamer, part of him an icy realist. It seemed impossible to combine the two.

What he was, what he did, made her uneasy. All her life she'd believed in right and wrong, good and evil. Until she'd met him, she hadn't considered there could be so many shades in between. Nor had she realized until she'd met him that she could be attracted to a man who lived his life in those shades.

But it was a fact—not a theory, not a hypothesis, but a fact—that she was attracted, that she did trust, that she did believe. She couldn't take her emotions into a laboratory and dissect them, analyze them. For perhaps the first time in her life, she was stuck with a problem that no amount of logic or experimentation could solve. And the name of the problem was Trace O'Hurley.

She'd been jealous, quite fiercely jealous, when that woman had draped herself all over Trace in the club. When she'd murmured to him in intimate French and put her hands all over him, Gillian had wanted, badly, to grab her by the hair and yank out a few lacquered hunks. That simply wasn't in her nature. Or rather she'd never known it was.

She'd been jealous of Flynn from time to time, but only in the way a sister might be of a favored brother. And her love for him had always been much deeper than her envy. At university she'd had a few jealous pangs over girls with straight blond hair and blue eyes. But that had been very much a surface thing, without passion or depth.

The jealousy she'd felt tonight had been hot and violent and very difficult to control. It had also been unfamiliar. She hadn't been jealous of the woman's exotic looks or of her sinuous body, but of the fact that she'd twined that body around Trace's and kissed him as though she could have eaten him alive.

And he'd seemed to enjoy it.

Gillian crossed her arms over her chest and looked out at the smattering of lights that were still glowing in the city. She didn't care for jealousy any more than she cared for confusion. Trace O'Hurley apparently equaled both.

She jolted at a quick scraping sound, then whirled to see the flare of a match on the terrace beside hers.

He was in the shadows. They seemed to suit him best. She wondered how long he'd been there, silently watching.

"I didn't know you were there." And she wouldn't have, she realized, unless he'd allowed her to. "I couldn't sleep." When he didn't respond, she fiddled with the tie of her robe and cleared her throat. "I thought you'd gone to bed."

"Time change throws your system off."

"Yes, I suppose that's it." She curled her fingers around the railing again, wishing it was that simple. "We've been in so many time zones in the past few days. I'd have thought you'd be used to it."

"I like the night." That was true enough, but he'd come onto the terrace because he'd been restless, and because he'd been thinking of her.

"Sometimes I'll go up on the roof of my building. It's the only way you can see the stars in New York." She looked up at them now. "Back in Ireland, all you had to do was walk outside." With a shake of her head, she looked out at the city again. "Do you ever miss it?"

"Miss what?"

"Your home."

He drew on the cigarette, and his face was washed in red light for an instant. "I told you, I don't have one."

She moved to the side of the terrace that ran along the

side of his. "Just the Canary Islands? How long can a man live on fruit and fish?"

"Long enough."

Though the night had cooled, he wore only baggy drawstring pants. Gillian remembered, quite clearly, the wild thrill of being held against that body. And the confusing emptiness of being pushed away from it. No, emotions couldn't be analyzed, but she could try to analyze their source.

"I wonder what it is you're running from."

"Running to." Trace pitched his cigarette over the balcony and onto the street below. "A life of luxury, sweetheart. Coconut milk and half-naked women."

"I don't think you can do it. You've already given a chunk of your life to your country."

"That's right." Unconsciously he rubbed at the scar on his chest. "What's left is mine." Her scent was soft again. The breeze carried it from her skin to his.

"You know, one of the things Mr. Forrester told me about you was that if you played by the rules more regularly you'd be running the ISS."

"Charlie had delusions of grandeur."

"He was tremendously proud of you."

"He recruited me. He trained me." Trace moved restlessly to the railing. "He'd want to think he'd done a good job of it."

"I think it was more than that. Affection and pride don't always go together." She thought of her father. "You should have the satisfaction of knowing he liked who you were, as well as what he'd made you. I know you cared for him, and that you're doing this as much for him as for the money. The reasons shouldn't matter to me, but they do. Trace?"

He didn't want to look at her now, with the moonlight

slanting down and her scent hanging in the air. He kept his eyes on the street below. "Yeah?"

"I know that Flynn and Caitlin will be all right. That they'll be safe soon because you're here." She wished he was close, that she could reach out and touch him. She was grateful he wasn't. "And when I have them back I'll never be able to repay you. So I want you to know now that whatever happens in the meantime, whatever has to be done, I'm grateful."

"It's a job," he said, his teeth clenched, because the low, warm voice tended to make him forget that. "Don't make me out to be some knight on a white charger, Gillian."

"No, you're not that, but I think I'm beginning to understand what you are, Trace." She walked to the terrace doors. "Good night." Because she hadn't expected him to answer, she closed the door on his silence.

"But how can you expect me to browse through shops and snap pictures as if I were nothing more than a tourist?"

Trace steered Gillian toward another display window. "Because today you *are* nothing but a tourist. Show a little enthusiasm, will you?"

"My brother and my niece are prisoners. I'm afraid it's a little difficult for me to work up any enthusiasm over a bunch of crockery."

"Authentic North African Art," Trace said.

"We're wasting time poking around when we should be doing something."

"Any suggestions?" His voice was low as he continued to stroll, her arm caught firmly in his. Brightly striped awnings shaded the wares spread on outside tables. There was leather, and there was the flash of metal and the smell of horse. "You want me to break into where your brother's being held, guns blazing, maybe a knife between my teeth?"

He did a good job of making her feel like a fool. Gillian shrugged it off. "It makes better sense than buying trinkets and taking snapshots."

"In the first place I don't know where they're holding him. Hard to break into something until you've got the address. In the second place, if I tried that kind of TV tactics I'd be dead and your brother would be no better off. Let's sit." Satisfied with the position, he chose a shaded table on the terrace of a small café. "Why don't you tell me what's eating you?"

Gillian pushed her sunglasses more firmly on her nose. "Oh, I don't know. It might have something to do with the fact that Flynn and Caitlin have been kidnapped. Or perhaps I just got up on the wrong side of the bed."

"Sarcasm doesn't suit you." He ordered two coffees, then stretched out his legs. "You played the game well enough yesterday."

Gillian looked down at her hands. The sun glinted off the gold band of her watch. She studied the play of light until their coffee was served. "I couldn't sleep. Most of the night I just lay there waiting for morning. There was this feeling I couldn't shake. Something was wrong, dreadfully wrong, and I was going to be too late to put it right again." She looked up at him then, certain she would despise him if he laughed at her.

"You've been through a lot in the past few days." He said it easily, without the sympathy she would have bristled at or the edge she would have resented. "It wouldn't be normal for you to sleep like a baby."

"I suppose not, but if I just felt we were doing something…"

"We are." He put his hand on hers, then immediately drew it away again. "Drink your coffee."

The touch had been quick, and he was already resenting it. The fact that she thought she understood made her smile. "Being kind makes you uncomfortable."

"I'm not kind." He lit a cigarette, knowing he'd do better if he kept his hands occupied.

"Yes, you are." A little more relaxed, Gillian picked up her cup. "You'd prefer not to be, but it's difficult to change your nature. You can become other people." The coffee was hot and strong, and exactly what she'd needed. "But you can't change your nature. Whatever name you use, underneath it you're a kind man."

"You don't know me." He let smoke fill his lungs. "Or anything about me."

"As a scientist, I'm trained to observe, to analyze, categorize, hypothesize. Would you like to hear my hypothesis about you?"

"No."

The tension that had been locked in her muscles throughout the night eased. "You're a man who looked for adventure and excitement and undoubtedly found more than he'd bargained for. I'd say you believed in freedom and human rights strongly enough to spend a great deal of your life fighting for them. And you've been disillusioned and you nearly lost your life. I'm not certain which disturbs you more. I don't think you lied when you told me you were tired, Trace. But you lie every time you pretend not to care."

She was close, much too close, to the heart of things, much closer than anyone else had ever stepped. He'd found that life was more comfortable with distance. When he spoke, it was with the single goal of reestablishing it. "What I am is a trained liar, thief, cheat and killer. There's nothing pretty or glamorous or idealistic about what I do. I follow orders."

"I think the question isn't so much what you do as why you do it." For now, she stopped asking herself why it was so important for her to believe that, and just believed. "The whys became less clear, so you have a fantasy about retiring to some little island where you won't have to think about it."

Trace crushed out his cigarette. "You said physicist, not psychiatrist, right?"

"It's simply a matter of logic. I'm a very logical person." She set her cup back neatly in its saucer. "Then there's the matter of your behavior toward me. Apparently you're attracted."

"Is that so?"

She smiled then, always more secure when things were spelled out clearly. "I think it would be foolish to deny that a physical attraction exists. That can be listed as fact rather than theory. Yet, even on that basis, your behavior is contradictory. On each occasion when you've acted on that attraction, you've chosen to back off in favor of annoyance and frustration."

He didn't care to have his attractions, physical or otherwise, dissected like some embalmed frog. Trace waited until the waiter had freshened both cups before he leaned toward Gillian. "You can be grateful I backed off."

Their faces were very close over the little round table. Her heart began to drum, but she found the sensation more unique than unpleasant. "Because you're a dangerous man?"

"I'm the most dangerous man you'll ever meet."

She wasn't about to argue with that. "I explained to you before, I can take care of myself."

She reached for her coffee, and Trace closed his hand

over her wrist. The grip was firm enough to make her eyes narrow. "You wouldn't know where to begin with me, Doc. And you sure as hell wouldn't know where to end. Count your blessings."

"My family's been kidnapped, I've seen a man die and had a knife to my back. There's little you could do to frighten me." She jerked her hand away and, with every outward appearance of calm, lifted her cup. Her heart beat fast and hard in her throat.

"You're wrong." This time he smiled. "If I decide to have you, you'll find out how wrong."

Her cup hit the saucer with a snap. "I'm ready to go."

"Sit." It was the sudden change in his voice that made her obey. "Drink your coffee," he said mildly as he picked up his camera.

"What is it?"

"Al-Aziz has a visitor." The camera was one of the few pieces of ISS equipment Trace was fond of. He pushed a button, and a man stepping out of a black car twenty yards away filled the viewfinder. He recognized the face from briefings, and he smiled again. Kendesa was the general's right hand, a man of taste and intelligence who just managed to balance the general's fanaticism.

"You know who it is?"

Trace took two shots out of habit. "Yeah." He lowered the camera.

"What does it mean?"

"It means they took the bait."

Gillian moistened her lips and struggled to stay calm. "What do we do now?"

Trace lit another cigarette. "We wait."

Al-Aziz's visitor stayed twenty minutes. When he came back out, Trace was up and moving. By the time Kendesa stepped into his car, Trace and Gillian were in a cab. "I want you to stay with that car," he told the driver, pulling out bills. "But keep a nice distance."

The driver pocketed the money before he started the engine. Gillian groped for Trace's hand and held on.

"He knows where Flynn is, doesn't he?"

"He knows."

She pressed her free hand to her lips as they drove. "What are you going to do?"

"Nothing."

"But if he—"

"Let's just see where he's going." Because her hand was icy, he kept it in his. The black car stopped at one of the more exclusive hotels in the business district. Trace waited until Kendesa was inside. "Stay here."

"But I want to—"

"Just stay here," he repeated, and then he was gone. As the minutes passed, fear became annoyance. Gillian slid to the door and had her fingers around the handle when Trace pulled it open.

"Going somewhere?" He let the door slam behind him. Settling back, he gave the driver the name of their hotel.

"Well?"

"He just checked in this morning. He hasn't given them a day of departure. I'd say that means he intends to stay until business is completed."

"Aren't you going to go in and make him tell you where Flynn is?"

Trace spared her a look. "Sure, I'll go on up to his room, rough him and his three guards up a bit and drag the truth out of them. Then I'll march up to wherever they're holding your brother and blast him out single-handed."

"Isn't that what I'm paying me for?"

"You're paying me to get him out—in one piece." As

the cab pulled up at the curb, Trace handed the driver more bills. "Let's play this my way."

Knowing her temper couldn't be trusted, Gillian remained silent until they were in their rooms. "If you have a plan, I think it's time you filled me in."

Ignoring her, Trace walked over to the bed and began to fiddle with what Gillian had taken for a compact portable stereo.

"This is hardly the time to listen to music." When he continued to say nothing, she stormed over to him. "Trace, I want to know what you have in mind. I refuse to be kept in the dark while you sit here and listen to the radio. I want to know—"

"Shut up, will you?" When he played back the tape, the voices came out barely audible, and speaking Arabic. "Damn." He adjusted the volume and strained.

"What is that?"

"Our friends talking, almost out of reach of the bug I planted yesterday."

"You… I never saw you plant anything."

"That boosts my confidence." He rewound the tape to the beginning.

"I can't think of any place you could have hidden it."

"I left it out in plain view. People find things a lot quicker if you hide them. Didn't you ever read Poe? Now be quiet."

The voices were barely distinguishable, but he recognized al-Aziz's. He could decipher the formal greetings, but from there on could translate only a few snatches. He heard Cabot's name, and some basic monetary negotiations.

"What does it say?" Gillian asked when he shut the tape off again.

"I don't know enough Arabic to make much sense of it."

"Oh." She tried to block off the disappointment. Running her hands over her face, she sat on the bed beside him. "I guess you'd hoped they speak in French or English."

"It would have been helpful." Trace removed the tape and slipped it into his pocket. "Now we need an interpreter."

Her hands dropped in her lap. "You know someone who'll help us?"

"Almost anyone's willing to help for a price." He checked his watch. "The club ought to be pretty quiet now. I think I'll go to see Désirée."

"I'm going with you."

He started to refuse, then thought better of it. "Just as well. I can use you as a cover in case Amir's around. With you hanging all over me, he won't think I'm trying to tickle his wife's fancy. Or anything else."

"I'm so glad I can be useful."

They found Désirée in the apartment above the club. Though it was nearly noon, she answered the door heavy-eyed and in a sexily rumpled robe that slipped provocatively off one shoulder. Her eyes brightened considerably at the sight of Trace.

"André. What a nice surprise." She spotted Gillian, pouted a moment, then stepped back to let them in. "You used to come visiting alone," she said in French.

"You used to be single." Trace glanced around the wide, dim room, with its fussy pillows and its china knicknacks. The room was crammed with furniture, and the furniture covered with things. Possessions had always been important to Désirée. Apparently she'd finally acquired them. "You've come up in the world, *chérie*."

"We make our own way in life." She walked to a table and chose a cigarette from a glass holder. "If you've come

for your information, you haven't given me much time."
She held the cigarette, waiting until Trace crossed the room
to light it.

"Actually, I've come on other business." She smelled of
perfume that clung from the night before, no longer strong,
but still overpowering. "Is your husband in?"

Her brow lifted as she glanced in Gillian's direction.
"You were never one for group games."

"No games at all." He took the cigarette from her and
drew on it himself. "Amir. Is he here?"

"He had business. He's a busy man."

"Your Arabic was always excellent, Désirée." Trace
drew the tape from his pocket. "Two thousand francs for
a translation of this tape, and a memory lapse immediately afterward."

Désirée took the tape and turned it over in her palm.
"Two thousand for the translation, and three more for the
loss of memory." She smiled at him. "A woman must make
a living where she can."

There had been a time when he would have enjoyed
negotiating with her. He wondered why that time seemed
to have passed. "Done."

"Cash, darling." She held out an empty hand. "Now."

When Trace handed her the money, she went over to a
stereo. "Amir enjoys his toys," she said as she slipped the
tape into the player. After switching it on, she adjusted the
volume. Almost at once, her expression changed. With the
touch of a finger, the player fell silent again. "Kendesa.
You said nothing of Kendesa."

"You didn't ask." Trace sat and gestured for Gillian to
join him. "The deal's struck, Désirée. Play it my way and
your name will never be mentioned."

"You mix in very bad company, André. Very bad." But
the money was still in her hand. After a moment's con-

sideration, she slipped it into her pocket, then switched the machine back on. "Kendesa greets the swine al-Aziz. He asks if business is good." She listened for another moment, then turned the machine off again. "They speak of you, the Frenchman Cabot, who has an interesting business proposition for Kendesa's organization. Al-Aziz has humbly agreed to act as liaison."

She turned the machine on again, then repeated the process of listening before turning it off to translate. "Kendesa is very interested in your product. His sources have confirmed that you are in possession of a shipment of American arms intended for their Middle Eastern allies. A shipment of this size and—" she groped for the word a moment "—quality is of interest to Kendesa's superior. And so are you."

She switched the tape on again and lit a cigarette as the two voices murmured through the speakers. "Your reputation is satisfactory, but Kendesa is cautious. His organization is most concerned with another project at this time, and yet your product is tempting. Kendesa has agreed to have al-Aziz arrange a meeting. They discuss commission. Then it becomes interesting. Al-Aziz asks of this Fitzpatrick. He tells Kendesa he has heard rumors. Kendesa tells him to mind his shop and his tongue."

Désirée turned the tape off. It ejected smoothly. "Tell me, André, are you interested in guns or in this Irishman?"

"I'm interested in the largest profit." He rose to take the tape from her. "And your memory, Désirée?"

She fondled the bills in her pocket. "Quite blank." She smiled, then ran a hand up his chest. "Come back for a drink tonight. Alone."

Trace cupped her chin in his hand and kissed her. "Amir is a large, jealous man who has a talent with knives. Let's just treasure the past."

"It was an interesting one." She sighed and watched him walk to the door. "André, the Irishman was in Casablanca."

He stopped, clamping his hand around Gillian's arm before she could speak. "And now?"

"He was taken east, into the mountains. That's all I know."

"There was a child."

"A girl. She's with him. It would have to be a great deal more profitable to ask questions now that I know who is involved."

"You've asked enough." He drew out bills and set them on the table by the door. "Forget this, too, Désirée, and enjoy your large husband."

When he closed the door, Désirée considered for a long moment, then walked to the phone.

"He was here," Gillian said, torn between relief and fresh terror. "They were both here. There has to be a way of finding out where they were taken. Oh, God, they were so close."

"Don't get ahead of yourself. The mountains to the east isn't a street address."

"But it's another step. What do we do now?"

"We get some lunch. And we wait for Kendesa to move."

Chapter 6

"I want to go with you."

Trace straightened the knot of the hated tie. "It's out of the question."

"You haven't given me a reason." Gillian stood planted behind him, scowling at his reflection. He looked so smooth, she thought, a world away from the man she'd found in the cantina. She wondered what dramatic turn her life had taken to make her prefer the rough, unshaven and slightly dirty man she'd first met to the urbane and cologned one who stood in front of her.

"I don't have to give you reasons, just results."

At least that much hadn't changed, she thought wryly, standing her ground. "I explained to you right from the beginning that I'd be going through this step-by-step with you."

"You're going to miss this step, sweetheart." Trace checked the plain brushed-gold links at his cuffs. "You just stay here and keep a light burning in the window." Turning, he gave her a friendly pat on the cheek.

"You look like a stockbroker," she muttered.

"No need for insults." Trace picked up a briefcase filled with papers and inventories he'd spent the better part of the night putting together.

"You're meeting with Kendesa, and I think I should be there."

"It's a business meeting—bad business. I take a woman along to a meeting where I'm talking about dealing arms to terrorists, Kendesa's going to wonder why. He wonders hard enough and he could check you out. He checks deep enough, he could find out that my woman is the sister of Hammer's most prized possession." He stopped long enough to wipe away a smudge on his shoe. "It's not a good bet."

It was because it was too logical to argue with that Gillian was angry. "I'm not your woman."

"They better think you are."

"I'd rather be buried up to my neck in hot sand."

He glanced at her. She stood by the window, spitting mad and stunning. "I'll keep that in mind. Why don't you spend a couple hours making up a list of alternatives? It might put you in a better mood."

When he opened the door, she prepared to hurl abuse. "Be careful," she said instead, hating herself for it.

He paused again. "Concern. I'm touched."

"It's nothing personal." But her palms were sweaty at the idea of him going alone. "If anything happened to you I'd have to start from scratch."

With a little laugh, he stepped into the hall. "Stay inside, Doc."

The moment the door closed at his back, he left Trace O'Hurley behind. He had a certain affection for each of his covers. Without that, it would have been difficult for him to play any of them convincingly for what were often long stretches of time. André Cabot was fussy, and often pompous, but he had excellent taste and extraordinary luck with women. Trace felt that redeemed him.

Still, Cabot's charm hadn't made a dent in Gillian's defenses. So she doesn't like Frenchmen, Trace decided as he settled into a cab. Apparently she preferred stodgy American scientists like that Arthur Steward she spent so much time with in New York. The man was fifteen years older than she, and more interested in white mice than romance. Trace had told himself it was simply standard procedure to check him out. Nothing personal.

Trace shifted his briefcase and reminded himself that Cabot was concerned only with making a profit. He wouldn't have given a woman like Gillian a second thought once she was out of sight. The trouble was, Trace O'Hurley was thinking about her entirely too much.

She was still a puzzle to him, and he was used to figuring any angle, any woman. They shared the same set of rooms, yet she gave the arrangement a sense of innocence and propriety. She was vulnerable and passionate, frightened and determined. She was logical, yet enough of a dreamer to feel the power of a Mayan ruin. She spoke easily, even clinically, of his attraction to her. But there had been a fire, hot and vital, when he'd kissed her.

She was right about one thing—he wanted her, and bad. What she didn't know, what he couldn't explain even to himself, was that he was terrified of what might happen if he acted on that need.

When the cab drew up to the curb, Trace pulled himself back. He was right about something, too. He was thinking about her too much.

He counted out bills as Cabot would, carefully. With obvious reluctance, he added the minimum tip. After straightening the line of his jacket, he walked into the lobby of Kendesa's hotel.

He spotted one of the bodyguards but walked to the bank of elevators without pausing. He was on time to the minute. That was another of Cabot's traits. The elevator took him to the top floor, to the executive suite, often reserved for dignitaries and visiting heads of state.

The door was opened at the first knock by a burly guard who looked uncomfortable in his dark Western suit. "Your weapon, monsieur," he said in stilted French.

Trace reached inside his jacket and removed a .25 automatic. Cabot carried a small pistol rather than chance ruining the line of his jacket.

The guard pocketed it before gesturing him into the parlor of the suite. A bottle of wine was open on the table. Fresh roses stood in a vase beside it. The room was cushioned from the noise and heat of the day. Noting that the terrace doors were not only shut but locked, Trace took his seat. Kendesa didn't keep him waiting.

He wasn't an imposing man. Whatever passions stirred him were kept firmly strapped down and controlled. He was small in stature and impeccably and conservatively dressed. Unlike the man he represented, he wore no ostentatious jewelry, no vivid colors. He was dark and blandly handsome, rather like a news anchorman, and moved with the steady grace of a career soldier.

He was a man who exuded trust and moderation, and in the past eighteen months he had been responsible for the execution of three political hostages. He was holding the wildly fanatical Hammer together by the skin of his teeth.

"Monsieur Cabot." Kendesa offered his hand. "It's a pleasure to meet you."

"*Monsieur.* Business is always my pleasure."

With a politely interested smile, Kendesa took his seat.

"Our mutual friend indicated you have some supplies that may be of interest to me. Some wine? I think you'll find it agreeable." Kendesa poured two glasses. Trace let him drink first.

"I've recently acquired certain military supplies that I believe your organization would find useful." Trace sipped and found the wine dry and light. Cabot's preference. He smiled. Kendesa had done his homework.

"My sources tell me that these supplies were intended for the Zionists."

Trace lifted a shoulder, pleased that the money he'd spent in the bidonville had been invested wisely. "I'm a businessman, *monsieur*. I have no politics, only a profit margin. The supplies could still be shipped where the Americans originally intended, if the price was right."

"You're frank." Kendesa tapped a finger on the side of his glass. "The United States had not admitted openly that these supplies were…confiscated. In fact, it's difficult to prove that they ever existed."

"Such things are embarrassing. For myself, I prefer that the entire business be kept quiet until the final transactions are complete." Setting his wine aside, Trace lifted his suitcase. "This is a list of the arms my associates are holding. I can assure you they are top-quality. I've checked samples myself."

Kendesa took the papers but continued to watch Trace. "Your reputation in such matters is unimpeachable."

"Merci."

Kendesa's brows lifted slightly as he scanned the list. Trace had made it irresistible. "This particular weapon, the TS-35. My sources tell me it was not to be completed for several months."

"It was completed and tested five weeks ago," Trace told him, knowing the news would be out in a matter of weeks in any case. "It is a beautiful piece of work. Very lightweight, and compact. The Americans are very clever in some areas." He drew out another sheet of paper. "My associates and I have settled on a price. Shipping can, of course, be arranged."

"The total seems high."

"Overhead. Inflation." He spread his hands in a purely Gallic gesture. "You understand."

"And I am a cautious man, you understand. Before negotiations can be initiated, it would be necessary to inspect a portion of your product."

"Naturally, I can deal with that myself, if you like." He moved his fingertip over his jawline consideringly. "It will take me a few days to make the arrangements. I prefer to do so in a place you have secured. In today's atmosphere, transactions of this nature have become only more delicate."

"The general is residing in the east. Such a transaction cannot be completed without his approval."

"Understood. Though I'm aware much of the buying and selling are your province, I would prefer discussing the matter with the general."

"You will bring your samples to us, in one week." In a week he would have a complete report on Cabot and the enterprise. "The general has established his headquarters in an area east of Sefrou that he has christened el Hasad. It will be arranged for you to be met in Sefrou. From there, your transportation will be seen to."

"I will contact my associates, but I see no problem with those arrangements. One week, then." Trace rose.

Kendesa rose, as well. "A question on another matter, *monsieur*. You inquired about a scientist who has recently joined our organization. I would ask what your interest is."

"Profit. There are several parties interested in Dr.

Fitzpatrick and his particular skills. The Horizon project, once completed, could generate an incredible amount of income."

"We are not only interested in money."

"I am," Trace said with a cool smile. "You might think of what the scientist is worth, if you can persuade him to complete the project. The arms we are currently negotiating over would be little more than toys." He folded his hands, and the gold at his wrists winked dully. "If your organization finds the proper partner, you could not only be rich, but as powerful politically as any developed country."

It was something he had considered already, though he would have preferred making the first move. "Your outlook is intriguing."

"Only speculation, *monsieur*, unless you can indeed convince the man to produce for you."

Kendesa brushed that aside easily. He was a man who was accustomed to cooperation—or submission. "That is only a matter of time. I will speak with the general on this, as well. Perhaps it can be discussed." Kendesa led him to the door. "I would tell you, Monsieur Cabot, that you might be more cautious in choosing your associates."

"I beg your pardon?"

"I speak of the French woman, Désirée. She thought a greater profit could be made through blackmail. She was mistaken."

Trace merely lifted a brow, but he felt a cold gnawing at his stomach. "She is as greedy as she is beautiful."

"And now she is dead. Good afternoon, *monsieur*."

Trace gave a slight bow. He held on to Cabot until he was back in his room. There he gave way to fury by slamming a fist into the wall.

"Damn the woman!" Couldn't she have been satisfied with the easy money he'd passed her? She'd killed herself.

He could tell himself she'd killed herself, and yet he felt the weight of another life on his hands.

For a moment he closed his eyes and forced the image of his island into his mind. Soft breezes, warm fruit, warmer women. The minute he had the cash in his hand he was getting out.

Trace went to the bottle of whiskey on his dresser, poured a double and washed the taste of Kendesa's wine from his mouth. It didn't help. Slamming the glass down again, he went into the next room to tell Gillian they were a step closer.

She was sitting on the bed, her back very straight, her hands folded in her lap. She didn't glance over as he came in, but continued to stare out the window at a slice of sky.

"Still sulking?" The whiskey hadn't helped, but maybe dumping a little excess temper on her would. "I don't know which is more tiresome, listening to you bitch or putting up with your moods." Yanking off his tie, he tossed it in the general direction of a chair. "Snap out of it, Doc, unless you don't want to hear what I found out about your brother."

She looked at him then, but he didn't see recrimination or temper in her eyes. There wasn't the anticipation he'd expected, but grief, raw and dry-eyed. He'd started to peel out of his jacket, and now he drew it off slowly.

"What is it?"

"I called my father." Her voice was quiet, hardly more than a whisper, but steady. It was the tone that stopped him from nagging at her for using an unsecured line. "I thought he should know we were close to finding Flynn. I wanted to give him some hope, some comfort. I know he felt helpless having to send me instead of doing it himself." She closed her eyes and waited for her strength to rebuild. "I got his nurse. She's staying at the house, looking after it. He died three days ago." She unlinked her fingers, then curled them together again. "Three days. I didn't know. I wasn't there. They buried him this morning."

He came to her in silence to sit beside her, to slip an arm around her. She resisted only a moment, then allowed herself to lean against him. The tears didn't come. She wondered why she felt so cold and numb, when hot, raging grief would have been a relief.

"He was all alone when he died. No one should die alone, Trace."

"You said he'd been ill."

"He was dying. He knew it, and he really didn't want to live the way he'd become. Weak and feeble. All his research, all his brilliance, couldn't help him. He only wanted one thing—for me to bring Flynn home before he died. Now it's too late."

"You're still going to bring Flynn home."

"He loved Flynn so. I was a disappointment to him, but Flynn was everything he wanted. The worry of the past days only made him worse. I wanted him to die easy, Trace. Even after everything, I wanted him to die easy."

"You did everything you could. You're doing what he wanted."

"I never did what he wanted." Her cheeks were hot and wet now, but she didn't notice. "He never forgave me for going to America, for leaving him. He never understood that I needed to breathe, needed to look for my own life. He only understood that I was going away, rejecting him and his plans for me. I loved him." Her voice caught on the first sob. "But I could never explain myself to him. And I never will. Oh, God, I didn't get to say goodbye. Not even that."

She didn't object when he drew her closer, to rock, to stroke, to soothe. He didn't speak, only held, as the tears came, fast and violent. He understood grief, the fury and the ache of it, and knew it wasn't words that dulled both, it was time. Gathering her close, he lay down with her while she wept out the first pains.

He understood the guilt. He and Gillian were as different as black and white, but he, too, had had a father who had made plans, who hadn't understood and hadn't forgiven. And he knew that guilt made grief more painful even than love.

He brushed his lips across her temple and held on.

When she was quiet, he continued to stroke her hair. The light was still strong through the windows. Wanting to draw the curtains closed, he started to rise. Gillian tightened her hold.

"Don't go," she murmured. "I don't want to be alone."

"I'll close the drapes. Maybe you can sleep."

"Just stay with me a little while longer." She brushed a hand over her face to wipe away the tears. Emotional outbursts were something she'd always been prone to, and one more thing her father hadn't understood. "He was a hard man, my father, especially after my mother died. She knew how to reach him. I'll always regret that I couldn't." Taking a long breath, she shut her eyes again. "Flynn and Caitlin are the only family I have left. I have to find them, Trace. I have to see that they're safe."

"I have a pretty good idea where they are."

She nodded. All her faith, all her hopes, were tied up in him now. "Tell me."

He gave her a brief sketch of his meeting with Kendesa, but stopped short of mentioning Désirée. That was still on his conscience. She listened but didn't move away. Her head stayed on his shoulder, her hand on his chest. As he spoke, something he'd closed off long before began to crack open. He couldn't explain why he felt stronger because his arms were around her. He couldn't explain why, even knowing what had to be done in the next few days, he felt almost at peace lying in the bright room with her hair against his cheek.

"You think Flynn and Caitlin are with this General Husad?"

"I'd give odds on it."

"And in a week you'll meet with him."

"That's the plan."

"But he'll expect you to have some of these guns. What will happen when you don't?"

"Who says I won't?"

She did move then, slowly drawing her head back so that she could see his face. His eyes were half closed, but the grimness around his mouth hadn't faded. "Trace, I don't understand. You told them you had a shipment of American arms. You don't. How can you take them samples of what you don't have?"

"I have to go shopping for a few M-16s, 40-millimeter grenade launchers and odds and ends."

"I don't think the local department stores carry them."

"The black market does, and I've got connections." He let the silence hang for a moment. "Gillian, it's time to let the ISS in on this."

"Why? Why now?"

"Because I've established cover, I've made contact. They'll be annoyed, but they aren't stupid enough to blow the operation at this stage. If something goes wrong, they'll need to have the information so they can move on it."

She was silent for a long time. "You mean if you're killed."

"If I'm taken out, a lot of time will be wasted in getting to your brother. With ISS backing from this point, we cover more bases."

"Why should they hurt you? You're selling them the guns they want."

He thought of Désirée. "The guns are one thing, Horizon is another. These people aren't businessmen, and they don't have the honor of a Manhattan street gang. If they think I know too much, or might infringe on their territory, eliminating me would be the best way of protecting their interest. It's a toss of the dice which way they'll play it. You don't want to risk your brother's life on a toss of the dice."

Nor did she want to risk his. It came to her now as they lay close, without passion, without anger, that she'd become as concerned for him as for her family. He wasn't simply an instrument to free Flynn and Caitlin with any longer, but he was a man who drew her, infuriated her, aroused her.

She looked down and saw that her hand had curled against his chest. Holding on, she thought, to something that wasn't hers. "Maybe we should let the ISS take over from here."

"Let's not go overboard."

"No, I mean it." She shifted away and sat up. She wanted more now. She wanted him to hold her, not in comfort, not in reassurance, but in desire. "The more I think about it, the crazier it seems for you to go in alone. Anything could happen to Flynn and Caitlin…to you."

"I've worked alone and come out in one piece before."

"And the last time you worked against them you nearly died."

Because this sudden attack of nerves intrigued him, Trace sat up and took her by the shoulders. "Don't you believe in destiny, Gillian? We do things to move it along, to protect ourselves from it, but in the end, what's meant is meant."

"You were just talking about luck."

"Yeah, I don't figure there's a contradiction there. If my luck's in, and I'm meant to come out, I will."

"You're not a fatalist."

"Depends on the mood. But I'm always a realist. This job is mine, for a lot of reasons." And she wasn't the least of them. "But I'm practical enough to know when it's time for backup."

"I don't want anything to happen to you." She said it quickly, knowing it was as foolish as it was useless.

His look sharpened. Before she could turn away, he cupped her chin in his hand. "Why?"

"Because... I'd feel responsible."

It wasn't wise to push, but he wasn't always wise. "Why else?"

"Because I'd be alone, and I've nearly gotten used to you, and..." Her voice trailed off as she lifted a hand to his cheek. "And there's this," she murmured, bringing her lips to his.

The light was still bright, but it seemed to her that the room went dim, the colors softened and the world tipped out of focus. The emotional roller coaster she'd already experienced went speeding around an unexpected curve, leaving her giddy and exhilarated. She pressed against him, already anticipating the next plunge.

She was as warm and sweet as any fantasy. She was real and vital. More than he'd ever wanted freedom or wealth or peace of mind, he wanted her. He felt reason slipping against the pull of need, and he held himself back. To need anything too much was to risk losing.

But her hands were so soft, so soothing. His own were in her hair, dragging her closer, even as he told himself it was wrong for both of them. Her scent was like a quiet promise, lulling him into believing he could have and keep. He ached from needing to touch her, to feel how her body might move against his hands.

He had to remind himself that there was no promise, neither from her nor to her. There couldn't be.

When he drew her away, she reached out again. Trace tightened his grip and held her back. "You listen to me. This is all wrong. You know it and I know it."

"No, I don't."

"Then you're an idiot."

She knew how to handle rejection. She braced herself for it. "You don't want me?"

He swore, once, then twice. "Of course I want you. Why shouldn't I? You're beautiful. You've got brains and guts. You're everything I've ever wanted."

"Then why—?"

He dragged her out of the bed. Before she could draw in the breath to protest, he was holding her in front of the mirror. "Look at yourself, you're a nice, well-bred woman. A physicist, for God's sake. You came from a nice upper-class family, went to good schools and did what you were told." When temper had her pulling away, he yanked her back again. "Look at me, Gillian." He gave her one hard shake until her head snapped up and her eyes met his in the mirror. "I spent most of my life dancing from second-rate club to second-rate club. I never spent more than a handful of days a year in a real school. I never learned to play by the rules. I've never owned a car or a piece of property, and I've never stayed with a woman for long. Do you want to know how many people I've killed in twelve years? Do you want to know how many ways there are to do it?"

"Stop it." She pulled away from him, only to whirl back. "You're trying to scare me, and it won't work."

"Then you *are* an idiot."

"Maybe I am, but at least I'm an honest one. Why don't you just admit that you don't want to be involved? You don't want to feel anything for me."

He drew out a cigarette. "That's right."

"But you do." She tossed her head back, daring him to deny it. "You do feel, and you're the one who's scared."

Her point, he thought as he blew out smoke. But he'd be damned if he'd let her know it. "Let's get something straight, sweetheart. I don't have time to give you the hearts and flowers you'd like. We've got a priority, and it's in the mountains east of here. Let's concentrate on that."

"You can't run forever."

"When I stop, you'll wish to God I'd kept going. I've got some things to do." He walked out.

Gillian did something she hadn't done in years. She picked up the nearest breakable and heaved it at the door.

Chapter 7

"After the number of years you've had in service, Agent O'Hurley, I'm sure you're aware that there's such a thing as procedure."

Captain Addison—British, balding and straight-line ISS—sat in Trace's room, drinking coffee and looking annoyed. It was his job to oversee and coordinate operations in this part of the world. After nearly fifteen years of field duty, he was quite content to do so from behind a desk. Under these particular circumstances, he'd been ordered to handle the business face-to-face. The break in routine did nothing to please him.

He'd been set to go back to London on holiday when the call had reached him at his Madrid base. Now he was in godforsaken Morocco, in the middle of an incident that would very likely keep him from his steak-and-kidney pie for some time to come.

"You have, I presume, some sort of valid explanation?"

"I was on vacation, Captain." Trace drew easily on his

cigarette. Types like Addison amused him more than they annoyed him. It was the possibility that he could become similarly straitlaced that had kept him away from desks and paperwork. "My own time. I thought the ISS might be interested in what I stumbled into."

"Stumbled into," Addison repeated. He pushed his rimless glasses up on his nose and gave Trace a very cool and very clear stare. "We both know you didn't stumble into anything, Agent O'Hurley. You acted on your own, without ISS sanction."

"The woman came to me." Trace didn't bother to put any emphasis into the explanation. He knew very well that men of Addison's type preferred agents to sweat. "I followed up an interesting story and came by some even more interesting information. If you don't want what I've got, it doesn't matter to me. I've still got a week before I punch in."

"The correct procedure would have been to inform the ISS the moment Dr. Fitzpatrick contacted you."

"I consider that a judgment call, Captain. My judgment."

Addison folded his hands. Though he'd been divorced for five years, he still wore a gold wedding band. He'd gotten used to the weight on his finger. "Your record shows a high percentage of infractions."

"Am I fired?"

A creature of habit and order, Addison bristled at Trace's careless arrogance. But he, too, had his orders. "Fortunately—or unfortunately, depending on one's viewpoint—your record also shows a high percentage of successful assignments. To be frank, O'Hurley, I don't care for showboating of this kind, but the Horizon project and Dr. Fitzpatrick and his daughter take precedence over personal feelings."

Trace hadn't missed the order of importance. Nor had he expected anything else. "Then I take it I'm not fired."

"You will maintain your cover as André Cabot, but from this point on we go by the book. You will keep in constant contact with the ISS base in Madrid on your progress. You will report directly to me." This, too, gave him no pleasure. One didn't easily keep a rogue agent under one's thumb. "We have arranged for one crate of American-made weapons to be delivered to you in Sefrou in four days. Your contact there will be Agent Breintz. Once you have confirmed Dr. Fitzpatrick's location and assessed the situation, you'll be given further orders. Headquarters feels you should keep the arms negotiations straightforward. If you do find yourself in Husad's lair, it's code blue."

Again, it was nothing he hadn't expected. Code blue meant simply that if his cover didn't hold the ISS would destroy his files, his identity. It would be as if Trace O'Hurley had never existed.

"I need a TS-35 in the crate."

"A—" Addison laid his hands carefully on the arms of his chair. "You told them about the TS-35?"

"The Soviets will know about it in a week—if they don't already. Everyone else will know before the month is out. If I dangle one in front of their noses, Husad might decide I'm a useful ally. He might loosen up enough about Fitzpatrick to let me have a tour, especially if I tell him that my associates are willing to help finance Horizon."

"They may be maniacs, but they're not fools. If they had a prototype, it wouldn't take them long to duplicate the weapon."

"If we don't get Fitzpatrick out and secure the Horizon project, the TS-35 isn't much more than a peashooter."

Addison rose and paced to the window. He didn't like it. He didn't like O'Hurley. He didn't like having his plans interfered with. But he hadn't reached his position by not knowing when and how to play his cards. "I'll arrange it. But the weapon is to be brought back out or destroyed."

"Understood."

With a nod, Addison turned back. "Now, about the woman." He glanced toward the door that led to Gillian's room. "Since Agent Forrester saw fit to tell her about you and she's now aware of the operation, she'll have to be debriefed."

Trace lifted the pot of coffee and poured himself a cup. "Good luck."

"Your humor eludes me, O'Hurley. I'd like to speak with her now."

With a shrug, Trace rose to walk to the door. He pushed it open and stuck his head inside. Gillian stopped pacing and looked at him. "Your turn."

Gillian swallowed, wiped her hands on her slacks, then walked through the doorway.

"Dr. Fitzpatrick." With the first congenial smile Trace had ever seen on his face, Addison crossed to offer her his hand. "I'm Captain Addison."

"How do you do?"

"Please, sit down. Can I offer you a cup of coffee?"

"Yes, thank you." Gillian sat, back straight, chin up, while Trace lounged in the chair beside her.

"Cream, Doctor?"

"No, black, please."

Addison handed her a cup, then sat down cozily with his own. Gillian was almost afraid he was going to talk about the weather. "Dr. Fitzpatrick, I must tell you how concerned the ISS is about your family's welfare. Our organization is dedicated to ensuring the freedom and basic human rights of people everywhere. A man like your brother is of great importance to us."

"My brother is of even greater importance to me."

"To be sure." He smiled again, almost avuncularly. "Though we believe you and Agent O'Hurley acted impulsively, we think we can turn these impulses to our advantage."

Gillian looked at Trace, saw by the lazy way he moved his shoulders that he would be no help and looked back at Addison. "I acted in what I believed, and still believe, is my brother's best interests, Captain. He and Caitlin are my only concern."

"Of course, of course. I can assure you that even now the ISS is putting all its skill and experience into freeing your brother. We hope that will be accomplished quickly. In the meantime, I'd like you to come back to Madrid with me and remain under ISS protection."

"No."

"I beg your pardon?"

"I appreciate the offer, Captain, but I'm staying with Agent O'Hurley."

Addison put his arms on either side of his cup and linked his hands. "Dr. Fitzpatrick, for your own safety, and for the security of this operation, I must insist you come under ISS protection."

"My brother and my niece are in the mountains east of here. I won't sit in Madrid and wait. I'm quite confident that Agent O'Hurley can protect me, if you feel protection is warranted. As to the operation's security, I was involved long before you or the ISS, Captain. I'm sure my clearance can be upgraded if necessary."

"My orders are to take you to Madrid."

"Your orders are of no concern to me, Captain." It was that tone of voice, used rarely but effectively, that had helped secure her a top position at the institute. "I have no ties to the ISS, or to anyone but my family. General Husad wants me, as well. As long as there's a chance that that can be used to get Flynn out, I'm willing to take the risk."

"Dr. Fitzpatrick, I understand and appreciate your emotional involvement, but it's simply not possible—"

"It is possible, unless the ISS also indulges in kidnapping private citizens."

Addison sat back to collect his thoughts, then tried another tactic. "Agent O'Hurley is highly trained, certainly one of our best." Trace merely lifted a brow, knowing that had stuck in Addison's throat. "However, his energies will be centered on the operation."

"And so will mine, as long as I can be useful."

"Agent O'Hurley will tell you himself that it's against policy to use a civilian."

"Go to Madrid, Gillian." Trace said it quietly, and broke a promise to himself by putting a hand over hers. It wasn't a matter of policy. He'd already said to hell with policy. But it was a matter of what would be best, and safest, for her.

"I'm going with you." She turned her hand over so that their palms met. "That was the deal."

"Don't be stupid. It could get ugly from here."

"That doesn't matter."

Because he thought he understood, he drew his hand away again. Rising, he walked to the window and lit a cigarette. What the hell had he done to earn that kind of trust? He didn't know the answer to that any more than he knew how to make her see reason. "I told you before, I don't have time to babysit."

"And I told you, I can take care of myself." She put the hand, still warm from his, in her lap as she turned back to Addison. "I've established myself as Cabot's woman. There wouldn't be any reason to question my traveling with him as far as Sefrou. If I have to wait there, I'll wait. Unless you intend to forcibly detain me, which I assure you would cause some nasty publicity, I'm going."

Addison hadn't expected resistance. His files on Gillian had indicated that she was a dedicated scientist, a woman who lived quietly and followed the rules. "I have no intention of forcibly detaining you, Dr. Fitzpatrick, but let me ask you this—what would happen if you were discovered and taken to Husad?"

"Then I'd try to find a way to kill him." She said it passionlessly. It was a decision she'd come to at dawn, after spending the night searching her soul. And it was because of the lack of passion, because of the simplicity, that Trace turned from the window to stare at her. "I would never allow him to use my knowledge or the skill I've worked all my life to attain against me. The Horizon project was never intended for a man like him. One of us would die before he got it."

Addison pulled off his glasses and began polishing them with a white handkerchief. "I admire your dedication, Doctor, and I appreciate your feelings. However, Agent O'Hurley will have his hands full over the next few days."

"She holds her own," Trace said from the window.

Addison pushed his glasses back on. "She's a civilian, and a target."

"She holds her own," Trace repeated as he and Gillian looked at each other. "I can use her. Cabot's been traveling with a woman. He always does."

"Then we'll assign another agent."

"Gillian's already established. She'll go with or without ISS sanction, so we might as well make the best of it."

It wasn't the fact that he was outnumbered. Addison had been outnumbered before. There was, however, the fact that any change of routine at this point could endanger the operation. Gillian Fitzpatrick wasn't one of his people, but if she insisted on risking her life, the ISS would use her.

"Very well. I can't stop you, but I can't approve. I hope you won't live to regret this decision, Doctor."

"I won't regret it."

"The notes. Since you refuse to come to Madrid with me, I must insist you give me your notes on Horizon so that I can secure them."

"Of course. I wrote them—"

"She wrote them in technical terms," Trace said, interrupting her. He aimed a long, cool glance at her that had her subsiding. "You probably won't be able to make much out of them."

"I'm sure our scientists will be able to interpret them. If you'll get them for me?"

"Of course."

"She's your responsibility," Addison said in an undertone when Gillian left the room. "I don't want any civilian casualties."

"I'll take care of her."

"See that you do." Addison rose and brushed back what was left of his hair. "At least without the notes she won't be able to make things worse than they are."

Gillian came back with her neatly folded papers. "This is all I have on the area I worked on."

"Thank you." Addison took them and slipped them into his briefcase. He turned the combination lock before straightening again. "If you change your mind, you have only to ask O'Hurley to contact us."

"I won't change my mind."

"Then goodbye, Doctor." He shook his head. "I hope that when this is over you and your brother can work on Horizon in peace." He gave a brief nod to Trace. "Report at six-hour intervals."

Gillian waited until the door had closed before she sat on the edge of the bed. "What an unfortunate man to work for. Do you deal with him often?"

"No, thank God." He went back to the coffee, but it was only lukewarm. "Not all ISS brass are like him."

"That's good news for the free world." She waited until he'd paced the room twice before speaking again. "I have some questions."

"Am I supposed to be surprised?"

"Could you sit?" In a gesture that might have been of annoyance or amusement, she waved toward a chair. "Over there. There's no danger of you touching me accidentally from that distance."

He paused long enough to give her a level look. "I don't touch accidentally."

"Well, that clears that up." She waited. Restless and edgy, he took the chair. "Why did you change your mind?"

"About what?"

"About taking me with you."

"Agreeing with Addison went against the grain."

Gillian folded her hand and spoke with the patience of a Sunday-school teacher. "I think I'm entitled to a genuine answer."

"That's genuine enough." He lit a cigarette. "And I meant what I said. I think you'll do okay."

"Your flattery leaves me speechless."

"Look, I figure you've got the biggest stake in this. Maybe you've got a right to stick around." He watched her through a haze of smoke. "That's all there is."

Or all she'd get, Gillian thought. She opted to accept it. For now. "All right. Now tell me why you didn't want me to tell Addison the notes had been doctored."

"Because the real ones are in your head. I figure that's where they belong."

"He's your superior. Don't you have an obligation to be straight with him?"

"First I go with the gut, then I go with regulations."

Gillian said nothing for a moment. She respected what he'd said, admired him because she knew he meant it. Hadn't that been the reason she'd chosen to trust him? "Once before you told me you thought you understood why Mr. Forrester didn't go directly to the ISS. I think it's time you tell me."

Trace tapped the ashes of his cigarette. The sun was dropping lower in the sky. Twilight was nearly on them. He remembered he'd been watching another sunset just before he'd seen her the first time. Perhaps he was doomed to think of her whenever night approached.

"Why don't you want Hammer to have the formula?"

"That's a ridiculous question. They're a group of terrorists headed by a madman. If they had the serum, nuclear war would be almost inevitable." She fell silent as he simply sat and looked at her. "Surely you're not comparing the ISS with one of the most radical organizations on the globe? The ISS is dedicated to ensuring international law and order, to saving lives, to protecting democracy." This time it was she who rose to pace. "I don't have to tell you what they represent. You're one of them."

"Yeah, I'm one of them. Weren't you the one who said it was an organization run by men, some good, some bad?"

"Yes." She couldn't have said why her nerves were beginning to fray. The room was dimmer, the light soft and pleasant. "And I still believe that if I had gone to them in the beginning, the project would have come first, my brother and my niece second. Meeting Captain Addison did nothing to change my mind. Still, the project was done under their auspices, and it was always intended to be handed over when completed. My father believed in the system."

Trace took one last long drag. "And you?"

"My family comes first. When they're safe, we'll go from there."

"Complete the project and hand it over to the ISS?"

"Yes, of course." A little paler, she turned back to him. "That was what my father was working toward. What are you saying, Trace?"

"Just that I figure the intent of the ISS is one thing and possible results another. Think about it, Gillian, a serum that protects you from the effects of nuclear fallout. A miracle, a shield, a scientific breakthrough, whatever you want to call it. Once it's proven, how much easier is it going to be for someone to decide to push the button?"

"No." She hugged her chest and turned away again. "Horizon is a defense, only a defense, one that could save millions of lives. My father— None of us who have worked on it ever intended for it to be used destructively."

"Do you figure the scientists involved in the Manhattan Project ever expected Hiroshima? Or maybe they did. They had to know they were busy creating a bomb in the name of a scientific breakthrough."

"We're creating a defense, not a weapon."

"Yeah, a defense. And some German physicists were just fooling around with experiments fifty years ago. I wonder if they'd have gone on with it if they'd known they were forming the basis of a weapon that has the power to wipe life off the planet."

"But the weapon's there, Trace. We can't go back and prevent its creation." She'd turned back to him now. The light coming through the window behind her had gone a pure rose. "Horizon's meant to balance that, to ensure that life will go on if that final button is pushed. Horizon is a promise of life, not a threat."

"Who decides who gets the serum, Gillian?"

She moistened dry lips. "I don't know what you mean."

"Do you plan to inoculate everyone? That's not practical, probably not even feasible. Maybe we should only shoot for the countries in the United Nations. Better yet, just the countries whose political beliefs mesh with ours. Do we use it on the very old or the terminally ill? It's bound to be expensive. Who pays for it, anyway? The taxpayers? Well, do the taxpayers want to foot the bill for the inoculation of criminals? Do we go in and give the mass murderers a shot in the arm, or do we get selective?"

"It doesn't have to be that way."

"Doesn't have to, but it usually is, isn't it? The world's not perfect, Doc. It ain't ever going to be."

She wanted to believe it could be, but she'd been fighting off those very same questions and doubts for a long time. "My father devoted most of his life to Horizon. My brother might lose his because of it. What is it you're asking me to do?"

"I'm not asking you to do anything—I'm just theorizing."

She came to him then, knowing he would distance himself, however hard she struggled to close the gap. "What disillusioned you, Trace? What made you stop believing that what you do can make a difference?"

"Because it doesn't. Oh, maybe for a while, maybe here and there, but in the long view, none of it really means a damn." He started to reach for another cigarette but pushed the pack aside instead. "I'm not ashamed of anything I've done, but that doesn't mean I'm proud, either. I'm just tired of it."

She sat across from him, no longer sure of her own

thoughts, her own goals. "I'm a scientist, Trace, not a politician. As far as Horizon goes, my input has been minimal. My father didn't share a great many of his hopes with me. I do know that it was his belief, his dream, that his work would bring some lasting good. Perhaps the kind of peace we all claim to want but do so little to secure."

"You don't get peace from a serum, Doc."

"No, perhaps not. Some of the questions you've asked I've asked myself, but I haven't gone very far with them. Maybe I haven't done enough with my life to be disillusioned." She closed her eyes a moment, because nothing seemed clear, and especially not her life. "I don't know enough of what you do—or have done—to understand. I have to take it on faith. I believe, in the long view, you have made a difference. If you're tired, if you're dissatisfied, it may be because you're more of a dreamer than you'll admit. You can't change the world—none of us can—only little pieces of it."

She wanted to offer him a hand, but she held back, knowing that rejection now would prevent her from finishing. "These last few days with you have made a difference with me."

He wanted to believe. And wanting, he discovered, could hurt. "You're romanticizing again, Doc."

"No, I'm being as honest as I know how. As logical as the situation permits. You've made a difference in the way I think, the way I feel, the way I act." She pressed her lips together. Did he have any idea how difficult it was for her to strip herself bare this way? She cleared her throat, telling herself it didn't matter. She was going for broke. "I've never thrown myself at a man before."

"Is that what you're doing?" He picked up a cigarette but only ran it through his fingers. He wanted to be casual, even amused, but the ache was spreading.

"It would be obvious to anyone but you." She had to get up, to move. Why did it always seem she had to beg and bargain for affection? "I haven't asked you for a commitment." Though she wanted one. "I haven't asked for a pledge of love or fidelity." But she would give one to him if he asked. "I've only asked you to be honest enough to…to…"

"Sleep with you?" When the cigarette snapped in his fingers, Trace dropped the pieces in the ashtray. "I've already given you the reasons why that's not in the cards."

"You gave me a bunch of foolishness about our differences. I don't want you to be my twin." She had to take a quick, steadying breath. "I want you to be my lover."

Need and longing twined so tightly inside him that he had to make a conscious effort to stand and walk toward her. He would make it quick, he promised himself, he would make it cruel and save both of them. "A fast tussle in the sheets, no strings attached? Some nice uncomplicated sex without the pretty words?"

Color flooded her face, but she kept her eyes steady. "I expect no pretty words from you."

"That's good, because I don't have any." He curled his fingers into the V of her blouse and dragged her closer. She was trembling. Good. Her fear would make it that much easier. "You're out of your league, Doc. A one-night stroll through paradise isn't your style."

She started to back away but made herself stand firm. "What difference does it make? You said you wanted me."

"Sure, and maybe I'd get a kick out of showing you what life's all about. But you're the permanent kind, sweetheart. If I ever start thinking about a house in a nice neighborhood, I'll give you a call. Meanwhile, you're just not my type."

It was, as he'd intended, a solid slap in the face. She

backed away, turned and started toward her room. She heard the sound of liquid hitting glass as she grasped the doorknob.

All her life, Gillian thought on a sudden wave of fury. All her life she'd taken that kind of casual criticism without a murmur. She'd grown up with it, come to expect it. But she was a grown woman. Her shoulders straightened. Her own woman, she added with a touch of malice as she turned back. It was time to stop freezing up or walking away and take the next risk.

Trace sipped warm whiskey and braced himself for what he thought would be a rousing argument. He'd have preferred it if she'd just gone into her room and slammed the door, but she was entitled to take a few shots. If she needed to, he'd let her aim and fire. He lifted the whiskey a second time. And choked on it.

"What the hell are you doing?"

Gillian calmly finished unbuttoning her blouse. "Proving you're wrong."

"Stop it." She let the blouse slide to the floor, then reached for the hook of her slacks. "Damn it, Gillian. Put your shirt on and get out of here."

She stepped out of her slacks. "Nervous?"

The teddy was virgin white, without lace, without frills. Her legs were creamier, with long thighs. Despite the whiskey, his mouth went dry as dust. "I'm not in the mood for one of your experiments." With damp hands he fumbled for a cigarette.

"Nervous, definitely." She tossed her hair back. One strap fell down her shoulder as she started toward him.

"You're making a mistake."

"That's more than a possibility." She stood in front of him so that the last light of day streamed over her hair and face. "But it'll be mine, won't it?"

If he'd ever seen anything more beautiful, he couldn't remember it. If he'd ever wanted anything more intensely, he'd long since forgotten it. But he was sure he'd never feared anything more than this small, lovely, half-naked woman with eyes like jade and hair like fire.

"I'm not going to touch you." He lifted his glass and drained the last drop. His hand trembled. It was all she needed to complete her confidence.

"All right. I'll touch you."

She had no guide to work with, no standard formula she had tested. Her experience with men wasn't nonexistent, but it had been limited by a strict upbringing and a demanding career. Somehow she understood that even if she'd known hundreds of men this time would have been different. Relying on instinct and need, she stepped closer.

Her hands were steadier than his as she ran them up over his chest. With her eyes on his, she enjoyed the firm, hard feel of muscle as she moved them over his shoulders. She had to rise on her toes to reach his mouth. Then her lips were soft and coaxing as they played across his. With her body pressed against his, she felt his heart thudding.

He held his body tense, as if he were expecting a blow. Once he caught himself reaching for her, but he dropped his hands again and curled them against the dresser at his back. He thought he knew her well enough to be sure a lack of response would humiliate her to the point where she would leave. To keep her safe from him. What he hadn't counted on was that she'd come to understand him, as well.

While her lips toyed with his, she unbuttoned his shirt so that her hands could move freely over the flesh beneath. Her own heart was drumming, her vision clouding, as she murmured her approval. If she had been an accomplished seductress, she could have done no better.

"I want you, Trace." Her lips trailed over his jaw to his

throat. "I have since the beginning. I tried not to." On a shuddering breath, she wrapped her arms around his waist, then ran them up his back. "Make love with me."

He put his hands to her shoulders before she could kiss him again. He knew that if his mouth was on hers a second time there would be no reason, no chance. "This isn't a game you can win." His voice had thickened. The words seemed to burn his throat. "Back off, Gillian, before it's too late."

The room was dark. The moon had yet to rise. He could see only the glimmer of her eyes as she looked at him. "You said you believe in destiny. Don't you recognize me, Trace? I'm yours."

Perhaps it was that and that alone he feared most. She was as inescapable as fate, as elusive as dreams. And now, just now, she was wrapped around him like a promise.

"Then I'm yours. God help you."

He lowered his mouth to hers with all the fire, all the force, all the fury, that he'd held back. He'd wanted to save her, and himself. Now it was up to fate, and luck. Whatever promises he'd made he'd break. He would touch her, would have his fill of her. The night would take care of itself.

He let his hands roam over her. The thin material slid under his palms. More enticement. It rose high on the thigh, so he could move from texture to texture, arousing them both. Her skin was like cream, cool, white, rich. Fascinated, he slipped his fingers under the material and found the heat. At once she dug her fingers into his back. Bracing her against him, he drove her up until her knees buckled. When she was limp, he swept her into his arms.

"This is just the beginning," he told her as he laid her on the bed. "Tonight I'm going to do all the things to you I imagined the first time I saw you." Her hair spread out like a fan of flame on the plain white cover. The first sprinkling

of moonlight filtered in, along with a breeze that smelled
faintly of the sea. "I can take you places you've never been.
Places you may wish tomorrow you hadn't gone."

She believed him. Excited, afraid, she reached up to
him. "Show me."

She hadn't known anyone could kiss that way. Before
he'd shown her passion, temper, restraint. Now the restraint
had been lifted, to be replaced by a devastating skill. His
tongue teased and tormented, his teeth aroused and pro-
voked. She found herself responding with a totality she'd
never experienced. Already more involved than she'd ever
been before, she dragged him back again and again.

Then he began to touch.

He had the hands of a musician, and he knew how to
play a woman. Fingertips stroked, pressed, lingered, until
she was breathless beneath him. Her murmurs were soft,
then urgent, then delirious. She reached for him, held him,
demanded with a strength that seemed to have been born of
the moment. She fumbled for the snap of his pants, ready
to take him to her, ready to give back this pleasure that
she thought could reach no higher. Then his fingers found
a new secret. Her body tensed, shuddered, then went lax.

No, she'd never been to this place before. It was dark,
and the air was thick and sweet. Her arms felt so heavy, her
head so light. She felt the trace of his lips down her throat
to where the material lay on her breast. He dipped his
tongue beneath to run over the peak. She could only moan.

He caught the strap in his teeth and lowered it slowly
while his hands continued to work their magic. This was
how he'd wanted her, weak from pleasure, drugged with
desire. He could taste where he chose. Such sweetness.
Even as her skin grew hot and damp, there was such sweetness. He could have fed on it for days.

The moonlight grew brighter, the passion darker.

He drew the material down and down, following the path with his mouth. He could make her shudder. And did. He could make her moan. And did. He let her sigh with quiet delight, murmur with easy pleasure, then shot her back to desperation.

Catapulted up, Gillian reached for him. They rolled together, caught in a need that was so close to being fulfilled. Again she struggled to undress him, and this time he made no protest. She moved quickly. When they were naked, he moved more quickly.

When he plunged into her, she let out a strangled cry. Half mad, she grabbed his hair and dragged his mouth to hers. He took her hard and fast, but she found herself more than able to match her rhythm to his. More than that, it seemed to her that their hearts beat in the same rhythm. She felt him form her name against her mouth, heard the sudden shudder of his breath as emotion merged with passion. She saw as her eyes fluttered open the dark intensity of his.

Then he buried his face in her hair and they took each other.

Chapter 8

It had been a mistake to stay with her. To sleep with her through the night. To wake beside her in the morning. Trace had known when they'd wrapped themselves around each other in the night that he'd pay. A man always paid for his mistakes.

The problem was, it felt so damn good.

In sleep she was as warm, as soft, as pliable, as she had been in passion. Her head was nestled on his shoulder as if it belonged there. Her hand, curled loosely in a fist, lay over his heart as if a claim had been staked. He wished, in those early morning moments, that such things were true. Knowing better wasn't easy, it just was.

The odd and uneasy thing was that the desire hadn't dissipated. He still needed, still craved, just as sharply as he had the night before, when she'd put her hands on him for the first time.

He wanted to gather her close, to wake her slowly, erotically, and send them both spinning back to where they'd gone before sleep had claimed them. He wanted, somehow more intensely, to gather her close, to stroke her hair and absorb the quiet excitement of dozing with her through the morning.

He couldn't do either. Though Trace would never have considered himself noble, he was thinking of her. He was a man who did his job and did as he chose. He lived as hard as he worked and had no ties to anyone. In Gillian he recognized a woman to whom home and hearth and family came first. He had no doubt she was good at what she did, that she was devoted to her work, but there were white picket fences and flower gardens buried inside her. A man who'd never had a home, who'd chosen never to have one, could only complicate the life of a woman who made one wherever she went.

But she felt so good curled around him.

He drew away more abruptly than he'd intended. When she stirred and murmured something, he rose to pull on his loose drawstring pants. He didn't have to turn around to know she was awake and watching him.

"You can sleep a while longer," he told her. "I've got some things to do."

Gillian drew the sheet with her as she sat up. She'd been half awake, or thought she had been. Perhaps she'd dreamed that he'd been stroking her hair. "I'll go with you."

"Well-bred ladies don't belong where I'm going."

Strange how quickly a chill could come. She'd lain half dreaming, warm and secure. Now she was cold and alone again. Her fingers tensed on the sheet, but her voice came out calmly. "I thought we were going to work together."

"When it suits, sweetheart."

Her fingers began to work on the sheet. "When it suits whom?"

"Me." He reached for a cigarette before he turned back

to her. It was just as he'd thought. She looked more beautiful now than she had any right to, with her skin pale, her hair vivid, her eyes dark and heavy. "You'd get in the way."

"Apparently I already am." She fought back humiliation as she tossed the sheets aside to gather up what she could find of her clothes. Holding them in front of her, she paused long enough to look at him. She would say what she had to say, she told herself. Too often in the past she'd taken an emotional slap with a bowed head. No more.

"I don't know what you're afraid of, O'Hurley, except yourself and your own feelings, but there's no need to behave this way."

"I'm just doing what comes naturally." He drew on the cigarette. It tasted as bitter as his thoughts. "Look, if you're going to order breakfast, get me some coffee. I'm going to take a shower before I go out."

"It's fine to regret what happened. That's your privilege." She wouldn't cry. That she promised herself. "But it isn't fine to be cruel about it. Were you thinking I'd expect a pledge of undying love? Did you have it in your mind that I'd be waiting for you to fall on your knees and tell me I'd changed your life? I'm not the fool you think I am."

"I've never thought you were a fool."

"That's good, because I'm not." It was satisfying, she'd discovered, very satisfying, to bite back. "I didn't expect those things from you. But I didn't expect that you'd treat me as if I were something you'd bought and paid for and had the right to discard in the morning. I didn't expect that, either, Trace. Maybe I should have."

She walked quickly into her room and, tossing the crumpled clothes aside, headed straight for her shower. She wouldn't weep for him. No, by the saints, there wouldn't be one tear wasted on him. Turning the spray up to near scalding, she stepped into the shower. All she needed was to be warm again, to wash the scent of him from her skin, to rinse the taste of him from her mouth. Then she would be fine again.

She wasn't a fool, she told herself. She was simply a woman who'd made an error in judgment and now had to deal with it. She was an adult, one who made her own decisions and accepted fully and freely the consequences of her own actions.

But she was a fool. As big and as stupid as they came. Gillian pressed the heels of her hands against her eyes as the water streamed over her. Damn him, and her. Who else but a fool fell in love with a man who would never give anything back?

When the curtain whipped back, her head snapped up. She turned and gave Trace a cool, disinterested stare. The hurt wasn't his problem, she told herself. And she'd see him in hell before she'd let it show. "I'm busy at the moment."

"Let's get something straight. Just because I didn't babble over you like an idiot this morning doesn't mean I think of you as someone I could have picked up off the street."

Gillian picked up the soap to rub it in slow circles over her shoulder. So he was angry. It was there, darkening his eyes and his voice. That, too, was satisfying. "It occurs to me that I'm better off not giving a damn what you think. Your pitiful excuses don't interest me, O'Hurley, and you're getting water all over the floor." She snatched the curtain back into place. It didn't even have time to settle before he tore it open again.

His eyes were furious, and his voice entirely too soft and steady. "Don't ever close a door in my face."

She wondered why she should feel like laughing at this point in her life. "It's not a door I'm closing, it's a curtain. A door would be more effective, but this will have to do." She pulled it closed again. Trace ripped it from the rod in one angry tug. As the little metal hooks jingled against the rod, Gillian tossed wet hair out of her eyes. "Well, now, that was a brilliant move. If you've finished taking out your foulness on an inanimate object, you can go."

He kicked the torn curtain aside. "What the hell do you want?"

"At the moment, to wash my hair in peace." Deliberately she stuck her head under the spray. Despite her determination, she let out a quick yelp when she was dragged back. He stood in the tub with her now, his cotton pants plastered to his legs. Water bounced off them both and onto the tile.

"I don't have time for this guilt trip. I've got a job to do, and we're going to clear the air so I can concentrate on doing it."

"Fine. The air's clear." She smacked the soap back in its holder. "You want absolution? You've got it."

"I've got nothing to feel guilty about." He stepped closer, and the spray hit his chest. "You threw yourself at me."

With one hand, Gillian dragged her hair back from her face. The steam rose, clouding the room. "Aye, that I did. You fought like a tiger, but I overpowered you." She shoved a hand into his chest. "Better clear out, O'Hurley, before I force myself on you again."

"You smart-mouthed little—" He'd started forward, then had the breath knocked out of him as her fist connected with his stomach. As the water beat down on both of them, they stared at each other in equal surprise. All at once Gillian let out a gurgle of laughter and covered her mouth with her hand.

"What the hell's so funny?"

"Nothing." She choked back another laugh. "Nothing at all, except you look like a bloody fool, and I feel like one." Still laughing, she turned her face into the spray. "Be on your way, O'Hurley, before I really get tough."

He touched a hand to his stomach for a moment, amazed that she'd gotten one in under his guard. He was slipping. Then, because the anger had disappeared, he laid a hand on her shoulder to turn her around again. "You pack a hell of a punch, Doc."

It might have been her imagination, or wishful thinking, but she thought he was speaking of more than her fist. "Thank you."

"You know you run the water too hot."

"I was in the mood for hot."

"Uh-huh." He touched her cheek, running his thumb over the light sprinkling of freckles. She wondered if he knew he was apologizing. "Why don't I wash your back?"

"No."

He slipped his arms around her. "Then you can wash mine."

"Trace." She brought her hands up in a small defensive gesture. "This isn't the answer."

"It's the only one I've got." He lowered his head to rub his lips over hers. "I want you. Isn't that what you wanted to hear?"

If only it were so simple. If only she cared less. She let the sigh come as she pressed her cheek to his. "Last night was special. I can accept that it didn't mean anything to you, but I can't afford to get in any deeper, because it did mean something to me."

He was silent for a moment, knowing they would both be better off without the words even as he understood that they had to be said. "It meant something to me, Gillian." He framed her face in his hands so that he could look at her as he took the risk. "It meant too damn much."

Her heart broke a little. "And that makes things hard for you."

"Hard for me, maybe impossible for you." He would

have let his hands drop, but she caught them in hers. "I'm no good for you."

"No, you're not." She smiled as she pulled his arms around her. "Neither's chocolate cake, but I can never resist that, either."

He wasn't sure it was wise to take Gillian to the bidonville, but he'd nearly convinced himself it was necessary. She might be better off seeing how low he had to sink in his job, and what kind of people he often did business with. What had happened between them that morning hadn't changed his mind about the senselessness of their relationship, but it had made him realize that a bond had formed, like it or not. It was up to him to be certain she had a clear-eyed view of what she was getting into.

So he took her on a roundabout route until he'd lost both Kendesa's tail and the shadow Addison had assigned to him. The first he not only expected but accepted as part of the game. The second proved to him that the ISS, or perhaps Addison alone, had decided against giving him a free hand. That only meant he had to take it.

Once he was certain he'd ditched both teams, Trace took one last circle before heading toward the shacks and squalor of the bidonville.

Because he wanted to go on foot, he carried a pistol under his jacket, another strapped to his calf, and a silent and very effective switchblade. Though his visit this trip had been brief, he knew his way here, just as he knew his way through so many other slums and ghettos.

There were plenty of unemployed men loitering in the narrow streets and cramped alleyways. But the two of them were never approached. Trace didn't walk like a tourist who'd lost his way or a curiosity seeker who'd come to take snapshots of the other side of Casablanca.

It stank. Gillian said nothing as she walked beside Trace. She wondered if he sensed it as she did. The smell was more than sweat, animal and rot. Over that there was the scent of anger and hatred. She'd seen poverty in Ireland, she'd witnessed the homeless and destitute in New York, but she'd never seen such misery and squalor as this.

There was blood here, newly spilled. There was disease waiting patiently to take hold. And there was death, more easily understood than life. She saw men watching her with hard black eyes. Veiled women never lifted theirs.

Trace approached a shack. It couldn't be called anything else, though it had glass in the windows and an excuse for a yard. A scrawny dog bared its teeth but backed away when Trace continued forward. There was a vegetable garden scratched into the ground. Someone had weeded it, and the rows were straight.

Trace knocked on the door of the shack before taking a long, sweeping view of the street. They were still watched, that was expected, but what went on in the bidonville stayed in the bidonville. Kendesa wouldn't find out about his visit unless Trace arranged it himself.

The door was opened by a small woman in a dark dress and veil. Her eyes showed the quick light of fear as she looked at Trace.

"Good morning. I've come to speak to your husband." His Arabic was rusty but competent enough. Gillian watched the woman's eyes dart here and there before she bowed the door the rest of the way open.

"If you would be pleased to sit."

Whatever filth and dirt were outside, the inside of the shack was neat as a pin. The floors and walls were scrubbed and still smelled lightly of the harsh soap used. The furniture was sparse, but without a speck of dust. In the center of the room sat a small boy in a cloth diaper. He grinned up at Trace and Gillian and pounded on the floor with a wooden spoon.

"I will bring my husband." The woman scooped up the child and disappeared through the back door.

Gillian bent to pick up the wooden spoon. "Why is she afraid of you?"

"Because she's smarter than you are. Sit down, Doc, and look a little bored. This shouldn't take too long."

With the spoon still in her hand, Gillian sat on a spindly chair. "Why are we here? Why did we come to this place?"

"Because Bakir has something for me. I've come to collect it." Trace slipped a hand inside his jacket as the door opened. He let it relax again when he saw that the man was alone.

Bakir was a little weasel of a man with a thin build and a narrow face. His eyes were small and dark. When he smiled, his teeth gleamed white and sharp. He was dressed in a gray robe that might have started off as spotless as the room. Now it was grimy at the hem. Two fresh grease stains spoiled the sleeve. Gillian felt an instant and uncontrollable revulsion.

"Ah, old friend. You were not expected until tomorrow."

"Sometimes the unexpected is preferable."

Though they spoke in English—Trace wasn't feigning an accent—Gillian said nothing. She wished quite fiercely that she had remained behind. The shack didn't seem clean and harmless now that Bakir had come inside.

"You are in a hurry to complete our business?"

"Do you have the merchandise, Bakir? I have other matters to attend to today."

"Of course, of course, you're a busy man." He glanced at Gillian and, with a grin, said something in Arabic. Trace's eyes went hard as stone. His reply was only a murmur, but whatever he said was enough to make Bakir blanch and bow. Pushing a table aside, he lifted a portion of the floor to reveal a wide trench beneath.

"Your assistance, please."

Trace bent to the task. Between the two of them, they hauled up a long wooden crate. Moving in silence now, Bakir pulled a crowbar from the trench and pried off the lid. Gillian's fingers tensed when Trace pulled out the first rifle.

It was black and oiled. She knew by the ease with which he lifted and sighted that he'd used one before. He broke it open and, in the practical manner of a man who understood guns, examined it.

"Almost like new," Bakir offered.

Instead of acknowledging him, Trace put the rifle back and drew out another. He performed the same careful examination on it, then on the next and the next, as he pulled them out of the crate. Each time he lifted a new one, Gillian's heart jolted.

He looked so natural with a gun in his hands. The same hands that had held and stroked and aroused her only a short time before. He was the same man. And yet as she looked at him now she wondered how he could seem so different in this place, with a crate of weapons at his feet and one in his hand.

Satisfied that the guns and ammunition were in order, Trace nodded. "You'll have the merchandise shipped to Sefrou. This address." He passed Bakir a sheet of paper. "Shipment tomorrow."

He reached into his jacket for an envelope fat with ISS money. He wondered what Addison's reaction would be when he learned Trace had requisitioned it.

The envelope disappeared into the folds of Bakir's cloak, but his hand remained on it. "As you wish. It may interest you that certain powers have offered great rewards for information on Il Gatto."

"Make the shipment, Bakir, and remember what would be done to anyone found to have done business with Il Gatto."

Bakir only grinned. "My memory is excellent."

"I don't understand." Gillian stayed close to Trace's side as they started down the narrow street. "Where did you get that money?"

"From taxpayers." As he walked he let his gaze swing right and left. "This is an ISS-backed operation now."

"But you gave him money for those guns. I thought Captain Addison was arranging for the weapons."

"He is." He took her arm to steer her around a corner.

"Well, if Addison's arranging for the weapons you're to show Husad, why did you pay that man for more?"

"Backup. If things don't go Addison's way, I don't figure on trying to get your brother out with a pistol and a charming smile."

Gillian felt the knot of tension in her stomach tighten. "I see. Then they're for you."

"That's right, sweetheart. Keep walking," he said when she hesitated. "This isn't the neighborhood for window-shopping."

"Trace, what good are those weapons going to do you, one man, alone?"

"Isn't that what you hired me for?"

"Yes." She pressed her lips together as she kept pace with him. "Yes, but—"

"Having second thoughts?"

She was having more than second thoughts. But how could she explain to him that the past few days had changed everything? How could she tell him that he was now every bit as important to her as the man and the child she wanted so desperately to see safe? He would laugh at her concern—or, worse, be annoyed by it.

"I don't know what I think anymore," she murmured. "The longer this goes on, the less real it seems. When it first started, I thought I knew exactly what had to be done. Now I'm not sure of anything."

"Just let me do the thinking."

A man in a grimy white robe stumbled in front of them. He only had time to gesture toward Gillian and mutter something in a drunken slur before Trace had the switchblade out. Gillian saw the sun glint off steel as Trace issued a quiet warning. Still grinning, the man lifted both hands palms up and teetered out of the way again.

"Don't look back," Trace ordered as he pulled Gillian along with him.

"Did he want money?"

He'd stopped believing anyone could be that naive. She was good for him, he thought. Too damn good. "For starters," he said simply.

"This is an awful place."

"There are worse."

She looked at him then as the beat of her heart began to calm again. "You know how to walk here, how to talk here, but that doesn't make you like that man back in that shack."

"We both make a living."

They skirted around the walls and went into the shopping district. "You know, I think you'd like me to believe you were like him. That would be more comfortable for you."

"Maybe. We'll get some coffee, hang around here long enough for the tails to pick us up again."

"Trace." Though it shamed her, she felt safe again away

from the sights and smells of the slums. "Is it just me, or do you fight off anyone who gets too close?"

He didn't know how to answer her. Worse, he wasn't sure he could afford to dig too deeply for the real answer. "Seems to me we were pretty close last night."

She met his look levelly, her eyes clear and serene. "Yes, we were, and you still haven't dealt with it."

"I've got a lot on my mind, Doc." He pulled out a chair at a small café and sat down. After a moment's hesitation, Gillian joined him.

"So have I. More than I bargained for." She let him order coffee and hoped that before long she would be back in her room, where she could pull down the shades, close her eyes and block out the morning, if only for a little while. "I have another question."

"Sweetheart, I've never known you not to."

She put a hand on his before he could light a cigarette. "That man, Bakir, he didn't know you as Cabot."

"No, I used him in an operation a few years back."

"He's an agent?"

Trace laughed but waited until their coffee was served before speaking again. "No, Doc, he's a snake. But reptiles have their uses."

"He knows who you are. Why would he deliver the shipment instead of simply keeping the money you've given him and telling Husad who and where you are?"

"Because he knows that if Husad didn't manage to kill me I'd come back and slit his throat." Trace lifted his coffee. Out of the corner of his eye he noted that the first tail had picked them up again. "Bad business risk."

Gillian stared at her coffee. It was black and thick. She knew that if she drank it it would take the chill from her skin, but she didn't pick up the cup. "I was raised to respect life," she said quietly. "All life. So much of the work

I've done has been to try to make life better, easier. I can't deny that science has had too much to do with destruction, but the goal has always been to preserve and advance. I've never in my life hurt anyone intentionally. It's not that I'm such a saint, but more, I think, that I've never had to make that choice."

She wrapped both hands around her cup but still didn't pick it up as she lifted her gaze to Trace's. "When Captain Addison asked me what I would do if Husad took me, I was telling the truth. I know in my heart that I could take a life. And it frightens me."

"You're not going to find yourself in the position where you have to put that to the test." He put a hand over hers briefly, because no matter how hard he tried he couldn't keep himself from offering comfort.

"I hope not, because I know not only what I would do, but that I could live with it afterward. I suppose what I'm trying to say is that we're not so different, you and I."

He looked away from her, because the need to believe she was right was too sharp. "Don't bet on it."

"I already have," she murmured, and drank her coffee.

Chapter 9

Gillian told herself that the move to Sefrou was bringing her another step closer to Flynn. He was close now. She could look out at the unfamiliar streets and mountains and almost feel how close.

It was a rare thing now for her to allow herself more than a few moments alone. Alone she would think too clearly of what had happened, what could be happening, to her brother and niece. The fear that she was too late, or would ultimately be too late, was a dark secret she kept buried inside her heart.

She didn't spend her nights weeping. The emotional release of tears wouldn't help Flynn. There were the nightmares, the sometimes hideous, often violent dreams she pulled herself out of on almost a nightly basis. Thus far she had been able to bring herself out of the nightmares without causing a disturbance that woke Trace. At least she could be grateful for that. She didn't want him to know she was weak enough to be frightened into cold chills by dreams. He had to think of her as strong and capable. Otherwise he might change his mind about letting her play any part in freeing Flynn.

Strange how well she had come to know him. Gillian watched a small compact car wind through the streets below while the silence of her hotel room hung around her. It was at times like this, when she was alone, that she worked hardest to concentrate on the practical aspects of Flynn's release. When that didn't work, she concentrated instead on Trace. Who he was, what made him tick, what secrets he kept locked in his heart.

She had come to understand him, though he told her little with words. More than once she had imagined them meeting socially in New York, under normal, even pedestrian, circumstances. A dinner date, a show, a cocktail party. She knew they would have become lovers wherever they'd met, but she also knew that under other circumstances it would have happened slowly and with more caution.

Destiny. She had never really thought about her own before Trace. Now she believed, as he did, that some things were meant. *They* were meant. She wondered how long he would continue to fight his feelings, the feelings she sensed in him whenever he held her. Words of affection wouldn't come easily from a man who'd deliberately shut those doors in his life. She was certain the reason for that had to do with his family.

If there was one thing Gillian was accustomed to, it was reticent males. She could be patient until he opened up to her. And she was optimistic enough not to doubt that he would.

She was so in love. She leaned on the windowsill with a sigh. All her life she'd waited for this feeling, the one that made the heart pound and the brain giddy, the one that made everything seem more vivid. True, she'd never expected to experience love for the first time in the midst of the biggest crisis of her life. But, crisis or not, the feeling was there, big and bold and beautiful.

Gillian knew she would have to wait to share it. There'd come a time when she could speak of it freely, laugh and steep herself in the feelings between them. She hadn't waited all her life to fall in love only to be denied the pleasure of expressing it. But she could wait.

One day, when Flynn and Caitlin were safe, when the violence, the fear, the intrigue, were nothing more than a vague memory, she would have her time with Trace. A lifetime. She couldn't afford to doubt that. What had happened in the past few weeks had taught her that happiness had to be grabbed with both hands and treasured with a full heart.

Yes, she would bide her time, and accept her destiny.

But how she wished he'd come back. How she hated being left alone.

Gillian understood he had a role to play and a job to do. Neither Cabot's mistress nor Dr. Gillian Fitzpatrick had a place in the morning meeting between Flynn and his ISS contact in eastern Morocco. The ISS agent would see that André Cabot received his supply of arms, just as Bakir would see that Il Gatto received his.

She could only wait while the man she loved armed himself and stepped into the hornet's nest.

Because her nerves were building quickly, Gillian searched for something to do. She had already unpacked and rearranged her belongings three times. Trace's case was open, but his clothes were jumbled inside. He'd taken out only what he needed that morning. For lack of something better to do, Gillian began to shake out, refold and put away his clothes.

She found she could enjoy the small task, smoothing

out a shirt, wondering where he'd bought it, how he looked wearing it. She could draw in his scent from his rumpled garments. His taste in clothes was certainly eclectic. There was everything from denim to silk, from bargain basement to Saville Row.

How many men did he carry around in this case? she wondered as she folded a T-shirt that was thin to the point of transparency at the shoulders. She wondered if he ever had to stop and think, to bring back to the front of his mind who he really was.

Then she found the flute, wrapped carefully in felt beneath a tailored shirt of satin piqué. It was polished but had the look of something old and well used. Experimentally Gillian lifted it to her lips and blew. The note came clear and sweet and had her smiling.

He came from a family that made its living making music. He hadn't left that behind, not completely, no matter how hard he pretended he had. She imagined he played when he was alone and lonely in some foreign place. Perhaps it reminded him of the home he claimed not to have, of the family he'd chosen not to see for years.

She placed her fingers over the holes, then lifted two at random, enjoying the sound that came when she blew into the mouthpiece. She'd always had an affection for music, though her father had considered the study of chemicals more important than the piano lessons she'd once hoped for. She wondered if someday Trace would teach her to play a real melody, something sentimental, from the country she'd left behind.

She set the flute on the bed, but didn't rewrap it. There were books in the case, as well, Yeats and Shaw and Wilde. Gillian picked one and leafed through familiar passages. A man who described himself in such harsh terms carried Yeats along with a weapon. She'd sensed that contradictory combination long before she'd seen evidence it existed; indeed, she'd fallen in love with the many sides of the enigma that was Trace O'Hurley.

Nerves forgotten, fears banked, she set the books on the table beside the bed. She was humming to herself as she put the last of the shirts away. When she started to close the case, she noticed a notebook tucked in one of the side pockets. Without thinking, she drew it out and set it on the edge of the dresser. She put the case in the closet beside hers, fussed to be sure the trousers were hung by the crease, then wandered back toward the window. As she passed the dresser, she knocked the notebook to the floor. The words and musical notes caught her eye as she bent to pick it up.

The sun rises, the sun sets, but I wait for the dream.
The nights are too long to be alone.
Days pass without sweetness in sunlight that streams.
The nights are too dark to be far from home.

Enchanted, she sat on the bed to read. Her hand went to the flute and rested there.

It had been a few years since Trace had worked with Breintz. They'd put together a tidy little job in Sri Lanka five or six years before, and then, in the way of people in their business, they'd lost touch. Outwardly Breintz had changed. His hair had thinned, his face had widened. There were folds of wrinkles under his eyes that gave him a lazy basset-hound look. He sported a sapphire stud in his ear and wore the robe of the desert people.

After an hour's discussion, Trace was reassured. However much Breintz's appearance had changed, inside he was still the same sharp-witted agent he'd worked with in the past.

"It was decided against using the usual routes for the shipment." Breintz's clipped English had a controlled musicality Trace had always found agreeable. "It would be too possible for another terrorist group to trace it, or even for an overenthusiastic customs official to cause problems. In this I have used my contacts. The shipment comes by private plane to an airstrip a few miles east of here. Those who need to be paid off have been."

Trace nodded. In the dim rear booth of the nearly empty restaurant he indulged in one of Breintz's Turkish cigarettes. Over the scent of rich smoke he could smell meat— some sort of sausage—grilling. "And once the shipment arrives, I move accordingly. The whole thing should be over in a week."

"If the gods permit."

"Still superstitious?"

Breintz's lips curved, more in patience than in humor. "We all hold on to what works." Breintz let out smoke in three puffs, watching the rings form and vanish. "I don't believe in advice, but in information. Understand?"

"Yes."

"Then I will pass on this information, though you are likely aware already. I am in my fourth year of association with terrorists in this small, beleaguered part of the world. Some are fanatically religious, some politically ambitious, some simply blinded by anger. Such things, when accompanied by a disregard for human life, are dangerous, and, as we have too often found, not easily controllable. There is a reason, old friend, why none of the more established revolutionary organizations recognize Hammer. Religion, politics and anger become unpalatable even to the radical when they are driven by madness. Husad is a madman—

a clever and magnetic one, but a madman. If he discovers your deception, he will kill you in any of several unpleasant ways. If he does not discover your deception, he will still kill you."

Trace drew again on the Turkish cigarette. "You're right, I'm already aware. I'm going to get the scientist and the kid out. Then I'm going to kill Husad."

"Assassination attempts have failed before, to the disappointment of many."

"This one won't."

Breintz spread his hands. "I am at your service."

With a last nod, Trace rose. "I'll be in touch."

Trace knew he would be moving toward a conclusion in a matter of days. He was grateful for it. Since his first assignment with the ISS, he'd accepted the fact that any job he agreed to take could kill him. It hadn't been a matter of his not caring whether he lived or died. Trace had always had a definite preference for living. It had simply been a matter of his acknowledging the risks and making damn sure he was around to collect his pay. Over the past few days, staying alive had become even more important.

He hadn't changed his mind concerning himself and Gillian, but he'd had to accept the fact that he wanted more time with her. He wanted time to hear her laugh, as she'd done so rarely since they'd met. He wanted time to watch her relax, as she did only when she'd convinced herself she could let go for short snatches of time. He wanted, more than he cared to admit, to have her care for him with the same depth and devotion that she cared for her family.

It was stupid. It was certainly wrong for her. But that was what he wanted.

He would give her back her brother, and the child she sometimes murmured for in her sleep. He would do what he had come to Morocco to do, and then he would have one clear night with her. One night, all night, without the tensions, the fears, the doubts, that hovered around her now. She thought he didn't sense them, but he did. He wanted to give her peace.

She hadn't wanted his sympathy, so he didn't offer it. The passion he did give should have been easy, yet it was tinted with the sweetest, sharpest ache he'd ever known. The ache was longing, a longing to give more than was asked, to take more than was given. To make promises, and to accept them.

He couldn't do that, but he could have that one night with her when her family was safe and the threat was past. Then he could give her the gift of backing out of her life.

To have that one night, to walk away with more than he'd ever had before, all he had to do was stay alive.

Kendesa's tail dropped him in the lobby. Trace felt secure knowing Kendesa was taking precautions. He felt even better knowing that his meeting with Breintz would be reported. The other agent's cover was as tight as they came. Trace strolled down the corridor to his room, thinking how glad he would be to get out of the suffocating suit and tie.

When he opened the door he was stunned, then furious.

Gillian looked up at him, her eyes damp and her smile brilliant. "Trace, I'm so glad you're back. These songs are so lovely. I've read them all twice and still haven't decided if I have a favorite. You have to play them for me so I can—"

"What the hell are you doing digging around in my things?"

The tone caught her so off guard that she simply stared at him, the notebook open in her lap. When he crossed to her to snatch the notebook, she felt the full brunt of his fury. She didn't cringe away. She just sat very still.

"I don't suppose it occurred to you that even though I'm working for you, even though I'm sleeping with you, I'm still entitled to my privacy."

She went very pale, as she did whenever stress took over. "I'm sorry," she managed in a very careful voice. "You were gone so long, and I needed something to do, so I thought I'd put your things away for you. I came across the flute and the notebook as I was finishing up."

"And didn't stop to think that what was written in the notebook might be private?" He stood, holding the book in his hand, as thoroughly embarrassed as he'd ever been in his life. What he'd written had come straight from the heart and was nothing he'd ever intended to share with anyone.

"I beg your pardon." Her voice was stiff with formality now. She didn't bother to tell him how the notebook had fallen open, since he was so obviously interested only in the end result. "You're right, of course. I had no business messing about with your things."

He'd hoped for an argument. A good shouting match would have helped him turn the embarrassment into something more easily dealt with. Instead, her quiet apology only made him feel more embarrassed and a great deal like a moron. Opening a drawer, he tossed the book in, then slammed it shut again.

"Next time you're bored, read a book."

She rose as her own temper bristled. She'd gotten such pleasure, such innocent pleasure, out of the words the man was capable of writing. Now she was being punished for discovering this secret part of him. But it was his secret, she reminded herself before she could open her mouth in anger. It was his, and she'd intruded on it.

"I can only repeat that I'm sorry, I was completely in the wrong, and you have my word that the mistake won't be repeated."

No, she wasn't going to argue with him, Trace realized as he walked over to wrap the flute in felt. There was too much hurt in her eyes, hurt he'd put there by being so unreasonably hard about an innocent act. "Forget it." He set the flute in the drawer beside the book and shut them both away. "The meeting with Breintz went according to plan. The guns are here. I figure Kendesa will make contact tomorrow, the next day at the latest."

"I see." She looked around for something to do, something to occupy her hands. She settled on clasping them together. "Then it should all be over soon."

"Soon enough." For reasons that escaped him, he wanted to apologize, to hold her and tell her he was sorry for being an idiotic ass. He stuck his hands in his pockets. "We can go down for lunch. There's not much to see in this place, but you could get out of the room awhile."

"Actually, I thought I'd lie down, now that you're back and I know everything's all right. I've really been more wound up than hungry." And though she'd thought never to feel that way again, she wanted desperately to be alone.

"All right. I'll bring you something back."

"Some fruit, maybe." They kept their distance, because neither had the nerve to take the first step. "I never seem to have much of an appetite when I'm traveling."

He remembered the first night, when she'd fallen asleep without dinner, how pale and drained she'd been when he'd carried her to bed. She was pale now, too. He wanted, very badly, to stroke the color back into her cheeks. "I won't be long."

"Take your time."

She waited until he was gone before she lay down on the bed. Curling into a ball always seemed to help somehow. It concentrated the hurt into one tight place where it was more easily dealt with. She wouldn't weep. She let her eyes close and tried hard to concentrate on nothing. She wouldn't let her emotions swing wild, the way they had when she'd been young and had thought to surprise her father.

She'd tidied up his office, polishing wood and shining glass. He'd been furious, too. She sighed and struggled to clear the memory from her mind. Furious that she'd infringed on his private space, touched his personal things. She might have broken something, misplaced something. It hadn't mattered that she'd done neither.

Sean Brady Fitzpatrick had been a hard man, and loving him had been one long exercise in frustration. Gillian sighed again. Apparently she was a very slow learner.

He hadn't eaten anything. Nor had he finished the whiskey he'd ordered. Trace had never known a woman who could make a man feel more of a fool when she was clearly in the wrong. Those songs had never been intended for anyone but himself. He wasn't ashamed of them, it was just that he'd indulged himself, or parts of himself, in the writing of them. They were his innermost thoughts, innermost feelings, dreams he admitted to having only on the rarest of occasions. He wasn't sure he could handle her knowing what was inside him, what he sometimes longed for on the longest of lonely nights. The songs could erase the differences and the distance between them, whether he wanted to or not.

He shouldn't have hurt her. Only the stupid or the heartless hurt the defenseless. Discovering he could be both left an unpleasant taste in his mouth. He'd have liked to blame that on her, too, but he thought too clearly once anger had passed.

He laid the rose on the little basket of fruit and opened the door.

She was sleeping. He'd hoped she would be awake so that he could make his gesture of apology quick and painless. Growing up with women had taught him that they forgave easily, often smugly, as though men's cloddish behavior was to be expected. It wasn't a sweet pill to swallow, but at least it was a small one.

Trace set the basket on the dresser before moving toward her. She was curled up tight, as if to ward off another blow. That was one more brick on his back. Muttering a curse, he pulled the spread up over her. She'd left the shade up. He walked over to draw it down and dim the room. It made a quiet sound that had her stirring in sleep.

"Caitlin."

Though the little girl's name came in a murmur, Trace heard the fear in it. Not sure what to do, he sat on the edge of the bed and began to stroke her hair. "She'll be all right, Gillian. Just a few more days."

But his touch and his reassurance seemed to set off a new reaction. He felt her begin to tremble. Even as he stroked the hair from her temple, sweat pearled cold on her skin. Though he let no more than a second pass, he could see she was fighting to pull herself out of the dream. Her face went a deathly white as he took her by the shoulders and drew her up.

"Gillian, wake up." He gave her a squeeze that had her muffling a scream. "Come on, Doc, knock it off." Her eyes were wide and terrified when they flew open. Trace kept his grip firm until he saw comprehension come into them. "You okay?"

"Yes, yes, I'm fine." But she couldn't stop shaking. All the other times she'd been able to control the shaking. "I'm sorry."

"You don't have to apologize for having a nightmare."

"For making a fool out of myself, then." She drew away,

just a little, but enough to make him realize what a twist rejection gave the heart.

"Want some water?"

"Yes. I'll get it."

"Sit down, damn it. I'll get it." He felt like a ham-handed jerk. Giving the tap a violent twist, he filled a glass to the rim with tepid water. Gillian sat on the bed, fighting back tears she was certain would put a cap on her humiliation and struggling to ignore a roiling stomach that came from holding back too long. "Take a couple of sips and relax."

But her hands were shaking, and she only managed to spill water on both of them. "I'm—"

"If you apologize again, I swear I'll belt you." He took the glass and set it aside and then, feeling an awkwardness he'd never experienced with women, slipped an arm around her. "Just relax. Why don't you tell me about it? It usually helps."

She wanted to lean her head against his shoulder. She wanted him to hold her, really hold her, murmuring something sweet and foolish, until the terror passed. She wanted a miracle, she told herself. As a scientist, she knew that the world was fresh out.

"It was just a dream, unpleasant, that's all. Like the rest of them."

"What rest of them?" He cupped her face in his hand so that he could turn it up to his. "Have you been having nightmares all along?"

"It's not surprising. The unconscious mind—"

He swore and tightened his grip. He remembered how she had trembled, how the sweat had beaded cold and clammy on her skin, how glazed with fear her eyes had been. "Why didn't you tell me?"

"I didn't see the point."

He let her go then, slowly, and rose to his feet. If she

had aimed a blow directly at his solar plexus, she wouldn't have been any more accurate. He gave a brief, humorless laugh. "Well, I guess I had that one coming, didn't I?"

A new fear was growing, one that warned her that she might be suddenly, violently, physically sick. She was too afraid to try to stand, too restless to stay where she was. "You'd just have been annoyed, as you are now. And I'd just have been embarrassed, as I am now." She shifted so that she could press a hand against the churning of her stomach.

"Seems you've got me pegged," he murmured. He opened his mouth to say more but was surprised to see that she'd gone even paler. Moving instinctively, he turned her toward the edge of the bed and pushed her head between her knees. "Just breathe deep. It'll pass in a minute. Come on, love, nice deep breaths."

Even as the faintness faded, the tears burned in her eyes. "Just leave me alone, will you? Just go away and leave me alone."

There'd been a time, not so long before, when he would've been only too happy to oblige her. Now he simply ran a hand up and down her spine, murmuring to her, until he felt her breathing even out. "I think we've both taken the easy way for too long." Gathering her up, he lay down beside her and held her close. He recognized more surprise than resistance and decided he deserved that, as well. "I think you should know I don't expect Superwoman. I know what you're going through, and I know that even someone as strong as you needs an outlet. Let me help."

She tightened her arms around him. Though the tears fell quietly, the release was complete. "I need you." Her body absorbed the warmth of his as tension fled. "I've tried so hard not to be afraid, and to believe everything really is going to be all right. Then the dreams... They kill all of you. And I can't stop them."

"The next time you have a dream, remember, I'm right here. I'm not going to let it happen."

She could almost believe in miracles when he moved his fingers gently through her hair, his lips gentle at her temple. "I don't want to lose you, either." She tilted her face up to his, hoping she would at least see acceptance.

"I've come through tighter spots than this." He touched his mouth to her forehead, realizing how comforting it could be to give comfort. "Besides, my retirement fund's riding on this one."

Her lips curved a little. "The Canary Islands."

"Yeah." Oddly, he couldn't picture the palm trees and calm waters. "I'm not going to let you down, Gillian."

She touched a hand to his face. "When this is over, I wonder if it would be an intrusion if I visited you there for a few days."

"I might be up to some company. The right company." He nestled her head in the curve of his shoulder again. The glass on the table beside them vibrated against the wood. Water sloshed over the edge again. Beneath them, the bed shook.

"What—"

"Earth tremor." He tightened his grip. "Just a little one. Morocco's prone to earthquakes."

"Is that all?" When the vibration ceased, Gillian let out the breath she'd been holding. "I could give you some scientific data on earthquakes, crustal plates, faults." She let out a calmer breath when the world stayed steady. "But I can't say I've ever experienced one firsthand."

"It's quite a show."

"One I wouldn't mind missing."

"Gillian…"

"Yes?"

"I'm…ah… About before… I guess I didn't have to come down so hard on you."

"I didn't think before I acted. That's always a mistake."

"Not always. Anyway, I overreacted about something that wasn't that big a deal."

"Your songs are a very big deal." She liked the way he brushed his hand under her hair to her neck. He'd held her so close when the earth had shaken. There was a need in him to protect. She wondered how long it would take before he recognized it. "I know you didn't like me looking at them, but I can't be sorry I did. They were so beautiful."

"They're only… Really?"

Because the question touched her, she shifted again so that she could look down at him. How nice it was, how sweet, to discover that he, too, knew self-doubt and the need for reassurance. "Now and again, and very briefly, I've seen true sensitivity in you. A real gift for seeing things, feeling things. I like that man very much. After reading those songs, I felt closer to him."

He moved his shoulders uncomfortably. "You're making me into something I'm not again."

"No. I'm just accepting that there's more than one side of you." She kissed him softly, reaching out as much to the man he was as to the man he'd had to be.

She moved him too much, too deeply. Trace drew her away again, though he knew they'd passed the last border. "I'm going to disappoint you."

"How, when I'm willing to take you as you are?"

"I guess there's no use reminding you you're making a mistake?"

"None," she answered, just as her lips met his.

He'd never kissed her like this, softly, quietly, as if he had a lifetime to indulge himself. The passion and skill that always excited and overwhelmed her was banked.

Instead, he gave her the affection she'd always fantasized about but had never expected to receive. She wondered if he realized how beautiful that gift was or how desperately she needed it now. Her sigh, as much from gratitude as pleasure, stole into the room.

He undressed her slowly, experimenting with the feelings that he'd finally let have their freedom. Strong, solid, inescapable feelings that filled him with power and serenity.

He could love and be loved, he could give and receive love, taste it, savor it, hoard it. For one day he could believe that a woman like her was meant for him, to keep, to cherish, to last.

By necessity the future had always been kept very close to the present. He could never allow himself to think in months, much less years. So even now, with her warm and willing in his arms, he refused to acknowledge the tomorrows. Today was timeless and theirs, and he would remember it.

His hands were the hands of an artist now. Skillful, yes, but sensitive. She hadn't known a man could love a woman with such restraint and still stir unbearably. His body was familiar now, so that when she undressed him she knew how to touch, where to stroke, when to linger. It was an adventure in itself to discover she could arouse him, make his body tense, his muscles bunch. It was thrilling to learn that even when aroused he could take care.

He held her differently, and though the difference was subtle, she reveled in it. Desire took on such fascinating, such miraculous angles when touched with emotion. Her name came almost musically through his lips as they glided over her. His murmurs were like quiet promises as she caressed.

He loved her. She wanted to laugh and shout it out with

triumph, but she knew the words had to come from him, in his time, in his way.

Such patience. She hadn't known he had such patience in him for a woman. For her. Given it, she felt herself blossom in his hands. All that she had, all that she felt, all that she'd hoped to feel, was his for the asking.

Such generosity. He hadn't known anyone could possess such a bounty of it. He hadn't expected anyone to offer it to him with such freedom. Whatever he could give, whatever was coming to life inside him, was for her. And only her.

When they offered, and accepted, they both understood that some miracles were possible.

The light crept around the edges of the shades but did little to chase away the shadows in the room. He'd never felt so at ease with anyone. They'd slept awhile—only minutes, really—but he'd found himself refreshed and renewed. Trace rolled over on his stomach, one arm wrapped around her, and thought that the best thing to do with his energy was to make love with her again.

"Remember that shower we took the other day, when you were in a snit?"

Lazily she shifted so that she lay half over him, her cheek on his back. "I don't recall being in a snit. I do remember being justifiably annoyed."

"Whatever, the result was the same." He closed his eyes on a sigh as she began to knead the muscles at the base of his neck. "I was just thinking how nice you felt, all hot and wet, particularly when you were mad enough to spit in my eye."

"Oh? Do you have plans to make me mad again?"

"Whatever it takes. A little lower, Doc. Yeah." He sighed as her fingers moved down his spine. "That's the spot."

"I could be persuaded to take a shower." She pressed

her lips to his shoulder blade, then moved them down to follow the path of her hands.

"I don't think it would take much persuasion."

"Really." She looked up at the back of his head. "Are you saying I'm easy, O'Hurley?"

"No." He grinned to himself. "I'm saying I'm good." He winced only a little when she pinched him.

"Such arrogance usually precedes a fall. Perhaps I should—" She broke off when she made a new discovery. "Trace, why do you have a beetle tattooed on your bottom?"

He opened one eye. "A scorpion."

"I beg your pardon?"

"It's a scorpion."

Willing to give him the benefit of the doubt, Gillian leaned closer. "I realize the light's a bit dim, but... No, this is definitely a beetle. A squashed beetle, at that." She gave it a quick, friendly kiss. "Trust me, I'm a scientist."

"It's a scorpion. Symbolic of a quick sting."

She pressed a hand to her mouth to muffle a chuckle. "I see. How appropriate. However, since my view is undoubtedly better than yours could be, let me assure you that your very attractive posterior is adorned with a squashed beetle."

"It's just a little out of focus," he told her, refusing to take offense, because her hands felt so good. "The tattoo artist was drunk."

Gillian sat up, resting one hand on his hip. "Are you saying you were mad enough to trust this very sensitive area of your body to a drunk tattoo artist?"

Trace rolled over. In a move that reminded her how quick he could be, he had her beneath him. "I was drunk, too. Do you think I'd let anyone come near me with a needle if I was sober?"

"You're mad."

"Yeah. And I was twenty-two." He began to indulge in the taste of her skin. "Nursing a broken heart and a dislocated shoulder."

"Did you have your heart broken, then?" Curious, she lifted his face to hers. "Was she pretty?"

"Gorgeous," he said instantly, though he couldn't really remember. "With a body that was almost as good as her imagination." He kept his face bland as her eyes narrowed.

"Is that the truth?"

"If it's not, it should be. Anyway, I did have a dislocated shoulder."

"Aw." Gillian ran her hand up to it. "Would you like another?"

"Threats?" Delighted, Trace grinned down at her. "You know, Doc, you sound suspiciously like a jealous woman."

Now the heat came into her eyes. "I don't know what you're talking about. I'd hardly waste any healthy jealousy I might have on the likes of you."

"Are you getting justifiably annoyed?"

"And why shouldn't I, when I'm lying naked in bed with a man who's cloddish enough to tell me about another woman?"

"Good." Trace rolled off the bed. Then, ignoring her struggles, he tossed Gillian over his shoulder.

"Just what do you think you're doing?"

"Now that I've got you in a snit, I thought we'd take that shower."

Gillian caught the beetle between her thumb and forefinger and twisted hard. "Bastard."

"I love it when you talk dirty."

He carried her laughing into the bath.

Chapter 10

When the arrangements had been made for Trace to meet Husad's men and be driven into the mountains, Gillian was torn in two directions. She wanted Trace to get to Flynn, to see him, to come back and tell her that her brother and her little niece were well and that he'd found a safe and simple way to free them.

It was because she knew there was no safe and simple way that she wanted to tell him not to go, not to risk being killed or captured. She was well aware that if she hadn't interfered in his life Trace would have spent these past weeks basking in the Mexican sun. Whatever happened to him now was her responsibility. When she'd tried to explain her feelings to him, he'd brushed her off.

"No one's ever been responsible for me, sweetheart. It would be stupid for you to start now."

So she kept silent about her fears, knowing they were of little use to her, and of no use whatever to Trace.

When they made love, it was with a quiet madness, a restrained desperation that spoke of what neither of them had said aloud. This might be the last time. She wanted to beg him for promises, but she settled for moonlight and rough caresses. He wanted to make her a pledge, but he settled for her warmth and generosity. She could have no idea what risks were involved when he walked into the lion's den armed only with a lie. Though he knew a lie could be as lethal a weapon as any, he would have preferred the cold company of his .45.

As Cabot, he would get nowhere near Husad with a gun or a blade. As Il Gatto... But Il Gatto would have to wait. He would go to Husad's mountain headquarters, and he would come back with Flynn and Caitlin Fitzpatrick. Or he would not come back.

Shifting, he listened to Gillian's quiet breathing beside him. No nightmares, he thought, grateful. In a day, perhaps two, it would be done. Then she could go back to her life in New York, her institute, her experiments. There would be no need for nightmares once her world had been put in order again.

He stroked her hair, but lightly, wanting to touch but not to awaken. He'd never asked her about her work. To ask would have brought himself another step closer. But he tried to imagine her now, laboring over some impossibly complicated calculations, a white coat covering some neat business suit, her hair tied back or pinned up, her eyes intense with concentration.

She really believed she could change the world with knowledge and logic and science. He let the tangled silk of her hair drift between his fingers. Maybe it was good that she did, that she refused to face the hard reality that nothing ever really changed. The grimness of that fact would steal something from her, as it had from him. He wanted to remember her as she was—strong, naive, full of hope.

He didn't know how to tell her what she'd meant to him, what, if he'd been different, they might have meant to each other. So he drew his hand away and left her sleeping.

But she was awake. She'd known he was restless and lost in his own thoughts, so she'd lain quietly. There was something so tender and sweet about the way he touched her when he thought she was unaware. That was something she could hold on to the next day, when he walked out the door.

If he couldn't sleep, she thought, perhaps if she reached out and offered to hold him he would rest. But when she heard him pick up the phone, she kept her silence.

He spoke in French, which left her in the dark, then lapsed into silence. She heard him strike a match as he waited.

"This is O'Hurley, number 8372B. Patch this call through Paris to New York, code three, phase twelve."

He needed to make the call, though he knew it was against regulations when he was on assignment. Going through the Paris operation would secure it. He knew the phone wasn't bugged or tapped, and if Kendesa was tracing his calls he would know only that Cabot had called Paris. From there, the call would be scrambled.

Now he could only hope she was home.

"Hello."

"Maddy." The sound of her voice had him smiling into the shadows. "No show tonight?"

"Trace? Trace!" Her quick, infectious laugh bubbled over oceans and miles. "How are you? Where are you? I was wondering if I'd get my semiannual call. I'm so glad I did. There's so much to tell you. Are you in New York?"

"No, I'm not in the States. I'm fine. How's the toast of Broadway?"

"Terrific. I don't know what the Great White Way is going to do without me when I take a year off."

"A year? You and Valentine going traveling?"

"No… I don't know, maybe. Trace, I'm going to have a baby." Her excitement was all but sizzling the wires. "In six and a half months. In fact, they're going to be doing some tests, because it looks like I'm having more than one."

A baby. He thought of the skinny, long-legged redhead, who had always seemed to have more energy than any one person was entitled to. She'd still been a teenager when he'd seen her last. And now…a baby. He thought of Abby and her sons, the nephews he'd never seen.

"You okay?" And he wished, more intensely than he'd wished before, that he could link hands with her and see for himself.

"Never better. Oh, Trace, I wish you could make it home, even for a little while, and meet Reed. He's so terrific, so upstanding and stable. I don't know how he tolerates me. And Abby, she's going to have the baby in just a few months. You should see her. I can't believe how beautiful, how content she is, since she married Dylan. The boys are growing like weeds. Did you get the pictures she sent you?"

"Yeah." He'd gotten them, pored over the faces of his sister's sons, then destroyed them. If something happened to him, he couldn't leave behind anything that could be traced to his family. "Nice-looking boys. The little one looks like a heartbreaker."

"That's because he looks like you."

She couldn't know how the statement shook him. Trace closed his eyes a moment and brought the face in the photo back into his mind. Maddy was right, of course. Family ties might be thin, almost invisible, but they were strong.

"You hear from Chantel?"

"That's the big news." Maddy paused automatically for dramatic impact. "Big sister's getting married."

"What?" He wasn't often thrown completely off balance, but Trace nearly choked on the smoke he'd dragged into his lungs. There had been rumors, of course. There were always rumors. But he hadn't believed them. "You want to say that again?"

"I said Chantel, femme fatale, star of stage and screen, has met her match. She's getting married in just a couple of weeks. We wanted to let you know, but we didn't know how to get in touch."

"Yeah. I've been—" he glanced over to where Gillian lay quiet in the bed "—tied up."

"In any case, she's really taking the plunge. It should be the glitziest wedding this side of the Windsors."

"So Chantel's getting married. I'd like to meet the guy," he said, half under his breath.

"He's perfect for her. Rough and tough and just cynical enough to keep Chantel on her toes. Trace, she's absolutely crazy about him. Seems there was a writer who'd developed an obsession about her, a dangerous one. Anyway, to keep the story short, she'd hired Quinn as a sort of bodyguard, and when the air cleared, she was making wedding plans."

"Is she all right?"

"She's fine, better than fine."

He wanted to dig deeper. He could use his contacts and sources to learn the details Maddy was leaving out. It would have to wait until he came out of the mountains— if he came out of the mountains.

"Trace, you know how much it would mean if you could come back for the wedding. It's been a long time."

"I know. You know I'd like to see you again, kid, all of you, but I'm just not suited to playing prodigal son."

"It doesn't have to be like that." She knew better than to press, but something told her she might not get another chance. "Things have changed. We've all changed. Mom misses you. She still has that little music box you sent her from Austria, and Pop…" Here she hesitated, because the ground was shakier. "Pop would give anything to see you again. He won't admit it—you know he can't—but I can see it every time your name's mentioned. Trace, every time we manage to get together, there's this hole. You could fill it."

"Mom and Pop still touring?" he asked, already knowing the answer, only to redirect the conversation.

"Yes." Maddy bit off a sigh. The son was as stubborn as the father. "They've got a gig coming up on public television. Folk dancing, traditional music. Pop's in heaven."

"I bet. Is he…is he okay?"

"I swear, he gets younger every year. If I had to make a bet I'd say music is the fountain of youth. He can still dance a teenager into the ground. Come see for yourself."

"We'll see how things go. Listen, tell Chantel and Abby I called. And Mom."

"I will." Maddy tightened her grip on the phone, knowing she was losing him. "Can you tell me where you'll be?"

"I'll let you know."

"Trace, I love you. We all love you."

"I know." He wanted to say more, but he knew there was nothing left. "Maddy?"

"Yes?"

"Break a leg."

He hung up the phone but didn't go back to bed for a very long time.

* * *

In the morning, Gillian watched Trace dress in Cabot's conservative European suit. She waited, nerves stretching, in silence while he deliberated over the proper tie.

What difference does it make? She wanted to shout it at him, rage it at him, while she tossed the hated, well-laundered clothes around the room. She watched him slip Cabot's little derringer into his pocket. It wouldn't do any good, she thought. He took it only because Cabot would take it. The pistol might as well have been filled with water for all the protection it would afford him.

He turned, and the man who had loved her so fiercely the night before had become André Cabot. He was sleek, well groomed and cold-eyed. She'd wanted to put off this moment, to push it back until it couldn't be pushed any longer. Now it was here, and she had to face it.

"If there is another way…" she began.

"There isn't." He answered with the same finality she'd heard when he'd spoken to his sister the night before. But then Gillian had been sure she'd heard a trace of regret. Perhaps he'd been too tired to stamp it out. But this morning he was in complete control.

"I have to ask. Is there some way you can take me with you?"

"You know there isn't."

She pressed her lips together, hating being helpless on the ground while everyone she loved walked a tightrope. "Is there some way I can contact this other agent, if things…if there's anything he should know?"

"You won't have to contact him."

She'd known that, too, and that she was dragging something out that should be done quickly. "So all I can do is wait."

"That's right." He hesitated a moment. "Gillian, I know that waiting is the hardest part."

"At least I'm allowed to pray, as well."

"It wouldn't hurt." He wished he didn't need to, but he reached out to take both of her hands. Things had changed, he realized, too much and too fast. For the first time in a dozen years, leaving was painful. "I'm going to get them out."

"And yourself." Her fingers tightened on his. "Will you promise me that, too?"

"Sure." He knew that often lies were needed. "Tell you what, once this is over, we'll take a little vacation. A couple of weeks, a month, pick the spot."

"Anywhere?"

"Sure." He bent to kiss her but only brushed his lips over her forehead. He was afraid that if he held her, if he really kissed her, he wouldn't be able to turn away. But he did give himself a moment, one long moment, to memorize her face—the milky skin dashed with freckles, the dark green eyes, the mouth that could be so sweet, so passionate. "Give it some thought while I'm gone." He let her go then and picked up his briefcase. "You've got two ISS guards, Doc, but don't do any sightseeing. I shouldn't be gone more than a day or two."

"I'll be waiting."

As he walked toward the door, she struggled to keep a promise to herself. She'd sworn she wouldn't say it. But he was leaving. In a moment he'd be gone and— "Trace."

He stopped, impatience just beginning to show as he turned.

"I love you."

She saw his expression change, his eyes darken, deepen. It seemed, for a heartbeat it seemed, that he would come to her. Then his face went carefully blank. He opened the door, and left without another word.

She could have thrown herself on the bed and wept. She could have thrown all the breakables in the room and raged. It was a huge temptation to do both. Instead, Gillian stood where she was and waited for calm.

The fact that he hadn't answered her was no more than she had expected. But he was gone now, and the wheels that had been put into motion couldn't be stopped. She could pray, and would, but for now there was something else she could do. Whenever it seemed there would be no tomorrow, it was best to make plans for the next day.

She went to the phone and asked for the number Trace had called the night before. Gillian dialed it and, calling on her photographic memory, gave the person who answered the same sequence Trace had recited. Her heart beating a bit unsteadily, she waited for someone to pick up. She winced when a sleepy and irritated masculine voice did.

"Hello, I'd like to speak with Madeline O'Hurley."

There was an oath, and a feminine murmur in the distance. "Do you know what time it is?"

"No." Gillian rolled her eyes and nearly laughed. Trace was on his way to Husad, and she didn't have the least idea what time it was in New York. "I'm sorry, I'm out of the country."

"It's 4:15 a.m.," Reed said helpfully. "And my wife is trying to sleep. So am I."

"I'm really terribly sorry. I'm a friend of her brother's. I don't know if I can make the call again." And Trace would surely murder her if he found out she'd made it at all. "If I could just speak with her for a moment."

There was static, and more muttering. Then the connection became so clear that Gillian could hear the bedsprings squeak. "Hello? Is Trace all right? Has something happened?"

"No." Gillian cursed herself for not waiting. "No, Trace is fine." She hoped. "I'm Gillian Fitzpatrick. A friend."

"Is Trace in Ireland?"

"No." She nearly smiled. "Ms. O'Hurley, well, I suppose it's best to be frank. I'm in love with your brother, and I think it would do him a lot of good to come home. I thought you might help me arrange it."

Maddy gave a shout of laughter, threw one arm around her very cranky husband and decided Gillian Fitzpatrick had been sent from heaven. "Tell me what I can do."

Trace sat silently in the car as it traveled east. He had directed the driver to the warehouse where Breintz had arranged for the ISS weapons to be stored. Retrieving them had been as simple as signing a form and passing a few bills. Now they were deep in the mountains. The ride was far from smooth. In the way that Cabot had, he muttered a few complaints but exchanged no conversation. There were no questions asked, no answers given. Trace sat back and, behind tinted glasses, marked the route as carefully as if he'd drawn a map.

He'd be back.

He knew the villagers in the scattered settlements they passed would keep to themselves. They had their own way of life, and their own way of dealing with what came. A man like him, passing through their land, was only so much wind. To be noticed, tolerated, then forgotten.

Trace glanced at his watch with a slight sniff of impatience. The homing device inside it would be transmitting his location to Breintz. If his luck—and ISS technology—held, Husad's security wouldn't detect it. If they did…he'd take that as it came.

There were times when it didn't pay to think too far ahead. It clouded the present, and it was always the instant that had to be coped with. That was why he tried not to think of Gillian, how she'd looked, what she'd said. If she meant it.

She loved him. Trace felt the emotion move through him, warm and strong and not a little frightening. She'd meant it. He'd seen it in her eyes then, and before, though he'd tried to tell himself that it was the intensity of the moment that had made her feel it, had made him want it.

When she'd said it he'd wanted to go to her, to hold her hard and tight and endlessly. He'd wanted to make promises he couldn't be sure he could keep. And, though he wasn't sure she would understand, it was because he loved her that he hadn't.

He'd never loved a woman before, so he hadn't known what a tug-of-war it could be between the selfish and the unselfish. Part of him wanted to take what she so recklessly offered. Another part of him felt it would be wrong, even sinful, for a man like him to take such pure emotion from her when he'd long since forgotten how to give it back.

Because he knew no other way at the moment, Trace decided to treat it as an assignment. He would give her what she had come to him for. Once she had her family back, he would…he would play it as it came.

Trace got his first sight of Husad's headquarters as the car drove over a rise. It was large, even larger than he'd expected, and built into the side of a cliff with rock carved from the mountains. Another ten miles in any direction and it would have been easily detected by air or land surveillance. But here it was isolated, almost merging into the wild desolation of the countryside. There was no land fit to farm here, no river to settle beside, no town to spread out from.

This was country for outlaws and renegades—and the hopeless.

Security seemed light, but Trace's eyes were sharp enough to spot the armed men stationed on the ridges. It was windowless and unfenced. Wise, because the reflection of glass or high-voltage wire could have been spotted from miles away. The driver signaled by punching out a code on a small box fixed to the dash. After a few seconds' delay, a wide door opened into the rock. The car drove into the mountain.

He was inside. Trace adjusted his cuff. His finger slid over and pressed on the stem of his watch to turn off the homing device. Either Breintz had his location now or he was on his own.

As he stepped out of the car, Trace took a long look around. The floor and the walls were rock. The tunnel seemed to go on endlessly and was dimly lit and cool. The door behind them had already closed, shutting out the sun and the heat. From somewhere came a low mechanical whine, telling him the air was circulated and processed. He heard, too, the sound of a door and footsteps. It was Kendesa who came to greet him.

"Again you are prompt. I trust your journey was not too unpleasant."

Trace inclined his head. "Business often causes some physical discomfort. The roads in your country are not yet as civilized as those in Europe."

"My pardon. Perhaps you would join me for a drink. I have an excellent chardonnay that should ease the memory of the journey."

"My samples?"

"Of course." Kendesa signaled. Two men seemed to come straight out of the rock wall. "They will be taken directly to the general, if you have no objection." His brow lifted at Trace's hesitation. "Surely you would not demand a receipt. We have no need to steal trifles from guests."

They both knew that the "trifles" included a TS-35. Still, his orders were to proceed with straightforward negotiations. "I would enjoy the chardonnay before meeting with the general."

"Excellent." Kendesa gave another signal, and the crate in the car's trunk was off-loaded. He gestured Trace forward. "I'm afraid a man of your taste will find our establishment crude. You will understand, of course, that we are a military operation and look not for comfort but revolution."

"I understand, though for myself I prefer comfort."

He led Trace into a small room whose walls had been paneled in light wood. The floor was carpeted, and, although the furniture was sparse, what was there was tasteful.

"We entertain rarely." Kendesa smiled as he drew the cork from the bottle. "When the general becomes more widely accepted, this will change." He poured wine into two Waterford glasses. "I confess that I have an affection for beautiful things, and the comfort and pleasure they bring."

"To profit, then," Trace said as he lifted his glass. "Because money gives the most comfort."

"I find you an interesting man, Cabot." Kendesa sipped his wine. Over the past few days he had employed the best equipment at his disposal in his search through Cabot's background. What he had found had pleased him a great deal. Such a man, and his connections, would be very useful during a period of transition.

"You've reached a level in power and wealth most men only wish for, yet you crave still more."

"I shall have still more," Trace countered.

"I believe so. You will understand that before doing business I used my resources to look into your current situation, as well as your background."

Trace merely sipped again. "Standard procedure."

"Indeed. What fascinates me, Cabot, is that you've reached this level of power while remaining almost unknown."

"I prefer subtlety to celebrity."

"Wise. There are some, even in our own organization, who criticize the general for maintaining such a high profile. Power amassed quietly is something more useful."

"The general is political. I am not." Trace continued to drink, wondering what Kendesa was fishing for.

"All of us are political, even if the politics is money. You expressed interest in Horizon."

"I did. And do."

"I have considered discussing this further with you. You are interested in the profit from Horizon. I am interested in the power."

"And the general?"

Kendesa lifted his glass again. He was nearly ready to play his cards. "Is interested in the revolution."

Unless Kendesa was playing a part, Trace sensed a slight disenchantment, and more than a little ambition. "Perhaps, with a kind of partnership, we could gain all three."

Kendesa studied Trace for a long, silent moment. "Perhaps."

The knock on the door echoed dully. "Come."

"The general is ready."

With a nod, Kendesa set down his glass. "I will take you to him myself. The general speaks no French, I'm afraid, but is quite proud of his adeptness with English. You will oblige him?"

"Certainly." Trace set his glass beside Kendesa's and prepared for the next step.

Gillian felt she'd waited for days, though it was only a matter of hours. She tried, unsuccessfully, to pass the time with Trace's books. Every time she started to read, she thought of him, and worried.

So she paced. And when she tired of that she sat and reminded herself of her conversation with Maddy. She would take Trace back to the States. In doing so, she would be able to give him what he'd promised her only a short time ago—a family.

For as long as she was able to hold off worry, Gillian concentrated on that. In a few days, a week at most, both she and Trace would have their families back.

And where would they go from there?

The Canary Islands? she thought, and nearly laughed out loud. She wondered what Trace would say when she told him that if he insisted on hiding from the world for the next fifty years or so she would be hiding right alongside him.

She wasn't going to lose him now, not to Husad, not to the ISS or his own stubbornness. If he wanted life in a hammock, it would be a hammock for two.

Gillian had learned a lot about herself in the past few weeks. She could do what needed to be done. She could face what needed to be faced. More, she could change what needed to be changed to find the happiness that had always remained just out of her reach.

When the fear began to edge back, she wondered what she would do if Trace didn't walk through the door again. Her life wouldn't be over. She knew you could lose what you loved and go on, but you could never go on in quite the same way. She knew there was no way to prepare herself for losing Trace. He'd opened doors in her, he'd caused the blossoming of love in her that had pushed her to open doors in him. She wouldn't lose him. Gillian promised herself that.

And went back to watching the clock.

She ordered room service only because she wanted something to do. Then she asked herself how in the world she could eat anything. She'd nearly decided to cancel the order when the knock came.

Experience had taught her caution. Even knowing she was guarded, Gillian checked the peephole for the uniformed waiter. Satisfied, she opened the door and looked disinterestedly at the tray.

"Just set it over there," she told him, gesturing because she wasn't certain he spoke English. Still, a check was a check in any language. Gillian leaned over to sign it.

She felt the prick in her arm and jerked back. The drug worked quickly, and she was staggering even as she grabbed for the table knife. The world went gray and dissolved to black before she could even think Trace's name.

Chapter 11

General Husad liked beautiful things, too. He liked to look at them, touch them, wear them. Still, the austerity of his headquarters pleased him. A military establishment required a certain ambience. A soldier's life could never be a soft one, or discipline was lost. He believed that, even when he dressed in silks and admired his wife's emeralds.

He was a small, spare man in his prime, with a mesmerizing voice and a glint in his eyes some took for genius and others took for madness. The title of general was self-bestowed, and, though he had indeed fought in wars, most of the medals he had pinned on his chest were self-awarded. By turns he treated his men like an indulgent father and a heartless dictator. They didn't love him, but they feared him enough to follow his orders without question.

He was dressed in a gold cloak for his meeting with Cabot. It was tied at the neck to reveal the medal-bedecked uniform beneath and the twin handguns at his hips. He had a striking face, hawkish, with silvered hair combed straight back. He photographed very well and spoke like an evangelist. His mind was slipping into a dark, violent area that even his medication no longer controlled completely.

His office wasn't sparsely furnished, as Kendesa's had been. The desk was huge, of polished oak, and dominated the room from its center. Sofas and chairs plump with pillows formed a circle around it. There were bookshelves and display cabinets. Trace studied them with what appeared to be a detached interest.

No windows, he thought, and only one door. Not likely.

There were a pair of épées crossed on the wall over an enormous aquarium in which colorful tropical fish glided in clear blue water.

"Monsieur Cabot." Husad held out a hand with the warmth and sincerity of a car salesman one sale away from his monthly quota. "Welcome."

"General." Trace accepted the hand and looked into the face of the man he'd sworn to kill. The eyes were black and full of odd lights. Madness. Could anyone stand this close to it and not smell it?

"I hope you didn't find the journey too inconvenient."

"Not at all."

"If you would be pleased to sit."

Trace took a chair and waited while the general stood with his hands folded behind his back. Kendesa stood silently at the door. For some moments, Husad paced, the sound of his highly polished boots absorbed by the carpet.

"The revolution needs both allies and arms," he began. "We wage a holy battle for the people, a battle that requires us to destroy the unworthy and the unbeliever. In Europe and the Middle East we have often been successful in bringing destruction to those who oppose us." He turned to Trace, head high, eyes blazing. "It is not enough. We have our duty, a sacred duty, to overthrow the oppressive governments of the world. Many will die in righteousness and sacrifice before we succeed. And we will succeed."

Trace sat calmly, noting that, as reported, Husad had a stirring voice, a strong presence. But even though he went on in the same vein for ten minutes, he basically said nothing. Trace noted, as well, that once the speech was over he glanced toward Kendesa. For approval? he wondered. For guidance?

"Your mission, General, if you will pardon me, interests me only as it concerns my associates and myself. I am not a patriot or a soldier, but a man of business." Trace folded his hands and continued. "You require arms, and I can supply them, for a price."

"Your price is high," the general said as he walked to his desk.

"My price includes the risk factor for securing, storing and delivering the merchandise. This same price can be quoted to others."

Husad reached down and came up with the TS-35. Even as Trace tensed, he heard Kendesa make a quick, surprised movement behind him.

"I find this weapon of particular interest."

The TS-35 was slim and amazingly lightweight. Even on a forced march, a soldier could carry it as easily as his food rations. The clips were slimmer than the average pack of cigarettes. Husad balanced its spearlike shape in his hands, then brought it up to sight it. In the middle of Trace's forehead.

If it was loaded, and Trace was certain that it was, the projectile would obliterate him where he sat, then go on to kill Kendesa and anyone unlucky enough to be standing in its path for the next fifty yards.

"The Americans talk and talk of peace while they

make such brilliant weapons." Husad was speaking almost dreamily now. "We are considered madmen because we talk of war. Such a weapon was made for a man of war. And the war is holy, the war is righteous, the war is food and drink."

Trace felt the sweat roll cold down his back. To die here, now, would be foolish, pitiful. "With all respect, General Husad, the weapon isn't yours until it's paid for."

The finger hovered on the trigger a moment, flexed, then retreated. With a charming smile, Husad lowered the gun. "Of course. We are warriors, but we are honest. We will take your shipment, Monsieur Cabot, and we ask, in the name of friendship, that you lower your price by half a million francs."

Trace's hands were damp as he reached for a cigarette. For survival's sake he wanted to agree and be done with it and get on with what he had come to do. But the man Cabot would never have agreed so easily. Nor would Husad, or Kendesa, expect it.

"In the name of expediency, General, we will lower the price by a quarter of a million, payment on delivery."

The weapon lay on Husad's desk now, and he stroked it as he might have a small child, or a pet. Again Trace saw his gaze shift briefly to Kendesa. "The papers will be drawn up. You will be driven back to Sefrou. In three days you will make the delivery, personally."

"It will be my pleasure." Trace rose.

"I am told you have an interest in our guest." Husad smiled. His teeth shone, and his eyes. "Personal interest?"

"Business is always personal to me, General."

"Perhaps you would be interested in observing the doctor. Kendesa will arrange it."

"Of course, General." Kendesa opened the door. Trace

saw him give both Husad and the weapon an uneasy look before they walked back into the corridor.

"The general amuses himself in odd ways," Trace commented as they walked.

"Were you afraid, Monsieur Cabot?"

"I have, as you have not, observed the power of that weapon. You may choose to die for your cause, Kendesa. I do not. My associates might find it unpalatable to continue to do business with one so unstable."

"The general is under some stress."

Trace crushed out his cigarette on the stone floor and decided to take the risk. "I am said to be observant. Who is it that wields the hammer, Kendesa? Who is it that I am actually doing business with?"

Kendesa paused. As was his habit, he wore a Western suit, without frills or jewelry. The decision came easily, because he had considered it for some time. If Cabot didn't continue to satisfy him, it would be a simple matter to arrange his disposal. "As is often the case, the one with the title is but a figurehead. The general's mental condition has become frail over the past year. It has become my duty to assume more responsibility." He waited to be certain Trace understood. "Does this change your position?"

Not the general, Trace thought, but Kendesa. Kendesa had ordered Charlie's death, Fitzpatrick's kidnapping. So he would deal with Kendesa rather than a half-mad puppet. "It satisfies me," Trace replied.

"Excellent." For the general's usefulness was almost at an end. Once Fitzpatrick had completed his task, Kendesa would take full power. And how much sweeter it would be with the backing of Cabot's organization, and the wealth that went with it.

Kendesa waved aside two armed guards. Taking a key from his pocket, he unlocked a door.

No research-and-development lab could have been better equipped. The lighting was brilliant, every surface was spotless. Trace spotted two surveillance cameras before he turned his attention to Gillian's brother.

It was the man from the snapshot, but he'd grown thinner, older. Strain had dug lines in his face and bruised the skin around his eyes. He was clean-shaven, but his hair, darker and deeper than Gillian's, was unkempt. His white lab coat hung loosely over jeans and a plain blue shirt.

Flynn pushed away from the microscope and stood. The hatred in his eyes brought Trace a wave of relief. He hadn't given up or given in. He was hanging on, and not by a thread, but by his teeth. If the man had enough strength to hate, he had enough strength to escape.

"Dr. Fitzpatrick, your work goes well today?"

"I haven't seen my daughter in two days."

"We discussed incentive, Doctor."

Flynn's hand closed into a fist. He had withstood their torture. He was all but certain Kendesa had known he would withstand it. It was only the threat that they would take his Caitlin into that dark little room that kept him in the lab.

"I'm here." His Irish brogue had barbs in it. "I'm working. I was promised that she wouldn't be harmed and that I would see her daily if I cooperated."

"I'm afraid the general feels you work too slowly. When there is progress, we will bring your daughter to you. In the meantime, I will introduce you to Monsieur Cabot. He is interested in your work."

Flynn turned dark, hate-filled eyes on Trace. "Go to hell."

Trace wanted to congratulate him, but he only nodded stiffly. "Your work here will put your name in the history books, Dr. Fitzpatrick." Trace looked around, osstensibly interested in the lab, while he searched for another exit. "Fascinating. My organization feels the profit from your serum will be enormous."

"Your money will do you little good once a madman has destroyed the world."

Trace smiled. So he understood. He kept his voice mild. "Your serum will ensure power and profit for those clever enough to earn it. There is progress?" he asked Kendesa.

"It is slow." This time Kendesa smiled and watched Trace carefully. "The missing link is Fitzpatrick's sister. She has in her possession certain notes, certain knowledge that will expedite the completion of this work. She'll be joining you, Doctor."

Trace felt the air stop pumping into his lungs. Before he could speak, Flynn was rushing forward.

"Gillian? What have you done with her?"

Kendesa had his gun out quickly. "Calm yourself, Doctor. She is unharmed." He turned a curious smile on Trace. "Were you aware, *monsieur*, that you traveled with the good doctor's sister?"

"I?" He could play it two ways. But if he went with instinct and attacked, Flynn Fitzpatrick would be dead. "I'm afraid you're mistaken."

"The woman you brought to Casablanca was Dr. Gillian Fitzpatrick."

"The woman I brought to Casablanca was a little American tart I picked up in Paris. Attractive, amusing and dull-witted."

"More sharp-witted than you know, *monsieur*. You have been used."

So that was it. For once Trace blessed the ISS for the strength and depth of his cover. "You're mistaken." There was a low edge of fury to his voice.

"No, I regret it is you who are mistaken. The woman

purposely sought you out, hoping you would bring her closer to us and her brother. I assume she played her part well."

"Very well. If you're correct."

"Quite correct. A short time ago she was in Mexico, where she sought out and enlisted the help of a certain ISS agent. We can assume it was he who instructed her on what course to take. Do you know the name Il Gatto, Cabot?"

Trace drew out a cigarette, making sure his hand didn't appear quite steady. "I know it."

"He seeks revenge on the general, and uses you and the woman to gain it."

"Who is he?"

"I regret I do not yet have that information." Anger broke through the sophisticated calm briefly. "The general was unfortunately hasty in executing three men who might have been able to identify him. But the woman knows, and will tell us. In time."

"Where is she?" Trace blew out a stream of smoke. "I do not tolerate being a woman's pawn."

"On her way here, if not here already. You are welcome to speak with her when you return. Once we have her notes, and she has identified Il Gatto, I may consider it a gesture of goodwill to give her to you."

"Bastard." Flynn raised his fist and would have struck if Trace hadn't moved more quickly. Grabbing Flynn's arm, he twisted it up behind his back and held him close, their faces an inch apart.

"Your whore of a sister owes me." Flynn bared his teeth but was helpless to strike back. "I'll take my payment from her, and from you, Doctor." He shoved him aside. "I've seen enough," Trace said curtly, and strode toward the door.

"Let me see Caitlin. Let me see my daughter, you son of a bitch," Flynn cried.

"Perhaps tomorrow, Doctor," Kendesa said calmly. "Perhaps then I shall reunite your family." In the same unhurried manner, he opened the door and locked it behind him. It gave him some pleasure to see the smooth, sleek André Cabot with his feathers ruffled.

"There is no need for embarrassment, my friend. The woman, under the guidance of Il Gatto, was a formidable enemy."

Trace turned on him. In an instant he had Kendesa against the wall. Even as the guards' guns clicked into place he had the key from Kendesa's pocket palmed in his hand. "I will not be made a fool. The woman is unharmed?"

Kendesa waved the guards aside as Trace's grip relaxed. "We did not want her damaged."

"Good." A muscle twitched in his cheek. "Very good. When I return in three days, I want her. Get the information you need, Kendesa. Get the information and then turn the woman over to me. The price of the shipment can be reduced another quarter of a million francs, between us."

Kendesa lifted a brow. "The price of your pride is high."

"Before I am through, she will wish, with a full heart, that you had killed her." Trace straightened his jacket and seemed to bring himself under control. "I assume the child is still alive."

"She is kept on the second level. Mild tranquilizers keep her quiet. They are full of passion, these Irish."

"Indeed." Trace saw the car and driver waiting where he'd left them. "I will report to my associates. If the papers are in order, we will finish our current business."

"Cabot." Kendesa rested a hand on the door of the car. "Does Il Gatto disturb you?"

Trace looked directly into Kendesa's eyes. "I feel he would have little interest in me, and a great deal more in you. I should watch my back, *mon ami*. Cats strike quickly."

Trace settled in the back seat and for the first time in years began to pray.

He would waste precious time traveling back to Sefrou, contacting Breintz and gathering the weapons. As the driver started down the mountain, Trace considered putting him out of commission and going back. But how far would he get alone, with a miserable peashooter of a .45?

Straining against his own impotence, he looked at his watch. Automatically he reactivated the homing device, but he was more interested in the time. He could be back, fully armed, by dark.

She'd be all right. She was strong. She was braver than she should be. He would come back for her and get her out, no matter what had to be done, no matter what had to be sacrificed.

But the cold sweat he was in reminded him what it was to fear for more than your own life.

When the tire blew out, he was thrown against the side of the car. Swearing, he straightened. Instinct had him reaching in his pocket as he stepped from the car. The driver got out, turned toward the damaged wheel, then dropped like a stone.

Trace drew out his pistol. Smelling ambush. Even as he whirled, Breintz rose from a rock. "Your mind's elsewhere, old friend. If I'd wanted you dead, you'd be dead."

Trace pocketed the pistol. "They've got Gillian."

"I know. One of her guards lived long enough to contact me." Breintz dropped agilely from the rock. "My orders are to give you twelve hours to get the Fitzpatricks out. If you're unsuccessful, Hammer's headquarters is to be destroyed."

"Give me your weapon."

"One rifle?" Breintz lifted a brow. "Such conceit."

"Twelve hours doesn't give me a hell of a lot of time. Give me the rifle."

"For once Il Gatto is not using his head." Breintz bent down to examine the driver's clothes. "Could it be the woman is more than an assignment?" Breintz drew off the driver's braided headdress and settled it over his hair. "An adequate fit."

Trace schooled his breathing until his head cleared. "You drive. We can take out the guards at the gate and use their weapons. The layout's simple enough. We get Fitzpatrick, I find Gillian and the kid."

"Agreed." Breintz gestured for him to follow. With the ease of a goat, he climbed over the rocks. Trace saw the case he'd purchased from Bakir. Breintz only smiled. "I have worked with you before." Breintz handed Trace a grenade launcher. "And this is my country. I say modestly that my contacts here are excellent."

Trace yanked off Cabot's raw-silk jacket and threw it in the dirt. He slipped the strap of the weapon over his shoulder and reached for another. "I'd forgotten how good you were."

"Old friend—" Breintz was quietly taping clips together "—I am even better now."

Trace strapped on an ammo belt. "We have to wait until dark."

Breintz sat cross-legged. "It will come soon enough."

"You don't have orders to go in with me."

"No." Breintz closed his eyes and began to drift into meditation. "Charles Forrester was a good man."

"Thanks."

Wishing he could find the same kind of serenity, Trace sat beside him. And waited for sundown.

Gillian awoke slowly, with her head throbbing and her mind fuzzy. Once or twice she nearly found consciousness, only to go into the grayness again. She heard weeping, quiet and heartfelt, and wondered if it was her.

She felt warmth against her side, then again warmth stroking along her arm. Instinctively she reached out for it.

"Aunt Gillian, please wake up. Please, Aunt Gillian, I'm so scared."

It was like the nightmare. Gillian felt her skin go clammy and fought it off. Just a dream, she told herself, but Caitlin's pleas were coming clearer and clearer. Opening her eyes, she saw her.

"I thought you were dead." Caitlin, eyes puffy and red, buried her face in Gillian's hair. "They dropped you on the bed and you lay so still I thought you were dead."

"Baby." She pushed herself up and nearly passed out again. The drug had been strong and had left her with a raging headache and traces of nausea. Unsure what was real, she reached out and touched Caitlin's face. "Oh, baby. It's you. It's really you." Gathering the child close, she rocked her. "Oh, Caitlin, little darling, go ahead and cry. Poor little lamb, how frightened you must have been, all alone like this. I'm here now."

"Are you going to take us home?"

Where was home? And where were they? As she looked around the dim room, Gillian remembered the waiter, the prick of the hypodermic. Closing her eyes, she cursed herself for her stupidity. Did they have Trace, too? Oh, God, did they have him, too?

"Can we go home now? Please, I want to go home."

"Soon," Gillian murmured. "As soon as I can. Caitlin, can you dry your eyes and talk to me?"

With sniffles and nods, Caitlin burrowed closer. "You won't go away?"

"No. No, I won't leave you." They'd have to kill her first, she promised herself as she kept Caitlin close. "Where's your da?"

"They keep him downstairs, in a laboratory."

"Is he all right? Be brave now, darling. Is your da all right?"

"He looks kind of sick. I can't remember when they let me see him last." She swiped her hand over her wet cheeks. "He cried once."

"It's all right. It's going to be all right. There's a—" She cut herself off as she remembered how carefully Trace had searched their hotel rooms for microphones. Someone could be listening to them even now. She couldn't mention his name or give her niece the comfort of knowing they had help. "There's sure to be a way out," she said instead. "We just have to be patient. We're together now." Then she lifted a finger to her lips, signaling to the child to be silent. As quietly as she could, she searched the room.

She knew it was more luck than skill that led her to it. When she found the mike, her first instinct was to smash it. Even that small sign of defiance would have been satisfying. But she made herself think coolly. Leaving the mike in place, she climbed back onto the narrow bed.

"I met a man in Mexico," she began, knowing whoever was listening would already be aware of that. "He said he'd help. He has a funny name, Caitlin. Il Gatto. It means 'cat.'"

"Does he look like a cat?"

"No." Gillian smiled to herself. "But he thinks like one.

When I don't contact him tomorrow," she said, "he'll come after us."

"And take us home?"

"Yes, darling. Do you know where we are?"

"It's like a big cave with lots of tunnels."

"I see." Gillian lifted Caitlin's eyelids and examined her pupils. Drugs. The fury rose and nearly overpowered her. "Do you ever go outside?"

"No. There aren't any windows."

Caitlin cringed as the door opened and a man with a rifle over his shoulder carried in a tray. He set it on the edge of the bed, gestured to it, then walked out again.

"I bit him once," Caitlin said, with some of her old spirit.

"Good for you."

"He smacked me."

"He won't smack you again." Gillian looked at the tray. There was rice and some cubed meat with two glasses of milk. She sniffed at it. "Have you been eating well?"

"The food doesn't taste good, but I get hungry. Whenever I eat, I get sleepy."

"You need to eat, darling." But she shook her head as she lifted the tray. "It helps keep up your strength." Gillian dumped the contents of both plates under the bed. "And you need to sleep, as well." Looking around for a likely place, she poured the milk on a pile of dirty linen in the corner. Caitlin watched her with wide eyes. "Come on, baby, try to eat a little more."

When Caitlin pressed a hand to her mouth and giggled, Gillian nearly wept from the sight of it.

"That's it. Now drink your milk." Grinning with her, Gillian climbed into bed again.

A trace of mischief lit Caitlin's eyes. "I don't like milk."

"It's good for your bones. You wouldn't want soft bones,

would you?" Gillian cuddled with her. Putting her mouth against the child's ear, she whispered, "They put something in the food to make you sleep. You have to pretend to sleep so they don't find out we didn't eat it. Do just what I say. If one of the men comes back, lie very still so they don't know we've fooled them."

Caitlin nodded. "Don't go away, Aunt Gillian."

"No, I won't go away."

Gillian cradled the child in her arms. In the dark, she stared at the ceiling and planned.

Sunset came with brilliance. The mountains went pink with it, and the sand gold. In the last of the light, Breintz changed into the driver's clothes after fixing the tire while Trace loaded weapons on the floor of the car.

They worked in silence now. Everything had been said. As the sun dipped below the high peaks, Trace stretched out on the floor in the back and Breintz climbed behind the wheel. They headed east for the last time.

Breintz began to whistle tunelessly as they approached. As Trace had, he noted the sentries on the ridges above the building. Following Trace's directions, he punched out the code and waited for the door to lift up.

As he stopped the car inside, he lowered his head to conceal as much of his face as possible. A guard approached as the door closed behind him.

"You made good time," he said, just before Breintz brought an elbow to his throat. Trace was out of the car and leading the way to the lab.

They pulled up short some twenty feet later. Two more guards were dealt with in utter silence. Trace knew they would have to move quickly once they broke into the lab. There the cameras would give them away. Trace shrank back out of sight as Breintz moved forward, weaving slightly.

"A cigarette," he demanded in Arabic, keeping his voice a bit slurred. "What good is wine without tobacco?"

As one of the guards broke into a grin, Trace and Breintz moved quickly. Not a shot was fired.

"You still have a light touch," Breintz commented as Trace slipped the key into the lock.

"And yours has improved." Taking a deep breath, Trace opened the door. "Keep working," he said in a low voice to Flynn the moment he spotted him. "Keep as much of your back as possible to the cameras."

Despite the order, Flynn set down his tongs and test tube. "You." There was a look in his eyes that told Trace he'd been pushed almost to his limit.

"For God's sake, if you want to get your daughter out, keep working. I don't want surveillance to see anything unusual until the last minute."

"Push it along," Breintz said mildly as he kept a lookout.

"Pick up the damn test tube, do something scientific. I'm ISS."

Flynn picked up the tube, but in a grip that threatened to shatter it. "You're a pig."

"Maybe, but I'm here to get you and the kid—and your idiot sister—out of here. Keep working. Do you want to see a goddamn badge?" Trace cast a look at the first camera. "Just do what I say, do it slow, and do it right."

Something in his tone made Flynn obey, but the strain was still evident. "I thought you were French."

"I'm as Irish as you are, Fitzpatrick," Trace said reassuringly, and grinned. "And, by the saints," he said, dropping into the easy brogue of his alter ego, Colin, "we'll be gettin' out and blowin' this place to hell."

Maybe it was simple desperation, but Flynn responded. "When we do, the first bottle's on me."

"You're on. Now move as far as you can to the left, the edge of camera range. Go after those papers."

Flynn set down the tube and obeyed. With his back to the cameras, he looked over the papers as if he were checking his equations. "How did you find us?"

"Your sister had a lot to do with it. If you've got half the guts she does, we're going to make it. Now keep reading. Something doesn't check out. Take out your pencil like you're going to make notes. I'm going to blow the camera out. When I do, you run. Breintz'll take you out while I go up for the kid and Gillian. Now!"

Trace blew the camera out with a single blast. When Flynn passed through the door, both agents had their weapons ready. "Give me twenty minutes," Trace said to Breintz.

"I'm not going without Caitlin."

"I'll get her." Trace shoved Flynn in Breintz's direction. "You're the key. If they get their hands on you again, none of us is going to make it."

"She's my child." Weariness and despair had frozen into icy determination. "I won't leave her behind."

"You're her brother, all right," Trace muttered. And time was running out. He shoved a rifle into Flynn's hands. "Can you use it?"

Flynn felt a ray of hope bloom like a sunrise. "With pleasure."

"Say a prayer to whatever gods work best," Trace told Breintz.

"I already have."

Gillian heard the door open and lay as silent and still as Caitlin. The child had truly fallen asleep, a natural sleep.

Gillian gripped the pitiful weapon in her hand. During the hour she'd lain in the dark, she'd tried to accept that Trace was gone. They'd discovered the deception, killed him and kidnapped her.

She wanted to mourn for him, to grieve, to rage. But first she would have her revenge, and her family's freedom.

With her eyes half open, she saw the man bend over her. Gillian held her breath and swung. The edge of the plate caught him full force on the bridge of the nose. She heard the grinding break, saw the spurt of blood. While he was blinded by it, she lifted the other plate and struck again. He staggered but grabbed at her arm as he went. Though her arm twisted painfully, she remembered what her neighbor in New York had told her.

Go for the eyes.

This time he yelped. The butt of his gun slammed into her side as he tried to bring it into place. And then she was fighting for her life.

It was through a red wave of fear and fury that she heard Caitlin begin to whimper. As she had in the nightmare. At the sound of it, Gillian fought like a madwoman. She gripped the rifle. So did he. It exploded with the most terrible sound she'd ever heard.

Then she was standing, holding it, and the man, whose face she had never seen, was at her feet.

"Aunt Gillian!" Caitlin climbed out of bed to grasp Gillian's legs. "Is he dead? The bad man, is he dead?"

"I think—I don't know." She swayed, as though the drug had taken over again. "I don't know. We have to go. We have to go now."

Then she heard the gunfire, close and coming closer. Shoving the child behind her, Gillian lifted the rifle again. Her hands were slick with sweat as she prepared to protect her own.

They'd found the first guard faster than Trace had counted on. The alarm was out, and if it hadn't been for luck and a brutal frontal attack they would have been cornered. They'd reached the second level.

"I'll hold them here." Breintz took his position behind a column at the top of the stairs. "Find the woman and the child."

Trace switched to the grenade launcher and sent three over the rail. "Keep down," he ordered Flynn, and began to move. He broke open a half-dozen doors, then saw the one that was already open. With his back pressed against the wall, he gripped the gun in both hands and took two deep breaths before swinging into the opening, prepared to fire. Gillian's bullet grazed his left shoulder. He was too shocked to feel the sting.

"Good God, woman."

"Trace!" With the gun lowered, she sprang forward. "Oh, Trace, I thought you were dead."

"Damn near." He brushed his fingers over his sleeve, disgusted when they came away red.

"Flynn." With a sob, she fell against him.

"Da!" Caitlin flew across the room and was scooped up by her father.

"Family reunions later," Trace told them. "Let's move. Breintz!" Trace sent another few rounds into the first level to cover the agent. "Get them out. I'll keep everyone busy." He unhooked the Uzi he'd taken off one of the guards. "Fifteen minutes," he said between his teeth. "Send it up in fifteen minutes."

"I would prefer to see you again."

"Yeah." Trace swiped sweat from under his eyes. He dashed back toward the stairs, sending bullets flying, before Gillian realized what he was doing.

"No! No, he can't!"

But he could. Gillian knew that he had to face his destiny, just as she did. "I'm sorry, Flynn." She kissed him quickly. "I have to stay with him. Go quickly." Then she was racing behind Trace.

He set off a series of explosions that not only cleared the stairs but nearly obliterated them. He was halfway down when he heard the noise at his back. For the second time, he turned on Gillian.

"What in the name of God—?"

"You know they have a better chance if we separate. I'm staying with you. That was the deal."

It was too late to send her back. If he'd had even seconds to spare, he would have shouted at her. Instead, he grabbed her arm and hauled her along with him.

They'd caused considerable damage, Trace saw with satisfaction. And more confusion. The general was out, waving and firing the TS-35. As he furthered the damage to his headquarters and added to the casualty toll among his own men, he ordered them to stand and fight the army of invaders. The unexpected attack appeared to have cut the bonds on his last hold on sanity. Trace lifted his gun. The general fell before he pressed the trigger.

"Fool." Kendesa stood over the gold-cloaked body. "Your time has passed." Bending, he retrieved the American-made weapon. "What you have cost us." He whirled to shout at the scattering soldiers. "To the front entrance, idiots!" he ordered. "Bar the front entrance!"

Too late, Trace thought grimly as he stepped out from cover. "You've lost, Kendesa. And the fool is you for believing that the woman duped me when it was I who duped you."

"Cabot."

"When it suits me."

Kendesa's expression changed. "Il Gatto, at last."

"Definitely at last. Our business is finished, Kendesa, and this is personal."

Perhaps he would have killed him where he stood. He'd been prepared to. But before it could be put to the test, the general raised his handgun. "Traitor." He wheezed as he fired. Kendesa staggered back, but didn't fall. Again Trace aimed.

This time, heaven interfered.

The ground shook, violently. Trace's first thought was that Breintz had set the charges early. He grabbed Gillian's hand and started to run. Another tremor had them both ramming into the rock wall.

"Earthquake," Trace said as he fought for breath. "A real one. The whole place is going to go."

"They got out, didn't they?"

"They had time." It was all the hope he could give her.

They raced down one passage, only to have it cave in in front of them. Gillian heard screams as the dust blinded her. Without pausing for breath, Trace pulled her down another. "There's got to be more than one way out. We won't make it to the front." Again he went with instinct and headed for the general's quarters. "He'd have an escape route," he said as he blasted the lock off the door. Pulling Gillian inside, he went for the obvious. "Look for a button, a mechanism," he shouted as he searched the bookcase. He could hear stone falling from great heights. Something was burning, and the fire was close. With both hands, he shoved aside books. Then he found it. The panel slid out.

The corridor beyond was narrow and vibrated from the tremors underground. But it was unguarded. Praying his luck was still holding, he shoved her through. In seconds they were out in the night.

Men ran and shouted, scattering. Behind them the building was splitting apart, huge chucks of rock tumbling down with a noise that seemed impossible. Then the noise grew greater with the first explosion. Without bothering with cover, Trace ran. No one came after them.

It seemed to Gillian that they ran for miles. He never let her stop to rest, and she didn't ask to. Then, like a shadow, Breintz rose from a rock.

"So we do meet again."

"Looks like." Trace dragged Gillian over the rocks to the makeshift camp.

"The gods made it unnecessary for me to complete our plan." With his usual calm, Breintz handed Trace night-vision glasses. Lifting them, Trace focused in the direction they had come from.

"Not much left."

"And Kendesa?"

"The general took care of him." Trace lowered the glasses again. "If not, your gods did. Hammer's smashed." He handed the glasses back. "Looks like a promotion for you."

"And you."

"I'm finished." He sat with his back to a rock and watched Gillian gather her family to her.

"I owe you." Flynn sat with his daughter curled on his lap and his sister close against his side.

"Just doing a job."

"In any case, I owe you. You have a name?"

Trace accepted the bottle Breintz handed him. The long swig he took had a kick he could have lived on for a week. "O'Hurley."

"Thank you, O'Hurley, for my daughter."

Caitlin reached up to whisper in her father's ear. Then, at his murmur, she rose and walked to Trace. "My da says you saved us."

"Sort of." She was thinner than in the snapshot, and her

eyes were too big in her pale face. Unable to resist, Trace reached up and tugged on one of her tangled red locks. "It's all done now."

"Can I hug you?"

Nonplussed, he shifted his shoulders. "Yeah, sure."

She cuddled against him and, with the resilience of childhood, giggled. "You smell," she said, not unkindly. "I guess I smell, too."

"Some."

As she pressed a wet kiss to his cheek, he held her, and his eyes drifted to Gillian.

"Just little pieces," she murmured to him. "All we can change are little pieces. But it's worth it." Because she was afraid she would weep, she rose to walk a little way into the shadows. She heard him come up behind her.

"I know you want to know how I got there and what happened, but I can't talk about it now."

"All right. It's all right." He started to reach for her hair, then dropped his hand again. "We have to get going. There'll be a plane in Sefrou to fly us to Madrid. The ISS will take care of you."

"I thought they'd killed you." It was anger, rather than tears, that sparkled her eyes as she turned. "I thought you were dead, and all you can talk about is planes and the ISS?"

Trace touched the blood drying on his shoulder. "The only hit I took was from you."

"Oh, God, I'd forgotten." She came to him quickly. "I might have killed you."

"Not with that aim."

"You're wrong." She wiped the back of her hand over her mouth. "I killed a man. With my own hands." She looked down at them now and shuddered. "I didn't even see his face, but I killed him."

"And you think you can't live with that." He cupped her chin in his hand so that she would look at him. Her face was filthy, and there was blood on it from a scrape along her cheekbone. "You can, Gillian. You can live with a lot of things. Believe me, I know."

"Trace, would you do something for me? One more thing?"

"Maybe."

Still cautious, she thought, and almost laughed. "If it wouldn't put you out too much, would you hold me? I don't want to cry, and if you hold me I won't."

"Come here," he murmured, and wrapped his arms around her. It was over, he thought, and she was safe. Maybe, just maybe, they had some time. "Cry if you want. It doesn't hurt anything."

He was warm and hard against her, and the night was quiet again. "I don't need to now."

Chapter 12

"After everything we've been through, I don't understand how you can be nervous over this."

"Don't be ridiculous. I'm not nervous." Trace yanked at the knot of his tie again. As far as he was concerned, Cabot was dead, and the ties should have gone with him. "I don't know why in the hell I let you talk me into this."

Enormously pleased with herself, Gillian sat in the rented car as they drove away from the Los Angeles airport. "You gave me your word we could go anywhere I wanted after things were settled again. And where I wanted to go was your sister's wedding."

"A shabby trick, Doc, after I saved your life."

It was precisely because of that that she was determined to save his, or at least a small part of it. "A man's word is his bond," she said solemnly, then laughed when he swore at her. "Oh, Trace, don't be cranky. It's a beautiful day, and I don't think I've ever been happier in my life. Did you see how wonderful Flynn and Caitlin looked when we left them? I can hardly believe it's all over, really over."

He relented enough to put a hand over hers. "It's over. Your brother and the kid can go back to Ireland and put all this behind them. With Husad and Kendesa gone and Hammer's headquarters destroyed, they've got nothing to worry about."

"Addison wasn't pleased about the Horizon project being destroyed, or Flynn's refusal to try to duplicate it."

Trace gave a short laugh. Maybe he'd been wrong about scientists—or at least some of them. Fitzpatrick had stood toe-to-toe with Addison, turning aside offers, pleas, bribes and threats. Gillian had taken the same stand, saying nothing about her memory and leaving Addison and the ISS with a handful of doctored notes. For better or worse, Horizon was finished.

"Addison wasn't pleased about much. He grumbled for an hour over losing a crate of weapons, including a TS-35."

"I think he was more displeased to be losing one of his best agents."

Trace lifted a brow. "I don't think he'd put it that way."

"But he did, to me." She ran a hand down the skirt of her dress. She'd fallen in love with the rich green silk. It was a bit more elaborate than her usual style, but, after all, this was Chantel O'Hurley's wedding. "He was hoping I could convince you to stay 'on board,' as he put it."

It was hard not to feel a nasty little streak of satisfaction at that. "What did you tell him?"

"That he was mad as a hatter. Oh, look how tall the palms are. In New York it's probably cold and sleeting."

"I guess you miss it?"

"Miss what?" She turned to look at him. "New York? Oh, I haven't really thought about it. I suppose everyone at Random-Frye thinks I've dropped off the edge of the earth." She sighed, content. "In some ways I think I have."

"I guess Arthur Steward wonders."

"Dear old Arthur," Gillian said with a smile. "I suppose he might, at the odd moment." It didn't surprise or even annoy her that he knew about Arthur. After all, she knew about his squashed beetle. "I'll have to send him a postcard."

"You'll be back in a couple of days."

"I don't know. I haven't decided." She wasn't going back to New York, or anywhere else, without him. He just didn't know it yet. "What about you? Are you winging straight off to the islands?"

Why was it she could make him so uncomfortable when she smiled that way? It was as if she could see what he was thinking. Or trying not to think. "I've got some business to take care of in Chicago first." He paused for a moment, because he hadn't taken it all in yet. "For some reason, Charlie left me his house."

"I see." She smiled again, brilliantly. "So it seems you have a home after all."

"I don't know anything about real estate," he mumbled. They were in Beverly Hills now with its mansions and trimmed hedges. This was the kind of place his father had always dreamed of. The O'Hurleys had come up in the world, he thought. Or some of them had. He yanked at his tie again. "Listen, Doc, this is a dumb idea. We can head back to the airport, take a flight to New Zealand. It's beautiful there."

And at the other end of the world. Gillian resisted the urge to lecture or comfort. "A promise is a promise," she said simply.

"I don't want to spoil this for Chantel, or the rest of them."

"Of course you don't. That's why you're going."

"You don't understand, Gillian." And he'd never been able to bring himself to explain it before. "My father's never forgiven me for leaving. He never understood why I had to. He wanted—I guess he needed for me to be a part of the dream he had. The O'Hurley Family, in big, bold lights. Broadway, Vegas, Carnegie Hall."

She was silent for a long moment. Then she spoke quietly, without looking at him. "My father never forgave me, never understood me. He wanted me to be one thing, and I was always another. Did your father love you, Trace?"

"Sure he did, it was just—"

"My father never loved me."

"Gillian—"

"No, listen to me. There's a difference between love and obligation, between true affection and expectation. He didn't love me, and I can accept that. But what I can't accept is that I never made peace with him. Now it's too late." She looked at him now, and though her eyes were dry they shone with emotion. "Don't make that same mistake, Trace. I promise you, you'll regret it."

He could think of nothing to say, no argument to give. He was here because he'd promised, but more, because he'd wanted to come. The ideas, or maybe he should call them dreams, that had begun to form couldn't be brought to fruition until he'd resolved his life. He couldn't do that until he'd closed the rift with his family. With his father.

"This could be the biggest mistake you've ever made," he said as he pulled up to the gates guarding Chantel's estate.

"I'll risk it."

"You're a stubborn woman, Doc."

"I know." She touched his face. "I've got as much on the line as you do."

He wanted to ask her to explain, but a guard knocked

smartly on his window. "You're early, sir," he said when Trace rolled down the window. "May I see your invitation?"

She hadn't thought of that, Gillian realized with a start. Before she could speak, Trace pulled out a badge. "McAllister, Special Security."

The ID looked official, because it was. The guard studied it, compared the laminated photo to Trace, then nodded. "Go right in, sir," he said, nearly snapping a salute.

Trace tooled through the gates and started up the long drive.

"McAllister?"

Trace slipped the ID back in his pocket. "Old habits die hard. Good God, what a place." The house was huge and white and elegant. The grounds were trimmed and rolling. He thought of the crowded hotel rooms they'd shared, the meals his father had cooked on hot plates, the airless dressing rooms, the audiences that snarled as often as they applauded. And the laughter. And the music.

"It's beautiful," Gillian murmured. "Like a picture."

"She always said she'd do it." The pride came through, deeper than he'd expected. "The little brat pulled it off."

"Spoken like a true brother," Gillian said with a laugh. She was helped from the car by a man in uniform, and was suddenly every bit as nervous as Trace. Maybe she should have made him come alone. She was hardly prepared to meet royalty, even the Hollywood variety. And his family might resent... As he came to her, she reached out a hand. "Trace, maybe I shouldn't."

The front door burst open and nearly cracked on its hinges. A woman with a wild mop of red curls and an exquisite dress of sapphire blue raced down the stairs. With something close to a war cry, she launched herself into Trace's arms.

"You're here! You're really here!" With her arms in a stranglehold around his neck and her mouth smothering his, Trace could do little more than absorb the scent and feel. "I knew you'd come. I didn't believe it, but I knew. And here you are."

"Maddy." Because he needed to catch his breath as much as he wanted to look at her, Trace drew her back by the shoulders. There were tears streaming down her face, but she was grinning. And the grin was exactly as he remembered. "Hi."

"Hi yourself." She pulled the handkerchief out of his pocket, blew her nose hard, then laughed. "Chantel will kill me if my nose is red." She blew again. "How do I look?"

"Terrible, but there's so little you can do with that face." With the laughter, they were close again. He held her and wished he could believe it would be so easy with everyone. "Maddy, I love you."

"I know, you jerk." Her breath hitched on a sob. "Stay this time?"

"Yeah." He brushed his cheek against her hair. "I'll stay this time." Looking over her head, he watched Gillian.

"I can't wait to show you off." Maddy drew back beaming, then glanced at Gillian. "Hi."

"Maddy, this is Gillian Fitzpatrick."

Still sniffling, Maddy turned. "I'm so glad to meet you." Gillian found herself enclosed in the same exuberant hug. "In fact, I'm thrilled." She drew away far enough to wink, then squeezed Gillian again. "You look wonderful, both of you, just wonderful." She slipped an arm around each of them and started up the stairs. "I can't wait for you to meet Reed. Oh, here he is now."

Coming down the hall was a leanly built man with hair shades darker than Trace's and more conservatively cut. He looked as if he'd been born in the tux. So this was

Reed Valentine of Valentine Records. Rich, well-bred and straight-line. Thinking of his free-spirited, unconventional sister, Trace decided he could have come up with no one less suited to her.

"Reed, it's Trace." Maddy gave Trace another quick kiss, then dashed to her husband. "I told you he'd be here."

"So you did." Reed slipped a protective arm around Maddy and sized up the brother even as the brother sized up the husband. "Maddy's been looking forward to seeing you again." With his arm still around Maddy, he offered a hand. Trace took it. It wasn't as smooth as he'd expected.

"Congratulations."

"Thank you."

"Oh, don't be stuffy, Reed. We have to kill the fatted calf, at least."

Reed saw the expression on Trace's face and smiled. "I have a feeling Trace might prefer a drink." He turned a smile of considerable charm on Gillian. "Hello."

"Oh, I'm sorry," Maddy began. "This is Gillian. She's with Trace. We should go in and sit down, and I'll find everyone. Things are a little confused."

To prove it, two boys raced down the hall, one in oblivious and desperate pursuit of the other. "I'm going to tell Mom."

"I'm going to tell her first."

"Whoa!" Maddy grabbed an arm each before they could come to blows. "Slow down. You'll have those cute little tuxedos filthy before we can start the wedding."

"He said I looked like a geek," the smaller of the two said.

"He kicked me," the older said righteously.

"I *tried* to kick him, only I missed." He looked across at his brother, hoping he'd have another chance.

"Kicking's not allowed. And, Chris, you do not look

like a geek. In fact, you look very handsome. Now, can you behave long enough to meet your uncle?"

"What uncle?" Ben, the oldest, looked up suspiciously.

"The only one you haven't met. Trace, this is Ben, and this is Chris. Abby's boys."

He wasn't sure whether he should shake hands, crouch down or wave from a distance. Before he could make up his mind, Chris stepped forward to give him a good study.

"You're the one who went away. Mom said you've been to Japan."

So crouching down seemed natural. "Yeah, I've been there."

"We studied about it in school. They eat raw fish there."

"Sometimes." Good God, he thought, he could see himself in the boy, just as he saw Abby's solemn eyes in the brother.

"Did *you*?" Chris wanted to know.

"Sure I did."

Chris made a face. He couldn't have been more pleased. "That's gross. Dad—that's Dylan—took us fishing, but I wouldn't clean them."

"I did," Ben said, tired of being left out. He shouldered Chris out of the way to get a good look for himself. "I liked the spaceship model you sent me. It was neat."

"I'm glad you liked it." Trace wanted to ruffle the boy's hair, but figured it was too soon.

"He only lets me play with it if I beg and beg," Chris put in.

"That's because you're a geek."

"Am not!"

Ben started to launch into a full-scale exchange of insults, then clammed up when he recognized the sound of footsteps.

"Trouble?" Dylan said mildly as he stepped into the hall.

"Dad, we've got another uncle, and he's here." Delighted to be in charge, Chris grabbed Trace's hand and dragged him forward. "This is Uncle Trace. This is my dad. We changed our name to Crosby and everything."

So this was the brother no one knew very much about. Dylan's writer's instincts were humming. "Glad you could make it. Abby's always showing the boys where you've been on Ben's globe. You get around."

"Some." Trace was pleased enough to meet the brother-in-law, but he was wary of the journalist.

"He eats raw fish," Chris supplied. "Hey, Mom, guess who's here?"

Abby came from the direction of the kitchen, her dancer's legs still graceful beneath the deep rose dress that draped over the child she carried. Her dark blond hair swung loosely at her shoulders. "The caterers want me to tell certain greedy little fingers to keep out of the canapés. I wonder who they might mean." Her brow was lifted as she smiled at her husband. Then, looking past him, she saw Trace.

"Oh." Her eyes, always expressive, filled as she opened her arms. "Oh, Trace."

"Mom's crying," Ben murmured as he watched his mother being held by this man he'd only heard about.

"Because she's happy," Dylan told him, placing a hand on his shoulder. "Imagine if you didn't see Chris for a long, long time." Ben considered it, and a gleam came into his eyes. "Monster." With a laugh, Dylan ruffled his hair.

"It's such a surprise. Such a terrific surprise."

Trace brushed a tear from her cheek. "Maddy already stole my handkerchief."

"It doesn't matter. How did you get here? Where did you come from? I've so many questions. Give me another hug."

"This is Gillian," Maddy announced, though Gillian

had done her best to stay in the background. "She brought him." At Trace's lifted brow, Maddy grinned. "I mean, he brought her."

"Whichever way, hello." Though she sensed some intrigue, it could wait. Abby kissed both of Gillian's cheeks. "I'm glad you're here, both of you. And I can't wait to see Chantel's face."

"Why wait?" With a laugh, Maddy hooked an arm through Trace's. "She's upstairs making herself more beautiful."

"Nothing changes," Trace commented.

"Not much. Come on. Gillian, you, too. Chantel will want to meet you."

"Maybe I should—"

"Don't be silly." Abby cut off her protest and took her hand. "This is a once-in-a-lifetime."

"Dylan and I will…check on Quinn," Reed said.

"Thanks." Maddy threw him a smile as she climbed the stairs.

"I wonder how Pop's going to react," Dylan murmured.

"That's something I don't want to miss. Come on, boys, let's see how the bridegroom is holding up."

With her usual flair for the dramatic, Maddy rapped on Chantel's door.

"I don't want to see anyone unless they have a bottle of champagne."

"This is better." Maddy opened the door and stuck her head inside. "Abby and I brought you a wedding present."

"At the moment, I'd prefer the champagne. I'm a nervous wreck."

"This'll take your mind off it." With a flourish, Maddy pushed the door wide.

Chantel sat at her dressing table in a long white robe,

her crown of pale-blond hair done up in intricate coils. She saw Trace in the mirror and turned very slowly.

"Well, well," she said in her dark, alluring voice. "Look what the cat dragged in." She rose to look at him.

She was every bit as beautiful as he remembered. Perhaps more. And was undoubtedly every bit as hard a nut to crack. "You look pretty good, kid."

"I know." She tilted her head. "You don't look too bad. A little rough around the edges, maybe."

He stuck his hands in his pockets. "Nice house."

"We like it." Then she let out a long breath. "Bastard. There goes my makeup." He met her halfway and swung her in one long circle. "I'm so glad you're here, and I hate you for making me cry so I look like a hag for my wedding."

"A hag?" He drew her away. "Fat chance."

"Trace." She brushed the hair from his forehead. "We always knew the day would come, but you couldn't have picked a better one. God, don't you even have a handkerchief?"

"Maddy took it."

"Figures." She used the heel of her hand.

"This is Gillian." Maddy all but shoved her into the room.

"Oh?" Always cautious, Chantel lifted a brow. "How do you do?"

"I don't want to disturb you." Chantel's brow lifted a little higher at the accent, and a smile came into her eyes. "I think I should go down or—"

"She's with Trace," Abby put in.

"Is she really?" In the way of triplets, the sisters communicated the rest. "Well, isn't that nice? Excellent taste, Trace." She took both of Gillian's hands. "Sorry I can't say as much for yours, but champagne is definitely in order."

"I'll get it."

"For heaven's sake, Maddy, I'll have one of the servants bring it. You can't go traipsing up and down the stairs in your condition. Take everyone into the sitting room down the hall. Quinn's barred from this wing, so I'm not risking any bad luck. I'll be there as soon as I fix my face again." She put a hand on Trace's arm. "Stay, please."

"Sure." He shot a look at Gillian, but she was already being washed away in the wave of his sisters.

"We missed you," she said when they were alone. "Is everything all right?"

"Yeah, why?"

With her hands in his, Chantel sat with him on the bed. "I guess I always figured you'd come home in absolute triumph or absolute destitution."

He had to laugh. "Sorry, it's neither."

"I won't ask what you've been doing, but I have to ask if you're staying."

"I don't know." He thought of Gillian. "I wish I did."

"All right. You're here today. I hate to be sloppy, but I can't tell you how much it means to me."

"You start crying again, you will look like a hag."

"I know. You always were a pain in the—"

"Chantel, Reed said you needed me. I've been trying to keep your father from fighting with the—" Molly paused halfway into the room.

He'd thought he'd prepared himself to see her again. She looked older, but not old. Changed, but somehow constant. She'd scolded him and comforted him, walloped him and soothed him. Whatever was needed. He felt twelve years old as he stood and looked at her.

"Mom."

She didn't want to burst into tears. That would be a foolish thing before she'd said so much as a word. With the strength that had gotten her through years on the road, she took a deep breath. "Let me look at you." He was thin, but he always had been. Like his father. So like his father. "It's good to have you back." She took the next step and folded him in her arms. "Oh, Tracey, how good it is to have you back."

She smelled the same. She seemed smaller now, more delicate, but she smelled the same. He buried his face in her hair and let himself feel. "I missed you. Mom, I'm sorry."

"No regrets." She said it almost fiercely as she held on. "There's to be no regrets. And no questions." She drew away to smile at him. "At least not now. I'm going to dance with my son at my daughter's wedding." She held out a hand for Chantel. Some prayers *were* answered.

"Molly! In the name of all that's holy, where did you run off to? Those so-called musicians don't know a single Irish tune."

Molly felt Trace stiffen. "Don't repeat mistakes," she said with a sternness he remembered well.

"What's the matter with that girl, hiring a bunch of idiots? Molly, where the devil are you?"

He bounced into the room the way he bounced through life. Sure of himself and on the edge of a dance. It was rare for Frank O'Hurley's feet to falter, but they did when he saw his son.

"I have to see about champagne," Chantel said quickly. "Mom, there's someone I want you to meet. Come let me introduce you."

Molly stopped at the door and looked into her husband's eyes. "I've loved you all my life," she said quietly. "And will no matter what foolish thing you do. Don't disappoint me, Frank."

Frank cleared his throat as the door shut behind him.

A man shouldn't feel awkward with his own son. But he couldn't help it. "We didn't know you were coming."

"I didn't know myself."

"Still footloose and fancy-free, are you, Trace?"

His spine stiffened. "So it seems."

"That's what you always wanted." It wasn't what he wanted to say, but the words came out before he could stop them.

"You never knew what I wanted." Damn, why did it have to be a repeat performance? "You never wanted to know. What you wanted was for me to be you, and I couldn't be."

"That's not true. I never wanted you to be anyone but yourself."

"As long as it fit your standards." Trace started to walk out, but then he remembered what Gillian had said. He had to make peace, or at least try. He stopped, still feet away from his father, and dragged a hand through his hair. "I can't apologize, I won't apologize, for being who I am, or for doing anything I've done. But I am sorry I've disappointed you."

"Wait a minute." Frank held up a hand. A moment before he'd been afraid he would lose Trace again, and he hadn't been sure he would be able to get him back. He'd had years to regret. "Who said I was disappointed? I never said I was disappointed. What I was was angry, and hurt, but you never disappointed me. I won't have you saying it."

"What do you want me to say?"

"You had your say once, twelve years ago. Now I'll have mine." His chin was jutted out. He, too, wore a tux, but on him it looked like a stage costume. Trace would have bet his last nickel there were taps on the bottoms of his shoes. He hoped there were.

"All right, but before you do, I want you to know I didn't

come to spoil Chantel's wedding. If we can't do anything else, I'd like to call a truce for one day."

The calm strength surprised Frank. His boy had grown up. Pride and regret pulled him in opposite directions. "It's not a war I want with you, Tracey. It never was." Frank pushed a hand through his hair in a gesture that surprised Trace because it mirrored one of his own habits "I—I needed you." He stumbled on the words, then cleared his throat. "You were my first, and I needed you to be proud of me, to look up to me like I had all the answers. And when yc wanted to find your own, I didn't want to listen. Knowing I was a failure to you—"

"No." Appalled, Trace took the first step forward. "You never were, you couldn't be."

"You sent your mother money."

"Because I wasn't around to give anything else."

The old wound remained, gnawing. "I never gave you—any of you—the things I promised."

"We never needed things, Pop."

But Frank shook his head. "A man's meant to provide for his family, to pass some legacy on to his son. God knows I never gave your mother half of what she deserved. The promises were too big. When you left, saying what you said, I had to be bitter. Because if I stopped being bitter, I couldn't have stood knowing I wasn't the father you wanted, or being without you."

"You've always be :n the father I wanted. I didn't think…" Trace let out a long breath, but it didn't steady his voice. "I didn't think you wanted me back."

"There's not a day that's gone by I haven't wanted you back, but I didn't know how to tell you. Hell, didn't know where you were most of the time. I drove you away, Tracey, I know that. Now you've come back a man and I've lost all those years."

"There are plenty more. For both of us."

Frank put his hands on his son's broad shoulders. "When you leave, I don't want it to be in anger. And I want you to know that just by looking at you here, I'm proud of what you've made yourself."

"I love you, Pop." For the first time in twelve years, he embraced his father. "I want to stay." He closed his eyes because the words brought such tremendous relief. "I need you. I need all of you. It's taken me too long to figure that out." He drew away. "I want my father back."

"Ah, Tracey, I've missed having you." Frank reached for his own handkerchief and blew smartly. "Damn girl ought to keep a bottle in here."

"We'll find one, Pop." Trace looked into his father's damp blue eyes. "I've always been proud of you. What you gave me was the best. I just had to see what I could do with it on my own."

"This time, my boy, we kill the fatted calf." He put his arm around Trace's shoulder. "And we'll have that drink, you and me. When this hoopla of your sister's is over, I might even risk your mother's temper and get a little drunk. A man's entitled to celebrate when he's given a son."

"I'm buying."

Frank's damp eyes sparkled. "That's my boy. Made a bundle, did you? And you saw all those places you wanted to see?"

"More than I wanted to see," Trace said and smiled. "I even sang for my supper a time or two."

"Of course you did." Fresh pride burst through him. "You're an O'Hurley, aren't you?" He gave Trace a slap on the back. "Always had a better voice than you had feet, but that's no matter. I expect you've got stories to tell." He winked as they started out. "Start with the women."

That hadn't changed, either. Though he hadn't expected it, it made him glad. "It might take a while."

"We've got time." He had his son back. "Plenty of it."

They were halfway down the stairs when Trace saw another tuxedoed figure. "I'll check it out," the man said into a phone with his back to the stairs.

"Quinn, my boy." Frank's call could have brought down the roof. "I want you to meet my son, Trace."

Quinn turned. He and Trace stared at each other. The shock of recognition came, but it didn't show. "Nice to meet you." Quinn held out a hand. "I'm sure Chantel's thrilled you're here."

"It's interesting meeting all my in-laws in one fell swoop."

"We need a drink," Frank announced. "Guests'll be trooping in before we know it." And he was going to show off his family. All his family.

"Pour me a double." Trace patted his father's shoulder. "I'll be right with you."

"We'll make it a quick one for now. I still have to straighten out those musicians."

"Small world," Quinn commented when they were alone.

Trace shook his head, studying the man who had once, in his early days with the ISS, been his partner. "It's been a while."

"Afghanistan was what—eight, ten years ago?"

"That's the ballpark. So you're going to marry Chantel."

"Come hell or high water."

"Does she know what you do?"

"I don't do it anymore." Quinn pulled out his cigarettes and offered one. "I've got my own security business. You?"

"Recently retired." Trace pulled out matches. "I'll be damned."

"You know, I'm amazed I didn't put it together, O'Hurley."

"We weren't using names in that operation, not real ones."

"Yeah, but the thing is, you look more like her than either of her sisters."

Trace blew out a long stream of smoke and laughed. "If you don't want to sleep on the couch for the next six months, I wouldn't mention that to her."

The O'Hurleys overwhelmed her. Gillian had never met anyone like them. She found herself sitting with the family as Chantel was married in the warm California winter under a white silk canopy while some five hundred guests looked on. There was champagne by the bucket, flowers by the truckload, and tears enough to swim in.

For hours she was caught up in the whirlwind they created until, head spinning, she sought out a quiet spot to let it all settle. She wasn't sure it was quite proper for her to slip into the parlor, but the music was muted here. And she could put her feet up.

"Sneaking out?"

With a gasp, she pressed a hand to her heart. "You scared the life out of me." She relaxed again as Trace came to sit beside her. "You shouldn't creep up behind a person."

"I've been doing it for years." He stretched his own legs out. "Feet hurt?" he asked as he looked at her discarded shoes.

"I feel like I've danced my toes off. Doesn't your father ever slow down?"

"Not that I've ever noticed." God, it was good to be back.

Gillian snuggled back against the pillows. "He likes me."

"Of course he does. You're Irish. Then there's the fact that you can do a fairly adequate jig."

"Fairly adequate?" She sat up straight again. "I'll have you know, O'Hurley, your father said I could go on the road with him and your mother anytime I wanted."

"Packing your trunk?"

She sat back again with a sigh. "I don't think I could keep up with either of them. They're all wonderful. Every one of them. Thank you for bringing me."

"I think I've figured out who brought whom." He lifted her hand and kissed her palm, leaving her speechless. "Thank you, Gillian."

"I love you. I just wanted you to be happy."

When he let her hand go again, she curled her fingers into the palm he'd kissed. "You said that before." Rising, he walked to the window. From there he could see the tables ladened with food and wine and hundreds of people milling around and dancing.

"That I wanted you to be happy?"

"That you loved me."

"Did I?" Very casual, she studied her nails. "Isn't that interesting? As I recall, you didn't have much of a reaction then, either."

"I had things on my mind."

"Oh, yes, saving my brother and Caitlin. We haven't quite finished there." She reached in her purse and drew out a piece of paper. Standing, she offered it to him. "The hundred thousand we agreed on. I had my lawyers send the check." When he didn't move, she walked over and pushed it into his hand. "It's certified. I promise it won't bounce."

He wanted to jam the check down her pretty throat. "Fine."

"Our business is over, then. You've got your retirement fund, a house, your family." She turned away, knowing she was very close to murder. "So where do you go from here, Trace? Straight to the islands?"

"Maybe." He crumpled the check and jammed it in his pocket. "I've been thinking."

"Now *there's* good news."

"Watch your mouth. Better yet, just shut up." He took her by the shoulders and kissed her hard. As he hadn't, Gillian thought, in much too long.

The door opened. Abby took one step in and stopped. "Oh, excuse me. Sorry." Just as quickly, she was gone again.

Trace swore lightly. "Maybe you *are* in love with me. And maybe you're plain stupid."

"Maybe." This time she swore, too, and made his brow lift. "Maybe I'd like to know how you feel."

"We're not talking about how I feel."

"Oh, I see."

Before she could move away he had her close again. It was amazing how quickly panic could come to someone who'd lived his life one step ahead of danger. "Don't turn away from me."

She gave him a straight, level look. "I'm not the one who's doing the turning, Trace."

She had him there. And, damn it, his palms were damp again. "Listen, I don't know how attached you are to New York, to that place you work. I could sell the house in Chicago if it didn't suit."

She felt the gurgle of laughter—or triumph—but swallowed it cautiously. "Didn't suit what?"

"Didn't suit, damn it. Gillian, I want—"

This time Maddy burst through the door and halfway into the room. "Oh, hi." At the expression on Trace's face, she rolled her eyes. "You didn't see me," she said as she began to back out. "I never came in. I was never here. Now I'm gone." And she was.

"Some things never change," Trace muttered. "I never in my life had a minute's privacy with those three around."

"Trace." Gillian put a hand on his cheek and shifted his face back toward hers. "Are you asking me to marry you?"

"I'd like to muddle through this in my own way, if you don't mind."

"Of course." Very solemn, she sat on the window seat. "Please go on."

Did she think one of her long, quiet looks was going to make it easy for him? He could write down how he felt, he could put it to music. The words would come then. But now, just now, he was fresh out.

"Gillian, I think you're making a big mistake, but if you're set on it, we could try it. I've got some ideas about what to do with myself now that the ISS is history." His hands were in his pockets again, because he didn't know what else to do with them. "Maybe I could pitch some of my songs—but that's not really the point," he went on before she could speak. "The point is whether or not you could handle—that you'd be willing to— You know, you really have no business getting tangled up with me."

"This time you shut up."

"Wait a minute—"

"Just shut up and come over here." He scowled, but crossed over to her. "Sit," she said, then gestured to the seat beside her. She waited until he sat down, then took his hands. "Now, I'll tell you exactly what the point is. I love you, Trace, with all my heart, and I want nothing more than to spend my life with you. It doesn't matter where. The house in Chicago is special, I know, and there are laboratories in the Midwest. What I have to know is that you'd be content. I won't start the rest of my life by holding you down."

There was no one else like her. And there would never

be anyone else for him. He wished he had the right words just now, something soft and sweet. One day, he thought, they might come easily.

"I told you when we first met that I was tired. That's the truth. I don't need to climb mountains anymore, Gillian. I already know what's at the top. I'll probably be a lousy husband, but I'll give you the best I've got."

"I know that." She took his face in her hands and kissed him lightly. "Why do you want to marry me, Trace?"

"I love you." It was a great deal easier to say than he had thought. "I love you, Gillian, and I've waited a hell of a long time to make a home."

She rested her head on his shoulder. "We'll make one together."

* * * * *